Additional Acclaim
No One Thinks of Gre

"Griesemer proceeds to savagely send up the military. . . . *No One Thinks of Greenland* effectively skewers the excesses of the early Cold War mentality."
—*The Washington Post Book World*

"An intelligent first novel . . . The book recalls the topsy-turvy military worlds of *Catch-22* and *M*A*S*H*. . . . Compelling."
—*Publishers Weekly*

"This is a terrific—possibly great—first novel. . . . A quirky, affecting, and powerful read."   —*Booklist* (starred review)

"A terrific and compelling first novel, haunting and beautifully imagined, that hovers between the real and the apocalyptic. Griesemer pulls off the enviable trick of creating a place that gradually becomes a place we recognize from our dreams."
—George Saunders, author of *Pastoralia*

"Absolutely the best tragicomic literary war candy since Terry Southern's *Dr. Strangelove*. Literary hijinks laced with the cyanide of truth."   —Tom Paine, author of *Scar Vegas*

"The sign of a great book? The urge to look ahead, to see if certain characters are still persevering, to see if the madness has abated or escalated. The tension in *No One Thinks of Greenland* was excruciating, and the characters were totally alive. This is *Catch-22*, Vonnegut, and as alluded to in the book, even a bit like *The Thing*! And at the core of it? A love story, and a wonderful one at that. . . . Holy shit, what a book!"
—Carl Lennertz, Book Sense

NO ONE
THINKS OF
GREENLAND

[a novel]

JOHN GRIESEMER

PICADOR USA
NEW YORK

To Be Commended for Distinguished Service:

Craig, William
Drosendahl, Glenn
Gray, Edward
Griesemer, L.C., MD
Kendall, Joshua
Metz, Don
Millman, Lawrence (*Last Places*, p. 141, the spark)
Soeiro, Loren
Tate, Cassandra
Weatherbees, The

www.picadorusa.com

Picador® is a U.S. registered trademark and is used by St. Martin's Press under license from Pan Books Limited.

For information on Picador USA Reading Group Guides, as well as ordering, please contact the Trade Marketing department at St. Martin's Press.
Phone: 1-800-221-7945 extension 763
Fax: 212-677-7456
E-mail: trademarketing@stmartins.com

Design by Michael Collica

Library of Congress Cataloging-in-Publication Data

Griesemer, John.
No one thinks of Greenland / John Griesmer.
p. cm.
ISBN 0-312-27457-2 (hc)
ISBN 0-312-28336-9 (pbk)
1. Military hospitals—Fiction. 2. Greenland—Fiction. 3. Soldiers—Fiction. I. Title.

PS3607.R54 N6 2001
813'.6—dc21   2001021932

First Picador USA Paperback Edition: May 2002

10 9 8 7 6 5 4 3 2 1

For
Faith

In the 1950s, the U.S. military maintained a hospital for the most severely wounded soldiers of the Korean War. They were flown from the battlefield to the hospital and held there until they died. This U.S. military hospital for Korea was at Narsarsuaq, on the west coast of Greenland.

While Qangattarsa is not Narsarsuaq, it is, in a sense, not far away.

NO ONE
THINKS OF
GREENLAND

ONE

"You'll want to scratch," said the nurse.

"Don't," said the orderly.

Corporal Rudy Spruance looked up at them from his bed. Something was wrong with his skin. He was having trouble opening his eyes; they were sticky and almost swollen shut. He could barely focus. Although the nurse and the orderly stood at the foot of his bed, they seemed much farther away, giving Rudy the illusion of being marooned in a vast place. He'd felt that way before.

"To keep you from scratching," the nurse said, "we put mittens on you."

"Winter issue," said the orderly. "They were the only things big enough to fit over your hands."

"You got bit bad," said the nurse.

There was movement near the limits of Rudy's vision, then a light shot into his eyes, making him wince. He tried to turn his head but the spot followed him.

"What day of the week is it?" This was a new voice, male.

"No trick questions, Doc," the nurse said.

Rudy couldn't see anyone, just light.

"All right then, what month is it?"

"Still a trick question," said the orderly. "Give the guy a break."

The spot kept harassing Rudy.

"Jesus Christ," said the voice. "All right, then. What year is it?"

"Nineteen . . ." Rudy said. The word sounded slushy; he barely understood it himself. "Fifty-nine."

The spot clicked off. Everything looked green and purple. The feeling of being stranded came back, this time worrying Rudy. He had a memory of a huge landscape, of being alone. Then, unaccountably, he remembered standing before a flickering television, and a pang of longing struck through all the other sensations. The pang wasn't comforting, but it was better than anything else he was feeling, so he tried to hold onto it. His mind jumped, though, when he heard receding footsteps.

"He'll be fine," the doctor said from afar. "I've got a plane to catch."

Rudy tried to rub his eyes and felt soft balloons against his cheeks. He held his hands up in front of his face. Two large, olive drab pillows hovered there: mittens as big as boxing gloves.

"Have I been asleep?" Rudy said, not sure if anyone was still in the room. The words came like staggering drunks out his swollen lips.

"Yep," said the orderly. "For hours." The orderly and the nurse were still at the end of Rudy's bed.

"We sedated you," said the nurse. "You were a little worked up."

"My skin feels funny."

"It's swollen," said the nurse. "Also we put calamine lotion all over you. Didn't anybody tell you about the bugs?"

"No," Rudy said. "Where am I?"

"Didn't they tell you?"

"No. They just let me out with a couple of mail sacks and took off."

"Why were you out wandering around?" the orderly asked.

"Nobody came for in-processing. I couldn't sleep. There was too much light. So I stepped out for a stroll."

" 'And pretty soon I heard a buzzing in my ears,' " said the nurse.

" 'It got louder and louder,' " said the orderly. " 'I started brushing them away.' "

" 'I brushed and brushed, but it was like I was signaling them to come and get it,' " said the nurse.

"*Yah!*" said the orderly, and he slapped his hip and snapped his fingers like a hepcat horn player jamming.

" 'I began to run,' " said the nurse.

" 'It was awful,' " said the orderly.

" 'I just wanted to get away.' "

" 'But there was nowhere to go.' "

" 'I didn't know where I was.' "

"Well, soldier, we'll tell you where you are," the orderly said. "You're on top of the world."

"That's it!" said the nurse. "Bitten on top of the world!"

"Ooooo, ye*ahhh!*" said the orderly. "Bitten on top of the world!" And they dissolved into laughter and self-congratulatory slaps and nudges until they both spun around and did a one-leg-forward, hot-cha turn toward the bed, hands out, grinning, almost gloating. Rudy thought for a moment that they were expecting applause for their vaudeville.

He twisted uncomfortably. Calamine lotion crinkled on his pillow.

"Did I say all that?" he asked.

"Nope," said the nurse, and she leaned down toward his face. "But it's what you *would* have said. Isn't it?"

They'd gotten that right. The mosquitoes had clouded the sky around him. They'd risen up out of the rivulets and grasses on the bright, sunny tundra where he'd been walking, trying to piece together where the hell he was and what had been happening to him since he'd left the States and, for that matter, since his enlistment, since the arrest, since *before* the arrest.

The mosquitoes had come at him so quickly and in such numbers that it was like hitting a wall. He couldn't see a thing, and he'd begun to run. The whining of the tiny wings had sounded as if it came from inside his head. That was what had finally panicked him. He thought they were boring into his brain through his ears. He was getting bitten everywhere. The pinpricks gathered into a fire all over his skin, down his collar, up his nose, in his pants. He started screaming, calling for help, inhaling mosquitoes, bellowing, crying. He'd had no idea where he was going.

Then someone had tackled him, and they fell onto the soft, lumpy moss and grass. Whoever it was had wrapped him in a wet towel. Moist OD terry cloth all around his head, a strong grip around his arms that he'd tried to buck against as his panic fought even aid. The person had yelled at him to get a grip. Whoever it was had hauled him to his feet and forced him to walk, blindfolded and whimpering in the towel, back to safety. He remembered picturing what he must have looked like as he stumbled along: a prisoner of war.

"What's your assignment . . ." The orderly was looking at the name tag on Rudy's fatigue shirt that was draped over a metal folding chair. ". . . Corporal Spruance?"

"PIO," Rudy mumbled.

"Public Information Office?" asked the nurse. "That's crazy. There isn't one. Not here."

"There isn't any public," said the orderly. "And there better not be any information."

"*Tenn*-hutt!" The nurse stabbed the orderly with her elbow, and they both immediately pulled back from Rudy's cot and shot to attention.

Rudy could see the door. For an instant he glimpsed a young woman there. She was wearing a nurse's skirt and a women's OD army blouse. She had red hair, almost strawberry blond, brushed back but about as long as army regs would allow. Rudy wanted to see more, when a tall, striding man filled the door and advanced on Rudy's cot. The man was a lieutenant colonel.

Since he couldn't come to attention, Rudy saluted, his balloon mitt chuffing against his brow and sending tiny flakes of dried lotion raining into his right eye.

"Corporal Spruance."

"Sir?"

"Colonel Lane Woolwrap. Base CO."

The colonel did not return Rudy's salute, and Rudy didn't know what to do with his hand. For a moment he let the mitt hover in the air off to the side of his head, then he let it plop onto the sheets.

"We've already met," the colonel said. "Out on the flats. I was your rescue party. Sergeant Teal here saw you doing the hurt dance out our window. I donned my M1-E1 OD mosquito bonnet and jeté'd my way with a wet towel across the arctic waste to save your ass. Didn't anyone tell you about the bugs?"

"No, sir."

"Well then, you got a little OJT. The lecture portion of the Bug Briefing goes something like this: Springtime is the worst, the first big hatch. Anytime the temp goes above fifty-two degrees Fahrenheit. They've been known to drive reindeer to leap off cliffs and to run musk oxen to exhaustion. They drove you so nuts, you were running away from the base. You'd've run straight for the ice cap if I hadn't stopped you. We hose the grounds down with DDT, and that helps, but obviously you walked out beyond the perimeter. So how do you like Greenland?"

"Sir?"

The colonel exploded into laughter. He was a handsome man, probably in his early fifties, big boned, blond, curly hair, balding on top, but somehow that looked okay with his muscular build. He had one boot up on the frame of Rudy's bed. He even slapped his knee as he laughed.

But Rudy was still dumbfounded by the word *Greenland*. He'd had no idea.

Now that he thought about it, though, it made sense. There *had* been mountains, huge ones, and ice in the distance, a flat plain with tufts of grass, him alone in the middle of vastness.

"No doubt," the colonel said. "We're not supposed to *like* Greenland. But we will endure Greenland, and Greenland will endure us. And while we're here, we have our mission. What would yours be, Corporal Spruance?"

"Sir?"

The colonel rolled his eyes. He cupped his hands around his mouth and made his voice sound as though it were coming through a loudspeaker. *"Why are you here?"*

"I don't know, sir."

"You don't know?"

"Honest." Rudy held up his mitt.

The colonel planted both feet on the floor. "Well, what's your MOS?"

"PIO, sir."

"You're kidding."

"No, sir." He held his hand up again. "I swear."

The colonel scratched his head, let out a sigh. "A fuck-up."

"Sir?"

"Not you. You're not a fuck-up. We don't even know you yet. Although that blood donation you pulled out on the tundra leaves you open to speculation. I'm talking about the army. Well, no, not the *army,* God love it. But something *about* the army. It always fucks up. Sends a chaplain's assistant to repair half-tracks. Sends an MP to direct a USO Christmas pageant. Sends a barracks thief just out of Leavenworth to run a recruiting office. And evidently . . . sends you to me."

Rudy looked at the colonel, who was shaking his head. Rudy had the impulse to apologize. He wanted to get another look at the woman at the door. The colonel had said she was a sergeant.

"Well," the colonel said, "you'll find out soon enough that we've got no P, no I, and no O."

"I was told that already, sir."

The nurse and the orderly shifted on their feet and shot Rudy a dirty look. The colonel didn't pay attention to this. "So it looks like we're in for a little holding action here," the colonel said. "Which should fit your recovery plans just fine. You look like shit, by the way. Hurt much?"

Rudy shrugged. "Some," he said, "sir." His eyes felt watery. Saliva might be dripping out the corners of his puffed lips. It was hard to tell.

The colonel took a step back as if he were about to leave.

"Sir," Rudy said. He didn't want to let the colonel go. Here he was, granted an audience with a commanding officer after days—or was it weeks?—of being shunted and shuffled through transient barracks, waiting areas, and holding detachments, getting the runaround or shrugs from Fort Benjamin Harrison to Fort Dix to McGuire AFB to Pease to Keflavik to a couple of God-knows-where landing strips to here. The last time he'd been near anyone with this much authority was when he stood before the judge who got him into this whole mess. And that time his lawyer had told him to keep quiet and take what comes. This time, though, he was speaking up.

"Begging your pardon, sir," Rudy said. "But I hardly know where I am or what this base is or anything."

The colonel stopped and raised his eyebrows. "No one told you?" he asked with a small upturn in his voice that made him sound almost British.

"No, sir."

"They just shipped you here? No explanation?"

"Yes, sir. They couldn't say. Or they shouldn't say. That's all they'd say."

"This is your first assignment, troop?"

"Yes, sir."

"You're fresh out of PIO school? An army-issue ink-stained wretch?"

"Yes, sir."

The colonel threw his arms out and whipped them back to

clasp his hands behind himself. He cocked his head back. "And the question on the floor from the freshman member of the fourth estate is, 'What goes on here?' Is that a good way to put things, troop?"

"That's fine," Rudy said.

"We're a hospital," the colonel said quietly and smiled. Then he went on, "But putting things any more precisely than that gets a leetle delicate."

The colonel paced some at the foot of the bed. The nurse and the orderly stepped back to give him room. As the colonel moved from side to side, Rudy could see the sergeant by the door. She was more relaxed, in a less military posture, than anyone else in the room. She leaned lightly against the door frame and watched Rudy. She had a half smile on her lips and fine, high cheekbones.

"A hospital," the colonel said. "Or a terminal. Take your pick."

The nurse and the orderly rolled their eyes. The sergeant cocked her head, her smile faded; she kept looking at Rudy.

The colonel hooked his thumbs in his belt and said, "There's a horror movie in the mess hall. Think I'll go catch it." He turned. The sergeant gave Rudy a little nod, then she turned too as the colonel passed her. Rudy saw Woolwrap's hand give a deft, sculpting stroke down and under the sergeant's ass as he went through the door. She was smiling as she followed him.

The nurse put a paper cup on the metal chair beside Rudy's cot.

"Well-breasted," the nurse said.

"Well-legged," said the orderly.

"Well-derriere'd."

"Well done, good and faithful servant."

"*What?*" Rudy said. He was getting tired of their stupid routines.

"Sergeant Teal," said the nurse. "The colonel's good and faithful aide. You noticed her? You noticed her."

Rudy folded the mitts over his stomach.

"Sure," he said.

"Take the pills in the cup about midnight, when the sun's at its lowest. You'll feel better in the morning. Up and at 'em in a couple of days."

"So, how many patients in this hospital?" Rudy asked. "Besides me."

The nurse and the orderly were on their way out the door. They both stopped and turned their heads.

"Oh," said the nurse. "You don't count. You're not a patient."

"Not by our standards," said the orderly.

"That's nice," Rudy said. "I suppose."

"Believe me," said the orderly. "It is."

"Well," Rudy said, "how many of your patients do you have?"

"Seventy?" the nurse asked the orderly.

"Sixty-five?" the orderly asked the nurse.

"Call it sixty-six and two thirds," the nurse said to Rudy. "It fluctuates."

"Downward," said the orderly.

"Ever downward," said the nurse.

"Who are they?" Rudy asked.

The nurse and the orderly looked at each other. Exchanging signals, Rudy thought. Something telepathic.

The nurse looked at Rudy.

"War wounded," she whispered.

The orderly nodded.

Rudy said, "There is no war. *What* war?"

"Korea," the nurse and the orderly whispered simultaneously.

"But why are they *here?*" Rudy asked. "This is Greenland."

"He's telling us," the orderly said to the nurse.

"War is hell," the nurse said to Rudy. "And we're what's next."

The orderly waved, the nurse blew a kiss, and together they left. In the distance a motor hummed. Hot air pulsed through the heating ducts overhead. Rudy lay back on his bed and began to itch.

T W O

His Baby Ben alarm had gone off at midnight. He'd managed, even with the mittens, to take his pills as the nurse had ordered. He'd noticed the pallid light outside, then had fallen quickly back to sleep. Now Rudy was awake again. The clock said 1:35, but he couldn't tell if it was A.M. or P.M.

He was still in the room where the CQ had dumped him. It was where he'd awakened to the nurse and the orderly, to the colonel and that sergeant with the red hair.

It wasn't a bad rack. It had a locker, a bed, and a couple of folding chairs. Packing crates and freight pallets were stacked against the far wall. Out the window, Rudy could see the bowed roof of a Quonset hut and in the distance, barren, gray mountains with the crowns of glaciers wedged between the summits.

With his teeth, he pulled off one mitten. His hand looked like a turnip, his fingers swollen to the size of sausages. There were bites on his arms and legs where mosquitoes had found their way inside his cuffs. He got out of bed and walked over to the locker to check himself in the mirror.

His face filled the little round glass. There were pink welts everywhere, bites upon bites upon bites. Some places were so bitten they looked pulpy. His eyelids looked punched. His cheeks pushed his mouth into a pucker and his lips bulged. There were a few flecks of dried calamine stuck here and there on his skin, but much of the stuff had found its way into his hair. He brushed at his scalp, and a faint, rose-colored snow drifted down across his reflection. He looked like a monster.

But he barely itched. That was one consolation. He decided to go to the latrine. He pulled out some brutally starched fatigues from his duffel bag. He had trouble working his hands through the sleeves, and his arms were like drinking straws in creased wrappers, but the stiffness of the cloth felt good as it brushed across the bites. It was useless trying to button the shirt or tie his boots with his swollen fingers.

He started out his door, but he couldn't remember where the damn crapper was. The hallway was angled and articulated with a turn or an incline every few yards as if the building's sections had bucked and heaved themselves into position. Walking through the twisted halls was like passing through an intestine. The ceiling was a maze of heating pipes, ductwork, electrical conduits, and commo wire. There was plenty of headroom, but it was such a mess up there, Rudy found himself ducking anyway as he flapped along, in his unlaced boots, hoping to find a latrine.

He went down one passage to a dead end. Every door was marked STORAGE. Another turn took him to an exit with double doors and scratched Plexiglas windows. He turned to try yet another hall when he heard the sound of a typewriter. It started, stopped, started again. Rudy headed toward the sound. More STORAGE doors. But one of the them was just barely ajar. Somebody had stenciled on it: BIRD LIVES.

The typing stopped, and Rudy could hear some soft, delicate sounds like the snapping of brittle glass or the breaking of small animal bones.

He slowly pushed the door open. Amid the storage shelves and crates were a desk and typewriter under a hanging bare bulb. Sitting behind the desk with his head tilted upward toward the light was a fleshy, sandy-haired corporal. He wore fatigues and a narrow-brim porkpie hat. He was cracking an ampule under his nose and snorting mightily.

Rudy said, "Excuse me," and the corporal yelped. In a massive sweep, he wiped everything—papers, pencils, a half dozen white bullet-shaped benzedrine inhalers, and at least a score of little gauze-wrapped glass ampules—off the desk and onto the floor.

"I'm an asthmatic!" the corporal blurted. He was on his feet. "I have asthma. This . . . this . . ." He paced around behind his desk, snapping his fingers, crunching on the glass and pencils underfoot. "This is my . . . my medication!" His voice cracked with surprise and relief as he found the word. "Dig. My medication."

"Oh," said Rudy.

"It *is!* And look, you made me spill it all."

"I'm sorry," Rudy said. "I only wanted to ask where the latrine is."

The corporal was no longer listening; he was now finally noticing Rudy's face. His jaw dropped. "What the hell *happened* to you, man?" he asked.

"Bugs," Rudy said.

"Ohhhh, yeaaahhh. Yeah. Dig. Yeah. I heard about you. Didn't anybody tell you about the bugs?"

"No," Rudy said.

"CQ should have told you, man. Or the officer of the day. Some cat should have told you. That's a shame, man. The way you look." The corporal began to rake up the debris behind the desk with his boot.

"So, you've got asthma?" Rudy asked.

"Yes!"

"And they let you in the army?"

The corporal looked at Rudy for a moment, then turned away. "All right. I don't have asthma. Big deal. Look, do me a favor and just keep it to yourself, what you saw. You're new here. You don't know everything. You don't even know where the shithouse is."

"You're right," Rudy said. "Where is it?"

"You'll keep cool? All you saw was me typing in here?"

Rudy nodded.

"Spruance, right?" The corporal came crunching around the desk and extended his hand. He smiled, droopy-eyed. "Henry Lavone. Clerk-typist."

Rudy held out his bulbous hand. Corporal Lavone touched it lightly. Rudy looked back at the desk and typewriter. "This is where they've got you working?"

"Not work," Lavone said, shaking his head. "I'm off duty. This is my studio."

Crates were stacked to the ceiling. Government nomenclature was stenciled on all the boxes: *Bandages/gauze/sterile; Enemas/rubber/complete/one each.* There were movie posters for horror and science fiction films tacked on some of the shelves where there were also dog-eared paperback books and piles of manuscript pages. A candle burned in a Chianti bottle. The place was a cross between a military-supply dump and a bopster hangout.

"So, how long have you been here?" Rudy asked.

"Since I got off duty," Lavone said. "I'm going all night. That's why I needed a little . . . you know, medication."

"I meant," Rudy said, "how long have you been here in Greenland?"

Lavone sat down and tilted back in his chair, thought a moment, then said with a vague smile, "I don't know."

"Seriously?" Rudy asked.

"Truth. I don't. It's not that uncommon here. I do know that it's been more than six months because I had a birthday recently, I think."

"You *think?*"

"Some things I'm exact about. You will be too," Lavone said. "Some things you'll let go. Some things will let go of you. Here in Greenland. Time's one of those things. They said you're PIO."

"For what it's worth," Rudy said.

"A fellow scribbler," Lavone said. He almost sounded forlorn. "I write poetry." He reached over to a shelf and put his hand on a thick pile of manuscript pages.

"I don't know how much a scribbler I'm going to be here," Rudy said. "They don't know what they're going to do with me, from what I gather."

"They'll think of something. The colonel will. I'm the Admin Company clerk, but he's also got me down as the Entertainment Liaison." He gestured at the posters: *The Thing, The Blob, The Day the Earth Stood Still.* "I book all the movies for the colonel and, by extension, for the rest of us. That's about all I do. I assigned you a rack down here in Storage Charlie. You should be grateful. No inspections. Quiet. If things go okay, you won't have to bunk in the barracks sector at all."

"Thanks," Rudy said.

"Privacy can come in handy around here," Lavone said.

Rudy could see a small box under a pile of papers on a crate behind Lavone's desk. Visible was the stenciling: *Ampules/amyl nitrite.*

"This is a hospital," Rudy said.

Lavone nodded. "Right-e-o."

"For war wounded," Rudy said.

Lavone nodded again, vague, not giving out too much.

"From Korea," Rudy said.

"Yeah."

"Korea was a long time ago."

"I was in high school," said Lavone. He turned to look at the manuscript page that stuck out of the typewriter like a speckled, white tongue. "This canto sucks," he said.

"You never told me where the crapper was," said Rudy.

"Sorry. Back to the left. Take the corridor that angles right."

Lavone dove into his typing. In a moment, he bent down, picked up an inhaler from the floor, took a snort, and said, "Yesssssss!" Then he went back to work at twice the speed. He never looked up to see Rudy leave.

In his room after going to the latrine, Rudy sat on his bed. He decided he'd better get transferred the hell out of here once he got well. He could feel the weight of his swollen face droop toward the floor. He saw a section of one of the base's buildings through his window. The glass of the windows over there reflected the twilight. He wondered if that was where they kept the wounded soldiers. Exhaustion was creeping back over him. But it was light outside. Two A.M. Daylight at night. Back home, Rudy guessed, allowing for time zones, Jack Paar would be signing off. Rudy thought of the flickering DuMont TV in his old living room, of other TVs in other houses in the old neighborhood. A dark, spring night in suburbia. Blue TV glow. The sign-off. The national anthem. The test pattern. He was in Greenland. Day. Night. Time lets go of you, or you let go of time, was what Lavone had said. Here in Greenland.

THREE

The low ceiling compressed the noise of the mess hall into a din that felt like a solid mass weighing on his swollen face. His hands weren't so puffy anymore—he could work his fingers—but his face was still bloated and dotted with bite scabs.

This was Rudy's first real trip out of his room, where he'd been for two, maybe three, days. He was losing track of time, just as Lavone had said. His clock had run down, and he wasn't even sure what meal this was.

The mess hall was jumping. Officers and enlisted men, medical personnel and everyone else, seemed to be getting up and settling in, jostling one another, standing in the aisles, talking, smoking. On a side aisle a lieutenant was trying to twirl a Hula Hoop. Rudy counted three card games. Many of the people wore a combination of hospital whites and combat fatigues like Rudy'd seen on the colonel's aide. A sergeant went by with a metal tray stacked with pancakes. So, the meal was breakfast.

Things looked crowded at the serving line. Rudy hung back and glanced at the bulletin board by the door. There were fire regulations, frostbite and polar bear warnings, a movie poster for *The Fly*, a For Sale sign for a used guitar "once strummed by PFC Elvis Presley in Grafenwöhr, Germany," and a notice for something called the Bash:

> CELEBRATE THE LONGEST DAY OF THE YEAR . . . THE SUN NEVER SETS. THE BEER NEVER STOPS . . . AT THE BASH! BE THERE! (COLONEL'S ORDERS)

As he read the notices, Rudy began to sense something coming through the general noise behind him. It was a high-pitched whining sound, a tiny, thin buzzing that snapped him back from the bulletin board. A remembered panic kicked in under his ribs, and the surface of his skin became caustic with a sheen of sweat. He almost raised his hands to swat the sound away from his ears. Then he turned and saw a staff sergeant at a table in front of him do that very thing.

The sergeant had a severe crew cut and an egg-shaped paunch. He waved arms that seemed too long for the sleeves of his uniform. He was flailing at the air around his head. He'd stood up from his place at a dining table and was wiggling his hips and making grunting sounds and yelps between the falsetto buzzing that came from his throat and the throats of the other NCOs sitting at the table. They were all imitating mosquitoes, and the staff sergeant was imitating Rudy out on the flats. If they weren't buzzing, the men in the group were laughing and clapping. People at the neighboring tables turned to look and chuckle. Soon most of the mess hall was laughing at the sergeant and turning to look at Rudy.

As the staff sergeant twitched and yelped, he reached across the table, grabbed a pitcher of water, and held it over his head.

"Pour it!"

"Help meeee! Help meeee!"

"Get those bugs!"

"Call the colonel!"

"Help meeee! Help meeee!"

The shouts came through the laughter from all the nearby tables. But the sergeant stopped the dancing and put the pitcher down. He raised his hand to signal the show was over. A chorus of boos, jeers, applause, and cries for more filled the mess hall.

Rudy was only able to stand and stare. He couldn't fix his eyes on anything. He had a moment's hope that the sergeant would turn around, make a gesture of truce and friendship, and solicit a round of good-sport applause from his audience. But he didn't. He just sat back down, laughing and shaking his head.

Rudy's swollen skin burned. He considered walking over to the sergeant's table, picking up the pitcher of water, and dumping it on the man's head. But that would probably mean a fight, and he didn't have a fight in him, certainly not upon walking into a mess hall for the first time at a new posting. He just proceeded, eyes straight ahead, to the steam tables back by the kitchen. The noise of the room had returned to its normal din by the time Rudy had his tray of French toast.

He found a seat near the wall at the back of the room. No one else was at the table. He sat facing the stacks of trays and utensil hoppers. It had been a mistake to leave his room. He should have stayed hidden until his face had returned to normal. Only the nurses and the orderlies who'd brought him his meals would have known he was around.

A mug of coffee plunked down next to Rudy's place.

"So which is worse here, the bugs or the assholes?"

Rudy turned. The colonel's aide was taking a seat next to him at the end of the table. She was wearing a T-shirt and fatigue pants. She'd pinned back her red hair to keep it away from her face. She was flushed and had the loose-limbed moves of a person just released from hard work. She flopped into the chair next to him.

"I got KP," she said. "I was wiping trays, and I saw the little show. I don't think we were introduced properly. I'm Irene Teal. I know who you are."

"Who doesn't, right?" Rudy said, and he worked up a weak, lopsided smile. It was all his swollen face would allow.

Irene leaned forward to sip from her brimming mug. Rudy found himself looking at the tiny, pale vortex of scalp at the crown of her tilted head. It was only inches from his eyes. Her hair swirled out from that point. Her whole being materialized from that point. Before his eyes she'd just appeared, swirling, a genie out of a lamp.

"Who are they?" Rudy asked as Irene looked up from her coffee. He nodded back toward the sergeants.

Irene shrugged. "Lifers. NCOs. Most of them aren't too bad, though. Razzing the new guy is just, you know, their idea of fun while living on a glaciated rock for a year at a stretch."

Rudy turned to look back toward the sergeants' table. The mess-hall crowd had thinned out. The sergeant who'd done the dance was gone. A couple of NCOs were at a pinball machine near the bulletin board and water fountain. No one was paying attention to Rudy.

He turned back to Irene. "How come you're on KP? If the colonel's aide's on KP, then no one is safe."

"I lost a bet."

"Who with?"

"The colonel."

"Over what?"

She smiled and pinged the handle of her coffee mug with her fingernail. "Can't tell."

Her coyness released a surge of feeling in Rudy that surprised him. He wasn't sure, but it seemed like jealousy, as if he suddenly couldn't abide anyone knowing more about her than he knew.

"You been here long?" Rudy asked.

"About a year," Irene said. "I never counted it exactly. Nobody does."

"So I've been told," Rudy said. "How do you make it pass? Time, I mean."

"Well," Irene said, and she leaned back in her chair but kept her forearms on the table in a circle around the coffee mug, "we have our movies in the mess hall. We have our rec room. We have our EM/NCO club. It's really just a detached Quonset, but you can get as juiced as you want there if that's your pleasure."

Rudy worked at a piece of French toast with his fork. He liked listening to her. He could almost enjoy his status being the poor, bug-bitten new guy. She might never have noticed him otherwise. He remembered what the nurse and the orderly had intimated about her, though, that she was more than just the colonel's aide, good and faithful. He wondered if it was risky sitting here talking with her.

"So, you work for the colonel," he said.

"I prefer to think of it as working *with* him," she said.

"You're a sergeant. He's a colonel. Sergeants work *for* colonels."

He felt the air between them instantly go still as if it were waiting for the snap in her voice he knew was coming.

"Well, you're quite the experienced soldier, aren't you, Corporal? I suppose you know all there is to know about the chain of command."

He looked up from the protection of cutting his toast and watched her. He hadn't set out to provoke Irene, yet he was glad that he had. He was reeling through this conversation, one instant jealous, another soothed, another deliberately annoying and edgy. It was crazy. He noticed that she had begun to blush. Maybe she was feeling the same way, but then again, maybe she was angry.

She swung her legs out as if to go. "You might even be looking good sometime," she said, "once your swelling goes down."

"No," he said suddenly. "I'm not. I'm not what you said."

She stopped and stared at him.

"I'm not an experienced soldier. Not at all. Sergeant."

A thin smile came to her face. It held a measure of tolerance and, he thought, of relief.

"Maybe then you just need to get your bearings," she said quietly.

"That's it," Rudy nodded and tried to smile. "That's exactly what I need."

She stood up. "I suppose I could show you around. The wind usually blows up the fjord in the afternoon, and the bugs aren't a problem. I'm free tomorrow. Meet me at the old C-47 at fifteen hundred. I'll give you a tour."

She reached down and drank off the dregs of her coffee. "I've got to get back," she said. "I'm on the grease trap."

"Man, when you lose a bet, you really lose."

"Yes," she said, "but when I win . . ."

And she glided away toward the clanging, boisterous kitchen, leaving him hanging.

"Where's the old C-47?" he called out. But she was beyond hearing.

"Dead airplane out by the hangar," came a voice from over by the pinball machine. A solitary, fat sergeant was pressing his gut into the machine and working the flippers. He never looked up. The game had him mesmerized, but he must have heard Rudy call out.

"C for cargo," the sergeant said automatically. "Twin engine. Workhorse of the air."

FOUR

Somewhere, back in the morass of paperwork the army makes soldiers fill out, Rudy had started leaving blanks in the spaces calling for the names of next of kin. He meant nothing by it really. It had just been an impulse that had seemed appropriate at the time. He'd wanted to feel he'd cut loose, that as long as he was forced to be in the damn army he wouldn't be dragging the past along with him. He even wrote *deceased* once in the next-of-kin blank as a little test to see if the bureaucracy would catch on. It didn't. The army never even blinked. Orphan soldiers must be no big deal, he'd thought. I'm one of many. It had made him feel less alone.

For three or four years before the army, he had felt stalled, or stunned was more like it; unmoved and unmoving. It had been as if he were stranded and invisible. Marooned. The feeling had followed him even after the judge had made him enlist. It had begun swallowing him. Then, in one stroke, by eliminating his kin on the army paperwork, he'd given himself new coordinates.

He suddenly stood out against the horizon; he had definition he'd never had before.

But now, alone out on the airstrip, the arctic's immensity all around him, Rudy began to get that marooned feeling once again. He kept listening for mosquitoes but only heard the breeze. He kept buttoning and unbuttoning his field jacket. The red wind sock atop the hangar pointed like an arthritic finger toward the mountains. The sun was warm, but the breeze was cool so he could never quite get comfortable.

It wasn't true he was an orphan. His father was dead from a car accident, true enough, but it was the booze, really, that had cut him down long before the tree had gotten in the way of his Studebaker. Rudy's mother was still alive and well. She had remarried and was living in Florida. Given the way Rudy and Roger had gotten along when they'd all lived together back in Jersey, Florida was barely far enough away, even from Greenland.

The airplane hangar was out at the end of the landing strip, and the sun had warmed the roof enough to make the metal tick and creak. Occasionally, a gust of wind would rattle a loose panel, and a clattering, tin belch would echo forth from the cavernous building. Above, thin clouds from earlier in the day had moved far to the east and had left an empty blue sky.

The C-47 was off the graded apron. Its starboard landing gear had been smashed completely, and its right wing tip had been sheared away. The OD paint on the fuselage was flaking and showed the pitted aluminum underneath. The starboard propeller blades were bent back like flower petals.

Someone had removed several seats from the old plane and had tossed them among the junk that was scattered around the edge of the landing strip. Rudy dragged one of the seats over to a sunny spot in the shelter of the plane's tail. He sat and was able to survey the hospital.

It was a little after three o'clock, but no one was coming up toward the old aircraft. The roofs of a couple of Quonset huts reflected the sun, and feathers of steam fluttered from the vents atop the main building.

About a quarter mile beyond the end of the runway was a Quonset with a large chimney made from stacked culvert pipe. A Jeep drove out from the building and headed up toward the foothills. A smear of dust-colored smoke stretched from the chimney in a long rope up toward the shining glaciers.

Rudy felt the sun bake his face. The warmth was good. For the first time since he'd arrived in Greenland, his face felt close to its normal shape and size. He looked back again toward the hospital. Still no Sergeant Teal.

He'd been jumpy ever since meeting her yesterday. Maybe it was the ridicule he'd run into in the mess hall. He'd taken to going to meals late, right at the end of the call, to avoid crowds. He sat by himself. He was still on medical exemption, so he'd hung around his room reading dog-eared magazines he'd dragged along with him from the transient barracks at Fort Dix. He'd wandered the halls some. He kept returning to his room expecting to see a buck slip or a memo telling him about in-processing or an assignment, but there was nothing. In his head, he composed his case for a transfer. He went looking for Lavone, but the storage closet/studio was locked. Finally a whole day had passed, and it was 1500 hours, so he headed out to the old C-47.

Of course, he'd been thinking about Irene. She'd come over in the mess hall to offer sympathy, but she'd teased him too. He'd felt comforted by her kindness, but he'd been compelled to probe at whatever she had going with the colonel. As the sun baked his face, he thought about the whorls and warm colors of her hair. He pictured her there with him. He looked again to see if she was coming. No. He closed his eyes. She'd be there soon. He felt the pleasant stirrings of a hard-on. His first since he'd arrived in Greenland.

"CORPORAL SPRUANCE . . ."

Rudy bolted forward. The volume of the voice almost sent him to his feet.

"CORPORAL SPRUANCE, CORPORAL SPRUANCE, YOUR

APPOINTMENT FOR FIFTEEN HUNDRED HOURS HAS BEEN CANCELED. WITH REGRETS AND APOLOGIES. PLEASE ACKNOWLEDGE THIS MESSAGE BY WAVING YOUR ARMS."

It was a man's voice coming from a loudspeaker mounted on the near corner of the airplane hangar. It might have been Lavone. It sounded like Lavone, but Rudy couldn't be sure. Each word was percussive and without echo. The emptiness of the sky and the tundra sucked up the booming sound.

"PLEASE ACKNOWLEDGE."

Rudy was still turned in his seat, facing the hangar behind him, looking at the loudspeaker.

"TURN AROUND AND FACE BUILDING A1-A. THAT'S THE HOSPITAL. WAVE YOUR HANDS. ACKNOWLEDGE MESSAGE."

Rudy turned, stood up and waved his hands over his head toward the hospital which was a quarter mile away across the open, gradual slope. As he stood beside the wrecked plane and waved, he felt like a downed pilot signaling his distress to an oblivious, passing freighter. He had no idea who was watching or from which window.

"THANK YOU. ACKNOWLEDGMENT RECEIVED."

Rudy let his hands drop to his side.

"NEXT: YOU HAVE A MEETING WITH COLONEL WOOLWRAP AT NINETEEN-THIRTY HOURS. THAT IS FOUR HOURS AND THIRTEEN MINUTES FROM NOW. PLEASE ACKNOWLEDGE RECEIPT OF THIS MESSAGE BY DOING THREE DEEP KNEE BENDS."

Rudy looked at the building below.

"PLEASE ACKNOWL—"

Rudy started to squat, automatically beginning with his hands on his hips and extending his arms forward as he hunkered down.

"THAT'S IT. ONE . . . TWO . . ."

"Jesus Christ," Rudy muttered.

"THREE. GOOOOOOD."

Rudy stood back up, with his fists clenched, knuckles jammed into his waist.

"NOW. YOU MAY TERMINATE THIS MESSAGE BY FLIPPING BUILDING A1-A AND THE ENTIRE QANGAT-TARSA U.S. ARMY HOSPITAL COMPLEX THE BIRD."

Rudy threw his arms up and turned about in a small circle like a flabbergasted coach on the sidelines after a bad call.

"YOU MAY—"

Rudy thrust his right fist and middle finger skyward.

"VERY GOOD. MY SENTIMENTS EXACTLY. OVER AND OUT."

There was a click from the speaker as the power shut off. The roof of the hanger made a few chirps of expansion; the wind blew some grit over Rudy's boots. Irene wasn't coming. With regrets and apologies. The hospital seemed as remote and opaque as the walls of glacial ice jammed between the mountains.

Rudy looked around and, now that he was up, decided to walk some more. He wasn't ready to go back to the hospital. He headed up to the landing strip and walked along the edge of the runway. He went out beyond the string of approach lights, crossed some soft hummocks, and followed a dirt track until he came to the Quonset with the smoking chimney.

The building had no windows. The large doors were locked. Lettered crudely across both of them was a hand-painted sign: FIRE DEPARTMENT.

Rudy tried to peek in at the crack in the door, but could see nothing. He wondered why there would be a fire department so remote from all the other buildings on the base. Just to get here and back to the hospital with equipment would take a good ten minutes.

While he had his face still pressed against the corrugated metal door, a Jeep burst around the corner. Rudy threw himself against the door, his heart walloping in his chest.

The Jeep never stopped. It roared and banged over a rise in the road to the hospital, and as it receded, Rudy could hear a couple of soldiers' voices laughing and singing under the Jeep's fluttering canvas canopy.

The voices and motor faded, and the valley became quiet. Smoke from the chimney still hung in a path toward the mountains. Rudy followed the Jeep track over to the next rise beyond the Quonset. From the crest, he was able to see down into the last protected basin before the foothills rose up toward the high peaks. About a hundred yards off were a half dozen stone rectangles in the grass. They looked like primitive foundations, overgrown, almost buried, splashed with the yellow blooms of dandelions.

Rudy walked down and paced around one of the perimeters, then strolled over to a grayish pile of rubble in the most distant rectangle. He thought he saw a wisp of smoke rise from the pile.

It was a broad heap of ashes about three feet high. At his feet, half buried among gray sticks and chips, was a small bowl. He knelt for a closer look and could see the bowl held an inch of water, a small stagnant pool in a jagged goblet. There was movement in the water, and Rudy could see tiny, fluttering beings wriggling there. Mosquito larvae. He winced. It was then that he noticed the gouges in the bowl. They were the eye sockets of a human skull.

He scrabbled backward and rose to his haunches to look at the whole pile. Amid the gray-and-white chips, he now saw the larger pieces unmistakably as the ends of bones, the heavier parts of skeletons, vertebrae, ball-and-socket joints. He shifted and felt his head spin. Everything began to prickle with blackness, and he began to lose his balance. He pitched to the side and tried to catch himself. His hand hit the ashes. He pulled it away. The place he'd touched was still hot.

Rudy stood and stepped delicately back a few paces. At that distance, the pile was pale and mottled and the color of rough paper. The dandelions in the enclosure all bobbed their yellow heads in unison as a breeze swept through the fjord and up the grassy basin. Rudy turned and sucked in the air. He walked quickly away, brushing off his hand as he went.

On his way back, he passed the outermost Quonset again and looked at its huge chimney and crudely lettered FIRE DEPART-MENT sign. The smoke had dwindled to almost nothing. He followed the Jeep track over the rise and down toward the hospital. Above the valley, the sun still glistened off the glaciers.

FIVE

"Where you from, troop?"

Rudy was about to answer when Colonel Woolwrap said, "Ahhh, I know every CO since Xerxes has asked that stupid fucking question, but hell shit, I'm curious. Where from?"

"New Jersey, sir."

"Town?"

"Mindowaskin."

"Damn. New Jersey has got the strangest friggin' names for its towns. Piscataway. Rahway. HoHokus. And—what?—Mindo—what?"

"—waskin."

"Never heard of it."

"It's not too far from New York. A suburb really."

"Fine. Fine. Okay. Fuck New Jersey. I'm from Phoenix myself. And this is Qangattarsa, Greenland, speaking of batshit nomenclature. And you, you're up and about. I'm glad to see it. You feeling better?"

"Yes, sir."

"You look better. Not great, but better. Accommodations okay?"

"Yes, sir. Fine."

"Food's not bad here, is it?"

"No, sir."

"That's one of the bennies of being stationed at this hospital," the colonel said. "You've got a CO in the Quartermaster Corps."

"That's you, sir?"

"That's me."

"You're not a doctor, sir?"

The colonel's eyes shot up from gazing at the backs of his hands, which were resting on the desk.

"No, troop," the colonel said quietly. "I am not a doctor." He pointed to the insignia on the wall. There was an eagle on it, a blue ring with stars and a sword crossing a key. Rudy thought it was screwy, all out of scale; for the key and sword to look that way, the key would have to be the length of a golf club or the sword the size of a fountain pen.

"*That* is the Quartermaster Corps insignia," the colonel said. "That should give you a clue that I am not a doctor. That and the fact there are no med school diplomas hanging all over my office. Those are the clues, Corporal. Those and the fact that you didn't have to wait six fucking months for an appointment to see me."

"Yes, sir."

"I've got an open-door policy."

"Yes, sir."

Somebody walked past the door to the outer office. Maybe it was Irene Teal. She hadn't been there when Rudy had arrived for his appointment. Whoever it was, Colonel Woolwrap glanced that way, nearly smiled, then frowned and said, "Well, *almost* an open-door policy."

Rudy was lightheaded. The colonel's severity had blown off the man in a gust. Now the colonel leaned back in his chair, suddenly relaxed. Two small disks of sweat darkened the armpits of his starched fatigue shirt.

"Have you been to college, troop?"

"Two years, sir."

"One of those junior colleges?"

"No, sir. A regular one."

"But you didn't finish?"

"No, sir."

"Care to say why?"

"Lost interest, sir."

"Did something else pique your interest, Corporal, and lure you away?"

"Not really, sir."

"So you just quit school and drifted."

"Not just, sir. I worked too. Some."

"Where?"

"Odd jobs." Rudy looked out the window. He wanted to change the subject. He could see the airstrip sliced by the colonel's venetian blinds. He thought of the bone chips out there, the skull.

"Also . . ." he said. The word leaked out while his mind was wandering.

"Also what?" the colonel asked.

"Also my mother got sick. I had to take care of her."

He hadn't meant to go down this route. It was just that he didn't want to talk about his knocking around, the marooned feeling, his working as a sales clerk in a toy store, the fights with his stepfather, the bombing out of college, his—and the colonel was right about this—his drifting. So he brought up his mother's "illness." She was fine, really; down in Florida with Roger now. But making her sick, just winging it here in the very seat of power, gave him the jump on the army, he thought. Same as filling out the next-of-kin blanks with *deceased*.

"I'm sorry to hear that. Is she doing better?" the colonel asked.

"You could say so, sir. She's dead."

Until now the answer had always been written, a bureaucratic ruse, but here Rudy was seeing its actual effects in performance. He so liked the way the news hit the colonel that it almost made

Rudy giddy. The colonel clamped his eyes closed, raised his brows, and nodded. He muttered he was sorry.

But before Rudy could say it was okay, the colonel threw him again by firing back, "Well, hell, this place is all about death, Corporal, as I guess I implied to you on your bed of pain. So maybe it's just as well you've had that little personal experience with the Big Finis and can be so cavalier about it."

"I didn't mean to sound cavalier, sir," Rudy said. "I'm sorry if that's the way it sounded."

"Don't apologize to me, troop. The apologies are due to your mother."

"Yes, sir."

"May she rest in peace."

"Yes, sir."

Now Rudy regretted the fib. It might screw up his chances of a transfer. What if the colonel checked up on him? There'd be more of these inquisitions, lots of squirming.

"But what the fuck are we talking about mothers for? That's what I want to know," the colonel said.

He stood up, gave his desk chair a spin and watched it revolve like a roulette wheel, then he slammed his hand down to stop it.

"A newspaper," he said. "I want one."

The colonel punched his fist into his palm. "A PIO lands in my lap," he said. "I don't bother to check with NATCOM as to *why*. I just figure, have Sergeant Teal write a rerouting order. Send this joker on to Germany or back Stateside. Treat him like an unauthorized hot potato and get him out of here. But then I think, hell shit. Why not take this fuck-up—not you, this army action— by the horns and get creative? You follow?"

"Yes, sir. So far."

"Good. Because I was thinking that even though we're here to keep the lowest of low profiles, so low that recordwise and cen- sorwise we don't officially exist, we could still use a PIO. But we would make it a *Private* Information Office. You could tell *us* about . . . *us*. For starters we could have an in-house newspaper.

I've always wanted one. It would be a booster. A way for us to keep in touch in a manner other than the all-too-common rumors and innuendos that buzz around this place like your blood-sucking friends out there."

The colonel turned to look out the blinds toward the airstrip, the tundra, and the mountains.

"It was right out there that I first saw you, by the by," the colonel said.

"Yes, sir. And I'm glad you did." Rudy's hand went up to his face. He felt the ripples of the bug bites.

" 'CO Saves Corporal from Mosquito Squadron.' How's that?" the colonel asked.

"I'd rather write the news, sir, than make it."

"Good attitude," the colonel said, spinning around and pointing at Rudy. "I like that. Now, let your army training run wild. Tell me how you'd run a newspaper here. Go. Be creative. Thrill me."

Rudy shifted in his chair. It seemed a bad moment to mention a transfer. The colonel was revved. Nothing back at Defense Information School, Fort Benjamin Harrison, Indianapolis, Indiana, U.S.A., had prepared him for this. He cleared his throat.

"Well, I'm assuming that the equipment you have here is something like a mimeograph machine?"

"Not *like* a mimeograph, troop. A mimeograph."

"Yes. Well, that limits us somewhat. But I figure you could do some things so that it doesn't come across looking like a, you know, a church newsletter."

"Okay," the colonel said.

"You don't want to settle for the mess hall menus and the chaplain's office hours and a list of the new magazines in the library, that kind of thing."

"No," said the colonel.

"You definitely want to go beyond that," said Rudy.

"Yes," said the colonel. "Where, then?"

"Good question," said Rudy.

"Answer it."

"Well, there are many possibilities. As you said, you want us to tell ourselves about ourselves, so you have to find out who those selves of ours are."

"Troop, why do I get the feeling you're vamping here?"

"Sir?"

"*Do* you have any ideas?"

"Yes, sir."

"Well, then, get on with it."

"Yes, sir. I thought I was."

"Not fast enough."

"Sorry, sir."

"And you keep saying 'you.' You. You. You. Start thinking 'we.' "

"Yes, sir."

"We. We. We . . ."

"Yes, sir."

". . . all the way home."

"Yes, sir." Rudy was sweating. He was parched. "Interviews, sir."

"What?"

"We'll do interviews. Profiles. 'Meet the Men and Women of Qangattarsa.' We'll find people with interesting stories and let them tell those stories."

"Go on," said the colonel.

"Well, we can probably pull some stuff from *Stars and Stripes.* And a culture page. I've already met a poet here. There's interest in the arts." Rudy was starting to roll at last. "We can't have photos, but maybe sketches. You can draw on mimeograph stencils, I think. And a crossword puzzle. We could do that. And—"

"This isn't going to work."

"Sir?"

"This sounds like shit. A mimeographed handout with a crossword puzzle drawn freehand on the back page?"

"Well, sir, we haven't even—"

"Plus they quit shipping *Stars and Stripes* here years ago. And what is this about culture? In a military newspaper?"

"I'm just—"

"I'm sorry, Corporal. I made a mistake. *I* was the fuck-up. I don't know what I was thinking. I'm going to get you transferred. Send you on to where your talent can be better used. I'm assuming you've got some talent. This was a bad idea. I'm sorry. Truly, I am sorry."

"No, sir. You don't have to apologize."

"You owe an apology to your departed mother. I owe an apology to you."

"That's not necessary, sir—"

"No, it is. I'm sorry."

"No, really—"

Rudy heard footsteps. He turned in his chair to see Irene walk past the door and go over to a filing cabinet in the outer office. She bent down to put something in one of the lower drawers, and Rudy got the kind of secretary-with-the-shapely-ass shot during which all the trumpets on the soundtrack go *whanh-wanh* with their mutes and the guy's mouth turns to flannel and he gulps in awe.

"No, really what, Corporal?"

"Hunh?"

"*What*, Corporal?"

Irene walked away from the file cabinet and out into the hall. Her heels clicked down the linoleum. Rudy snapped back to face the colonel.

"I want to stay here. I don't want to go, sir. Please."

"You want to *stay* here?"

Rudy could still hear the heels clicking ever so faintly. He couldn't believe what he was saying, but he knew he meant it. "I want to stay."

The colonel turned to look out his window again. "What would you call it, this paper?"

"The *Times?*" Rudy ventured. "The *Mirror?* The *Herald?*"

Colonel Woolwrap shook his head. "*I* had even thought of those names," he said.

"Oh," said Rudy. He thought of his old high school paper, the *Quill*. In the room next to the guidance counselor's office, looking out on the football field, the sound of slamming pads coming in through the open window on fall afternoons. He thought of the yeasty, acid smell of the fresh ink filling the room the day the bundles of a new issue came back from the print shop.

"The *Quill?*" he said.

"The Qangattarsa *Quill,*" the colonel repeated slowly. He tilted his head back and forth as if he were letting the name roll around inside while he considered it. "Nah. A quill's too flimsy. This is the military we're writing for, after all."

The colonel picked up a piece of something like ivory or bone from his desktop. It was about the size of a large carrot. Rudy thought again of the ash pile out by the hills. He noticed a penknife on the desk too. Some nicks and curves had been cut into the object. The colonel hefted the piece.

"Whalebone," he said.

"Ah," said Rudy.

"The natives kill them around here," the colonel said.

"Oh."

"I carve the bones," the colonel said, and he pulled some polished pieces out of his desk drawer and spread them on the green blotter. They were all body parts. Arms, legs, hands, a heart, even a torso that looked like a lumpish Venus de Milo. They were all polished and as pale as soap.

"My hobby," the colonel said. He studied the bones, turned a couple over and over, began to look dreamy. He sucked in a quick breath and flashed a surprised grin.

"The *Harpoon,*" he said. "Whalebone. Whales. Harpoons. The Qangattarsa *Harpoon.*"

"The *Harpoon?*"

The colonel stood up from his desk. He swept his hand across the air as if he were unfurling a banner. " 'It goes to the heart of the matter,' " the colonel said.

"The *Harpoon,*" Rudy said softly.

"That's the name," the colonel said. "You've got a name. You've got a motto. What more do you need? Put out a paper."

"The *Harpoon?*"

"It's basic to this godforsaken place. It's indigenous. It's also an armament, thus lending itself to our military posture here. I like it."

"The *Harpoon,*" Rudy said again.

"Christ, troop, don't make me do all the work."

"No, sir. Sorry, sir. I was just saying it over, getting used to it. I like it, actually."

" 'Actually'? How about that? The young tyro likes something the old man comes up with. *Actually.*"

"I'm sorry, sir."

"You do a hell of a lot of apologizing, troop. And none of it to the one person who deserves it most."

"Sir?"

"Your mother."

"Sir, could we—"

"I know. I know. '—leave my mother out of this?' That's the secret anthem of every soldier in the world. 'Leave my mother out of this.' Okay. Fine. But all this apologizing is not going to help you much as a newspaperman. You've got to be able to plunge in, maybe draw some blood."

"A harpoon."

"You've got it."

"Okay, sir."

The colonel began to pace again. He paced before the windows with views of mountains and glaciers. He paced over to a corner window that looked out on the fjord where the glaciers in the mountains picked up a rosy hue from the evening sun.

"Now, try this on for size: I've got you working with a mimeograph machine for starters, but I want to do better. This is the way the quartermaster mind works. I want this paper to have some class. I'll pull some strings. We'll make ourselves a real newspaper here."

"Sir, I might need a little help."

"Who?"

"Well, Corporal Lavone expressed some interest in writing."

"Sure. The more the merrier. I'm even beginning to like your artsy-fartsy idea, Corporal. Culture. Run with it." The colonel was rubbing his hands together. "We *needed* something like this to bring us out of our stasis."

"Stasis, sir?"

"Even worse than stasis, Corporal. Our decay. We're decaying here, Corporal. That's not for print. But it's true."

The colonel was running his fingertips over a heavy, red, floor-to-ceiling curtain Rudy hadn't noticed before against a side wall of the office. The curtain was closed. Stepping over to a standing globe by the window, the colonel turned away from Rudy. He looked pensive, maybe even melancholy. His hand rested on the globe and covered Siberia; his fingers stretched over the pole. It was, Rudy thought, a fine loneliness-of-command pose.

"This is a secret hospital, isn't it, sir?"

The colonel looked at Rudy. "It is," he said quietly.

From outside and far off, Rudy could hear the thumping of an approaching engine, a helicopter, probably coming up the fjord.

"Troop, I'd like the first issue of your paper out in a week."

"Wow, sir."

"You can do it."

"Yes, sir."

The colonel now heard the chopper too. He had his head cocked slightly. Rudy listened for Irene's heels on the linoleum outside, but all he could hear was the thrashing of the helicopter rotors above the hospital. The noise beat down and made Rudy jumpy. He had an impulse to run. Instead, he asked a question.

"Sir, will I get to go into the restricted part of the hospital?"

The colonel stared at Rudy from across the room. "What, troop? Say again?"

The colonel seemed preternaturally still. Rudy wasn't sure he could speak. "Never mind, sir."

"No! Say again, troop." The colonel had a slowly growing smile that began to gleam even next to all the light pouring through the window.

"Sir," Rudy said quietly, "will I get to go into—"

"The Wing, Corporal. We call it the Wing." And then the colonel reached up with both hands and began to pull the venetian blind cords, making the slats open and close. Rudy blinked as the daylight shuttered on and off.

"I'm answering you in code, Corporal." The colonel kept fluttering the blinds.

"I don't understand, sir."

"The answer to your question. About the Wing. Morse code, Corporal. Secret. I never said a thing."

As the blinds shuttered, Rudy could see that the helicopter had landed out on the strip. A man in a ski parka and civilian clothes had gotten out of the aircraft. A Jeep had picked him up and was heading down toward the Wing. Had the colonel even noticed this? Woolwrap kept pulling at the blind cords.

"Sir, are you saying yes?"

"Corporal, I'm saying, 'Dah-Dit-Dah-Dah . . . Dit . . . Dit-Dit-Dit.' "

SIX

He found Lavone down a roller coaster of a corridor in a small, brightly lit office in the Admin section. Lavone was typing, a Chesterfield dangling out of his mouth. He'd replaced his off-duty bopster porkpie with a regulation fatigue cap. On the walls of the office were charts covered with large sheets of celluloid on which were crayoned the names of soldiers who'd drawn CQ, guard duty, and KP. In the orderly room next door, Rudy could see a couple of PFCs playing darts.

"Was that you on the loudspeaker out by the airstrip yesterday?" Rudy asked Lavone.

Lavone looked up dreamily from his work. "It wasn't Arthur Godfrey."

Rudy told him the *Harpoon* would be out in a week.

"The *Harpoon,* hunh?"

"Yep."

"I like it."

"Good. You're on it."

Lavone's eyes dilated. "Colonel says?"

"Colonel says."

The PFCs next door were arguing about scoring.

"What am I supposed to do on it?" Lavone asked. He looked apprehensive. His eyes still on Rudy, he was rummaging for something in his shirt pocket. He pulled out one of the little white inhalers.

"Write," Rudy said.

"Journalism?" Lavone asked.

"There's nothing to it," Rudy said. "The army trained me in it."

Without taking the cigarette from his lips, Lavone took two deft hits on the inhaler. "Oh, the army," he said. "When do we start?"

Rudy went down a list of things they'd need to requisition. Lavone said he'd set it up so Rudy would have the storeroom where his bed was for his office-living quarters. Lavone went over to crank up the field phone to call Maintenance and Supply. Next door, the arguing got louder. One PFC poked the other on the shoulder with his fist. Rudy fiddled with the straps on a couple of octagonal motion-picture shipping containers that were on the edge of Lavone's desk.

After a couple of calls, Lavone said, "I got you a mimeograph. You can pick it up from Sergeant Genteen this afternoon. He'll tune it up. Lemme see about ink and paper." He held the phone in his hand and paused. "Jesus Christ, what am I going to write about for a goddamn newspaper? I write poetry."

"We could publish it," Rudy said.

Lavone looked toward the ceiling tiles. " 'Twat of winter night beast / Covers us all / As polar bear-hyena giant squats upon us for months / Smothering, darkening / Returning us to frigid birth canal of primal night . . .' It's from my 'Arctic Sutra,' " he said. "Canto Six."

Rudy looked at the film containers. "Maybe you could write something about the movies."

Lavone wagged the phone receiver. "Yeahhh. Maybe a little criticism, a little theory. Be kind of the post cineast."

It cheered Rudy to see Lavone warm to the idea of the paper.

"Dig it," Lavone said. He cranked the phone vigorously and began to make some more calls. Meanwhile, Rudy walked around to see what was in the typewriter. It wasn't poetry. It was a letter, on Department of the Army stationery.

. . . Because of the unusually difficult and protracted
negotiations with the Communist government of North
Korea, and thanks to the determination of American
military officials, your son's death in action can now be
confirmed. Security requirements limit our ability to
disclose details, but he was on a mission involving what is
now North Korean territory. . . .

The letter was to a Mr. and Mrs. Louis Santucci of Mineola, New York. It said it would be impossible for the army to return Louis Jr.'s remains. The army would be forwarding the Santuccis an American flag and would offer the family a grave marker at Arlington if they so desired.

Louis Santucci, Jr., gave his life in the service of his
country, and the United States Army in which he so
honorably served regrets the long and trying wait his
loved ones have endured.

Rudy had gotten so absorbed in the letter he didn't hear Lavone hang up the phone or notice that he had come around to look at the letter too.

"I'm out-processing the guy," Lavone said. "He Qangattarsa'd." Lavone made winglike motions with his hands fluttering up toward heaven. Rudy didn't get it.

"Qangattarsa," Lavone said. "It's Inuit. Eskimo. It's the name

of the base. It means 'Let us fly up.' The guy Santucci, he Qangattarsa'd." Lavone fluttered his hands again.

Rudy looked at the page.

"He was from the Wing?" Rudy asked.

"Mm-hm."

"He died?"

"Gone."

The window in Lavone's office looked out on the corrugated
flank of a Quonset annex ten yards away. There were a couple of
tufts of tiny flowers in the tight space between the buildings.
Rudy thought of the dandelions.

"Beyond the airstrip," he said. "There are these stone walls
almost grown over. There's a pile of—"

"You got it," Lavone said. "Santucci died, and yesterday the
cremation detail took him out there. He died in Greenland yesterday and in Korea eight years ago. He died here; they found
him there. Missing no more." Lavone tapped the letter in the
typewriter. "It's how we do it with all the guys when they go."

The PFCs in the orderly room were swiping at each other, on
the verge of throwing punches.

"What did he die of?" Rudy asked Lavone. "Really."

Lavone flipped through some papers. "Heart failure." He read
some more in silence, then began to mumble, "Missing arms, legs,
jaw, lower intestine . . ."

Rudy thought of the flag Mr. and Mrs. Santucci would get,
folded into a tight triangle of blue with a few stars visible on
the top.

"You ever been in the Wing?" Rudy asked.

Lavone shook his head solemnly. "Nope. No, thanks. I have
the clearance but . . ." And he drummed his fingers on the typewriter keys. They made a little puttering sound.

"But what?" Rudy asked.

After a long pause, Lavone said, "I lack the desire."

At that moment, a dart flew past Rudy's nose and thunked into the duty roster behind him. He ducked. Another dart pinged into the typewriter. The PFCs were screaming at each other. The largest one burst through the door first, running from the smaller one, who was cursing him and hurling darts. One of the darts bounced off the big guy's buttocks. He howled and tried to turn on his pursuer but flinched as two more darts and a flood of curses whizzed at him. The two PFCs raced through the office between Rudy and Lavone, knocking down a chair and pulling papers off the desk.

"Hey, assholes!" Lavone yelled, but the two guys were gone down the corridor. Their noise was quickly swallowed by the twists and turns of the hall.

Lavone began to pick up the papers. Rudy helped him.

"And right now everybody's happy," Lavone said. "Wait 'til it starts getting dark."

Rudy had a page of Santucci's medical report in his hand.

"Guys like Santucci die, we won't be printing their obits in the *Harpoon,* I suppose," Rudy said.

"Hell, no," Lavone said. "Of course not. It's a military secret. They aren't even here." He pointed the little bullet-shaped inhaler up his nose and sniffed. "For that matter, neither are we."

That afternoon, Rudy headed out to the machine shop to get the mimeograph. The shop was a small squared-off Butler hut adjacent to the larger semicylindrical Quonsets that were the motor pool garages.

The door to the shop was open, and from inside Rudy could hear an oscillating, metallic scraping. In the dimly lit room, he saw a man in goggles hunched over a whirling grindstone sending out a rain of sparks as the man drew something across the wheel. The sound of the metal on the wheel reminded Rudy of subway cars straining around a curve. It gave him a taste in his mouth like sucking on a key.

The man must have sensed someone standing in the door. He stepped back from the stone. Rudy recognized the paunch, the long arms.

"You Sergeant Genteen?" Rudy asked.

The man blinked. He had removed the protective goggles.

"Yeah," he said. His head moved back and forth on his neck almost like an Egyptian dancer as he tried to get a look at Rudy's backlit face, or at least discern his visitor's rank.

"I've come for the mimeograph," Rudy said.

"You ever hear of knocking?" Genteen asked.

"The door was open," Rudy said.

Genteen looked at the opening and at the light pouring through. He sniffed a wad of mucous back into his sinuses. He turned off the grindstone and stepped far enough to the side to get a look at Rudy.

"He-e-e-e-y," he said. "It's the Bug Man."

Rudy said nothing.

"Well, how you doin, Bug Man?" Genteen did a couple of little twitches. He giggled. Then he made the high-pitched whine. He giggled again.

"Sergeant, my name is Corporal Spruance. I have orders to pick up a mimeograph."

Genteen straightened up. "Oh," he said. "Oh. You do? Well, there it is." He pointed over to a hulking black and chrome machine sitting on a side workbench. "Pick it up."

Rudy looked at the large object with its printing drum, paper trays, dials, and crank.

"I'll need some help getting it over to my office," said Rudy.

"Your office?"

"It's in Storage Sector Charlie."

"Well, I dunno," Genteen said, making a show of stroking his chin with one hand and twirling the safety goggles by the strap with the other hand. "I'm a very busy man."

Genteen spoke with a drawl or twang that made Rudy guess he came from somewhere out in the midwest. One of those places where the land is huge and flat and featureless and they divide it up into sections.

"I mean," Genteen went on, "you want to tear me away from my work here. You want me to let things pile up. We're not accustomed to walk-in trade. We do things here by *appointment*."

"You had an appointment to fix the mimeograph," Rudy said.

"True," Genteen said. "I did. And it's fixed."

"Well, now it is needed in Storage Charlie."

"Is it now? And what for?"

Rudy knew this might be opening him up, but he figured at some level he had the colonel's backing. "For the post newspaper," he said.

"Ooooo, I heard about that," said Genteen.

"Great," said Rudy. "Now, would you help?"

"Gee, I'm awful sorry, Corporal. But I got my hands real full here. You'll just have to help yourself." He picked up the thing he'd been sharpening. It was a bayonet. He gave a helpless shrug and gestured at the shop, a man hopelessly swamped by demands.

For the first time, Rudy noticed that the place was shockingly neat, almost pathologically so. Every tool hung on pegboards within white outlined silhouettes. There were aisles and work areas limned on the floor with white lines. A flammable materials area and a paint locker had black-and-yellow diagonal warning stripes. The floor was spotless. Even rags, in their pile labeled "utility cloths," were neatly folded and stacked on a little shelf.

Genteen had gone back to sharpening the bayonet. Sparks flew from the wheel. Off to his right, in a sector marked "Grounds-keeping," Rudy noticed a wheelbarrow leaning against the wall. He grabbed it and pushed it over to the side bench. He embraced the mimeograph and muscled it into the barrow, smashing his fingers when the machine slipped. When he grabbed the handles of the barrow again and spun around, Genteen was there.

"Read that." The bayonet pointed to a sign hanging from the ceiling by two small chains.

NEITHER A BORROWER NOR A LENDER BE.
—William Shakespeare
SO DON'T EVEN GODDAMN ASK!
—Sgt. R.G. Genteen

Genteen tapped the barrow gently with the flat of the bayonet blade.

"I didn't ask," Rudy said.

"No, stupid, you just took. You were going to just take my goddamned wheelbarrow."

"You said help yourself."

Genteen winced and shook his head as if Rudy's very presence caused a stinging pain in his skull.

"Jesus, you are one dumb ass. No wonder you got all bug-bit. All right, I'll bend my own rules 'cause it sounds like the colonel's got a hard-on for this newspaper of yours. Take the wheelbarrow. Just be sure you put it back exactly the way you found it."

"Thanks a million, Sergeant."

Rudy wheeled the barrow by Genteen, who spoke softly, almost inaudibly, as he passed. "You know, I hate dumb asses. Only thing I hate more than a dumb ass is a wiseass, and you look like you're both."

Rudy left the shop and headed down toward the hospital with the machine thumping and shifting precariously in the barrow every time he hit a rock or a tuft of grass. The effort and aggravation were making him sweat. Genteen's voice stuck in his head. The day was almost hot, so Rudy took off his field jacket and wrapped it around the mimeograph. He noticed Genteen had done a good job servicing the thing. It was spotless; the chrome practically vibrated in the arctic sun.

At the door Rudy made a ramp out of discarded freight pallets. He rolled the barrow down the crooked halls to Storage Charlie and into his room. He was able—barely—to muscle the mimeograph up onto some empty packing crates that he and Lavone had gotten from Supply. Then he rammed back through the hall with the barrow and went back out to the machine shop.

Genteen wasn't there. Just to be sure, Rudy called in through the open door, "Anybody home?" No answer. The sergeant must have been down at lunch. Even out here, Rudy could hear the clamor of the mess hall.

A little breeze coming through an open window made the Shakespeare sign squeak on its chain. Rudy looked around the shop at all the perfectly ordered tools and equipment.

On the workbench, near the grindstone, he noticed the bayonet aligned neatly with some knives and entrenching tools. He picked the bayonet up and in a swift, pivoting swing brought it down on the anvil at the end of the bench. It made an echoless clank, and a tiny spark flew off the steel.

In the sunlight coming through the window, he looked at the weapon's edge. There was a small chip now on the blade; a pin-prick star gleamed there. Good. He placed the weapon back exactly as he had found it on the bench and left the shop.

SEVEN

Trotting out to the parade ground with a recorded bugle call blaring over the loudspeakers, Lavone was talking a mile a minute. He must have popped a fistful of whites with a gallon of morning coffee. He did little scat runs off the bugle's notes. He twitched and stutter-stepped as he jogged along. He told Rudy that these formations were at the colonel's pleasure. Sometimes they had them every few days, other times there'd be weeks between them. He couldn't remember when they'd last had one. Then he started reciting some verses of his "Arctic Sutra," doing it in a Lord Buckley voice. Then he wanted to know how Rudy became a fellow writer. They were out on the parade field. Troops were shuffling and jogging around them on the gravel.

"I'm only PIO," Rudy said.

"Yeah, but how'd you land that?"

"I liked the sound of typewriters."

"You're shitting me. They sound like whip cracks to me." Lavone winced and jerked and snapped his fingers. "I *bleed* my words out, man."

"Typewriters sounded better than M-1s."

"True. True. The man speaks true."

"So I asked the clerk in basic to put me down for something that required typing."

"And the man ends up here!" Lavone swept his hand in a full three-sixty around the horizon. "The army! You gotta dig it."

"*Fall in!*" a sergeant bellowed.

The soldiers dressed their lines, came to attention, and saluted as the flag went up. The formation was the first time Rudy had seen the hospital's entire troop strength. Rudy was at attention next to Lavone in the second line of Admin Company. There was the Medical Detachment across the parade ground with the Technical-Tactical Support Company: motor pool guys, maintenance, the mess hall and supply sergeants, transport guys, commo specialists, and a few Corps of Engineer mechanics and electricians. All together there were more than a hundred fifty men and women.

The parade ground was the clearest, flattest spot between the hospital and the fjord beach. Beyond the troops, Rudy could see the water sparkling a milky blue. There was a breeze blowing down from the mountains; it was cool and carried a light, cavelike odor from the glaciers.

Irene Teal was in a small squad on the open side of the formation. A couple of headquarters clerks, a chaplain, and a sergeant major were there. The colonel was nowhere to be seen. The sergeant major stepped out after the officer of the day called order arms. The sergeant major was named Dawes. He was large, black, and had a thick Louisiana accent. He announced movie night in the mess hall and a new laundry drop-off time. Then he launched into a diatribe against mess-hall pilfering.

"Any more food gets thieved outta there, y'all gonna be gettin nothin but ice sandwiches for lunch and for a hot supper we gonna serve you bowls of steam!"

There were a few snickers around the formation.

" 'Nuff said," Dawes went on. "Now Chaplain Captain Brank got his news repawt."

The chaplain stepped from his place in the line near Irene. Rudy noticed that with her back to wind, Irene's skirt fluttered out from her legs and curved around the backs of her thighs. He wondered if she knew—or cared—where he was in the formation.

Chaplain Captain Brank was short and stocky and had platinum hair sticking out in tiny feathers from the back of his fatigue cap. He had almost pink skin. Rudy wondered if he was an albino and if they even allowed them in the army. The gold crosses on Captain Brank's collar glowed; in his hands was a pack of three-by-five cards. As he stepped forward he kept flicking his wrists as if he were shooting his cuffs.

"Reverend Ed Norton," Lavone whispered in an Art Carney voice.

"Good morning, men . . . and women," the chaplain said.

"Good morning, Your Holiness," someone in the back muttered in a schoolkid singsong voice.

If Captain Brank heard it, he paid no attention and began: "I've picked up a little news from around the globe on the old wireless, so without further ado, let's turn to sports."

The chaplain reported that the Montreal Canadiens were the Stanley Cup winners, beating the Toronto Maple Leafs four games to one. He reported that the Bolivian government crushed a Falangist revolt, that the 116th patriarch of the Coptic Church in Cairo had been named, and that northern Greenland would be the site of four new Distant Early Warning radar stations. "To protect the free world from missile attack by Communist Russia," he said.

"Where's he get this stuff?" Rudy whispered to Lavone.

"And speaking of missiles," the chaplain went on, "you remember how the nation was thrilled back in April with the naming of the seven astronauts? Well, they're doing fine, and they're busy with the hard work of training for manned space flight."

"Off his shortwave," Lavone said.

The chaplain shuffled through his cards.

"And speaking of the hard work of training, both Ingemar Johansson of Sweden and Floyd Patterson of New York are readying themselves for their upcoming heavyweight-title bout in Yankee Stadium."

"Maybe," Rudy whispered, "we could get him to cover international news for us."

"Shut up in the ranks," a sergeant growled from down the line.

"And finally," the chaplain said, "our nondenominational worship service will be held Sunday at ten hundred hours, outdoors, right here, weather and insects permitting. Otherwise it will be in the mess hall."

There was some desultory clapping as Chaplain Captain Brank went back to his place in the formation. Rudy noticed Irene was looking right and left, as if searching for something beyond the formation. As he watched her, he was surprised by an incongruous smell mixed with the cool, sterile exhalations from the glaciers.

"Detachment . . ." Dawes bellowed. "A-tten-*hawn!*"

The smell was horse shit.

The entire garrison stiffened up, and from around the side of the hospital, on a roan mare complete with cavalry saddle and tack, came Colonel Lane Woolwrap at a canter.

"Hiyo, Silver. Awaaaay," muttered another voice from somewhere in the formation.

Cinders and dust kicked up as the colonel reined in the horse at the flagpole. He smiled, tapped at his mount with a crop, and had the horse walk along each side of the formation. He towered over the men.

Back at the flagpole, the colonel raised himself up in his stirrups, then settled back down and said, "Looking good, troops. I've got nothing of moment to tell you other than to announce the upcoming annual Qangattarsa Midnight Sun Bash, which will be held on the longest day of the year. That's the summer solstice for you Druids out there. There'll be further details in the *Harpoon*.

The *Harpoon,* for those of you who don't know, which should include just about every troop within the sound of my voice, is the soon-to-be published post newspaper. Watch for it. Carry on, Sergeant."

The colonel whipped a quick salute to Dawes, turned on his horse, and was off in a cloud of dust.

Dawes had the troops fall out. Rudy, Lavone, and the others in the Admin Company had police call. They stretched out at arms' width and walked in a line across the parade ground, picking up stray cigarette butts and gum wrappers.

"What's with the horse?" Rudy asked Lavone as they shuffled along, looking at the ground.

"It's purely for effect. Think Custer. Think Patton. Think San Juan hill. Woolwrap got the horses flown here on a cargo transport for his equestrian pleasure and for our morale." He bent down and picked up a cigarette butt.

"There's more than one?"

"There's a couple. His and hers. He's got them up in a paddock and barn behind the hangar by the airstrip. And if that's not enough, remember, it ain't easy getting a winter's worth of hay and feed shipped to a hospital in Greenland on the army's nickel."

"His and hers?" Rudy asked.

Lavone nodded. They were at the trash barrel now, dumping butts and wrappers in. They looked out toward the airstrip. The colonel was riding along the ridge. Rudy noticed over by the Headquarters entrance Irene had stopped at the door and was watching the colonel too.

"The guy's a wizard at hanky-panky," Lavone said, brushing the bits of tobacco off his hands. "Logistical and otherwise."

A white eye, flickering. A cone of illuminated cigarette smoke stretching the length of the room. On the screen, the flying-saucer door closed seemlessly, leaving the giant robot standing guard outside.

The mess hall was jammed. Rudy had to stand against the side wall. He was trying to make out Irene's silhouette. He thought he'd seen her sitting down front with a couple of the nurses.

On the screen, a soldier in a tank had shot his .45 at the space-man bearing a gift for the President. The spaceman fell, wounded; the gift was shattered. The robot's visor opened, and a beam of light vaporized soldiers' rifles, pistols, even one of the tanks.

Suddenly the film stuttered, and at the back of the mess hall the projector made a fractious clattering. Groans went up around the room. The images on the screen froze, tilted, then burned into an aureole of mauve and yellow around a white-hot core. The orderly running the projector cursed; the screen went blank. The broken and burned film reeled through the sprockets, and the machine began to purr again, empty.

In the reflected screen light, Lavone appeared on his way back to the projector, an exasperated Entertainment Liaison.

Along the center aisle, hands had gone up making shadow pictures of ducks, dogs, birds, and middle fingers fornicating with fists.

" 'A delightful amateur puppet show at the Qangattarsa Bijou greatly enlivened the Saturday screening of *The Day the Earth Stood Still*,' " Lavone muttered as he passed Rudy. "How's that for fuck-ing culture news?"

Some NCOs started clapping and chanting, "We want da movie. . . . We want da movie. . . ."

The orderly fussing with the projector looked up long enough to flip them the bird. Rudy noticed that there was a pile of film around the orderly's feet. Lavone began winding it onto the take-up reel by hand.

Down front, a couple of second lieutenants began singing lim-ericks. Other officers nearby joined in with the old frat house melody for the chorus:

> *Ay-yi-yi-yi*
> *In the Arctic we never get pussy.*

We've only got Eskimos
And they only rub your nose
So waltz me around by my willie.

Rudy saw Irene in the second row chatting and smoking with a couple of nurses. They were doing their best to ignore the goings-on around them. Irene turned to exhale and looked Rudy's way. She smiled; he did too. When she looked away again to answer one of the nurses, Rudy looked around. For the first time he noticed the colonel was sitting on an aisle seat just behind him. He was looking toward the second row too, smiling, arms folded, preoccupied. He hadn't noticed Rudy. Rudy wondered which one of them Irene had been smiling at.

The house lights flickered, the singing and stomping ceased, and the movie started up again, but people were losing interest. The door to the mess hall kept opening and spilling light into the room as people came and went.

"Shit," Lavone said. "These yahoos are ruining good cinema."

Rudy thought he saw Irene get up and, bent over to stay beneath the projector's light, work her way out a side door. He stayed a couple more minutes in deference to Lavone. The space man had survived his bullet wound and was living anonymously among the earthlings.

"I gotta get some air," Rudy whispered to Lavone.

As he headed out the door, he noticed that the colonel's seat was vacant too.

Rudy crossed the hall. In both directions he could see couples mashed up against the walls in crooks and alcoves, making out and copping feels. He pushed open the exit door to the outside. He went down a couple of wooden steps and stood looking at the fjord. A couple of gulls wheeled in the sky over the milky blue water. Then he noticed something moving out at the far end of the narrow bay, out where the fjord curved around a steep mountain slope. Something white and obtuse was working its way slowly into sight, like a letter being slipped tentatively under a door. At first Rudy thought it was a ship, but soon he realized it was something else altogether.

"Iceberg," he said aloud in astonishment.

The berg was bigger than the airplane hangar or any building at the base, maybe bigger than all of them combined. It was white, gray, and blue with crevasses and pinnacles and several winglike projections soaring from its top. It was beautiful.

He had no idea how long he'd been staring at it when he heard footsteps. Around the corner of the building came Irene, alone. She looked surprised to see him.

"Not watching the movie?" she asked.

Rudy shook his head. "Watching that." He nodded toward the iceberg.

She looked out at the fjord. "They wander in here every now and then. Like strays. It's amazing that they get this far inland."

They watched it creep further into the fjord. It still wasn't in full view around the point.

"I'm sorry about ditching you the other day," Irene said. "Did you get the message?"

Rudy said he did. He told her about Lavone on the speaker. She laughed. He told her he'd done a little tourism on his own.

"I got tied up with some work," she said. "I really did want to show you around. Did you get to see anything?"

"Yeah. A place called the Fire Department. A pile of bones and ashes."

"Jeez," she said. "All the hot spots. So to speak."

She put the ball of her right foot up on the first wooden step and flexed her heel. Rudy watched her calf tightening and loosening. She was wearing army low quarters, brown.

"You're learning about the place, then," she said.

Rudy nodded.

"It's not as bad as it sounds," Irene said. "Lane's done a lot to help them." She nodded toward the Wing, which was visible beyond a couple of storage sheds.

"Lane?" Rudy asked.

"The colonel," Irene said.

"He gave me clearance to go in there," Rudy said.

"I know. I was listening."

She must have tiptoed back after Rudy'd heard her footsteps go down the hall when he was meeting with the colonel. So she wasn't above a little eavesdropping, he thought. A kindred spirit. And eavesdropping on *him* at that. It made his skin tingle.

"I also know that was bull what you told Lane about your mother being dead," she said.

Rudy's breath caught. The tingle became a rush of blood to his face.

"I read your 201 file," Irene said. "Sometimes your parents are dead. Sometimes they're not." She smiled. Coyly, Rudy thought, and not without some warmth in her eyes. She hovered between interrogating and asking. "You like making up stories?" she wanted to know.

"Not usually," he said.

"You didn't make up that stuff in your 201 about enlisting on a judge's order as a way of having a sentence suspended," she said.

This dug right in. Rudy didn't know whether he was glad or scared shitless.

"What was it for?" she asked.

"Housebreaking," Rudy said.

"Robbery?"

Rudy shook his head.

"You just broke into houses?"

He nodded. "When people were on vacation. When things were lousy at my place."

"Then what?" Irene asked.

Rudy shrugged. "I'd look around."

"That's *it?*"

"Read their mail. Watch their TVs. See how they lived from the inside. Sound crazy?"

Irene looked at him and thought for a moment. "What do you mean, lousy at your place?"

"Fights," Rudy said. "With my stepfather. That kind of thing."

Irene slowly shook her head. She was staring, he could feel, hard at him, wanting him to know something about her.

"No," she whispered. "It doesn't sound crazy. It sounds like it makes sense."

Neither of them moved, and Rudy had the sensation they were floating like the iceberg that hung in the fjord.

Then Irene said, "The swelling's gone way down."

Rudy sucked in a deep breath. "Yeah," he said. "I probably can start shaving again soon." He rubbed at the stubble on his cheeks.

"Winter they relax the regs. Guys can grow beards if they want," Irene said. "Protection against the cold. A morale booster. I think they sometimes let guys in submarines do the same thing."

Irene looked up toward the glaciers. "In a way," she said, "winters here are like being in a submarine. Close. Closed in. Dark outside. They call it the Stark Raving Dark."

"My dad was in a submarine," Rudy said. "World War Two. He didn't mention beards, though. What do they do for women here to boost their morale?"

"Good question," Irene said, and she let out a quick, choppy laugh.

"Well, then," Rudy said. "What do you do for your morale?"

"Lose myself in my work," Irene said. Her hands, thrust in her fatigue jacket pockets, pulled down on her shoulders. She had jutted out her chin a little. She wasn't going to say any more.

He turned and looked out toward the flats. "When I was walking up there," he said, "and I saw the ash pile, there were some low stone foundation things in the grass. Lots of dandelions. It was pretty."

"That's the old Viking farmstead," Irene said. "The main house. The byre. Sheep pens and things. It's about a thousand years old. There was a whole colony. They did well for a couple hundred years, then the plague hit Europe, and ships stopped coming. The settlers here were left stranded. Cut off completely. The weather changed. The natives started closing in. The Vikings called them Skraelings, maybe because of the sound they made when they attacked. Anyway, the climate got cold. Crops failed. Hunting went to hell. I read that when a ship from Europe finally did get here, there were only a few stunted, inbred people left, practicing some weird kind of Christianity. A real lost civilization."

For the first time, Rudy noticed the soundtrack of the movie coming from the building. Eerie space music. A soft pink light spread across the tundra and made the mountains deep violet and the glaciers lavender. There were a couple of women's screams from the soundtrack. A panicked crowd scene probably.

"I have to go," Irene said.

"Where are you from?" Rudy blurted.

"What?"

"Where's home?"

"Over in the women's quarters—"

"No. I mean back in the world."

Irene took a hand out of her pocket and ran her fingers through her hair. The twilight had brought out an umber color in it. Normally it had looked more strawberry.

"The West," she said.

"Where?" Rudy asked.

"Idaho mostly," she said. "We moved around a lot. Me and my ma."

"What about your dad?"

"The war got him."

"Which one?"

She gestured over to the Wing. "That one. He didn't get shot or die or anything. He just didn't come back. Well, he came back, but he didn't stay. They got a divorce."

"So what did your mother do, moving around?"

Irene grinned. "Uranium prospecting."

"You're kidding."

"Used to be the big thing. Had a Geiger counter. Rock hammer for each of us. The whole bit. She was going to strike it rich. She used to say, 'Reenie, we're gonna get us a piece of those Atoms for Peace.' "

"Did you?"

"Well, she works in a fabric store in Spokane now, and I'm here. That's how we did."

Irene seemed amused by the story. Rudy, though, was spinning around one little part of it: her mother's pet name for her—Reenie. He wanted to say it, but he knew it would be a breach of something if he did, for now anyway.

"I better git," she said.

"I've never been west of Indianapolis," Rudy told her, wanting to keep her there, realizing he was grasping at straws.

"Well, it's a big country," she said. She was backing away some, trying to exit graciously, but smiling. There wasn't any of the prickliness and parrying like the time he'd met her in the mess hall. Maybe because she'd stood him up. Maybe because of the soft light.

"See you," he said.

She nodded.

He watched her go. She didn't head up the steps and inside. Instead, she turned and trotted, hands in pockets, across the cinder and stubble yard toward the far ell of the building, to the Headquarters sector, where the colonel had his office. There was a light on in one of the windows. Irene went in the door at the end of the building.

Rudy stood and listened to the movie some more. It was just a muttering jumble of dialogue now. The people sounded earnest and confused.

Shadows moved in the lighted window over in the office wing. Between there and where Rudy stood was a broken screen of empty fuel tanks, the mess hall trash sheds, and a parked deuce-and-a-half.

Rudy started walking as if heading toward the back door of the kitchen. He could soon smell the rancid fat in the tallow barrels. Someone was whistling in the storeroom. He walked past the loading dock and grease-slick steps. He quickened his pace as he traveled along the part of the building that faced the blind side of the Headquarters sector. He bent over as he ran to stay below window level and scissored his arms and legs like Groucho Marx.

Jesus, he thought, what *am* I doing? He had a fleeting picture of being in all those houses back in New Jersey. That had taken a little skulking too and some pretty sharp prowling tactics. He'd gotten good at it. Of course, it was darker there. He didn't have to mess with the midnight sun in New Jersey. He could move about and feel the glow of all the lights shining from the windows of the houses in the neighborhood. Lights that said, In here are people together. Lights like the one shining now in the colonel's office. In New Jersey, Rudy had to pick the houses with no lights—the unoccupied ones. When he got inside, moved around, pulled some shades and switched on a lamp or two, he felt pleasantly settled, at last a part of things, even as he was jumping with nervousness over breaking into places he didn't belong.

Now he was under the colonel's window. For a moment he wondered if it was open. If it was, had he made any noise? If it wasn't, what was he going to do: look inside? Stick his bug-bitten nose up against the glass and peep in? Kilroy is here?

This is crazy. The thought came so resoundingly into his head that he wondered for a moment if he hadn't actually said the words aloud.

"Where?" Irene's voice. Indistinct, but recognizable. The window was open a crack.

"The desk," the colonel said.

Irene laughed. "La-ane," she said with amused disbelief. "We can't there."

"Wanna bet?"

"No bets. No more bets."

Rudy was bent over, face almost at his knees, eyes closed. He could picture Irene with her hands on her hips, mirth flushing her cheeks, making her eyes flash. Her eyes were green.

There was a clatter of objects falling to the floor.

"All clear for landing," the colonel said. Irene laughed again.

Rudy heard furniture moving, feet shuffling, then nothing. Or almost nothing. He might have heard breezes blowing down from glaciers. He might have heard skin in contact with skin. Sighs. He didn't want to know.

He heard one word from the colonel: "Reenie . . ."

That did it. Rudy spun on his toes and, bent over, raced blindly along the building. He didn't pay attention when he shot across a small stretch of yard and headed in a different direction than he'd come. Dazed, he scuttled along up against attached Quonset sections and over to some steps that faced out toward the airstrip and the mountains. He thumped down at a doorway, out of breath.

As he sat panting, he began to realize he was looking at the mountains from a perspective he'd never seen before. The steps he was sitting on went into the Wing. He was about to stand up when something slammed into his back. It was a screen door.

"Whoa," said a voice. "Sorry, soldier."

Rudy turned. Behind him, in the haze of the screen, was a man in civilian clothes, wearing a ski parka. "Little help?" He tapped the door into Rudy's back. Rudy slid off the side of the landing.

The man came outside and looked down at Rudy. He was short and compact and had a severe, silver crew cut. His eyes were pale blue and his face was pocked with acne scars. He was smoking, and he had an attaché case in his hand.

"This area's off limits, in case you didn't know," the man said as he walked down the stairs and squeezed the burning coal of his cigarette ash onto the cinder path, then rolled the paper and shreds of unburned tobacco between his thumb and forefinger: field-stripping his smoke one-handed. He put the little white pellet in his pocket. "Strictly," he said. "Off limits."

He wagged his finger at Rudy as he strode by, heading for the airstrip. For the first time, Rudy realized there was a helicopter out by the hangar. It must have flown in while he was watching the movie.

Suddenly the man stopped, turned, and came back so close to Rudy they stood nearly toe to toe.

He grinned and almost hissed in Rudy's face. "I saw you from in there, soldier," he said with a glee that came out in his voice like escaping steam, "scooting along all bent over by the colonel's windows. What was it, a high-speed police call you were doing over there, or were you just running away from a butt-fuck?"

He didn't wait for Rudy to answer. He laughed and went on his way. Out at the airstrip, the chopper's engine was starting up with a whine as the rotors began to slice the air. Behind Rudy, someone closed the inner door to the Wing and locked it. In the dirt, the cigarette ember's last smoke rose in a tiny, disintegrating blue ribbon.

EIGHT

Rudy had to bust hump to get the paper out. He led with the Bash:

TITLE FIGIIT, GETTING TIGHT
TO HIGHLIGHT
POST FEST NIGHT

QANGATTARSA, Grnland.—A radio hookup to the Patterson-Johansson heavyweight championship bout, numerous local sporting and imbibing contests plus all-night revelry will highlight the annual Qangattarsa Midnight Sun Bash set for June 21st.

Commanding officer Lt. Col. Lane G. Woolwrap announced recently that the events will "pull out all the stops."

"The troops should be ready for a major offensive," he said.

"This goes back to a long tradition
started by our Scandinavian cousins," Col.
Woolwrap said. "The solstice is a time for
unbridled fun, for tossing off inhibitions,
for cutting loose. It's time to make up for
the long winter we must endure here."

Leading with the Bash for the *Harpoon*'s first edition had been
the most politic thing to do. The Bash was the colonel's baby; so
was the paper. Rudy had gotten all the information about the
party in a buck slip from the colonel that had come to him via
Lavone.

Rudy had been sitting at the typewriter, staring out the window at the glaciers. The mimeograph was in one corner on the
trestle table they'd fashioned from pallets and packing crates. Lavone had requisitioned a desk and typewriter for the other corner.
Rudy's living area with his bunk, footlocker, bedside crate, and
lamp was over against the far wall. Nice accommodations by army
standards, especially for north of the Arctic Circle.

Lavone had come in with the colonel's press release and a For
Sale notice from the GI who wanted to unload the guitar Elvis
had allegedly strummed. He also had a stack of three-by-five cards
from the chaplain: the world news roundup. At Rudy's request,
Captain Brank had sent over items about Queen Elizabeth's visit
to the U.S., Arthur Godfrey's battle with cancer, and Democratic
presidential hopeful John F. Kennedy's pledge to support the sep-
aration of church and state. "He's a Catholic!" the chaplain had
written in the margin.

When they'd finished running off the paper, sometime around
0300, Rudy had told Lavone to knock off; Rudy'd said he'd dis-
tribute the copies himself. He didn't expect to do it for every
issue—dawn delivery—but for this one, he felt like thumping
stacks of the early edition down on doorsteps around the post.

He lugged the bundle of *Harpoon*s into the deserted mess hall.
The place was quiet and a little humid still from the steam tables

and the previous evening's dishwashing. He took a large portion
of the papers, placed it on the pinball machine, and weighted the
stack down with a napkin dispenser.

Just before they'd run off the stencils, he and Lavone had
worked on the masthead. They'd settled on the title "Culture
Editor" for Lavone. Using an illustrated edition of *Moby-Dick* that
he'd found in his locker, Lavone sketched out a harpoon piercing
an unfurling banner with the paper's motto. For a while, they'd
tried to come up with something better than the colonel's slogan.

"Making a Stab at the News."

"A Whale of a Paper."

But it had been late, they soon gave up, and Lavone had lettered
in, "It Goes to the Heart of the Matter."

In a box on the front page, Rudy had placed his first editorial.
He called it the paper's "Statement of Purpose."

> We're here for you. The *Harpoon* is your pa-
> per, but it won't work without you. Help
> us. Keep us abreast of what's happening in
> your unit. If it's news, we need it. If it's a
> rumor, we'll track it down. Keep us posted.
> We'll do the same for you. We want to be
> your voice.

Rudy left the mess hall and headed toward Admin Company.
He liked walking the halls in the early morning. The undulant
floors were deserted; no one came around any of the sudden turns
or angles in the corridors; all the doors were closed; everything
was quiet, save for the far-off noise of the electric generator that
throbbed through the low-slung hardware of pipes, wires, and
conduits strapped to the ceilings.

Down in Admin, he left a stack of papers and gave a copy to
a sleepy PFC named Hinojosa, who was on CQ for the night.

"Fock is thees?"

"Your morning paper," Rudy said.

Even though they'd led with the Bash, it was Lavone's culture news that took up the most column inches. Lavone had stayed up two entire nights working on the piece. When he'd finished he looked frazzled and twitchy. He kept fingering his benzedrine inhalers and making jerky runs down to the latrine. Whatever he'd been taking, it had enabled him to produce reams. Enough for an entire series. Henry Lavone on American cinema. It was a gnarled, jittery, frantically digressive dissertation that placed science-fiction horror films at the center of the cultural moment and honored them as the safety valve protecting an endangered America from overheating in the race for nuclear superiority.

Rudy had no idea how the colonel or anybody else would take the piece. He wasn't even sure what Lavone was driving at, and from Lavone's hopped-up look, Rudy figured Lavone probably didn't know either. But . . . We want to be your voice.

After Admin, Rudy left bundles on folding chairs at the hall junctions to each of the barracks sections. He then followed the serpentine path down to the Headquarters area and slid some papers under each door until he got to the outer door of the colonel's office. While he was hunkered down there, close to the linoleum, he listened a moment, wondering if the two of them could possibly be inside. He half hoped they were. He'd slip the papers under the door. Make them start with surprise. Go to the heart of the matter.

But he heard nothing, save the sound of the distant generator. Still crouched, he saw his convex reflection in the polished brass of the doorknob. He looked like some kind of homunculus squatting there. Like Lavone's arctic winter night beast. He reached up. His hand grew large in the reflection. He turned the knob. As he was almost certain it would be, the door was open.

The shiver he felt was the same that came over him back home when he'd jimmied a lock or opened the unlatched window of a vacant house. It came from the certainty that he was about to cross the threshold into something forbidden and that with stealth and balls he would be able to juxtapose danger and the inexpressible peace of being in someone else's life for a little while. He wanted to go inside more than anything in the world.

The outer office contained only a couch, chair, and a rug with the Quartermaster Corps insignia on it. He remembered everything from his visit there to see the colonel, but now it all seemed bigger; every object had more mass and substance. Even in the shadows. The only illumination in the room came from the yard floods and twilight beyond the venetian blind. They left a dim grid on the walls. He saw the door to the inner rooms was ajar.

Rudy had a way of gliding when he trespassed. It was a form of floating, and he liked it. Even when he knew the house was deserted and its family was somewhere off at the Cape or in New Hampshire at the lake, he moved quietly and smoothly, levitating, the way he did now. It was his own brand of magic.

The offices were empty. He could smell it. Irene or the colonel had forgotten to lock up. He was the beneficiary of the oversight. He'd secure the place for them when he left.

He stood before Irene's desk. Backed by a palisade of file cabinets, it was nearly bare, save for a field phone, a blotter, and a lamp. No pictures. No mementoes. Very "strac." He went over to her typewriter and put a piece of paper in the machine. He didn't sit, but bent over and typed out a note:

WISH YOU WERE HERE.
                    —The Housebreaker

He left it in the machine and went into the next room, the colonel's office. Sometimes when he was trespassing back home, Rudy would pull the shades in a house and turn on the lights. He'd sit and read a book or watch some TV, maybe go through the mail with his feet propped up on the coffee table. It was risky, but strangely relaxing. He'd push his fear and loneliness outside the warmly lit room into the darkness beyond the home. He'd never felt so safe in his life.

He didn't turn on any lights in the colonel's office. He just moved around the room, hands behind his back, as if he were looking at artifacts in a museum. He sat for a while at the colonel's desk and resisted the temptation to pocket something, a pen, the little whalebone carving of a crooked arm that leaned against the lamp base. Instead, he walked over to a section of wall he'd noticed when he'd been there for his meeting about the *Harpoon*.

Between two bookcases was the floor-to-ceiling red velvet curtain. Rudy felt around and found the rope. He tugged it, and the drapes parted.

They were all military photos. Some were official, some nothing more than informal snapshots of soldiers. In the center were two company flags from the Third Infantry Division, Able and Baker Companies, Sixth Battalion. The pictures were arrayed around the flags as if radiating out from them. Many of the photos had black ribbons taped to their corners.

He stepped back and looked for a while at the men and the flags. Geographers said there was a place in Missouri or Kansas or someplace that was the exact center of the United States. Rudy didn't know how they measured it, but he knew what they meant. He had the feeling that this sanctum, or whatever it was, was at the exact center of Qangattarsa. It was a feeling he'd get sometimes when he moved through empty houses. There was always a center.

He crossed the room and closed the curtains. He couldn't help but think of the faces staring at the back of the drapes. He checked the area for any signs of his presence, went through each office, and carefully reentered the hall. He locked up behind himself and slipped a couple of copies of the *Harpoon* under the door.

NINE

During the warm months at Qangattarsa, polar bears sometimes came to the dump to forage. The bears were a nuisance and
dangerous, so the dump was off limits, but occasionally the colonel authorized Periodic Ursine Harassment Details (PUHDs).

When word went out one afternoon that two bears were rummaging in the trash and that a PUHD was on, Rudy and Lavone,
relaxing after putting the paper out, drove the Admin Jeep out
to watch the action and catch a few rays. They parked on a hill
above the dump, which was in a glacial depression about a mile
from the main post. Troops who had clearance for vehicles had
taken off over the tundra and were roaring around among the
garbage piles.

A pleasant breeze blew in from the fjord. Lavone lay shirtless
on the ground atop a shelter half. He had his porkpie tilted down
covering his eyes. Rudy sat on the Jeep's hood and leaned back
against the windshield. He was scanning the dump through the
viewfinder of a beat-up old Zeiss with a 200mm lens. Lavone had
brought the camera along for use as a telescope.

Several Jeeps and a half-track were chasing the two white bears around smoldering heaps of garbage. Up from the valley floor came the sound of the Jeeps' horns and GIs' shouts. Lavone leaned over to grab a beer out of the ammo box they were using as a cooler.

"There's something very Rome, four A.D., about all this," Lavone said. "An amphitheater. Beasts. Soldiers in chariots." He raised his beer aloft. "Emperor Caius Augustus Woolwrap, we salute thee."

Rudy tracked a peeved bear racing ahead of a Jeep. He fiddled with the focus, keeping the bear's shoulder in the crosshairs. There was a ponderous grace to the way the beast lumbered ahead of the jolting vehicle.

"Beer and circuses," Rudy said. "Or bear and circuses." He lowered the camera. The dump looked flatter and wider to the naked eye. "You ever been in the emperor's office?" he asked.

Lavone was drawing the icy beer can across his brow. "Nope," he said. "I avoid the place. Always have. Always will. It's off the map of the known world for me. Why?"

"Just wondering about some pictures I saw in there."

"When were you in there looking at pictures?"

"I saw them when I first met the colonel," Rudy lied.

"What kind of pictures? Ze feelthy kind?"

"Na. Just snapshots of soldiers. Third Infantry Division."

"That was the colonel's outfit in Korea. They're probably just old drinking buddies."

"Probably," Rudy said.

Down below, one of the bears reared up on its hind legs.

"Oooo, mama," Lavone said, sitting up. "That baby is pissed."

The Jeeps fanned away from the towering beast but quickly zoomed back in and started chasing him again. They bounced around, making figure eights. Sometimes they'd veer away and head for flocks of seagulls, sending the birds screeching and wheeling into the air. Occasionally the bear would roar, sounding like a truck with moaning air brakes. That would make the GIs cheer louder.

"You know," Lavone said, "I gotta thank you, man. I'm digging the hell out of this journalism gig you got me doing." Lavone was back down, spread-eagled on his shelter half, baking. "I mean it's a kick seeing your stuff in print, you know? Like who knows when my poetry will receive its due, right? But the paper, man, it's instantaneous. I write it, and, bingo, the next day people read it. I dig that. I'm wondering, though, you gotten any letters to the editor or anything about my stuff?"

"No. Not yet."

"Not yet, hunh? No comments? No reactions? No nothing?"

Rudy looked up from the viewfinder and shook his head. "You can't expect too much," Rudy said. "After all, this is the army." He went back to sweeping the viewfinder across the mottled and sparkling hills of refuse. It was kind of touching that Lavone wanted an avid readership so badly.

Then, coming around a trash pile, one of the Jeeps cornered too quickly and turned over. Both Rudy and Lavone sat up when they heard the shouting. The soldiers in the Jeep jumped clear and took off screaming for the half-track that was behind them making a wider sweep on the turn as a bear came loping around a hill of cardboard. The men, still shouting, dove headfirst into the half-track. The driver panicked, lost control of his machine, spun it wildly around with soldiers clinging to the outside, and drove it right up and over the toppled Jeep. The bear stood and watched.

"Shit," Lavone said. "More paperwork."

With the half-track off in the distance grinding gears, the bear walked up to the crushed Jeep, sniffed, and began to urinate on the right rear tire.

"Score one for Nanuk," Lavone said.

Soon another Jeep swung back into view, and the chase continued off to the far side of the dump. Rudy and Lavone had another drink while things were quiet. Rudy picked up the camera and swept the lens back and forth across the dump. He swung it out to scan the fjord, the mountains, the glaciers. It was a sparklingly sunny day, and seeing everything through a foreshortening lens made it seem as if he were watching a travelogue. He tilted down to focus on some white flowers shuddering nearby in the breeze, then back up to the arctic grandeur and the blue-white of a distant glacier. He skipped over the homely huddle of army buildings at the head of the fjord and caught someone walking down from the airstrip.

It was Irene. She was out there alone, a blithe farm lass espied on a country lane.

"You know what I'm wondering?" Lavone said in a dreamy voice from down on the blanket. "We've got one of our bears down there getting its periodic harassment by the U.S. Army. What I'm wondering is, where's our other bear?"

The answer was in Rudy's viewfinder. Even as Lavone spoke, the second bear popped into sight. He came steaming up the road. He must have slipped through the harassment detail's perimeter and escaped the dump. He was heading for the open spaces between the airstrip and the base, heading for Irene.

Rudy scrambled over the windshield of the open-top Jeep and flung himself behind the wheel. He fumbled for the keys and started grinding the engine.

Lavone turned around to check on the commotion.

"*Start,* dammit!" Rudy shouted.

"What are you doing?" Lavone yelled.

The engine kicked in, and Rudy slammed the Jeep into gear. He popped the clutch, and like a cartoon start, the vehicle leaped off all four wheels at once. Rudy was gone before Lavone was on his feet.

When he hit the first few bumps of the tundra, Rudy flew off his seat and smashed his head on the windshield top. He saw stars, felt for blood, but there was none. He was charging overland and had to balance his haste with his need to stay in the vehicle. The bear was about three hundred yards off to his right, moving fast. Another Jeep appeared at the crest of the dump road, the Jeep that had been pursuing the bear.

Rudy started blowing his horn. Maybe the beast would get scared and turn away. He didn't. He kept his course, heading for Irene. Responding to the horn, Irene turned, and Rudy could see her freeze, her arms shoot out, her knees buckle a little: the startle response.

Instantly she began to run. Irene was fast, but the bear was picking up speed and closing on her. Rudy, though, was gaining on the bear. He could see ropes of saliva hanging out of the animal's black chops. The bear's muscles pulsed in waves under his white fur.

Rudy was able to cut the angle down between his Jeep and Irene, and soon he was within shouting distance.

"Jump in!"

He pulled alongside and then ahead of Irene on her right. He let off the gas so she could match his speed. Her eyes were wide with fright. He held the wheel with one hand and reached for her with his other. She clutched at him, and together they flung her into the Jeep, over his lap to scramble for the other seat.

"Oh, God!" she cried. She rose to her knees and looked behind them. "Go! Go! Go! He's right there!" She was frantic. She looked as if she might jump out and start running again.

"Get a picture!" Rudy shouted.

"*What?!?*"

"Get a picture!" Rudy thrust the camera at her. He shook it before her face. She took the thing. He could see the bear, a throbbing white shape at the edge of his vision. Close. Almost at the Jeep's tailgate. "Hurry up!"

He could hear Irene on the seat next to him gasping and shooting pictures. "Asshole!" she yelled.

Him or the bear?

The Jeep jolted horribly when Rudy hit a rock. He checked: Irene was still aboard, still clicking away.

"All right, stop shooting!" he shouted. "Hang on!"

Rudy swerved to the right and felt the Jeep heel stiffly. Irene slammed into his shoulder; her head blocked his view for a moment. Christ, he could actually smell her hair, the shampoo and the slight odor of horses. She must have been on her way back from currying or feeding the colonel's stock up in the paddock.

The Jeep struggled to stay upright through the turn, made it, and Rudy thrashed the vehicle toward the nearest dirt track, where he could make better time.

The bear swerved too, but zoomed left again when the pursuit Jeep with its cheering crew of GIs nearly smashed into it. The troops threw beer cans at the bear and waved at Rudy and Irene. The gang must have picked up Lavone because he was now standing up holding onto the windshield, giving them the thumbs-up sign. The pursuit Jeep began to drive the bear away from the post and down toward the water.

Rudy slowed his Jeep, swung it around, and pulled it to a stop on a rise overlooking the base and fjord. He could feel his arms start to tremble and his heart pound. Irene was sitting on the seat, camera in her lap, eyes squeezed shut; she was hyperventilating and holding her head between her fists.

"Oh, man oh manohmanohman!"

"Hey, you okay?" Rudy asked.

"You're nuts!" Irene said. She looked up. Her face seemed unable to settle on an expression; it flashed emotions in quick succession like a sped-up movie. Finally, she started to laugh. "Oh, man! You are really, really *nuts!*" she said and looked out toward the distant bear and the careering Jeep behind it.

"And an asshole too?" Rudy tried to stifle his own shaking.

Irene let out another long laugh of relief. There was joy in it and a little leftover hysteria.

"Sure. All that and more," she said. "Jesus Christ, am I glad you were out here. Oh, man . . ."

"Me too," Rudy murmured.

Irene looked at the camera in her lap. She picked it up. "What was *this* all about? 'Get a picture.' "

Rudy shrugged. "I don't know. A nose for news, I guess."

Irene worked the cocking lever. "Well, you're out of film. I shot the roll."

"It was empty."

"*What?*"

"It's Lavone's. There wasn't any film in it."

"You *are* an asshole!" Her face shone bright with indignation but even more with exhilaration, as if she couldn't help but admire his mettle.

"It kept you busy while we fled."

Irene threw herself back against the Jeep's seat, her head flung back, eyes closed; she looked as if she were trying to piece together what had just happened, trying to settle down.

For Rudy, with Irene reclined in the seat like that, everything around him seemed to hold still for her. Then, hearing her breathing steady itself, he felt everything begin to turn slightly, begin to move again, but slower, as if the bear chase and the excitement, maybe everything in his life before this moment, had happened long ago. Now was a new time. Out in the fjord, the two bears were swimming away; their heads white dots, their wakes a pair of chevrons.

Rudy felt heat rise in his face. It was risky, he didn't know who could see them, he didn't know how she would take it, but he reached over and placed his hand on hers. She accepted his touch, then turned her hand into his and tightened on it. She shook her head and slid down in the seat with her eyes still closed and her head back. "Ooooo," she sighed.

"Yeah," said Rudy.

"Eeeyow."

They sat, holding hands, as Rudy watched the bears swim farther into the blue water. A calm settled over the hill. Even the breeze died down.

After a while, Irene whispered, "Thank you."

She turned her head to look at him. They could have been lying somewhere, side by side, just talking.

"Sure," Rudy said. "Any time."

Soon a sly look came over Irene's face. "By the way," she said. "I saw your newspaper."

"You like it?" Rudy asked.

"Well, I don't know. I barely got to read it. I was distracted by a note I received. . . . 'Housebreaker'? . . . 'Wish you were here'?"

Rudy smiled. "I did wish it."

"So, how'd you manage to get into the office to leave the note?"

"I was delivering papers, slipping them under doors. Your door was open."

Irene's face darkened for a moment. "Shame on me. A breach of security. I must have been distracted. Working after hours or something."

He didn't want to think about what after-hours work might mean, and so he looked away. He noticed for the first time he had parked at the center of a star of intersecting roads that ranged outward toward places all over the post. Irene hadn't let go of his hand, and their grasp, suspended there between them, had become an infinitesimally small point at the center of those diverging roads.

"Can we meet?" he asked quietly. "Again?"

Irene looked down at their clasped hands. She sighed and pulled her hand away, and Rudy let it go. She looked about, swept her glance in an arc of frustration across the whole of the base. "Damn this place," she whispered. Then she looked at him and shook her head no and half laughed, almost helplessly. "Damn me."

Rudy could have kissed her just then, she might have even let it happen, but it was way too dangerous. He'd have to let her go. All roads led to where they sat. They were visible from everywhere.

"I better get down there," she said, nodding toward the buildings.

"Sure." He was lightheaded. His voice came to him tinny and distant, the cry of a man lost far out to sea.

He started the Jeep, and they drove down toward the post buildings without speaking. Rudy pulled up in a cinder-strewn parking area. He turned off the motor. She went up the Headquarters steps. Rudy watched her from the Jeep. Irene's feet scraped on the wooden planks. At the door she turned. She made an almost military about-face and marched down the steps. She stopped at the far side of the Jeep.

She spoke firmly. "I will meet you," she said. "I will."

And then she went in. He was left staring at the closed door, and lingering in his mind was the look on her face: a smile colored with resolve but tinged, too, with uncertainty.

He turned to start the Jeep again and hadn't even put his hand on the key when he heard from one of the open office windows, down in the Headquarters area, the rattle of a venetian blind.

TEN

The EM/NCO club was smoky, loud, and in full swing. There were a few women around, but mostly it was men at the tables and at the bar made of oil drums topped with planking. Japanese lanterns hung over the lightbulbs dangling from the curved masonite ceiling that covered the triple-thick insulation of the Quonset. On the walls were travel posters of guys fly-fishing in streams around the United States. Stuck among the posters were airbrushed cheesecake paintings from old Ditzler automotive calendars.

One of the cooks was running the beer taps. The crowd was sitting four, six, or even more to a table. There was a jury-rigged juke box in the corner that played for free. Music and outbursts of boisterous laughter vectored in every direction.

Rudy came in with a copy of the *Harpoon* in his pocket. The colonel had sent it over earlier in the day. It had been slipped under his door while Rudy was at lunch. There were a few scratch marks here and there on the issue and a big question mark on Lavone's article, but there was also a buck slip that said,

FINALLY GOT AROUND TO READING
THIS. LOOKING GOOD. KEEP IT UP!
—Lt. Col. L. G. Woolwrap

Rudy saw Lavone sitting with two other men at a table near the juke. They waved him over.

Petri and Beef were the PFCs whom Rudy had first seen throwing darts. They roomed down the corridor from Lavone, in the men's barracks.

"Editor-in-chief," Petri said, "join us. Or are you out hunting down a story?" Petri had a weightlifter's build and was popping sunflower seeds into his mouth from his fist, which shot up like a spring-loaded catapult out of his lap.

"No story," Rudy said. "Off duty."

"Maybe he's out huntin' bars," Beef said in an affected drawl. "Polar bars."

"Or damsels in distress," said Petri. "Lavone's been telling us about your fancy driving out by the dump."

"His fancy technique for picking up broads."

"Scoop 'em up."

"The colonel's broad."

"Grin down them bars. Like Davy Crockett."

"Grin down them broads."

"A toast," Beef said, wobbling to his feet. "To the gentlemen of the press. And to bars."

"And to broads."

"And to Davy Crockett."

They threw their heads and glasses back, guzzling what beer didn't trickle down their chins or back to their ears. They all looked a little gone, especially Lavone, whose bopster porkpie was badly askew.

Rudy sat in the empty chair at the table and poured himself a drink from the pitcher. He felt uneasy that everybody had been talking about his polar bear encounter with Irene. A lot of people must have seen them out there. Or heard about it.

"Corporal Spruance," Petri said after his chug and a lengthy belch, "we're doing a survey. Might be interesting for your paper. As a man of proven driving ability, you own a car?"

"No," Rudy said.

"If you *could*," Petri said, "own a car, any make, any model, what would it be?"

"A Jeep," Rudy said.

"Asshole choice," said Petri. He flipped a seed at Rudy with his thumb. Rudy caught it, ate it.

"What'd you guys pick?" Rudy asked.

"Corvair," Lavone said.

"Prissy choice," Petri said.

"But a convertible," Lavone said.

"I want one of the Fords with the retractable hardtops," said Beef, scratching his nose.

"What about you?" Rudy asked Petri.

"DeSoto Firesweep," Petri said. "With the illuminated Indian figurehead on the hood."

"It takes something like seven motors to get that top to retract into the trunk," Beef said.

"A Corvair convertible or a TR-3 or a pre-'fifty-seven T-bird before they got all bloated," said Lavone.

"I like fins," Petri said, popping more seeds. "DeSoto's still going with fins, and I'm a fin man."

"Seven motors and, I don't know, ten relays and a dozen or so limit switches."

"You spend all your free time studying that shit," Petri said, whirling on Beef. "Limit switches."

Beef was a skinny lifer. Only about five years older than Rudy, he'd already been in the navy, gotten out, then reenlisted in the army after a three-month look at civilian life. He said he was considering sampling all the branches of the service. He was an electrician and fire tender and, although he had a bunk in Petri's room, he spent most nights on a cot down in the boiler room.

"So the fuck what?" said Beef.

"We seem to have a division here between the fins and the nonfins," Lavone said. "DeSoto and T-bird. Ford and Jeep."

"Aren't we all getting monorails sometime soon?" Rudy asked. He was scratching at his beard stubble and gazing up at a picture of a guy with a rainbow trout on his line in the middle of a pebbly stream somewhere in the Rockies. The jumping fish looked fake, a cutout added later in the darkroom. On the far bank, by a perfect campsite, a leggy blonde clapped with excitement. There was something else about the picture besides the fake fish that bothered Rudy.

"Fins," Petri said, "are aerodynamic. They help a car's stability."

"Bullshit," said Beef.

"Mr. Limit Switches says bullshit to fins," Petri announced.

"Jet packs," Lavone said. "Monorails and jet packs. We're supposed to get 'em."

"I want my jet pack with fins," said Petri.

"I want my monorail."

"I want another round."

As Beef got up to fetch more beer, the other three men listened to the music. It rumbled *bomp-de-bomp-bomp, bomp-bomp*. "Bo Diddley Bo Diddley," the record kept saying, but Rudy couldn't understand any more than that. The beer was getting to him. He liked the thick, fuzzy feel of the music.

"Did I ever tell you I was stationed with Elvis over in Germany?" Beef was back with the pitcher.

"Of course, stupid," Petri said. "They ran your goddamn guitar ad in their paper."

"Same unit," Beef said, ignoring Petri.

"What was Elvis like?" Lavone asked. He had an amyl nitrite ampule in his fingers just below the table, but stuffed it back in his pocket, pulled out an inhaler, and took a whiff.

"Quiet," said Beef. "Country."

"You talk to him much?" Rudy asked.

"Not a word," said Beef.

"He borrowed your fucking guitar," Petri said. "Supposedly."

"Guy in the bunk next to me loaned it to him while I was on guard duty. Never even asked my permission. Guy told me about it later. Said Elvis returned it and told him if he had started out with a guitar like mine, he would've had to quit music and be a Jeep driver in the army from the get-go."

"How do you know the guy in the bunk next to you wasn't bullshitting?" Petri asked.

Beef smiled. He rummaged in his pocket, pulled out his wallet, and began going through it. "Because," he said, "of this."

He held up a tortoiseshell guitar pick embossed with the script letter E. All the faces at the table crowded around the object in Beef's hand.

"It was in my guitar case when I got back from guard duty," Beef said. "*He* left it there."

There was a moment of silence at the table. The music throbbed on.

"Is he still in Germany?" Rudy asked.

"Still is," Beef said.

"Did you ever wonder why you got sent here instead of Elvis?" Petri asked Beef.

"Not for a moment," Beef said.

"Security," Lavone said. "Think of the security nightmare: Elvis here."

The drinking had made Rudy muzzy and relaxed. The conversation around him could have slipped into gibberish, and he'd have been happy just to sit there and drift along with it. He pictured Elvis walking around the base with a throng following him everywhere. Flashbulbs, soldiers, civilians. He saw photos. Faces. Rudy saw the curtained altar in the colonel's office. There were the faces behind the curtain. And he saw Irene's face. The look when she was fleeing the bear. Then the smile. Resolved. But uncertain.

But then he noticed a lanky figure at the bar, and even from the rear, Rudy knew it was Genteen. Rudy felt a sudden tightening in his gut. He hadn't noticed Genteen come in. The sergeant had his back to Rudy's table; he was sidled up to the bar talking to a couple of nurses.

"Spruance," Petri said, "you gotta do better than a Jeep. Pick something else."

"What kind of car does Elvis drive?" Rudy said, turning away from the bar.

"Cadillac, of course," said Beef. "About a dozen of them."

"A Cadillac, then. One will be fine."

"They got fins," said Petri.

"Where's Lavone?" Beef asked. There was the faint, quick odor of rotten apples in the air.

Rudy looked down. Lavone had bent over beneath the table to crack an ampule. He was taking a mighty suck through his nose. It made his back arch until he knocked the table and the glasses teetered. He popped up with a garish smile on his face.

"Plunk your magic twanger, Froggy," Petri said, catching his drink.

"Christ, Lavone," Beef said. "You'll turn yourself into a hophead for sure."

"The Thomas De Quincy of Greenland," Lavone said.

Rudy looked back at the bar and Genteen was gone. The two women were still there with a space next to them where Genteen had been. Rudy glanced around the room. No Genteen. He looked back at the bar. The women were laughing as they lit cigarettes together.

Petri turned around to see what Rudy was looking at.

"Got your eye on someone, Spru?" he asked.

"Nah," Rudy said, and he leaned forward, took a drink.

"He tried with Sergeant Teal, but the colonel's got polar bears guarding her," Lavone said.

"You considered the native population?" Beef asked.

"I haven't even seen any," said Rudy.

"They'll be around," Beef said.

"Beef likes red meat," said Petri.

"So the fuck what? I'm not alone in this."

"And that's why the tribe is called the Inuit," said Petri. " 'Cause with their women it's easy to get 'Into It.' "

"And what the fuck do you know?" asked Beef. "All you do is try to build up your body." He made the masturbating sign with his fist. A hail of seeds rained down on him from across the table.

The music changed from a slow tune to something actually by Elvis: "Jailhouse Rock." The women at the bar said something to the bartender, and he went over to the juke and turned up the volume. People all over the club started dancing. If they weren't dancing, they bopped to the music in place. Above, tacked to the curved ceiling, the man fished. As stupid as it seemed, Rudy found himself wishing he was in that poster, catching that fish, and the woman on the far bank by their perfect campsite cheering him on would be Irene.

"So why'd *you* get sent here?"

The voice sounded almost fierce and so close to Rudy's ear, he expected to turn around and see Petri leering an inch or two from his face. But the beer and the noise must have been playing tricks, because Petri was sitting back in his chair looking at him, hands folded on the table. Beef was looking at him too, bobbing his head to the beat, his palm slapping time on the table in a way that made him look as if he had all the time in the world for Rudy to answer. Only Lavone was ignoring him; he was counting ampules below the tabletop.

Rudy pulled the folded copy of the *Harpoon* out of his pocket.

"To put out a paper?"

Beef and Petri looked quickly, almost furtively, at each other, then back at Rudy. They studied him.

Finally Petri nodded, squinting his eyes. "You probably were."

The words spread like a slick, then sank immediately beneath the commotion. Together, Beef and Petri tossed back their beers. The bottoms of their glasses stared at Rudy. The music seemed to pound down from above. Rudy looked up at the poster. He'd asked the colonel to let him stay on. He could have been shipped out, transferred, but he'd asked to stay on.

Then he realized what it was about the poster that had bothered him. The fisherman had a silver-gray crew cut, just like the hissing man in the parka Rudy'd met on the steps of the Wing.

Rudy wanted out. He said good-bye, but too quietly for any of the others to hear. He was up before their glasses were down and they'd noticed he was gone. He pushed and strained his way through the crowd to get to the door. It took forever. Elvis was rocking the whole cellblock.

She was in his room when he got back. He hadn't read the regs, but this had to be a breach. Standing in the middle of the floor, between his bed and the desk, Irene didn't seem alarmed in the least to be caught there when he walked in. She just held up a copy of the *Harpoon* and said, "Looking good."

Rudy stood in the doorway.

"Those were the colonel's words too," he said.

Irene shook her head. "They were mine. I wrote the buck slip."

"Thanks," Rudy said. The bleariness from the beer sucked away in a furious rush inside his head. A high-altitude clarity was roaring in to replace it. She was in his room.

"The door was open," she said. She walked over to the desk and leaned on its edge. "So is it officially housebreaking?"

She looked at him and smiled, checking his reaction. He tried to stay composed, but this was happening too fast. All he could muster was a shrug. He stepped over and sat on the edge of his bed. He was lightheaded. He needed to settle down. His heart was hammering in his chest. There seemed to be a vast, windswept range of linoleum between them.

Irene walked a little around the office area, almost as if she were on an inspection tour.

"I wrote the buck slip," she said. "But it was the colonel's opinion too. I know that for a fact. He liked the paper. He couldn't make heads or tails of that piece about the movies, though."

Rudy chuckled. "He wasn't alone. But he'll have a second chance. And a third and a fourth and fifth, probably. Lavone's planning a series. If the paper lasts that long."

"It will," Irene said. She tested the crank of the mimeo. "Lane's got plans to ship a real press in here. I've been telexing bases all over Germany for the past two days. He's going to make the *Harpoon* a real newspaper."

"What the hell for?" Rudy asked.

"Why the hell not?" Irene said. "It's something to *do*. We need that here. You'll see."

Rudy ran his hand through his hair and rubbed his eyes. He actually liked the idea of a real paper. It seemed absurd, and how they'd pull it off was beyond him, but he didn't care at this point. Even if it was the colonel's idea. Irene seemed enthused, and that was enough.

She had entered the neutral zone of linoleum between the office area and the bunk where Rudy sat. She pointed over toward his bedside crate, then folded her arms in front of her. "No pictures of family," she said.

Rudy looked over to the crate. All that was on the OD towel was his Baby Ben, silent, rundown, and unwound.

"You don't have any photos of your family, your dog, your car, the girl you left behind," Irene said. "How come?"

"No dog. No car," Rudy said. "No family exactly. Dad died when I was fourteen. Mom and Roger, they're in Florida."

"He's the stepdad you fought with?" Irene asked.

"Tooth and nail," Rudy said.

"Over what?"

"The usual. Haircuts. Homework. Curfew. Money. He was tapping into what little money Dad had left Mom." Rudy leaned back on his elbows on the mattress, striking an insouciant pose, thinking he'd leave the story there. But then he noticed Irene looking at him, expecting him to say more, or maybe wanting him to.

"See, after Dad died," he said, "Mom got a job as a secretary in Roger's office. He's a dentist. She was a widow and, I guess, you know, lonely. 'My wife doesn't understand me,' is his story I'm sure. The standard bullshit. They have an affair. Roger leaves his wife and two little girls, gets engaged to Mom. His practice flounders. The whole town knows the deal. Mom starts loaning him money from her savings. I object. She sides with Roger. Marries him. And that was that."

Rudy felt now as if he'd been knocked down, dazed. He realized he had never once, ever, told this story in one short encapsulating burst to anyone. He'd dribbled it out occasionally, revealing bits and pieces, but never all of it. The memory of the anger and of the bereft loneliness left his chest feeling trampled. He tried to shake it off.

"Of course, the irony is," Rudy said, "Dad would have pissed away the money eventually anyway if he'd lived."

"So, how'd your dad die?" Irene asked.

"Booze. A car accident."

Irene winced. "It must be hard when they go suddenly," she said. "The shock."

"In a way it wasn't all that sudden. He'd been building up to it," Rudy said. "Funny thing was, I saw him in the hospital after the accident. He was in a coma, and he didn't look much different than when he came home after work and had had a few drinks. Asleep in his chair. Unconscious. He died quietly."

Irene was silent. Rudy stared at the inert clock on the bedside crate. He could feel the stillness in the room. He glanced at Irene, and she was staring at him, head turned slightly, looking a little curious. He leaned forward on the bed and stood up.

"It's true," he said. "What I just told you. Not like what I told the colonel. You can check my file."

"I know," Irene said.

Rudy had his hands in his pockets. Irene was half the room away.

"How about the girl you left behind?" she asked. "That wouldn't be in your file."

Rudy shrugged. "None. You'll have to take my word for it."

Irene smiled. "I will."

They stood another moment like that, across from each other, then Irene turned to place the *Harpoon* she'd been holding back on Rudy's desk.

"Thanks again," she said, "for, you know, with the bear."

"Sure," Rudy said.

"I better . . ." and she made a sign toward the door.

"You told me you'd meet me again sometime," Rudy said abruptly. "Was this it?"

"Men's billeting is off-limits to female personnel. And vice versa. I shouldn't be here at all. I just wanted to thank you."

"I'm glad you did," Rudy said. "But maybe we could still get together? Some place not off-limits."

She faced him, still holding the paper, just looking.

"What?" he said quietly. "Is *every* place off-limits?"

Irene didn't answer immediately but lowered her gaze toward the floor. It was as if she had retreated behind an invisible curtain.

"How about the Bash?" Rudy asked. Instantly the idea seemed preposterous. Here he was with her in his room—off-limits, against regs—and he was proposing a date with her for an all-installation party.

She was perfectly still, and he was sure she was about to turn incredulous and ask him if he was kidding. But then her head moved slightly, and soon she was nodding and saying, "I'll be there."

"You won't be with the colonel?"

This brought a flush to Irene's face. She put the paper on the desk and drilled her fingertip into the article about the Bash as if she were fastening it down.

"The colonel is often busy," she said. "He'll probably be cutting loose in the traditional ways after the long winter."

"Well, I got here late and missed the long winter," Rudy said.

Irene smiled a half grin. "And I'm not too interested in all those traditions."

"The Bash then," said Rudy.

Irene nodded; her expression seemed lighter. Maybe she was relieved at what they'd just accomplished. Rudy certainly was. The Bash couldn't come soon enough.

She started for the door.

"Sorry I dropped in unannounced," she said without turning around, "but I just couldn't resist breaking in on the House-breaker."

"The door was open," Rudy said. "So it's not officially house-breaking. For either of us. More like trespassing."

"Forgive us our trespasses," Irene said. She nodded once as she left, just as she'd done the first time Rudy had seen her, only this time there was no colonel there to pat her ass. Just Rudy watching her go.

He got ready for bed. He pulled the shade to block out the light. He leafed through an old issue of *Look,* then tossed the magazine to the floor. He played back the visit from Irene a few times. Its images began to blur. He saw close-up views of her finger boring into the *Harpoon* on his desk; her eyes checking over his room; her questions; her eyes again, by turns guarded and accepting. Then, for a moment, he saw his father, sitting in his chair. His father's eyes staring through him, then closed, unconscious. He thought of his mother and Roger. The hissing man. The chopper. The pictures in the colonel's office. He saw Irene again and felt better. Her teasing and slyly pleased references to the note he'd left her. Her nod wave and smile. He was asleep. It was a deep sleep. His beers at the club, the unceasing dusk outside, and the darkness inside made it difficult for him to know exactly how long he'd been out when the attack came.

ELEVEN

He felt the cinching on his chest first. Whoever it was had brought a large strap, probably the kind used to fasten loads to flatbed trucks, and had passed it under Rudy's bed and up over his body. The strap tightened across his midsection, pinning his arms and squeezing the air out of his lungs. His head jerked up. Instantly, his mouth was jammed full of cloth. He gagged. His tongue was pushed against the back of his throat. He tried to scream, but he made almost no noise. Even to himself, his voice sounded distant and pitiful.

His assailant quickly had Rudy blindfolded, and Rudy felt rope going around first his left wrist then his right, as the attacker tied Rudy's arms to the bed frame. Rudy bucked and kicked, hoping at least to make the bed bang around and create some noise, but his legs were quickly pinned and his ankles tied to the foot of the bed.

Rudy tried to wriggle and loosen the bonds, but it was useless. He was fastened down in too many places.

He stopped. He tried to pick up a telltale sign out there in the darkness: a smell, a noise, anything. He could hear his attacker's heavy breathing; maybe there was the odor of tobacco on his breath, but then again, it might have been the fetid smell of Rudy's own fear. Then he realized that the odor was the scent of oiled metal. At that moment, a fist grabbed Rudy's hair, yanked his head down against the pillow, and a terrible burning began on the side of his face.

Something was scraping across his left cheek. It was catching and pulling at his beard, ripping down the remaining mosquito scabs. Rudy flinched, and the hand that held his hair yanked at his scalp even harder, sending crashes of red flame across his retinas. The tearing continued around and under his jaw. He was being dry shaved.

The blade, the razor, whatever it was, scraped upward now from the top of Rudy's T-shirt along his windpipe, heedless of the contours of his neck. It was yanking, pulling, cutting. Rudy waited for a lateral move of the steel, a crosswise cut that would slit his windpipe. He was sure it was coming. He stifled a whimper that he felt building in his chest.

When the slicing didn't happen and the blade moved to the right side of his face to do its tearing and ripping over there, Rudy became enraged. He began screaming again. He writhed, heedless of the pain either on his cheek or scalp.

Blood trickled down toward his pillow. It tingled around his ears. Each place that a scab was torn felt like a chilled pool flowing out of the general burning of his skin.

When the shaving stopped, Rudy kept up his gagged screams and curses. He ceased, though, when he felt his blindfold being removed. He blinked and tried to focus his eyes. Floating out of the pulsing blur was a man in a winter-issue watch cap pulled down to cover everything but his eyes. He wore a pair of goggles. The lenses had been painted with lurid spikes and whorls, making it impossible to see anything of the eyes behind them. His field jacket was on inside out so there was no name visible above the pocket. Next to his face the attacker held up, toward Rudy, a hand mirror. The barber was letting the customer inspect the job.

In the mirror, Rudy caught the briefest glimpse of the three enormous, white circles that were his dilated eyes and his rag-stuffed mouth. There was blood on his cheeks. Blood had stained his pillow.

The attacker pulled the mirror away and brought into view a blade. The bayonet.

The man tapped Rudy's cheek with the steel. Two gentle pats. He held the bayonet out and pointed to the nick on the edge. Then he walked over to the desk, grabbed a copy of the *Harpoon* and wiped the weapon clean on it. He tossed the paper to the floor and came back to the bed to pull Rudy's blindfold back down over his eyes. In the darkness Rudy began to wriggle his ankles free. He thought about kicking but decided against it. Now that he knew it was Genteen, Rudy didn't want to show him anything. He wanted to turn to stone, to wait, to keep from Genteen the satisfaction of seeing him panic or struggle.

His ankles were free. He heard Genteen moving around, picking up the straps; he heard the clink of the bayonet blade, soft footsteps, the door clicking closed, then nothing. The generator. Nothing.

Rudy waited maybe ten seconds before he began to struggle. He worked maybe fifteen minutes, but couldn't break free. Instead, he threw his feet over the side of the bed and had enough leverage to bring the whole bed over on top of him.

Lying flat on the floor, he was able to nuzzle his head against the linoleum and work the blindfold off. He ground his cuts into the grit and dust on the floor, but he got his vision back.

Next, he worked his knees up under his body, and with the mattress and bedding drooping around him, he struggled to his feet. He stood like a furniture mover with a badly balanced load on his back. The bed teetered, and Rudy made it to the door by crashing into the desk, his locker, and the far wall. He had to tilt and strain to fit through the opening.

Once in the hall, he stopped to catch his breath and listen as best he could with the sheets, blankets, and mattress hanging around his face. He hoped to hear Lavone off typing in his studio, but there was no such sound. So, he centered himself in the hall and headed down toward the Admin office where he'd find the CQ—the soldier on all-night charge of quarters.

He came upon the Admin office quietly. He wasn't able to tell how much noise he was making, but it couldn't have been great because he didn't disturb whomever was inside. They were locked in a classic office hanky-panky position: he, sitting in the desk chair leaning back until the springs strained; she, in his lap, legs crossed, foot kicking up in excitement, his hand pushing her skirt far up her thigh, chirps and pleasure groans coming from their throats.

Rudy called, "Hey!" It was a gagged, muffled grunt, and he had to do it twice before the woman straightened her back and began to twist around with her hands on the man's shoulders as if she were a driver and had turned to speak to someone in the backseat of her car.

Rudy recognized her as one of the women he'd seen at the EM/NCO club bar. She seemed calm, almost amused, as if getting interrupted while necking on duty was no big deal.

But her composure fell apart when she saw Rudy in skivvies, standing there with a bed on his back, a rag jammed in his mouth, face covered with blood and grit.

"*Ho-ly-shit!*" she yelped.

She sprung out of the man's lap and sent him lurching, chair and all, back against the duty roster charts.

"What the—?"

It was Sergeant R. G. Genteen.

When he saw Rudy, he stood up and gently moved the woman out of his way by placing his hands on her shoulders as he came around from behind her.

"Jesus Christ, troop," he said. "What happened to you? Here, let me give you a hand."

And he walked toward Rudy, arms out, all kindness.

TWELVE

Dawes, the Fisher King.

When he saw the sergeant major down on the dock at the fjord's edge, Rudy thought of his one college poetry class. They'd read *The Waste Land*. The old king with his back to the shore, fishing. The Grail Legend. The Chapel Perilous. The young knight has to ask the right questions.

Rudy had orders to go see the sergeant major about the incident. He'd gone to Dawes's office, where the clerk there told him Dawes was down at the dock.

"You look like shit," the clerk said. "Again."

Rudy ignored him, went out the west side of the building, and crossed the parade ground where the flagpole rope clanged softly. He headed down to the beach.

He had a half dozen Band-Aids on his face. His cheeks were chafed red and his shirt collar hurt where it rubbed against his neck. He had a black eye. He was, however, clean shaven.

The night before, when Genteen had come toward him in the hall and freed his hands, Rudy had attacked. He hadn't waited to get the bed off his back. As soon as his hands were free, he lunged, and he and Genteen rolled onto the floor with the bed and bedding tangling around them. Rudy took some wild swings and landed a couple, he thought, on Genteen's face. A fist wrapped in sheet landed on Rudy's eye. The nurse had started yelling, and a couple of guys came down from the guard-duty billet to pull the two men apart.

Genteen cursed Rudy, but had made a big show of brushing himself off and displaying an air of shock about Rudy's behavior. Rudy had lost control and was yelling that Genteen was a son of a bitch who ought to have his ass court martialed. The OD, a warrant officer who was the detachment's meteorologist, came down and told Genteen to relax, to get back to the office and file a CQ report. He ordered Rudy to pick up his bedding and to get back to his quarters, where Rudy was restricted, save for a trip to the latrine to put some astringent on his cuts.

"I'll let Dawes get to the bottom of this," the warrant officer had said.

Dawes was sitting out on the end of the small pier that jutted into the ford. It was a rickety pontoon dock with a deck that floated about five feet above the clear, brackish water.

Dawes had a spinning reel and never looked back when he cast his line. He sat hunched on a crate, cocked the rod behind him, then whipped the lure out into the water. It made a little *bloop* in the fjord each time it hit. Dawes was a low, dark hulk in his field jacket, set against the immense towers of the gray mountains. Beyond Dawes, near the far shore, was the fluted, pinnacled iceberg. It had drifted in and had taken on an ashen hue under the high overcast of the sky.

The planks thunked under Rudy's boots as he walked out onto the pier. He stopped far enough behind Dawes to be clear of the lure and its hooks. He told the sergeant major that he was reporting as ordered. Dawes still didn't turn around. He flipped the lure out into the water. The line whispered through the rod guides. *Bloop*.

"A CQ repawt," Dawes said, "filed by Sergeant Genteen says that he tried to he'p you, an' you attacked him."

"He attacked me, Sergeant Major," Rudy said. "He did this to me first."

Dawes turned. He kept cranking the reel as he squinted at Rudy. "Well," he said. "Your face ain't exactly up to spec. You say Genteen did that?"

"He dry shaved me with a bayonet, Sergeant Major. He tied me up to do it."

"Genteen was on CQ duty."

"I know that, Sergeant Major."

The plug clicked against the rod tip. Dawes flipped it out again. *Bloop*. He began reeling in.

"Genteen repawts he didn't hear nobody," Dawes said.

"Of course not," said Rudy.

"So you say he left his CQ post and walked down an' attacked you and tied you up and dry shaved you?"

"Right."

Click. Whir. *Bloop*.

"A nurse from medical was there," Dawes said, "dropping off the night repawt. She didn't heah anything either."

"She probably came by after the attack. It took me, I don't know, twenty minutes to get free enough to make it down the hall. Besides, they were necking."

Dawes stopped reeling in.

"Who was, Genteen and this nurse?"

Rudy nodded, and Dawes laughed. "This is *good*, Corporal. You got our CQ leaving his post, cutting you up, *and* gettin some sugar from a nurse while on duty. Whyn't you throw in a charge of tax evasion too just for good measure?"

Dawes chuckled some more, until he realized his line was snagged. Rudy looked off toward the iceberg. He knew he'd sounded like a squealer. He wished he'd shut up.

"I don't mean to make fun, Corporal," Dawes said. "But you know what I see heah? I see a barracks squabble 'mong the troops.

Kind of thing there ain't a hell of a lot I can do anything about without I go and pour salt on wounds by initiatin' disciplinary action an' whatall. But tell me this: *Why* would Sergeant Genteen want to dry shave you so bad?"

Rudy wasn't sure he should go into this or, if he did, how he should go about it. He edged toward it.

"Because he thinks I damaged some property of his."

"What property?"

"His bayonet."

"The one he shaved you with? Supposedly?" Dawes was patient. He didn't mind Rudy's evasiveness. He was happy casting about for information. The Fisher King.

"Yes. I nicked it."

"Well now, why'd you go and nick his bayonet?"

Rudy's face prickled. And not just where he'd been shaven, but all over.

"Because," Rudy said, "he was being a pain in the ass about supplying me with the mimeograph he was under orders to supply me with for the post newspaper."

"Did you get the mimeograph you was after?"

"Yes."

"An' how long did it take for you to requisition this said mimeograph you needed for the post newspaper?"

"Not long."

"How long?"

"Five minutes."

Dawes held the rod still. He looked up at the sky. "Well, Corporal, we're kind of snagged heah, ain't we?"

"Look, Sergeant Major, Genteen and I . . . Well, I guess you could say we kind of have a history."

"A *his*tory. You ain't been heah all that long. How much history can you have? How many times you talk with Genteen?"

Rudy didn't answer. Dawes began tugging at the line, but he was waiting for a response from Rudy.

"Once," Rudy said.

Dawes whistled. "Some history."

Rudy shifted on his feet.

"Corporal, we ain't in the most pleasant of surroundings heah." Dawes nodded out toward the mountains. "Ice. Snow. Dirt. Lookit them damn waterfalls. They dump so much sweet water into this fjord thing, don't know whether we got a lake or a ocean heah. Shit for catching fish. 'Cept salmon. An' salmon avoid this fjord cause they ain't a river they can swim up to lay they eggs. Just them waterfalls, an' them waterfalls is too steep for salmon. Lookit them drop right down. An' the streams over there, they fan out and trickle across the rocks. Too damn shallow. What's a fish to do?"

Rudy looked out at the white cataracts lacing the mountain-sides and cliffs of the fjord. The falls were like dozens of pale arteries carrying some anemic bodily fluid.

Dawes went on, "Now, I'm not condoning what happened. But I don't think there's a hell of a lot I can *do* about it. You say it's Genteen, but no witnesses and no evidence says that's the case. Witnesses and evidence say Genteen was the only person around trying to *he'p* you. I think maybe you should let this whole thing settle and your time heah'll pass a lot quicker for you."

"So that's it?" Rudy asked. "Let it settle?"

Dawes nodded. "That's it. Let it settle."

THIRTEEN

At first it was impossible to tell where the cannon fire was coming from and where the rounds were landing. At the first shot, Rudy rolled out of bed and, still sleep dazed, low-crawled to the window. He peeked out.

He couldn't see anything unusual—no shell craters, no smoke—only the edge of a crowd near the far corner of the hospital. Like the gallery at a golf tournament, all their heads swiveled in unison the next time the gun's report boomed around the valley. The mountain walls of the fjord threw the sound of the explosions in every direction. The crowd cheered and pointed toward the water.

Rudy quickly got dressed and went outside. Down on the parade ground, between the hospital and the water, were four OD regimental hospital tents. Their sides were rolled up and tied. Troops milled around the encampment. From the poles of two of the tents hung a hand-painted banner: MIDNIGHT SUN BASH!

As Rudy stood looking at the sign, another shot went off. The gun was several hundred yards up the road toward the Fire Department. It was one of those howitzers towed by a Jeep. The muzzle was pointed over the hospital, toward the water. Down by the shoreline, the flank of the beached iceberg burst with a white detonation.

"YAAAHHH!!!" the crowd cheered. Chips of ice rained into the water around the berg.

Ka-blam! Another shot, and Rudy could swear he heard it whistling over his head. It splashed down beyond the iceberg.

"BOOOO!!!" the crowd jeered.

"You guys suck!" It was Petri hollering from the edge of the crowd near Rudy. He was already drinking a beer.

Rudy was thinking how he probably should cover the Bash in some way for the paper when another shot went off. The top of the iceberg was obliterated in a burst of smoke and shavings. The guys around him cheered.

Down by the tents there was a loud electronic clicking and tapping, then a thudding whoosh of amplified breath.

"TESTING. TESTING . . . MATTHEW, MARK, LUKE, AND JOHN . . . TESTING. TESTING."

"Sounds like the chaplain's all wired up for the broadcast," Petri said. "You bet on the fight?"

"Not yet," Rudy said.

"Take the spade," Petri told him. "What the fuck do Swedes know about prize fighting? The only prize they got is the Nobel Prize, and that's a *peace* prize. Think about it. Go get yourself a beer."

Petri turned and immediately started jeering at the gunners even before they'd fired another shot.

Down at the tents, the beer bust was beginning. There were rows of tables and chairs in each shelter. Chunks of milky glacial ice blasted by the howitzer filled tubs containing beer cans. Cases of beer were stacked near each tub. In the quadrangle formed by the tents were a pit and spit where several cooks were roasting a musk ox. The slabs of meat rotated slowly over a fire made of burning freight pallets. A cook basted the meat with barbecue sauce he shot from an Indian pump fire extinguisher strapped to his back.

A voice boomed from behind Rudy. "Spruance! Good to see you on the job."

The cooks gave a quick salute, but the colonel told everyone to stand at ease.

"At ease for the next whole friggin' day and night," he said. "This is a *party*. Sporting event too. How's your sportswriting acumen, Spruance?" He pushed up his sleeves and took a long-handled fork from one of the cooks. The colonel was wearing a University of Arizona football jersey over his fatigue shirt and a coonskin cap on his head. He reached across the fire, stabbed the fork into the ox, watched fat ooze from the punctures.

"Pretty good, sir."

"Excellent. Because the Great Shit-Face Race goes off at noon." He grinned at Rudy with a flush of excitement, or the glow of a couple of early beers. Rudy couldn't be sure which.

The colonel left the fork stabbed in the meat and began to stride away from the fire, indicating Rudy should attend him.

"I want you to say that I'm pleased with the help from all the units that we've had getting this shindig ready and that . . . Well, hell shit, you'll think of something for me to say. Right, troop?"

"Sure, sir."

"That's the spirit. What the fuck did we decide on having a newspaper for anyway?"

"Morale," Rudy said. "Communication."

"My idea."

"Right, sir."

"And that's what all this is for." The colonel swept his hand toward the four tents. "You have to give them *that*," he said nod-

ding toward the tents, "because we have to live with *that*." And
he pointed toward the main building of Q-Base with its shabby
walls and hodgepodge of additions and extensions. Rudy looked
beyond the building to the sheds and Quonsets around the valley,
the scrap metal and military detritus on the flats, the gray, barren
mountains and the ice.

"It's all pretty depressing, I guess," Rudy said.

"Not all *that*, troop," the colonel barked. "Just *that*." And he
leaned in so Rudy could practically sight down his long, sinewy
arm. It pointed to the far end of the hospital, to the Wing.

"You been in there yet?" the colonel asked.

"No, sir."

"You've got clearance."

"Yes, sir."

"Go in there."

"Now, sir?"

"No. Jesus Christ, not *now*. Enjoy yourself *now*. Indulge your
weaknesses *now*. Go in there when you're feeling strong. Your face
is looking almost regulation, by the way. Except those bugs didn't
give you that black eye."

"I ran into a door in the dark, sir."

"Ah," said the colonel. "That can happen around here. More so
in the winter. The Stark Raving Dark, we call it. People run into
doors. So to speak." He started walking away.

Rudy kept looking at the Wing. He rubbed his cheek. Only a
couple of Band-Aids were still necessary; the scrapes were almost
gone; the shiner now was just a pale OD crescent.

"I heard about your daring rescue," the colonel said. "You planning to put that in the paper?"

"Sir?" Rudy called.

The colonel turned around, looking surprised. He'd assumed
Rudy had kept walking with him. He raised his voice. "Your
rescue of Sergeant Teal out on the tundra, Corporal. Impressive."

"Oh, well—"

"I save you from some bugs. You save her from a bear. You

trying to upstage me, Spruance?" He strode back to where Rudy stood.

"No, sir."

"Good. Now, next item: fight." The colonel stopped squarely before Rudy.

Rudy's heart skipped. "Sir?"

"The heavyweight fight, Corporal. You bet on it?"

"No, sir."

"Who you for?"

Rudy hadn't thought much about it, so he went with Petri's tip. "Patterson, sir."

"I'll take the Swede," the colonel said. "He's got a killer right. They call it the Hammer of Thor." He raised his own right fist and looked at it.

"I heard he got disqualified from the Helsinki Olympics in 'fifty-two for not trying," said Rudy. "Word is he's lazy."

"That was before he turned pro. Now he's serious," said the colonel. "So, how about a wager? I love a good bet."

"I don't know, sir."

"Come on, where's your spirit? I'm the guy who saved your ass from the mosquitoes."

"I feel I already owe you, sir, for that."

"So indulge my weakness. Oblige my betting urge. Put some money down on your man."

"How much?" Rudy asked. He figured about five, ten bucks.

"Hundred," the colonel said, and he didn't put it as a question.

Rudy choked. "Sir, I make a corporal's pay."

"You're right. Forget it," the colonel said. He started to walk away. "Carry on."

There was something so insulting about the way the colonel had hastily dismissed him that Rudy called toward the man's broad back, "Well, hell shit, sir, why not?"

The colonel turned and smiled. "Corporal, you got balls."

And they shook hands.

Instantly, Rudy regretted the bet. The colonel was walking

away, whistling, with his hands in his pockets. Rudy felt mana-
cled to him now, win or lose. He sank down to sit on a rock. The
colonel was looking up at the sky as another artillery shell sailed
overhead. He could have been out for a stroll in the park, stopping
to notice a passing warbler. The round bit into the iceberg dead
center.

As Rudy sat alone, amplifer static and shortwave oscillations
swooped up from the tents. He looked over and saw Lavone walking his way. Lavone plopped down, winded, on a rock near Rudy's.

"What'd the emperor have to say?" Lavone asked.

Rudy told him about the bet.

"Eeeyow." Lavone winced. "Why'd you do it?"

"I don't know," Rudy said. "Force of the man's personality. His
rank." Rudy didn't want to get into whether it had anything to
do with Irene.

"Well, the old man does like to gamble," Lavone said. "Shit.
Maybe you'll win."

Some rock 'n' roll was coming over the speakers. Rudy got up
and went with Lavone down to one of the tents where the cooks
had set up a mess area. There were vats of boiled hot dogs for
troops who didn't want to wait for the musk ox. Rudy and Lavone
sat at a table with their metal mess trays. All around them, teams
for the Shit-Face Race were gulping milk to coat their stomachs.

There were about a dozen guys on each team with a couple of
the bigger female nurses thrown in here and there. The race was
going to be a treasure hunt, and the teams were to run around
the valley looking for clues and drinking beers at each stop. "No
brew, no clue," was the rule. There was a group of mechanics
who'd shaved their heads and had painted "TERMINAL
DRUNKS" on their skulls. Genteen was among them. His shorn
head looked tiny on his shoulders. It matched the egg shape of
his gut.

Rudy and Lavone went out to watch the start. Colonel Woolwrap was standing on the back of a Jeep with his .45 automatic

drawn. He explained the rules for the teams, which were huffing and prancing in place.

He held up the prize, a gold-painted bedpan.

"Plus," he bellowed, "for all the teams that finish less than first . . . two extra weeks' duty here in Greenland."

The contestants let out roars and cheers and catcalls.

The colonel fired his pistol into the air, and the sixty runners scuffed and skidded on the gravel as they raced across the parade ground to the far side, where five nurses and WACs threw off their overcoats to reveal bathing suits. The women struck cheese-cake poses as they held out each team's first clue. The running horde saw this and screamed deliriously. One of the women was Irene.

After the runners streamed by, the colonel's Jeep bounced past Rudy and Lavone on its way toward the ridge above the base. Rudy started walking across the parade ground.

"Hey, where you going?" Lavone called.

"See somebody," Rudy said, not turning around. He was focused on Irene, who was cradling beers and handing them out to the racers like bones to hounds.

By the time Irene saw Rudy coming, most of the racers had headed off toward the next clue, having tossed back their beers and thrown their cans to the ground. Irene pulled her overcoat back on, waved to the other women, and started walking toward Rudy. She pulled a pack of cigarettes out of her pocket and lit up. Her boot laces were flapping.

When he got close enough, she offered him a drag. He hardly ever smoked, but he took it anyway, and he felt the silky residue of her lipstick on the filter as he put it to his lips.

"I didn't expect you to be part of the day's proceedings," he said. He quickly exhaled the smoke out the side of his mouth, but the breeze shot it back into his eyes.

"The girls agreed it would be fun," she said.

"Was it your idea?" he asked.

"Why, yes, it was," she said, then smiled, but with her eyes narrowed.

The brittleness of her tone and the need to clear his head made Rudy look away.

Irene was back with a warmth in her voice. She touched the Band-Aid on his neck. "Shaving cut?" she asked.

Rudy was edgy, and her quick touch almost felt hot.

"I guess," he said.

"I heard you got a call from a late-night barber," she said.

Rudy nodded.

Irene brushed his sleeve. She said nothing, but she gripped his arm in a small, abrupt gesture of sympathy. This touching was exciting but nerve-wracking. Who was watching? Rudy looked around. GIs were everywhere but occupied with partying. The other women were walking back toward one of the beer tents. The colonel's Jeep was out of sight, over the ridge, following the Shit-Face racers.

Rudy felt embarrassed for casting furtive glances about. He lowered his eyes and caught a glimpse of Irene's beautiful, freckled calves that showed between the tops of her unlaced boots and the hem of her coat. Her boots pivoted, she nudged him once on the shoulder, and she started walking toward the waterfront.

"Come on," she said.

Rudy followed her long strides. He asked her what five women were doing bringing bathing suits on assignment to Greenland.

"We didn't bring them," Irene said over her shoulder. "Lane got them shipped up."

"Just for this?"

"Sure," Irene said. "He's a real showman."

"Obviously," said Rudy, feeling a burning in his chest. "So, what's it like working for him? Or *with* him? Or whatever you call it."

"Fine," she said. "Whatever you mean, it's fine."

She shot him a quick, sharp glance and kept walking.

When they were at the water's edge, at the beginning of the

pier, Irene took a last drag on her cigarette. She bent down and dipped it into the water, then field-stripped the butt and put the filter into her overcoat pocket. The same thing the crew-cut man in the civilian clothes had done.

"I've never seen a woman do that," Rudy said.

"My ma taught me," Irene said. "Those couple of months there when we were out looking for uranium. She was pretty finicky about leaving any trace behind."

"She was afraid of claim jumpers?"

Irene laughed. "No. She just said smoking wasn't a ladylike habit and that if I was going to do it with her, then we should at least be ladylike and not leave a trace."

Irene stepped up onto the pontoon dock. Rudy joined her, and they thumped over the planks. Looking down the fjord, he could see the blue-black water, the corridor of mountains, the gray sky, and one remaining piece of the iceberg.

Near the end of the pier, Irene threw off her coat and took a few more strides, stepping out of her boots. She arced into space, pale in her swimsuit, elongated in a slicing dive, almost pulling the water in behind her instead of making a splash.

She burst to the surface, let out a shout, and swam directly back to the ladder.

"You're crazy," Rudy said as he waited, holding her coat.

Her teeth were chattering even before she'd reached the last rung. Her skin prickled with goose bumps and looked as rough and white as pebbled glass. He wrapped the coat around her and couldn't help glancing at her breasts, with the beads of water tracing down into her suit. He looked at the fuzzed ruddiness of her thighs, with every tiny hair standing on end. She was no longer smooth and lithe and striding, but had become knotty and clenched. He squeezed the coat around her before he let go. She nodded thanks.

The smell of cooking meat wafted down to the dock. Along with it came a Frankie Avalon tune and some raucous shouting from the drinkers.

"You feel great once you get out," Irene said through chattering teeth.

Rudy looked up at the antic festivities by the tents and then at Irene. She was raking her fingers through her wet hair, head bent forward. He reached into his back pocket and pulled out his wallet. He grabbed her hand and slapped the wallet into it. Hopping and skidding as he unlaced his boots, he barely got them off before his momentum had carried him to the end of the dock. He knew this was going to be a cold and painful act of whimsy, but he didn't care. A mad flourish was called for here. He threw off his hat and jacket and leaped. He made no pretense about trying to enter the water gracefully. He grabbed his knees for a cannonball.

The water crashed around his head. It was so cold it seemed to claw at him, to hold him under, to pull him away from the dock as he tried to swim for the ladder.

"Oh Jeezohjeezohjeezohjeez," he said as he reached the bottom rung. Irene was applauding.

When he'd made it up to the deck, he pulled on his jacket and boots and trotted, dripping and shivering, back toward the shore. Up by the tents they saw some GIs pointing out toward the water. They turned and saw, off the last barren point of the fjord, about a dozen boats—kayaks, rowboats, and outboard launches—approaching.

"Inuit," Irene said. "Coming from their settlement out by the Davis Strait."

From the flotilla came some indecipherable chanting across the water. It was a rhythmic groaning that kept time with the strokes of the oars and paddles.

Up in the tents, the GIs had broken into song themselves. They were pounding picnic tables and singing from one tent to another. Some of the singers had even locked arms and were rocking back and forth on their benches, German-beer-hall style. They sang limericks and cadence marching songs that all blended into a cacophonous roar.

Rudy looked over at Irene. Her hair was still damp. Her cheeks stood out against the paleness of her skin. Color had even risen into her freckles.

With a screech, the rock 'n' roll came back on at nearly twice the previous volume.

"I guess the chaplain had enough of the singalong," Rudy shouted.

But Irene was looking out toward the flats where the colonel's Jeep was bouncing in from the airstrip. Woolwrap was standing, holding the windshield and cheering one of the Shit-Face teams on. The tail of his Davy Crockett hat streamed straight out behind him.

Rudy had started to shiver and said he had to get changed. Irene looked away from the airstrip, told him to come on, and together they began to run toward the hospital.

They bounded through the nearest entrance and stood inside the main corridor. When the door closed, the sounds of the Bash were muffled almost to silence. Rudy's uniform dripped a crescent of puddles at his feet.

"See you after you change?" he asked.

"Sure," Irene said.

Neither of them moved. The building was practically deserted. Their solitude was palpable. Rudy wondered if he should suggest something.

But Irene broke the silence. "Meet me down by Delta Corridor," she said.

Rudy said he'd be there, and he listened as her boots thudded and flopped down the hall, her coat open and winging out at the sides as she went.

Delta Corridor led to the women's quarters, and it ended near an intersection that was only a few doors down from the hall that led to the Wing. Rudy waited at the intersection. He was warm now, hair combed, happy in dry clothes.

He heard footsteps and a metallic rattling. An orderly was coming down the hall. He was black, a corporal like Rudy, and he was pushing a utility cart with a bum wheel that wobbled and made the whole wagon chatter.

"No partying, soldier?" he asked as he went by.

"Going to in a minute."

"That's my man."

As the orderly went past, Rudy noticed that the cart was piled with enema bags and rubber tubing.

Rudy stood where he was and listened as the cart went around the corner and rattled down the hall. He heard the orderly unlock the door to the Wing and go through. Rudy ran the few steps to the intersection to see if he could get a glimpse through the closing doors, but when he got there, they were clicking shut. First one, then the other. He could hear the cart's muffled noise on the other side.

Rudy looked around at the hallway. He'd never been down here. There were a few old issues of the *Harpoon* still lying on a folding chair. He walked down and picked the papers up.

TITLE FIGHT, GETTING TIGHT . . .

He folded the *Harpoon*s and stuffed them into his back pocket. He didn't like seeing unread, outdated issues lying around.

Through a small, vertical window in the corridor, he could see dark figures surging and congregating under the tents outside. A dragging, disoriented bunch of howling GIs stumbled across the foreground. A Shit-Face team in the home stretch.

Rudy walked quietly over to the doors to the Wing. He gently tested them. Locked.

He turned and saw Irene watching him from down by the intersection of the corridors. She was wearing her combination of WAC and nurse's uniforms. Through the walls came the low boom of the howitzer.

"The end of the race," Irene said. "Now the real partying can begin."

Rudy didn't respond.

"You were checking the door," Irene said.

"I'd like to go in there," he said. "I've never been."

"Now?"

Rudy nodded. It was because of her, he realized. The bet with the colonel, the dive into the fjord, and now being here at the door to the Wing with her. Go in when you're feeling strong. Well, he felt strong, or crazy. It was that same surreptitious, fuck-all attitude that had transported him into vacant houses to become part of something other than what he was, that had propelled him out of his own marooned panic and into some kind of peace, or if not peace, then at least some momentary high-strung calm. It was as if he were trespassing into his own self. And here she was with him. He felt strong because of that. Or crazy.

There was another boom from outside. Without speaking, Irene walked toward him and reached into her pocket to pull out a key ring. Rudy stepped aside, and she unlocked the door. He tried to fathom her mood from her face, but she was unreadable. There was no trace of malicious glee or pity or foreboding. She just looked detached, as if she were unlocking nothing more than a linen closet for him.

He stepped through the door into an anteroom where stretchers, IVs, enameled steel carts, and wheelchairs were parked.

Irene buzzed an intercom. "Teal and Spruance," she said.

The doors at the far end clicked. Irene nodded to Rudy to push through them.

The room he entered was long, as long as the Wing itself appeared from the outside. And while he knew it was filled with hospital beds, each one holding a body, that wasn't what struck him first. He had expected a room of hard surfaces, pale green paint, chrome and glass, traction racks, drip bottles, and surgical tubing; a room as functional as a freight terminal. Instead, what he noticed first when he stepped through the doors was all the oak paneling and the dawn-colored glow from the Tiffany lamps.

FOURTEEN

The first few men Rudy saw had no eyes. Their heads were either swathed in bandages or had been skin-grafted to a marbly pink over whatever was left of a brow. They appeared to have had scoops of flesh and bone taken out of their skulls or faces. They looked like unfinished plasticine busts thumped, dented, or squeezed by a child in frustration. In every case, noses were mere nostril holes: sometimes two, often just one, a large, flanged opening. Most of the eyeless heads had no lower jaw; their faces, such as they were, ended at the roof of the mouth with a tooth or two and surgical tubing entering the throat in a wad of gauze dressings.

Tinted glass on the windows reduced the light coming from the sky and mountains outside. There were heavy drapes and pale white sheers on thick brass rods above each window. The paneling wasn't cheap rec-room veneer, it was the real thing: thick, dark-stained oak. The half dozen Tiffany lamps that hung from chains down the center of the ceiling cast individual pools of light on the floor and kept the rest of the room in shadow.

There were men with no limbs. Of the patients Rudy saw, every one was a torso and a portion of a head but little, often nothing, more. Many men were no larger than an overnight bag.

The air was quiet and still. It had the weight of air in an old library or club room, the only difference being it smelled of bleached sheets, floor wax, twinges of human waste, and the bitter scents of medicine and disinfectant instead of pipe smoke, leather, aged brandy, and old vellum.

From somewhere in the ward came a groan. It was a soft sound, a sigh almost, like a coo of a pigeon. Rudy couldn't locate the source. The groan faded, and the only sound left was the distant hum of the generator.

In an enlarged space in the middle of the room was an octagonal wood-and-glass kiosk about ten feet in diameter. Green case-glass banker's lamps illuminated a black orderly and a nurse playing cards inside.

Heedless of Irene, Rudy began walking down the center aisle. On both sides were standard hospital beds, each in its own private alcove of low wood partitions. The partitions made the alcoves look like witness boxes in an old courthouse.

Each patient had an array of equipment around his bed. Bottles and enema bags hung from racks and from the bed frames; every person was connected to the IVs or rubber bags by hoses that attached to every recognizable orifice and many that weren't recognizable but had been made by surgery or perhaps warfare in Korea years before.

Rudy moved through sectors of lamplight and a couple of areas where the curtains were only partially closed so daylight fell in vinegar-colored umbras. He could hear Irene's footsteps along with his own, but then he began to notice another sound. It traveled with them down the aisle and made him think at first he was dragging something behind him. It was a swishing sound that followed them in a wave. The skin stiffened on Rudy's back when he realized what it was. The bodies were calling to him. They were hissing through tracheotomy holes or making *gna-gna-gna* sounds with portions of tongues and jaws as Rudy and Irene went past. Sightless though they were, the bodies must have sensed Rudy and Irene's presence. The calling was soft, not a plaint or a cry, but a simple rushing sound really, like surf on gravel, like water calling to land.

Without realizing it, Rudy had reached the far end of the ward. He felt unbearably weary, and when he leaned against the wall, Irene stood beside him. Down in the kiosk, the black orderly was up feinting and jabbing the air, probably instructing the nurse in the finer points of the Patterson-Johansson fight.

Irene touched Rudy's cheek. He raised his eyes to look into hers. He remembered the first time he'd seen her when she'd stood in the door of his room and he'd looked out of mosquito-bitten eyes to see this woman watching his reaction, interested in him. She looked at him the same way now, interested. Only here she held his face with her hand. His cheek was cupped in her palm. Her thumb stroked his temple. Rudy had his hands in his pockets. His hands were far too heavy to move.

"Did he design this?" Rudy whispered.

Irene nodded. "This place used to be just what you'd expect," she said. "Lane pulled some strings. Got what he could. Went behind the scenes. Special quartermaster channels."

"It's strange," Rudy said.

"This place?"

He nodded.

"Of course it is," Irene said.

"But also . . ." and Rudy's voice trailed off. He could hear the faintest thrumming of party noise coming from somewhere outside. It was like a hornet's nest in the wall, and he was safe in here away from it.

". . . it makes you want to stay," he said. "It's so different from everything else."

"Not so strange," Irene said. "I sometimes come in here just to sit. You'll see others do it too. It works on you that way."

She turned her hand and brushed the backs of her fingers across his lips, and his breath stuttered with the tingle and smell of her.

"Stay," she said softly. "I'll look for you out there later."

Rudy watched as she walked toward the exit. She waved at the nurse and orderly behind the glass. They waved back and resumed fooling around: the orderly was showing the nurse how to spar. They were laughing, but Rudy couldn't hear them.

The colonel must have known what he was doing, designing the place the way he did. Rudy felt unexpectedly peaceful. He let his gaze float like a bubble around the room. Men were lined before him in two receding files of beds and partitions. They had lived here quietly for years. They had come to this place from the other side of the world, from interstices of excruciating noise and pain. From battlefields and ambushes; sniper fire and land mines and flame throwers. Some of these guys probably got here because of American ordnance called in accidentally on their own positions. Rudy'd heard of that happening. Battle is chaos, his dad liked to say. But now chaos was hard to understand because everything here seemed to calm him, make him tired, make him lose the will to move.

He thought, They once felt like this too. It was shock. That sliding feeling, that letting go, that dropping away from pain and terror. Is that what I'm feeling? he wondered. Did the colonel know that? Did he know how these guys felt in their last conscious moments in Korea nearly a decade ago, and then did he duplicate it here in Greenland so that the guys would rise again into whatever thoughts they were capable of and never feel the horror of what they'd become?

Rudy was beginning to wonder if he himself was slipping into some kind of shock, when the door at the other end of the ward rattled, opened, and a pair of orderlies came in with a nurse. Once they rounded the kiosk, Rudy realized that the nurse was the woman he'd seen with Genteen. She was taller than both the men.

They were all laughing about something. They didn't notice Rudy until they were practically on top of him.

The nurse said hello. The two orderlies went over to an empty bed.

"Harder'n hell pulling together a detail that's sober enough to do a burial today," she said. Her hoarse, smoky voice seemed deflected, as if she were talking to a space somewhere to one side of Rudy. He wondered if she recognized him.

Over at the bed, the orderlies were detaching hoses and wrapping the top sheet around a body. Rudy had thought the bed was empty. He hadn't noticed the tiny corpse on it.

"Which window?" one of the orderlies asked. He was holding the body as if it were a swaddled, sleeping child.

The other orderly looked outside. "The end one," he said and pointed to a window where a Jeep had backed up to the building. A PFC was leaning against the vehicle, smoking a cigarette and drinking a beer.

The nurse opened the window and called to the driver, "Little help?" He tossed the can, belched, and scuffled toward the building.

Inside the ward, from down by the kiosk, came the warbling notes of a harmonica. The black orderly had stepped out of the nurses' station and was playing taps. With the window open, the sounds of the Bash mingled with the tune. The colonel was on the PA announcing the names of the Shit-Face winners.

The nurse and the orderlies passed the body out to the PFC. He laid it down gently in the back of the Jeep. It nestled between the tailgate and a tool box. Everybody—Rudy, the nurse, the orderlies, even the driver—stood still until the black orderly had finished playing.

When the tune was over, one of the orderlies started to detach the IV bottle from its hose. He brought the equipment over to a cart near Rudy.

"Why'd you do it out a window?" Rudy asked.

"Tradition," the orderly said. "The Inuits told the colonel that's the way they do it. Pass the body out a window instead of a door so the spirit can't find a way back in the building and trouble the living. The colonel liked the idea. Now we got orders to do it."

"What'd the guy die of?" Rudy asked.

"The usual," the nurse called from over by the bed, which she was stripping. "Pansystemic failure."

Rudy walked over to her.

"He goes from here up to the Fire Department?" he asked.

"That's right," she said.

Rudy started to take the soldier's chart off the foot of the bed, but the nurse stepped over from her pile of sheets and quickly grabbed the clipboard out of Rudy's hand. "You'll excuse me," she said with a snap to her voice. She put the clipboard with the sheets and began folding a blanket. Rudy watched her for a few moments.

"You told Dawes you never knew Genteen had jumped me and dry-shaved me," Rudy said.

The nurse stopped folding. It was just dawning on her who Rudy was. "That's right," she said. "I don't know Genteen did that. Genteen never said a word."

"You never saw him leave the orderly room?"

"Look, I'd only just gotten there when you showed up."

"Well, from what you were doing when I showed up, I'd say you work pretty fast then."

The nurse pursed her lips into a thin line and tossed the folded blanket onto the mattress. It brushed Rudy's legs when it landed.

"What is this; you want to be a muckraker now, Mr. Editor?"

"No. I just thought maybe you could have helped a little more."

"Hey, I've got nothing against you. I've got nothing in particular *for* Genteen either, for that matter. It's just life on the ice, you know? You do what you can to get by. That's all. I told Dawes what I knew. If Genteen did anything, he did it before I got there. And that's the truth."

They stood facing each other until Rudy gave in. She probably was right. He said no big deal. She said she had to go.

Rudy stayed after they'd left. He went over to the window by the stripped bed and watched the Jeep bounce up the road toward the Fire Department. A last Shit-Face team was straggling up from the shore to the tents. A throng of bald men was running around the party cheering and carrying the gold bedpan. Genteen's team had won. Rudy figured he better get out there and find Irene.

He was about to go when he heard a croaking. It was a human noise, a nasal, rasping quaver coming, he thought, from the next alcove. Rudy was afraid it might be a death rattle. But then, he wasn't sure how a death rattle should sound.

"She . . . she . . . c—c—c—"

It was a voice, cottony, padded, in need of saliva.

Rudy looked over the partition and below him, on the next bed, he saw a wispy-haired skull. From that angle, Rudy and the patient were staring at each other upside down, and Rudy was seeing a mouth ringed with dried spit above a single, unbandaged eye. The patient was wearing a physician's head reflector, and an arm waved like a tentacle in the air above the sheet.

Rudy stared in silence. The eye was observing him. The arm beckoned.

Rudy crept slowly around so he and the man could face each other right side up. He could see now that the man was only a torso and an arm. His hair was thin strands, gray or just colorless in the weak light that came from a lamp on a bedside table. The reflecting mirror on his head looked like a blind, glistening saucer of an eye next to the man's seeing one.

Like a cold engine, the voice turned over, and the words puttered out of the mouth softly and clearly, if still a little dry.

"She called you Mr. Editor."

The eye blinked once, waiting. Rudy felt pressed to say exactly the right thing, whatever that was, the way he would if he were before the throne of a despot in a strange and far-off kingdom.

The eye continued to scrutinize him.

"I run the post newspaper," Rudy said.

The arm uncoiled and reached over to the bedside table. The man turned his head slightly on the pillow. His skull seemed unnaturally flat in back. He pulled out some papers. He held them in front of his face, and he began to read aloud. " 'Keep us abreast of what's happening in your unit. We want to be your voice.' "

The arm brought the papers down to the bedsheets. The eye looked at Rudy.

"That's me," Rudy said.

"The post newspaper," the man said. "Cute."

"Those are my orders," said Rudy.

"Come on over here," the man told him. "Please."

Rudy walked around the partition and came over to the foot of the man's bed. The chart on the rail said SOLDIER X—DEC. '52.

"You're a corporal," the man croaked.

Rudy nodded. The man's reflecting mirror bounced some lamp glow into Rudy's eyes.

"I was corporal," the man said. "Once. I was a major about to be promoted. Got busted, though. Back to corporal. I fell to the rank to which you have risen. I assume you weren't busted."

Rudy shook his head no.

"I got busted. Then I got caught in a bombardment in Wonju, and that was when I *really* got busted." He giggled and wheezed so much that the IV tube shook and rattled the bottle on its rack. The man held the side rail of the bed with his one hand. Rudy noticed that the hand had only three fingers and half a thumb.

When the man's laughter subsided, he sighed. It was the singular pigeon coo Rudy had heard earlier. The man closed his one eye. His fingers stroked the bedsheet.

"Your name," Rudy said. "Your chart only says X."

" 'Whereof one cannot speak, thereof one must be silent,' " the man said, eye still closed. "I go by X. Just as it says."

"Don't they know your name?"

The head shook. "There was somebody over there," and the man pointed across the ward, "some time ago, gone now, and they didn't even know its *gender*. Too much blown away. I've only lost a name."

Rudy almost whispered, "Do *you* know your name?"

The eye clicked onto Rudy, the head followed. There was a small nod, silence.

"But you go by X," Rudy said.

"I'm just a guy. Soldier no more. Just a bedridden guy," the man said. "Call me Guy X."

"Guy X," Rudy repeated.

"And what might your name be?"

Rudy told him. Guy X blinked a slow, satisfied blink.

"Any relation to Admiral Spruance? Back in World War Two?"

"No," Rudy said. "They used to ask my dad that a lot when he was in the navy. Back in World War Two."

"You know, Rudy Spruance, I don't know what year it is," Guy X said. "And I'm kind of proud of that."

"You don't want to know?"

"They won't tell me."

"I can—"

"No! Don't. The point is not to know."

Rudy looked at the copy of the *Harpoon* on the bed sheets. There was no date on the masthead. He and Lavone must have forgotten it. Typical. Here in Greenland.

"And sometimes," Guy X said, "I forget where I am. I forget for long stretches of time. Whatever that means. But it doesn't matter. I'm often elsewhere. Which leads me to believe they think I can't talk. But I can talk to you, can't I? You're hearing me. Right now, right?"

"Yes," Rudy said.

Another disembodied sigh. "Good," said Guy X. "I can believe this."

Suddenly the eye looked at Rudy sternly. Then, without a move from the rest of the body, the eye glazed over. It was an almost imperceptible change, but Rudy felt a bolt of panic. He could see Guy X was still breathing, still alive, but he was no longer conscious. His eye was no more sentient than a cooked egg. There were tiny muscle twitches in his fingertips.

Rudy wasn't sure what to do. He moved his hand in front of Guy X's face. The eye never blinked.

"Hello?" Rudy whispered. No answer. He was about to run down to the nurses' kiosk when the eye fluttered, and Guy X spoke in the same tone as before.

"You want to know what's going on in my unit?"

"What?"

"You want to be my voice?"

"Are you okay?"

"Fine. Never felt better. Do you want to know what's going on in my unit? You want to be my voice?"

"Well, yes. . . ."

"Then come back."

Guy X stared directly at Rudy. No longer stern, back from its blindness, the eye looked earnest now and close enough to desperation that Rudy knew he had to oblige. Rudy could see his own image in the head reflector.

"When?" he asked.

Guy X's shrug was a lopsided contraction of his shoulder muscle. "Whenever it suits you," he said. "I don't even know what year it is. I'll never know if you're early or late."

Rudy couldn't find Irene down at the tents. People had gotten drunk, and the mood at the Bash was on the verge of ugly. Fistfights were erupting, and no one was bothering to break them up. Troops threw ox meat at each other and reeled around braying, covered with gore. People shook beer cans, then opened them and sprayed them about the tents. They threw full, unopened cans at each other like grenades.

Rudy couldn't find anyone he wanted to sit with, so he drank alone, sucking beers down fast. Lavone was passed out on one of the tables with an inhaler stuck in each nostril, and Petri and Beef were busy hitting each other and laughing. They stopped long enough to say hello. In one of the tents, troops had pulled tables back and had set up a boxing ring. Four, sometimes five pairs of black and white fighters were matched off and punching each other in mock Patterson-Johansson fights. Everywhere, couples were making out sloppily. Women pushed men away and slapped them, then they'd both go back to necking.

Rudy thought of the silence in the Wing, of the faces in there, the parts of faces. They murmured to him. Their faces sloshed back and forth. He couldn't find Irene.

Somebody put "The Ballad of Davy Crockett" on the speakers. Rudy couldn't see the colonel anywhere either. He drank another beer. He had never drunk at this pace. King of the Wild Frontier. He began to see the faces, to hear them call to him as he walked down the aisle. He shook his head. He was drinking too much. He saw Guy X. Rudy'd mentioned his father in there, his own unconscious dad, his dead dad. He'd told Guy X that he would come back.

Rudy loaded some beers into his pockets and staggered away from the tents. Now he was looking down across the flats toward the water and the remains of the beached iceberg and the mountains behind it.

The Inuit were down there. About a hundred yards from the tents and the party, the natives had set up a small encampment of bundles under skins stretched into makeshift lean-tos. Their boats were pulled up on the beach. There were some children scampering around, older people standing and smoking, a few GIs bent over looking at things spread on blankets. Rudy walked toward them. Getting away from the tents seemed to clear his head a little, steady him as he crossed the field.

The Inuit were selling carvings and bone. They had them spread on the blankets. A few of the men were drinking beer. Rudy looked at the pieces on the blankets. There were necklaces, knife handles, a small statuette of a woman, and figures of bears, igloos, and kayaks.

The Inuit watched Rudy as he walked from blanket to blanket. The natives had broad, flat faces and deep umber flesh. They wore a hodgepodge of clothing made from skins and pelts and stuff obviously bartered from GIs.

Rudy looked at the small carving of the woman. It was gray and smooth and about the size of a hefty Swiss Army knife. It had a small featureless face, armless shoulders, and its legs ended at about the knees. It had breasts and a vulva.

"What's it made of?" Rudy asked the Inuit man standing nearest him on the other side of the blanket.

Rudy had no idea if he'd been understood, but the man answered, "Walrus ivory."

"How much?" Rudy asked.

"One dollar," the man said. "One beer."

Rudy squatted and picked up the statuette. He hefted it in his palm and let his fingers curl around the stumps of the limbs and the small head. He liked the feel of it.

"Did you make it?" Rudy asked.

The man shook his head.

"Who?" Rudy asked.

The man shrugged. He swept his hand toward the fjord and the mountains and to the other natives. He shrugged again.

"What's your name?" Rudy asked.

"Alley Oop," the man said. He grinned a squinty smile with only three or four teeth visible. "Ululluik. Alley Oop."

Rudy gave the man a dollar and a beer. He thanked him. They both nodded at each other.

Rudy pulled out another beer as he was walking away. He was woozy, but the little doll that he now held in his pocket soothed him. Stroking it was pleasant, calming. A charm, he thought.

He leaned against the tailgate of a deuce-and-a-half that was parked about fifty yards from the tents. Elvis was on. Everyone was dancing to "Hound Dog." Even some of the Inuit were dancing down by their spread.

Rudy looked up toward the hospital. He remembered the weariness he'd felt in there, the strange unwillingness to leave. He stroked the doll. He felt the doll's breasts, the lobes of its vulva. Elvis sang on. Someone near the truck tried to do a chorus of the limerick tune—*Ai-yi-yi-yi*—but he gave up.

On the last ridge, out by the hangar, Rudy saw them riding. Two figures on horseback, cantering a traverse along the height of land. His and hers. They broke into a gallop. Rudy could see the woman lean down and hug her horse's neck and pull into the lead. They rode over the ridge and out of sight. Rudy blinked, and they were gone.

He looked down at the doll he held. He opened his fist and stared at the doll's curves. He saw a couple of tiny white flakes land on his sleeve. He first thought it was snow, but that was crazy. It was far too warm, and the stuff didn't melt. He looked toward the tents. Against the olive drab of the canvas where scores of GIs were dancing and yelling and drinking he could see more tiny flecks falling. They were sifting down over the whole Bash.

Even before he turned to look, he knew where the flakes were coming from. When he did look, he saw the cloud of smoke against the gray sky. It stretched all the way back up to the Fire Department. The Jeep was bouncing its way back from burial detail. The little white flakes fell from the crematorium smoke. No one at the party seemed to notice. A couple flakes had landed on the doll, and Rudy ground them into the ivory with his thumb. He smoothed the ash into the breasts and belly and genitals until it was gone.

The flakes were still falling when Chaplain Captain Brank cut into the music to announce on the loudspeakers that the heavyweight fight between Floyd Patterson and Ingemar Johansson was called off. It was raining heavily at Yankee Stadium. There would be no fight tonight.

It took a moment for the news to sink in, but then the revelers began to boo. And not just a brief hoot of disappointment, but a sustained and building gush of anger flooded out of their mouths. Rudy felt it too. Soon everyone—men, women; officers, enlisted men, and NCOs—were booing in unison. Howling, shaking their fists. Genteen stood up on a table and pointed his face toward the sky, booing. The Inuit, down at their encampment, booed.

Rudy booed. He walked away from the deuce-and-a-half and stood in an open spot and booed toward the hospital, toward the ridge where he'd seen them riding, booed toward the Fire Department, toward the whole damned place. He had a fleeting image of the men in the Wing. And then, strangely, it flickered into a thought of the curtained altar in the colonel's office, the company banners, the faces in the photos. He heard the clucking and hissing for him and Irene from the ranks of beds. But in a moment he erased all that with the sound coming out of his own chest. He felt the arteries in his neck distend, his eyes flash red, his balls suck up tightly as he yelled to the end of his breath. He inhaled and drank and yelled again and again, along with all the other soldiers and natives in the midnight sun, howling every last thought out of their minds.

FIFTEEN

A C-47 was taxiing in from the runway. A deuce-and-a-half and a forklift were rumbling up from Transport. The colonel was already there in his Jeep, rubbing his hands together as Rudy approached.

Out at the edge of the cinder apron, a ground crewman was signaling wig-wag to the pilot, bringing the plane in toward the Jeep. When he got closer, Rudy realized the crewman was Irene. She was in coveralls and gliding backwards as she watched clearance around the wings, the wheels, and props. She almost seemed to pull the plane toward her. When he feathered the props and throttled back, the pilot gave the thumbs-up and pulled open his window. Irene tossed a clipboard full of forms up to him. She had an efficient competence that made Rudy inexplicably glad.

"On the double, troop!" the colonel shouted to Rudy. "This is a touch-and-go procedure here. This plane isn't supposed to be anywhere near our humble fjord."

The colonel sprung from the Jeep into the plane's cargo bay. Over the noise, Woolwrap hollered that Rudy'd just received a

Goss flatbed printing press and a mint-condition Weimar-era lin-
otype machine routed from Germany via Paris, through Glasgow
to Greenland.

"The bills of lading on these babies read like a Baedeker," he
yelled. "Sergeant Teal was the real brains behind all this."

The colonel signaled to Rudy to start helping the PFCs from
Transport load the crates onto the forklift and then into the deuce-
and-a-half. Inside of five minutes, they had the cargo out of the
plane. Irene had stayed outside; Rudy caught glimpses of her
filling out forms on the hood of the Jeep. When the plane was
secure, she guided it out toward the runway and gave it a wave
and a quick Qangattarsa let-us-fly-up with her hands. The engines
kicked up cinders and dust as the plane roared away from her.

Rudy rode in the Jeep, on a jerry can in back, with the colonel
and Irene up front. Rudy had only managed brief looks at Irene.
She kept quiet, graceful but a little edgy too, maybe.

"What's even more miraculous," said the colonel as he drove,
"is that Sergeant Teal here went through the 201s and found a
guy on post who can actually run this stuff. You believe that?"

"No, sir. That is miraculous."

Irene kept her eyes straight ahead, not looking at either
of them.

"You know Desmond?" the colonel asked. "He's a spoon."

A spoon was a cook. Rudy said he didn't know him.

"You will," the colonel shouted as the plane roared past them
down the runway and up into the air. "He's going to be your
printer."

The colonel watched as Rudy and the PFCs unloaded the crates
in an unused motor-pool Quonset that was a few yards away from
Genteen's machine shop. When they got everything out of the
truck, the PFCs drove away. The colonel told Irene he'd be right
out and to wait in the Jeep. He called her "Sergeant." All very
proper, military. Irene gave a nod, not a salute. She had to pass
by Rudy on her way out, and Rudy jumped over to open the door
for her. "Miraculous," he whispered. She grimaced. At him? Well,

he'd just have to wait and see. The colonel turned, and Rudy closed the door.

Being alone with the colonel made Rudy fidget. He could hear the Jeep idling outside. He glanced out one of the scratchy plastic windows, but it was facing the door of Genteen's shop. Sparks were flying off a cutting torch in there.

The colonel pointed to the crate with the press inside. "I suspect," he said, "one of the first articles that comes rolling off that thing might go something like . . . 'The Swedish heavyweight stunned Floyd Patterson, Yankee Stadium, and the entire boxing world with his devastating right. . . .' "

It took Rudy a moment to catch the colonel's drift. He swallowed. "The fight?" he said. "You want the fight covered?"

The colonel shrugged. "You're the editor. More to the point is your bet. I want your bet covered."

The Patterson-Johansson fight had gone on the night after the cancellation. Johansson clocked Patterson after seven knockdowns in the third. Most of Qangattarsa had been too hung over to listen to the broadcast in the mass hall, Rudy included. He'd heard about it later. It meant he was into the colonel for a hundred bucks.

"I'll give you and Desmond a little extra time to get this equipment up and running," the colonel said as he left. "Same goes for your debt."

"Thanks, sir."

As the Jeep drove away, a breeze blew cinders from the yard against the corrugated metal walls of the Quonset. Rudy sat on a stack of old tires and looked at the hulking pieces of machinery Irene had gotten for him, caged in their rough wood crates like traveling carnival beasts.

"Hello, ol' X. And how are we today? Feeling better? I'd say we're getting our color back, yes I would. We were looking a mite peaked the past few weeks, but now we're looking like the picture of health."

The nurse was changing Guy X's bedding. She deftly rolled him to one side of the mattress, stripped that side, rolled him back, stripped the opposite side, then reversed the procedure to put new sheets on. Rudy offered to help, but the nurse said no, she could do it quicker by herself. She was a plump woman with remnants of acne scars on her cheeks that, from a distance, looked rosy. There was something of the kindly kindergarten teacher about her. She'd been coming down the aisle changing the beds the whole time Rudy had been sitting with Guy X. She chortled and babbled for each patient, getting no response other than an occasional cluck.

Rudy had come back to the Wing intending to make good on his promise to return, and to see if he could recapture some of that calm he'd felt his first time on the ward. The lamps, the luxurious wood, and all the alcoves were still as startling as when he'd first opened the door; but then, as he'd walked softly down the aisle and the patients' chuffing and whispering sounds had followed him, he'd begun to notice something new about the room's smell. He was picking up a substratum in the odors, a smell deeper than whiffs of wax, medicine, and waste. It was a close, sweet smell that any stronger would have had the power to turn his stomach. Strangely, though, it was a private smell too, a little like the odor of his own saliva or the smell of his crotch. It was, he realized, the odor of the men's wounds, the places that wouldn't heal.

Guy X appeared to be asleep. Rudy sat next to his bed and watched the slight rise and fall of the man's chest under the sheets. His eye was closed. His hair lay in filaments on the pillow. When the nurse came along to move him, he didn't wake up.

"Out," the nurse said as she worked. "Seizures. He's had them for years."

"He mentioned them to me," Rudy said.

"You're kidding," said the nurse.

"No."

"He *talked* to you?"

"Yes."

The nurse stood with her arms akimbo and her jaw dropped. "Get outta here," she said.

Rudy said he wasn't kidding. He told her about his conversation with Guy X.

"Amazing," the nurse said. She looked at the comatose patient, then went back to making his bed. "He's never done that the whole time I've been here. He *spoke?*"

"To me."

"In English?"

"Every word."

"I heard he once wrote notes some," the nurse said pointing to the papers on the bed stand, "but even that's cut back. I thought maybe we were losing him. They slip away on you. Whatever they've got begins to go, and one day you come in here and they're gone."

"Pansystemic failure," Rudy said.

"It happens," said the nurse. She made the fluttering sign, her hands like wings. "Qangattarsa."

She finished making the bed and adjusted the head reflector on Guy X by gently lifting his skull off the pillow.

"Why does he wear that?" Rudy asked.

"He used to use it to call the duty nurse. He'd bounce light off it like a signal mirror. We let him keep it even though he's been sort of out of touch with us." She stepped back to look at her work. "He talked to you, hunh?"

"A little bit," Rudy said. He felt uncomfortable, as though they were invading Guy X's privacy by discussing him right there in front of him.

Rudy was glad when the nurse shook her head and walked away to do more bed changes. He had come into the Wing feeling jittery; he hadn't expected to talk to anybody besides Guy X, and now he realized he was relieved that he didn't even have to do that.

Guy X lay quietly, his eyelid fluttering slightly, his fingers twitching on his chest as if they were playing an invisible instrument, a clarinet or a harp. Rudy had the feeling the fingers were twitching and probing at his own nerves.

Being in the Wing wasn't making him more peaceful today; if anything he was more agitated. He wanted to resolve something. He didn't really know what, though. So much around him was vague and confusing: his very presence at Qangattarsa for starters; this room, the Wing; the colonel's unnerving capriciousness, the bet, the paper; Genteen's asshole behavior. Even Irene. He thought about her all the time now, and it rattled him. He just wanted to be near her, unhassled, unafraid. Just simply with her. And without *her* jitters and nerves either. She was spooked, he could tell. They were both jumpy and awkward because they both seemed to be taking orders from circumstance. He thought of the moments after the bear chase: the draining calm they'd both felt, the peace after the frenzy and fear, how they both sat there in the aftermath, close, together. *That* was something he'd resolved. He'd seen a threat and dispatched with it. How often had he done that in his life? His solution had always been to sneak into other people's empty homes and sit there, just watch TV there, drift away from his own life, then sneak back to it, calmer. And where had it gotten him? Arrested, then conscripted, then dumped on his ass in Greenland.

Rudy looked over at the bedside table. On it were some wrinkled, yellowing papers and a couple of pencils. Most of the papers had scribbles on them, but one had writing. It was messy, almost childlike, but legible.

Dear MR. EDITOR,

it said,

What will become of us when they are done here? *And they will be done.* What will become of us? There is talk. THIS IS NO RUMOR! With my own ear I've heard the powers that be talking. Have you?

Is this letter for publication? *YES!!!* Which is why I must be vague. As far as I can tell I am the only one who can speak. But you can publish. Ask the questions. All of them. And soon.

A fellow SOLDIER

Guy X didn't come out of his seizure. He lay still, eye fluttering, fingers twitching, face upturned as if scanning for something with the radar pulses of his delicate tremors. After about an hour of sitting there, Rudy stood up, pocketed the letter, and left the Wing.

Desmond was just a kid. He confided to Rudy that he hadn't yet turned seventeen. He'd lied about his age to get into the service. His father had a printing business in Terre Haute.

"So I printed my own birth certificate," he said. "Backdated."

Desmond drank too much; for a sixteen-year-old, he consumed a frightening amount. Rudy's staff now consisted of a would-be hipster hophead and a boy drunk.

Rudy spent several days with Desmond trying to set up the equipment and learn how it worked. The assembly instructions were all in German, but Lavone had taken a year in high school, so they muddled through. When the equipment was up, Rudy would read copy aloud to Desmond who would type it into the machine. Desmond was often too drunk to read, but he could still touch-type like a dream. Even better, he knew a pharmacist's assistant in the med detachment who could make photo engravings with equipment the colonel got shipped in.

The first new, improved *Harpoon* was a four-page broadsheet that led with a Bash wrap-up and a photo of the winning Shit-Face team. Inside were the chaplain's "World News Round-Up" and a continuation of Lavone's film criticism article, "The Red Scare and Scary Movies":

What color does the Blob turn into when it devours the helpless townspeople? RED. Thus the filmmakers posit the idea that we are facing an all-devouring, amorphous threat from without. . . .

There was also an article that Rudy had found one day left on his bunk. It was handwritten on three-ring binder paper.

MY MOST UNFORGETTABLE CHARACTER

was the title, then came,

Respectfully submitted to the *Harpoon* Newspaper by PFC Charles T. "Beef" St. Beeve.

And the story:

He was a young truck driver from Memphis who recorded a birthday song for his mother at his own expense. He went on from there to fame and fortune.
But I knew him as a simple country kid who was polite and quiet and who had a bunk at the far end of the barracks.
It was only back in January of this year that he arrived in Baker Company, 7th Battalion, 3rd Armored Division in Grafenwöhr, Germany.
I had four weeks left to serve there. I was never with him for long, but I'll always remember the rainy night he arrived, a new Jeep driver assigned to our company. He came through the door, dripping wet, his duffel on his shoulder. We'd all been expecting him, but he introduced himself anyway.
"Excuse me," he said quietly. "I'm PFC Elvis Presley."
Some joker standing next to me at the far end of the

barracks squealed like a teenage girl. So I punched him in
the gut. . . .

People were actually submitting articles. It looked like the paper was beginning to take off. Amid his enthusiasm, Rudy remembered the letter from "A fellow SOLDIER." It was still in
his pocket. He hadn't printed it yet.

The day they went to press, they were cranking the old flatbed
and pulling off the sheets one by one. Desmond was busy running
the press; Rudy was reading the copy, incredulous and proud of
what they'd accomplished, but still looking for proofreading mis-
takes. When he had a full bundle of papers, he gathered them up
to make the first delivery.

He was out in the alley between the print and machine shops
when the whomping sound of a helicopter bounded over the
buildings. The chopper was making a low pass above the base.
When it was over the Quonsets, the helicopter hovered as if examining something. Its rear rotor twitched back and forth like
the tail of a dog picking up a scent. Rudy couldn't see who was
in the aircraft because the windows were glazed with reflected
light from the low sun, and because the down draft kicked up
such stinging whirlwinds of grit he had to bury his face in his
shoulder and turn away from the gusts. The blast tore some of
the papers from his bundle; he tried to claw them back under his
arm but several issues of the *Harpoon* flew down the alley. The
cinders bit into his skin and hissed against the corrugated steel
walls of the Quonsets.

After a few moments, the chopper charged away down the
fjord. The drumbeat of its rotors echoed off the mountains, but
faded quickly. When Rudy wiped his eyes and straightened up
again, he saw Genteen standing at the door of the machine shop.
A copy of the *Harpoon* had curled around his ankles. He bent down
and peeled it away from his legs. He strolled toward Rudy, reading the paper as he came.

His shaved hair had begun to grow back, but unevenly. Small, white scars flecked his scalp the way minor dents and creases mark the fenders of cars parked for years on city streets. He looked at both sides of the paper, studied his own picture in the Shit-Face team photo, then pulled out a utility knife so sharp he could cut the paper without even laying it down. He just held the broadsheet in front himself and made four quick slashes around his photo.

"You can have this," he said and stuffed the little square of paper in Rudy's shirt pocket. "The rest I can use. I gotta go take a shit." He wadded up the newspaper and took it with him as he walked away down the alley.

SIXTEEN

Guard duty finally got him. The PFC who was on the shift
before Rudy was waiting at the ammo dump gate when Rudy
and the sergeant-of-the-guard pulled up in a Jeep. The sergeant
was a heavy, red-faced NCO from Support who talked the whole
way out about foods he missed since coming to Greenland. The
PFC was a pale, almost blue-skinned Southern kid with a whiny
Ozark accent.

"I was like to die of boredom," the PFC said. "Left you some
donuts in the shack if you want any."

Rudy said thanks and locked himself inside the fence. Once
the sergeant and the PFC had driven away, there wasn't a sound.
The breeze silently ruffled the tiny clumps of purple saxifrage
outside the chain-link fence.

The fence, topped with coils of barbed wire and running up
and down the wrinkles in the tundra, enclosed three bunkers and
a guard shack. A footpath, worn by soldiers walking sentry, traced
the quarter mile around the inside of the perimeter.

The bunkers rose like a trio of waves in the soil. The doors into two of them were black holes. The third was locked. What ammunition the hospital had was stored in there.

Rudy walked up to the guard shack, which was at the height of land. It was another brilliant day. There'd been a string of them; Rudy'd lost track of how many. All the endless light. The sky had the near-purple hue of the stratosphere, and beyond the hillocks that hid the hospital, the rock and ice of the mountains shimmered like new metal.

Rudy entered the shack. Everything inside was olive drab. The clipboard, the stool, the nails from which flashlights and the emergency air horn hung, the initials and words carved into the wood—everything was the mud-green color of the army. The paint was so thick in some places it looked as if it had been applied with a trowel. Rudy pulled a donut out of the bag the PFC had left and took it outside. He figured he might as well stroll around.

The whole idea of keeping ammunition at a hospital seemed absurd. Wasn't it supposed to be against the Geneva Convention or something? Lavone was probably right: they left the ammo dump here just so the officers of Q-Base could bug the enlisted men with guard duty. Otherwise it wouldn't really be the army, Lavone had said.

Rudy looked into one of the bunkers. He could see empty wood shelves along the walls. There were military code numbers penciled in on the planking, but they were obscured by graffiti: guys' names, hometowns, women's names, obscenities, blunt penises ejaculating dotted lines into women's crotches with cartoon tornadoes of pubic hair, a couple of limerick verses, a Kilroy face, and three or four references to Jesus being Lord.

He walked past the other open bunker and went to the locked one. He tested the door, and it made a thud that reverberated in the chamber within. A boom under the tundra.

He reckoned it was late evening. The continuous daylight still amazed him, but he kept hearing about the Greenland dark from guys who'd been there a while. It'll come soon enough, they all

said. They called it by the same name both the colonel and Irene
had used: the Stark Raving Dark.

But tonight everything was in twilight as the sun shifted just
along the horizon from west to east. Guys would stay perpetually
awake during the summer. There was activity at all hours around
the base. There was even enough light for painting, because it
appeared Chaplain Captain Brank was out on the ridge between
the dump and the hospital with an easel set up. He would stare
out toward the fjord, turn, daub something on the canvas, and
stare back out. At that distance, he looked like a bird pecking at
a backyard feeder.

Near Rudy, two sparrows made a quick, flickering flight from
a thicket of dwarf rowans past the gate and landed on the chain-
link fence. They were small enough to perch between the links,
and they looked like pieces of brown paper that had blown in and
had gotten stuck in the holes. Rudy whistled to them, sputtering
out a fusillade of donut crumbs. They cocked their heads, then
flew away.

Out on the ridge, the chaplain had stopped painting and was
at attention, snapping a salute. In a moment, the colonel appeared
on horseback coming over the ridge, riding past the chaplain and
heading toward the ammo dump.

Rudy knew what this was about. He'd been expecting it.
He'd managed to scrape together the hundred dollars—he'd had
to borrow twenty from Lavone—and he'd been carrying the
wad around in his pants pocket for several days. He hadn't
wanted to avoid the colonel, and yet he hadn't been seeking
him out either. The money bulged in his pocket like a bad
tooth in his skull: an annoyance that he couldn't bring himself
to extract.

"No need to open up the gate," the colonel called as Rudy
trotted toward the entrance. The horse was shuffling from side to
side the way policemen's mounts do at parades.

"Lovely night," the colonel said. "If you can call this night."

He raised himself in his saddle and dropped back down again, making the leather creak. He looked up at the sky and sighed. He wasn't going to stoop to requesting the money.

Rudy pulled the folded bills out of his fatigue pants and pushed them through the fence links. The roll was the size of one of the sparrows. The colonel reached down from his saddle and plucked the money away.

"It was bad form, Corporal, to leave it to me to chase you down for this little wager."

"I know, sir. I was busy. I apologize."

"Were you hoping I'd forget?"

"It crossed my mind, sir. But I didn't think it likely."

The colonel chuckled. He rested his hands on the saddle horn and thumbed through the bills, counting them as smartly as a seasoned bank teller. He thrust the money into his breast pocket and turned his mount to go, but the mare kept pivoting. Despite his efforts, the colonel ended up facing Rudy again.

"The *Harpoon* looks good, by the way."

"Thank you, sir."

"The reporting needs a little strengthening, but the production is terrific. I've got to admit the paper's a class act visually."

"Thanks, sir. Getting that printing press helped a lot."

"You're welcome, troop. Glad I could help."

Now the guy was taking credit for getting the press himself, Rudy thought.

The horse twisted, but this time the colonel got her under control and calmed her. Then Woolwrap sat in a pose of stagy contemplation, looking off toward the sound of the hospital generator, making Rudy wait. Birds twittered in the brush.

"Troop, I'm wondering something."

Rudy's thoughts flashed briefly to Irene. He felt his chest tighten, but he maintained outward calm. "Wonder away, sir."

The colonel looked down at Rudy, who had hooked his fingers through the fence.

"I'm wondering if you've followed my directive. Have you been in the Wing yet?"

"I have, sir."

"And your thoughts?"

"Well, sir, I was impressed."

"Not what you expected?"

"Hardly, sir."

The colonel smiled, satisfied. "You've come a long way from being a swollen sack of mosquito bites full of questions, wouldn't you say?"

"I would, sir."

"Now you know a little more of what we're about here."

The horse got restless and began to pivot some more. She brushed the fence, and the colonel's stirrup pinged against the links.

"I do, sir. I know a little more."

"Yes, well, a little knowledge can be a dangerous thing, can't it?" Woolwrap stared down at him and then looked toward the base.

"I suppose so, sir," Rudy said.

"Therefore it behooves me to continue to keep my eye on you, troop. 'Eternal vigilance is the price of freedom.' "

"That's an interesting motto, sir. Yours?"

Woolwrap shook his head. "Strategic Air Command's, but it'll do."

"And whose freedom are we talking about, sir?"

"Why, mine, troop. Mine and only mine."

Abruptly Woolwrap spurred his horse, and the animal made a grunt like a drummed barrel. In a moment, the colonel and his mount were at a canter, heading over the hill.

He probably should have thought of the consequences or at the very least of the pattern that was emerging: whenever the colonel got imperious, Rudy would get impulsive. But his first thought as he watched the colonel ride away with his money was that he would publish the letter from "A fellow SOLDIER."

*   *   *

It wasn't a wise idea to lie down in the bunker, but it felt so good. The planks were firm under Rudy's back. He squirmed to work the ammo pouches and his canteen around so they wouldn't jab him in the kidneys. His rifle was snug against his side.

It was toward the end of his shift, and the weather had changed completely. From blue skies with chips of white clouds blowing eastward, things had deteriorated to a lowering gray mass shoving its way up the fjord. A frigid precipitation streaked diagonally across the bunker's open door. Sometimes the stuff was rain, sometimes tiny particles of ice. The empty bunker was underground and was warmer than the shack up on the knoll, where they'd taken out the propane heater for the summer.

Rudy whistled. He wasn't going to sleep, no sir. Just resting the old back. The whistle died in the empty cement room. Outside, the sleet's hiss changed to a purring. Rain again. Then back to a hiss. Sleet again. Rudy yawned. The rain or sleet or whatever it was continued to purr and hiss away. It was a soothing sound. He probably should check outside; it probably wasn't a good idea to lie here, but he felt so relaxed on the planks.

He may have slept. Something about the sound of the rain was altered for a few moments, as if the noise were obstructed coming through the open door. Rudy turned his head to look.

The man standing there told him he wouldn't court martial him, though he had every right to. The man said he could understand getting lulled into a false sense of security, locked in a two-bit ammo dump in the middle of an arctic nowhere. Any soldier could get smug about the lack of an enemy, God knows, or even about some officer coming around and checking up. The man told him that someday Rudy might even joke with his pals about how he once snoozed on guard duty and had a major general jump in his shit.

This had to be a dream, except Rudy was standing at attention, dizzy and trembling from having shot to his feet, from dropping his rifle and then scooping it up so fast he smacked his own forehead with the muzzle.

Shit, a major general. What was this? They lock him in an ammo dump and then send a procession of field grade officers out to harass him? First the colonel rattles his cage, now this guy climbs right in with him.

The man was leaning against the door frame. Rudy was beginning to notice things now. The man's hands were in the pockets of his blue ski parka. His bristly gray crew cut was the color of the sky outside. Shit, a major general.

"Follow me," the major general said.

Rudy went with him out into the sleet. A hoary gray slick covered everything. And this was summertime.

"The weather station down at Red West says the sun will be back out in a day and all this crap will melt," the general said.

There were two Jeeps inside the fence, idling up near the guard shack. The officer of the day, a lieutenant from Transportation, came around from behind the shack. He must have been looking for Rudy.

"A-okay, Lieutenant," the general called out. "He was running a check on one of the empty bunkers. Didn't hear us. I'll take it from here."

The lieutenant saluted and gave Rudy a look. The guy was skeptical, but he got in his Jeep and drove out through the gate.

"Saved your ass, soldier. Be thankful," the general said.

Rudy couldn't speak.

The general took a closer look at him.

"You're the same swinging dick I saw tippy-toeing outside the colonel's, aren't you?"

"Yes, sir." It came out like a peep.

The general shook his head. He told Rudy to meet him at the locked bunker. The general got in his Jeep, drove to the bunker, and pulled up with a flashlight, a clipboard, and a key for the door.

The door slid sideways on rusted metal rails, but it resisted mightily, and the general had to help Rudy push it open.

The general went in. He zipped the flashlight beam around the

musty room. In the darting light, Rudy could see shelves like the
ones in the empty bunkers. Here, though, they were loaded with
wooden cases. He caught the labels as the general read them: M-1
ammunition, .50-caliber machine gun belts, plus box upon box
of grenades and mortar rounds.

The general was muttering to himself. He was reading code
numbers on the wooden box ends. He pulled a couple of the crates
out and pried open the tops. He looked in the metal cases inside,
and over the general's shoulder Rudy could see the brass and steel
of shell casings.

"Out-fucking-dated. All of it," Rudy heard the general mumble. The general stood up and shoved the box he'd been examining
back onto the shelf with his foot. "History repeats itself. Woolwrap, what am I going to do with you?"

The general turned around and looked almost surprised to see
Rudy, but he went back to checking the shelves and all the boxes.

"Should just detonate the whole shitarree when we go. Make a
nice send-off. Good-bye, Korean War. *Boom!*" The general strode
past Rudy and out into the sleet. "Except it's all outdated and
would probably just go *pffft.*"

"Sir?"

"Nothing. Never mind. Close the door when you leave, Corporal. And your mouth too."

SEVENTEEN

The lock clicked softly in the door after Rudy announced his name into the intercom. He gently pushed the door open and stepped into the sanctum of the Wing. The light was subdued, as usual; the lamps glowed; the smells were the same, and as he walked, Rudy heard the usual murmuring. Tonight, though, there were several other GIs on the floor. Only a couple of them were orderlies working at changing IV bottles. Of the rest, one stared out a window at the mountains. Another sat on a gurney and looked at the floor. One was asleep in a chair.

The colonel had said the Wing was what the base was all about. Irene had said it worked on you. She'd said she came there sometimes just to sit. Other people did too.

The patients' murmuring stirred a couple of the GIs to turn and look at Rudy as he passed. They nodded to him. He half saluted with the rolled-up *Life* magazine he'd brought with him. No one spoke.

Guy X appeared to be asleep. His single arm lay atop his chest.

The three fingers twitched. The reflecting mirror obscured half his face. With the white sheets and pale skin around it, the mirror looked like a silver pool of ice.

Rudy walked closer and stepped into the alcove. Still no reaction. Outside, it was almost dark. The season was beginning to change noticeably now. During the night, there was actual darkness, and it would grow by ten or fifteen minutes every twenty-four hours.

Rudy sat and opened the *Life*. He'd brought it along figuring he'd read it aloud if Guy X was unconscious. It was probably a stupid choice—reading aloud from a magazine devoted to pictures—but he figured it was the sound of his voice that counted. When his dad was in the hospital after the accident, a nurse had told Rudy patients in comas could hear you. He talked to his dad sometimes. It hadn't saved him, but it was something Rudy was able to do while his father slipped away.

The cover story was about the seven Mercury astronauts. Rudy read aloud to Guy X and described the pictures of the astronauts in their jet cockpits, in centrifuges and immersion tanks and out doing PT in the desert. Rudy had to admit, they looked great: crew-cut, can-do motherfuckers. They were heroes already, and they hadn't even been in space yet. Rudy looked at Guy X. Gone. He looked around the ward. Quiet, still. The end of the can-do line.

There was one shot of all seven astronauts at their introduction to the press. They were wearing suits and ties and were sitting behind a long, cloth-covered table lined with microphones. They all had big grins, and their hands were in the air. One guy had two hands up.

Rudy stopped and leaned over Guy X. He could see his own face in the reflector, but behind the small eyehole in the center of the mirror, he was being watched. Guy X was awake; his eye moved in the shadow behind the mirror.

"Hello?" Rudy whispered.

Guy X sighed. Rudy was close enough to smell his breath. He expected it to be foul, but it wasn't. It smelled like wet wool.

"Let's see the picture," Guy X croaked.

Rudy held it up.

"It says they've just been asked who wants to be first in space," he said. "They all raised their hands."

Guy X looked at the photo from behind the reflector. The spot of light danced across the astronauts' smiles. Guy X turned his head away.

"Bring books," he said. "Next time you come. Bring books. Bring the classics. Read to me from the classics."

"Okay," Rudy said. He closed the magazine. "The classics."

Guy X looked back at him.

"So, the corporal returns," he said in a soft, padded voice. He licked his chops a couple of times to lubricate his mouth, and he raised his arm to tilt back the mirror.

"I was here before," Rudy said. "You were out. I found a letter addressed to me."

"You took it?"

Rudy nodded. Guy X looked relieved for a moment, then stern.

"Why didn't you print it?" he asked.

"I am. I will," Rudy said. "I'm just not sure what it means."

"What it says," said Guy X.

"It's about closing the place?"

"You got it, Sherlock."

"And something's got to be done about you guys."

Guy X stiffened a little on his pillow, as if to raise himself up. "I heard that little civilian shit talking," he said.

Rudy leaned forward in his chair, placed his forearm on Guy X's bed. "He wears a parka, crew cut?"

Guy X nodded.

"He's not a civilian," Rudy said. "What's he do in here?"

"Looks around. Hums. Takes notes. Talks to the colonel."

"And you heard they're closing the place?"

"*Thinking* of. I hear lots of 'If we . . .' and 'Should we . . .' I figure it out from there."

For a moment Guy X sounded sad, and Rudy did something that surprised himself. He got up and sat down delicately on the very edge of Guy X's mattress. Guy X's body seemed even more insubstantial now that Rudy was on the same bed with him.

"You think something's going to happen to you?" Rudy asked.

Guy X wasn't paying attention. He seemed to be staring at something beyond the ceiling. Rudy wondered if he was trying to signal with the reflector, but Guy X's stare had gone blank. He was still breathing but in tiny, rapid puffs. His whole body trembled in a seizure that vibrated him in the way loud noises can vibrate a glass of water. If Rudy hadn't been sitting right there on the mattress with him, he might not have noticed that Guy X was shuddering at all.

A tiny squeal began to rise from within Guy X's throat. Rudy had the crazy thought that the motor driving the man's trembling was running out of lubricant and the bearings were screeching. For a second it reminded Rudy of the sound the respirator made next to his father's deathbed. Those machine noises—inside or outside you—brought on the end; they confirmed everything he knew about the world. That was what he'd thought at fourteen, and he didn't want it confirmed again now.

He stood up. He didn't know whether to go get a nurse or to try to hold Guy X down. The trembling was getting more pronounced.

Then suddenly it stopped. The current, or whatever it was, had been shut off. Guy X's arm rose off the mattress. He opened his eye.

"I do, I do," he gurgled. His arm hung in the air.

Rudy knelt down. "What?"

"I do."

"You do what?" Rudy asked.

"I want to be the first in space, asshole."

Guy X let his arm drop back down, and soon he breathed the deep, steady breaths of slumber.

When Rudy got up to go, he noticed that the orderlies had all left. All but a couple of the Tiffanies had been shut off. A nurse sat in the kiosk, head down, reading or doing charts. The Wing was closed for the evening.

Rudy walked quietly up the aisle. Then he stopped. Someone was with one of the patients. They were in shadow, but Rudy could tell they weren't changing tubes or dressing wounds.

Rudy stepped closer. He could make out the lowered, balding head of the colonel. He was on his knees near the foot of the bed, and his hands were clasped. He was praying. Rudy stood a moment, staring at the man, when out of the shadows by the window came another person.

Irene stepped into the light. She looked alarmed. She silently began to signal Rudy to get moving, to get out of there, be quiet. He started to go, but he kept looking back at her and just before he reached the exit, he blew her a kiss. The colonel started to look up, and Irene laid a hand on Woolwrap's shoulder as Rudy slipped out the door.

Chaplain Captain Stu Brank had inherited the hospital library for his quarters. The room was a hodgepodge of metal shelving stacked with books and old magazines and back issues of *Stars and Stripes*. In one barren corner, with a cross tacked above it, was the chaplain's bed.

Captain Brank met Rudy at the door. The chaplain had blue eyes, so he couldn't have been an official albino. Still, his skin was as pale as candle wax. He was in his T-shirt and fatigue pants. He had white, woolly hair on his forearms that made them look as if they were wrapped in excelsior.

Rudy could hear broadcast static and the pinging, swooping, twisting noises of radio interference. The chaplain's shortwave rattled on a table where oil paint tubes, brushes, rags, and a solitaire hand lay.

"Corporal!" the chaplain said. "I've got the news-of-the-week column all typed up for you. Come in. Come in."

The chaplain rushed across the room, turned the radio down,

and picked up a sheath of papers. It was the first time Rudy had been inside the chaplain's quarters. Right away he noticed the windows. There was no light coming in. Covering every window was a canvas, and on every canvas was a painting. They were seascapes. Or so it seemed.

The chaplain caught Rudy looking at them.

"You like?" he asked enthusiastically. "It's my oeuvre."

"They're of the ocean?" Rudy asked.

"Yes!"

The pictures caught the blue of the sky Rudy'd seen over Qangattarsa before, but they looked nothing like the fjord and mountains outside. There were rocks and water in the paintings, all right, but each painting contained a small stone hut on a treeless island amid roiling waters of the broad sea. Rudy thought they looked pretty good.

"Ever hear of Saint Brendan?" the chaplain asked.

"No, sir."

"Ah-ah-ah . . ." The chaplain wagged the papers at Rudy.

"Stu," Rudy said. The chaplain hated to be called Captain or Chaplain or sir.

"Saint Brendan was the original Irish rover. Born late fifth century. It's believed he sailed as far as Greenland from Ireland. In these little boats called curraghs."

The chaplain said the word so harshly, Rudy thought he was about to hawk on his boots.

"Like teacups with sails," the chaplain said, tapping a cup on the table for emphasis. "If true, it was a navigational feat that would even put the Vikings to shame."

The chaplain put the papers down and wiped a brush with one of the rags. "Now, I'm not a Roman Catholic by trade," he said. "Episcopalian. But I read about Brendan and became fascinated. The *drive*. The *will*. The mad urgency to do what he did. Picture it, son."

The chaplain squinted at Rudy out of one eye, a pirate's glare. It made Rudy want to back up a step.

"*I* picture it," Captain Brank said. "Constantly." He waved his rag at the canvases. "I picture it so thoroughly, I want to look at nothing else. Brendan's cell had windows only up top, facing the sky—God's dwelling. I face only Brendan's dwelling."

"That's why they're covering the windows?" Rudy asked, nodding toward the canvases.

"Precisely!" Captain Brank said. "These are views of Brendan's hermitage. Or my interpretation of it. For inspiration. Just a skerry somewhere. Ocean. Rock. God." The chaplain rubbed at the brush furiously. It looked like he was almost trying to yank the bristles right out of the thing. "There's a theory that says great visions of the holy come only to desert anchorites, and that mysticism is linked to the sun. To that I say, Bull! Here in the arctic we also have our visionaries and our visions. I'm waiting for mine. Perhaps you will have yours. What do you think?"

The chaplain leaned toward Rudy.

This was not a rhetorical question.

"I don't know," Rudy said.

"Of course you don't," the chaplain said. "No one does. We just have to be ready for it. We're here. It will come to us in its own good time. Here's your news." He gave Rudy the sheaf of papers.

Rudy thanked him. He glanced at the shelves and remembered why he'd come. He asked the chaplain for some books.

"The classics," he said. "If you've got any."

Captain Brank brightened. "Planning on stocking up for the winter?" he asked.

"Yeah," Rudy said. "It looks like it's coming on pretty fast."

The chaplain seemed happy to have a task and went off ahead of Rudy to rummage. Rudy ambled through the stacks. Things smelled dusty and close back among the shelves, the odors of basement rooms of old churches, choir robes in closets, altarpieces kept in felt bags. He came across a couple of aisles full of forgotten, USO-donated novels and score upon score of *Reader's Digest* condensed books. He stopped and ran his fingers along the spines of some military histories. Stacked on the lowest shelves were old piles of *Stars and Stripes*.

Captain Brank came back with *Tom Sawyer, Ivanhoe,* and *Leaves of Grass.*

"I'll look for more for you. I've got an extra *Life of Saint Brendan* by the Venerable Bede if you're interested," the chaplain said.

"I'll just start with these," Rudy said. "Thanks."

Rudy spied a two-volume work on the shelf near the chaplain's shoulder—*A Divisional History of the United States Army, Revolutionary War Through Korea.*

"Would it be possible for me to borrow a couple of things here?" he asked.

"From military history?" Captain Brank asked, looking around the aisle.

"I'm getting interested in it," Rudy said.

"Be my guest," the chaplain said.

So Rudy pulled some books and newspapers out, added them to the classics and, in a couple of trips, lugged them all back to his room.

It took several hours, but he uncovered something. He had the books and papers spread out over the floor of his quarters. He used the *Divisional History, Vol. 2,* to track battalion locations in Korea. Then he dug into the *Stars and Stripes.* The Sixth Battalion of the Third Infantry Division had suffered serious losses in action north of Seoul in '51.

There were references to "equipment failure" and "faulty ammunition" on the battlefield. The PIO said the case was "under investigation." Later issues of the paper made scant mention of the incident. The investigation "uncovered some irregularities in procurement" which may have "hampered the GIs' ability to fight."

The equipment and ammunition irregularities were an "internal matter for the Quartermaster Corps," according to the PIO.

"Nearly two companies were lost," the PIO said. They were listed as A and B—Able and Baker—Sixth Battalion, Third Infantry Division.

EIGHTEEN

It was dark outside the EM/NCO club, the first real darkness Rudy could say he'd seen since he'd come to Qangattarsa. The season was changing.

He'd been pondering what the lead should be for the next issue of the *Harpoon*. Maybe something innocuous: helpful hints for getting through the winter ahead—drinking games, the chaplain's art classes, a pinball league. It was a dispiriting prospect for an issue. He had another idea, though. The "fellow SOLDIER" letter and the articles he'd read in the library books had given him the notion. He wasn't sure he should run with it, however, so he'd gone out for a beer to let the idea sit.

The club was percolating along on its weeknight setting— Tony Bennett on the juke, a couple of enlisted men, two or three nurses, but nobody Rudy knew—so he sat alone at the bar. He sipped at his beer and eventually pulled out the little statue that he'd bought from Alley Oop, the Eskimo trader. He'd been carrying it with him every day since the Bash. He'd often run his thumb over it in his pocket. He'd squeeze the figure tightly in his fist as if the action might bring him luck, or might squeeze the longing he felt right out of him.

At the bar, he held the figure in his palm, looking at it until he began to worry that the bartender or someone else might notice. Drinking a beer alone and clutching an Eskimo totem seemed in their own way dispiriting, so he paid up and left.

Outside, as he looked south, he could see the cloud banners streaming from the summits of the mountains. They seemed to flutter as if whipped by a stiff breeze in the moonlight. But the air was still. And there was no moon. Something was amiss.

Rudy turned to look behind him. In the sky over the club, gigantic, blue-green, white-and-violet curtains of light streamed and throbbed up from the mountain range forming the north wall of the fjord.

The northern lights.

Rudy almost lost his balance leaning back trying to see the whole spread of light sucking away, right up toward the apex of the night sky. The aurora hadn't been there when he'd gone into the club. Now it was so bright it nearly obliterated the stars.

He began walking on the gravel path. Soon his eyes became adjusted so that he could see human silhouettes. There were maybe three dozen men and women in groups, in pairs and singly, standing or sitting, spread around the grounds, all looking at the spectacle. They'd come out while he'd been in the club. Occasionally, someone would point heavenward, and when the lights gave off a particularly vivid pulse, there'd be a chorus of low ooohs and ahhhs. A violet glow shone everywhere. It was a like a drive-in movie without the cars.

Over in the Headquarters sector, a light was burning. Rudy dodged around some of the people sitting on blankets—there were even a few Inuit mingling with the GIs, everybody was drinking beer—and he made his way to the building. The sky watchers were all a good distance away and looking in the opposite direction. He glided up to the one lit window. He could hear the sound of typing, fast and fluent, coming from inside. He slowly brought his face around to the corner of the window.

Irene was alone in her office. She was at her desk, a pencil in her mouth like a pirate's dagger, and she was typing. Rudy watched for a couple of minutes. There was a marvelous competence to the way she moved. He could almost feel a rhythm to it. He knew it was just office work, but she seemed so direct and economical about it. He was surprised at the pleasure he was getting just from watching her. It was the same feeling he'd had fleetingly when he'd seen her with the cargo plane the day the press had arrived. He tapped on the glass.

Irene looked up, too cool to be startled. She cocked her head. Rudy waved. She squinted to see through the reflection, then smiled. He motioned for her to come over. She did and opened the window a few inches. He stood in the apron of fluorescent light spilling from inside.

"Working late?"

"Afraid so."

"Boss go home?"

She nodded.

"You see what's out here?"

"You are."

"I mean the sky."

Irene tried to look up through the glass but obviously couldn't make anything out.

"Turn off the lights," Rudy said.

She went back and flipped the switch. The aurora's radiance shone everywhere.

"Jesus . . ." Rudy heard her say from somewhere in the darkness of the office.

"Come on out," he whispered.

She rustled around some. Rudy heard the door lock. He thought maybe she'd left, but then she was at the window. She opened it all the way and climbed out into his arms. For a moment they stood there, in that hokey bride-and-groom-crossing-the-threshold pose. Rudy could feel her hand on the back of his neck. He could see her face in the light from above, and he could tell for certain by looking in her eyes that she was amused, just as he was, by the corniness of him holding her there, but that she enjoyed it too. He put her down gently and helped her close the window. For a moment they stood looking at the lights sweeping and unfurling overhead like a huge, windstruck, luminous flag. It was hard to imagine something so big and animate without sound.

"I've never seen them so beautiful," Irene whispered.

"Let's walk," Rudy said.

"Where?"

"I don't know. That way." And he pointed across the end of the runway out toward the mountains.

They strolled over gravel and lichen without speaking until they were well beyond the scattering of people. Once they were away from the base and the rest of the troops, Irene slipped her arm through Rudy's. He shuddered with pleasure at the gesture. He wondered if she noticed. She leaned into him as they walked.

They climbed the berm at the end of the runway and caught themselves looking right and left, like a couple of schoolkids watching for traffic before they crossed a street. They followed the Jeep track out to the large rectangles of stone, the place Irene had told Rudy was once a Viking farmstead. They passed the mound of bone chips and ash.

At one of the stone walls they stopped, and Rudy stepped up on the rocks. He let go of Irene's hand.

"How long ago did you say the Vikings were here?" he asked.

"A thousand years."

Rudy looked at the enclosures.

" ' . . . are but as yesterday when it is past,' " Irene said, " ' . . . and as a watch in the night.' "

Rudy turned to her.

"From the Bible," she said.

"You religious?" He was walking along the stones, balancing, hands out. She was keeping even with him down on the ground.

"My father was. He used to read the Psalms over and over, made us listen."

"Us?"

"Ma and me."

She called her mother Ma. Rudy had called his mother Mom. In a suburban neighborhood full of Moms. But here he was with a woman from the high desert. Flatness all the way to peaks on the horizon.

"You said your father left your mother. Wasn't he religious enough to believe 'until death do us part'?"

Irene shook her head and sat down on the wall next to where Rudy stood. They were both facing away from the post, up toward the mountains.

"No," she said. "Not after Korea, I guess. I don't know. After the divorce he took off. We're out of touch."

"Missing in action since Korea," Rudy said. "Like those guys." He nodded back toward the hospital.

Irene whispered, "You could say."

Rudy sat down next to her and told her about his father, how he'd been in submarines during World War II, how he'd grow quiet sometimes and terribly still, how he'd tune out by sitting and staring at the floor or up at where a wall met the ceiling. "It was like he was listening to sonar or trying to hear the propellers of a destroyer overhead or waiting for a depth charge to hit."

"Did you ever ask him about it?"

"Yeah. Sometimes. When I was a kid. 'What are you doing, Dad?' 'Thinking.' 'What about?' 'The war, I guess.' 'Don't you know?' 'Nope.' "

Rudy stood up and threw a stone against the far wall of rocks. It clinked when it hit the low boulders. The aurora was still flickering. Something inside him was flickering and jittering too, and it wasn't from being with Irene. Talking about his father had agitated him. He winged another stone at the boulders. It clinked, then ricocheted and made a *thup-thup-thup* noise as it hopped across the tundra.

"My mother got like that sometimes," Irene said. "Being a uranium boomer did it, I guess. I remember watching her when we were on the move. She'd smoke cigarettes and stare out the back window of some motel, looking at the desert. I could tell it all seemed nuts to her. And horrible too. Like she was the butt of some huge joke. Some rock gives off invisible rays that make a Geiger counter click, and it turns you into a millionaire. It just made her lonely was all. She'd never say it. She boomed on, but I could see it. Like *she* gave off invisible rays, and they made something in me click—a warning: *Don't end up alone like that.*"

Rudy was about to throw another stone, but let it drop. He sat down again on the wall. Irene moved close to him. He looked at her and gently turned her face to him. She seemed to be coming back from far away.

They kissed delicately at first. Rudy was surprised at the warmth and softness of her mouth. It was a sudden, shocking awakening to how cold and hard everything around him in this arctic place was: the light, the land, the military. He could feel her breath across parts of his face. It sent those shudders through him again, so he reached for her. In a moment they were pressing hard against each other, kissing.

Eventually they rose and began to walk again. The aurora shined down. Rudy felt giddy as he listened to Irene tell him how she'd read that the Vikings believed the lights were the reflections from the golden shields of the Valkyries, the warrior-maidens who escorted the souls of heroes through the sky, over the Rainbow Bridge, to everlasting life in Valhalla.

They stopped on a hummock that overlooked the rectangles of stone. The dandelions Rudy had seen his first time there had now gone to seed. Some of the stones on the walls had sunk below the tundra, leaving gaps, dotted lines, showing where the perimeters of the enclosures had been.

She told him again about the lost colony of the Greenland Vikings, the remnant, inbred people left practicing their strange, metamorphosed Christianity.

Together, hand in hand, Rudy and Irene arrived at the junction of Jeep tracks above the base.

"We better not get any closer," Irene whispered.

"You mean to the base," Rudy said, and Irene laughed.

"No," she teased. "To each other." And she pulled him toward her, and they kissed long and hard with rushed caresses, kissed lips, hands, necks, faces, searched each other's eyes, kissed more, and then with clutching embraces, they parted, barely able to let go of each other.

They couldn't risk being seen approaching the post together, so Rudy stood alone and watched Irene walk down the path, under the aurora borealis, toward the barracks sector.

Then he turned and looked up one last time at the sky, and at the lights flung across the heavens. It was the same for him: he'd never seen them so beautiful.

"A couple of things, Corporal."

Rudy had answered the door in his skivvies—he was off duty—and found himself standing before his commanding officer. The colonel held a copy of the *Harpoon* and drew the fold of the paper through the pincer of his index finger and thumb. The front-page headline hovered before him.

RUMOR MILL
RUNS OVERTIME

The colonel let the paper fall face up onto Rudy's bunk so they both could view it.

"Correct me if I'm wrong, Corporal, but didn't we decide to have a *news*paper here?"

Rudy didn't know what to do with his hands. Clasping them

behind his back at parade rest seemed to leave him too exposed. Holding them in front of his genitals seemed too prissy. So he just stood there half naked, arms dangling.

The colonel had stepped back from the bed. He kept his gaze fixed on the *Harpoon,* but looked as if he were viewing a stool specimen.

"This isn't," the colonel said with a dismissive flick of his wrist, "what I would call news. We have here a lead story about *rumors,* Corporal. What kind of *news* is that?"

Rudy sucked in a breath. "I admit it's unusual, sir."

The colonel nodded derisively.

"But," Rudy said. "I thought a feature story might be in order. I mean, after the Bash, there haven't been any sweeping events around here."

The colonel's face jelled into a concentrated stare.

"And, sir, there *have* been a lot of rumors around. And we did decide that we'd have a newspaper that would tell us about ourselves. A 'private information office,' I think you called it. 'About us, for us'? And I began to notice this about us: the rumors. So I thought I'd do a story about it. Rumors. Army hearsay. Innuendo. The skinny. The wildest rumor you ever heard. Women's rumors versus men's rumors. The rumor you wish was true. The basis in fact of the rumors around now. The rumors that—"

"I know the article, Spruance. I read it."

"Yes, sir."

The colonel walked over to Rudy's desk, picked up a paper clip, and unbent it. "Maybe I should be screening the stories before you go to press. I'd hoped that wouldn't be necessary. I liked that element of surprise. The little frisson I'd get when a new issue of our paper was on my desk in the morning. But . . ." and the colonel shook his head, sighed a heavy sigh.

"Sir, what is it about the article that specifically . . ." Rudy groped for a word. ". . . displeased you?"

The colonel twisted the straightened clip around his index finger and pointed the wirebound digit at Rudy. "You can't know that, Corporal."

"No?"

"No. Because if I told you, I might be disclosing, indirectly, information that is secret."

"Oh. Well. Sir, we wouldn't want *that*."

The colonel's gaze narrowed further. "Nobody likes a wiseass, Corporal. Least of all the U.S. Army."

The colonel paused, perhaps waiting for an apology, but Rudy was silent. Skivvies or no, he didn't want to give ground.

"Now then," the colonel said, "there's this too." And he picked up the paper and folded it back to the "Letters to the Editor" column. He pointed to the "fellow SOLDIER" letter.

"Do you know who wrote this?" he asked.

Rudy hesitated a moment. "No," he said.

The colonel twisted the paper clip around his finger some more and eyed Rudy from head to toe. "You print unattributed letters? No can do, Corporal. Not in this man's newspaper. No anonymous letters. The *Harpoon* is not going to be a repository for graffiti, and that's all unsigned letters amount to."

"Yes, sir."

"Other than that," the colonel said, "carry on." He started for the door.

A question popped into Rudy's mind. It was nuts to ask it, but he'd been caught almost bare-assed, so dignity was out the window. He'd been busy with the paper for several nights and hadn't seen Irene, but she'd been on his mind constantly. He was lucky, he thought, that he hadn't had an erection when the Colonel knocked. Still, it must have been the memory of her kisses that made him feel reckless, invincible.

"Sir?" Rudy asked. "Sir, what *will* become of certain people here when they're done with this place?"

"What?"

The colonel had heard him, Rudy knew damn well.

"Anonymous or not, the letter poses an interesting question. Since I'm running the paper that tells us about us, I thought it was my place to ask. Maybe, say, off the record?"

The colonel turned. "Corporal, I would hate to think you're playing around with this newspaper I've given you. You've got a pretty cushy job in this man's army, Greenland or no Greenland. I think you know that."

"Yes, sir."

"So, it's *not* your place to ask, Corporal. Is that clear?"

"I guess so, sir."

"Now I'm going to forget you posed that question because it's of no concern to you or to whomever else was wondering about it. We're doing just fine here. That's the news. Any other questions?"

"No, sir."

"Good."

"Except one, sir."

Rudy licked his lips. He felt weirdly exhilarated; it was that feeling as if he were breaking into a house again, only this time someone was at home, making the trespass all the more audacious.

"Sir, what can you tell me about Able and Baker Companies, Sixth Battalion, Third Infantry Division, Korea?"

The colonel squeezed the paper clip with his thumb until his wrapped finger swelled and turned almost purple with trapped blood.

"Able and Baker of the Sixth?" Rudy asked again, adding an innocent lilt to the words. This was like breathing pure oxygen. He was wondrously lightheaded. It was worth losing the bet, worth getting caught with his pants down.

"I've been doing some reading." Rudy pointed over to the *Divisional History* and the ragged pile of *Stars and Stripes*.

The colonel leaned toward Rudy, hands on hips.

"Corporal, as good as the work is that you've done, there is something of the fuck-up about you. I saw it from the start. A Public Information specialist, and you get assigned Greenland.

Then there's the mosquito attack. Plus, I hear about a blanket party somebody gave you. These are fuck-ups. Not necessarily your fault, but they occur around you. A miasma. You have a way, it would seem, of skating out onto thin ice. So, as to your question: it's of no concern to you. I say again: no concern. Copy that?"

"Loud and clear, sir," Rudy said, maintaining his poise. This made the colonel's voice clench even more.

"Just put out your paper, troop. Got that? Stay off thin ice and don't fuck up. Plus, something else occurs to me, Corporal. It's only a faint suspicion, so I can't be sure, but I'll add this too: Don't fuck around. The army's bigger than you are, Corporal. And up here, I am the army."

Woolwrap flicked the twisted, coiled paper clip off his index finger, and it pinged from the desk to the seat of a metal chair to the wall and ended up spinning on the linoleum floor. Rudy watched, spellbound by its gleaming ricochets, as the colonel strode out the door.

NINETEEN

For Rudy there was Before Irene and After Irene. In Before Irene, it had been hard enough to tell what hour or day it was. In After Irene, it was impossible. It was as if time had become embedded in one of the glaciers. Somewhere, under that ice, Rudy came to believe, was time, frozen and nearly still. He dreamed that if he were to walk up to the bulbous, protruding snout of the glacier towering out there, he would be able to see time in the ice; time, perhaps coiled like a heavy steel spring; time, perhaps as an organ, a heart, blood-blue and barely pulsing; or perhaps time, a polished brass pendulum locked in midswing.

Rudy sensed that days were now much shorter than nights. That meant it was autumn, or what passed for autumn up here. It was getting cold, but then it had never been all that warm. This was the arctic; heat and light played by different rules this far north.

He knew it was going to be hard to see her. They would have to be careful. It might be a while. But with no sense of time, "a while" meant nothing. Day and night meant nothing. There was only wakefulness and sleep.

In sleep, he had dreams about the Wing. Strange, disjointed dreams, amputated and partial like the patients. The dreams often had him floating. It was the same feeling he had when he glided through those houses trespassing, or when he moved about the colonel's office. In the dreams he drifted over the beds, looking at the men. Or the men would be floating, and he would be in bed, his body whole but unable to move. One dream had his father duplicated in every bed on one side of the ward, and his mother in every bed on the other side. Everyone was breathing in unison—inhale . . . exhale—Rudy included, while he floated.

He lost sleep because of the dreams. He wondered if maybe it was a debt he had to pay for the somnolent, restful feeling that slid over him whenever he was in the Wing. In all the dreams, whether he saw him or not, Rudy would hear Guy X's arid, stuttering voice. When he woke, he would lie in his bunk, trying to recall what Guy X had been saying.

The first chance he got, Rudy went back to the Wing.

"The . . . books!" Guy X said in his raspy voice. ". . . You've brought them."

"I thought I would read," Rudy said.

"How long has it been?" Guy X asked, then he burst out with one wheezy laugh. "Don't tell me!"

Guy X looked at the volumes in Rudy's hand.

"That's the best the army has to offer?" he asked.

"The chaplain said he'd look for more."

Guy X sighed and chose the Whitman. He asked for specific poems. "Crossing Brooklyn Ferry." "When Lilacs Last in the Dooryard Bloom'd."

"You know this stuff?" Rudy asked.

"I've read my share."

Rudy began to go through the poems. The rolling, teeming language made him feel crowded in the little alcove with Guy X, who nodded as Rudy read, closed his eye sometimes, but never slept or slipped away into one of his fits.

He asked for "I Sing the Body Electric."

Rudy began:

> "I sing the body electric,
>   The armies of those I love engirth me and I
>   engirth them,
>   They will not let me off till I go with them,
>   respond to them,
>   And discorrupt them, and charge them full
>   with the charge of the soul."

"Stop," Guy X said. "Read that again."

Rudy did. Guy X had him do it twice more. Then Guy X repeated it back to Rudy.

"That was good," Rudy said.

"I want to learn the whole thing," Guy X said.

Rudy flipped ahead in the book. "It's pretty long."

"So what? I want to go with something new in my head. Something besides the same old stuff."

"Go where?" Rudy asked.

Guy X didn't answer. He repeated the first few lines, then stopped and looked off toward the darkened end of the Wing. Rudy wondered if a fit was coming on, but Guy X seemed concentrated in thought, not about to go into a seizure.

" 'They will not let me off,' " he murmured. "Now we get to the Wonju salient. January 'fifty-one. The Chinese are coming down below the Thirty-eighth Parallel. We're hearing anywhere from four to seven corps. A total strength of a hundred twenty thousand men. The Second is fighting at Wonju and holding well.

"The Eighth Army, under orders, pulls back from Seoul, Official word is that the Eighth is leaving because the Second over at Wonju might give way and leave the Eighth outflanked.

"But the Second holds. Son-of-a-bitch, we hold. Altogether, we hold the enemy's advance for sixteen days. Caused him thousands of casualties."

The words just spilled out of Guy X with more ease than anything Rudy had ever heard him speak. It occurred to Rudy that the story had been running inside Guy X's head, perhaps for years, and had surfaced into audibility just now. Perhaps the poem had done it.

Guy X breathed heavily. He looked dazed.

"You want to learn some more of the poem?" Rudy asked. "You want to talk?"

The eye flicked over toward Rudy with a trace of annoyance.

"You wouldn't have recognized me," Guy X said. "I had everything. I had battle gear. I had a rifle. I had letters from my lover in my pocket." He tapped his chest. "I had six pence to spend and six pence to lend. I had all my body parts—I sing the body electric—eyes, skull, legs, arms, fingers, dick, guts, even a beard. And so we come to the nut of our little story . . . the beard."

Rudy was still pondering that bit about a lover, trying to imagine it. But Guy X was continuing:

"All of the field officers and a lot of the men of the Second had let their beards grow. We'd been growing them since the Reds crossed the Thirty-eighth two weeks before. The beards were against regs, but they were a badge of honor for us. We weren't going to shave until we drove the enemy back across the parallel. General McClure said okay with him. We were the heroes of the Wonju salient.

"But then headquarters command in Tokyo yanked McClure out of the Second. Fired him. We couldn't believe it. Here's the guy who led us against the Reds in one of the finest damn stands of the whole war. Fired.

"Word whispered out that we'd done the job *too* well. Word was MacArthur *wanted* a retreat, an all-out retreat. A big-time, clear-the-peninsula retreat so he could bomb Manchuria. And we fucked it up. We stood and fought like heroes and botched his plan. So he shit-canned the culprit."

Guy X stopped. He tried to lick his lips. On the table, Rudy found a plastic ketchup squirt bottle. It was labelled H_2O on a strip of surgical tape. He held it for Guy X who guided it as Rudy squeezed the water into Guy X's mouth. It was the first time Rudy had ever touched him. Guy X's fingers wrapped around Rudy's. The fingers felt mechanical, not enough of them to be a human hand. Dry, old man's skin. Guy X patted Rudy's sleeve and nodded thanks. It had been like drip-feeding an injured bird.

"I organized a protest," Guy X said. His voice clear and moist again. "I told a bunch of the other field officers, 'Let's shave the beards. Don't say anything. Just shave. They'll get the point.' So we did, and we made sure press correspondents caught sight of it. They knew what was up, but censorship stopped the story from getting out. America's fighting men don't protest."

Guy X was wearing out. His head lolled back and forth on the pillow. Rudy started to close the book.

"No," Guy X said. He recited the opening lines again, fluttering his fingers the two times he needed Rudy to prompt him. He had Rudy work with him for nearly a half hour more. They learned most of the first stanza.

> And if the body does not do fully as much as
>   the soul?
> And if the body were not the soul, what is the
>   soul?

Guy X began to sag. His eyelid drooped. His attention wandered, and he began to stutter seriously. Rudy suggested they take a break.

"No."

"I've got to report for work," Rudy said. It was a fib, but he wanted to end the visit with some dignity for Guy X, who was getting desperate and agitated.

"Fuck you," Guy X said. "I should have never told you my story."

He tried to roll over, but all he could do was turn his head away. At that angle, his skull showed the worst of its deformity. It looked like a half-crushed, rotted melon lying on the pillow. Guy X's wisps of hair looked like the mycelia of mold.

Rudy felt hopeless. Helping a wounded soldier learn some poetry seemed idiotic, almost cruel. Guy X obviously was taking on too much.

"Go," Guy X said.

"I'll be back," Rudy told him. "Another time."

"Yeah. Yeah. Yeah."

TWENTY

The season's first blizzard roared down from the north like a squadron of approaching aircraft. It came off the ice fields and sluiced through the mountain passes. On the parade ground, the flagpole rope started clanging frantically. The generator noise curled in and out on the changing winds. When the squall line had cleared the mountains, the storm made a hasty march across the outwash and tundra. One moment there were a few flakes dodging about the windows of the hospital; the next moment everything was a gushing, punishing white.

After the colonel had lowered the boom on the rumor edition of the *Harpoon,* dispiriting innocuousness seemed to be the line of least resistance. Rudy went with a "How to Get Through Winter" issue. He and Lavone were about to start work on it when Rudy drew the Manure Tour. It was officially listed on all rosters as "Outer Building Maintenance Duty," but the GIs at Qangattarsa called it the Manure Tour. It meant shoveling shit.

"I gotta give the colonel credit," Lavone had said. "He includes himself on this one detail. I've seen him up there with a shovel too. Of course, they are his damn horses, and he's still making all of us clean up after them. Wear your boots."

Rudy did. He put on his Mickey Mouse boots—the bulbous, polar-issue, insulated rubber jobs that looked like they were drawn by Disney and felt like they were made of lead—threw on his winter parka, and trudged up toward the hangar.

He'd been thinking constantly of Irene. Quick glances in the mess hall had been the best they could do lately. Contact was risky. He was losing track of when he'd last spoken with her. Time lets go of you. Longing was upon him with a vengeance.

There was easily a foot and a half of snow on the ground, and the storm didn't show any signs of quitting. Maintenance crews had set up the storm lines: ropes and cables strung from six-foot poles with cloth flags attached. The lines went from building to building so that GIs could hang onto them in a blinding, dark blizzard and not lose their way. They looked like gimcrack telegraph lines strung up around the post.

Rudy could see the lights of the main buildings behind him as he walked knee-deep in the snow; ahead was the yard light rocking on its stanchion up by the hangar. A Sno-Cat was parked under the light. Ice crystals scratched down Rudy's neck as he shuffled through the drifts. This first snow was a hint of the desolation a storm could bring down on the place. How to get through winter, indeed.

There was a sheet of instructions in a celluloid envelope tacked inside the door of the two-stall stable. The room smelled richly of dung and litter. It was a smell that comforted Rudy; it was so different from the other smells around the post: the odors of the Wing, of cigarette-butt cans in the barracks, of floor wax all through the halls and Pine-Sol in the latrines, of mess hall grease, of GIs' sweat and farts, of Lavone's amyl ampules and nasal inhalers, and of the occasional sniff of perfume Rudy'd catch whenever a nurse or WAC passed him in a hall. And, of course, this barn smell was one of the first whiffs he'd had of Irene. Faint traces of it had clung to her hair. Now it would cling to him too. One nice thing about the Manure Tour.

There was only one horse in the barn. A tan gelding. That was strange. Helluva night to be on horseback, Rudy thought. He hoped Irene wasn't out there riding around.

He set about the tasks as listed: muck out the stalls, replace the drinking water, two cans each of grain, fresh hay in the mangers and in each stall. The gas heater up by the ceiling kicked in and purled out a wave of warm air.

He was taking a break, patting the side of the horse, enjoying the soft sounds of the animal's chewing and of his chuffing breath, when Irene came through the door that led to the rest of the hangar. Not even giving him time to react, she walked directly to Rudy and, with her shoulder, shoved the horse farther over in the stall to give them room. She threw her arms around Rudy. They kissed right there in the stall. They kissed and held each other, and Rudy had a sudden image of them as two long-separated lovers meeting on the platform of a busy rail terminal and the horse was a big locomotive and steam swirled around them hiding him and Irene from all the inconveniences, all the alibis, the threats and worries of what they were about, leaving them alone for a moment in a cloud of charmed intimacy. He loved the feeling of her body fitting against his. Irene was holding him so tightly he began to feel she almost clutched at him. He tried to comfort her, to let her know with his embrace he would hold her for as long as she wished. He felt her shudder in his arms.

She steadied, and they embraced like two dance partners and talked softly over each other's shoulders. She said she knew he'd be here. She'd seen the roster. She had to come out.

"Am I glad you did," he said. "I've missed you."

Holding her like this, he was getting aroused. He could feel her press into him, but then he remembered there was only one horse in the barn.

"I kept going over to the Wing to think," she said. "I thought maybe I'd see you there, but we must have kept missing each other."

"What were you thinking about over in the Wing?" he asked. They had pulled back some from their embrace, but she was gripping his arms tightly.

"Thinking about?"

"Come on, you said you went over there to think."

She nodded and looked down at the floor. She seemed resigned to giving up any pretense of dodging his questions. "The works," she said. "How I got here. How it all happened. You."

"Good thoughts?" Rudy asked.

The horse thumped the floor of the stall and jangled his halter. Instinctively Rudy and Irene both put their hands on the animal's flank to steady him.

"Some. Some good thoughts."

"Sad ones too?"

"Who said anything about sad?" She pulled away a little. But then she leaned with her back against the planks of the stall divider. She eyed him, assaying the moment, then nodded.

"Sad too, I suppose," she said. "You're not in the sad part."

"Glad to hear it," Rudy said.

"You're different. That's what's got me so mixed up."

She slid out of the stall, patting the horse's rump, and went over to the small, foggy window that looked outside.

"Lane is riding around out there," she said.

Before Rudy could respond, Irene turned away from the window and made long, agitated strides across the floor, then back. She folded her arms across her chest as she paced. She slowed down, calmed herself. Rudy had never seen her so keyed up.

"I was thinking how it used to be I'd always go for the most powerful guy in the room, you know? The cheerleader who dated the football captain."

She said that was actually the way things started. She got married when she was seventeen. To the high school quarterback. It lasted just under two years.

"He got a job as a sand hog out at the test site in Nevada. Hot-shot heavy-equipment operator. He dug tunnels for the underground blasts," she said. "I was a kid, of course. Convenient, though, living in Nevada, for a divorce. Actually, getting married wasn't a bad idea at all back then. It's just that getting a divorce was a better idea."

She said she couldn't go back to her mother, who was getting a little batty after failing at uranium prospecting.

"So, it was the army in a wild moment. I regretted the hell out of it for a long time. But at least I wasn't alone. Three hots and a cot, as they say. I bounced around assignments stateside. Then I met Lane. . . ."

"The most powerful guy in the room," Rudy said.

Irene shrugged, neither accepting nor denying Rudy's comment. "He got me posted here. Said I should see a part of the world with him few people will ever see. And so I have."

Rudy could just barely hear the storm outside.

"But things change," Irene whispered.

"How do you mean?"

"I mean us, for one," she said. "And me."

Rudy felt his chest tighten. She was going to tell him it was over. She'd hooked him; now she was going to dump him. That was why she'd clung to him. She couldn't betray her mighty colonel. Rudy could barely draw a breath.

Irene seemed not to notice. "I . . . I was caught," she said. "Lane had changed. Or I had. I don't know. Then you showed up, and that unhinged everything."

Rudy drew a breath. She wasn't saying what he'd thought she'd be saying.

"What do you mean?" he asked.

"I don't know. I'd always sort of known in the past why I'd go for a guy, but now . . ."

"Well, I sure wasn't the most powerful guy in the room," Rudy said. He was now leaning on the post at the entrance to the stall.

Irene smiled, took his hand, and planted a quick kiss on his knuckles. "Maybe that was the point. Who *is* this guy? Why do I keep *thinking* about him? That's why I snooped through your files—to find some clue."

She let go of his hand. "Some things even a 201 file can't explain," she said.

Rudy smiled and brushed his fingers through her red hair. The storm kicked up a little, and a darkness crossed Irene's face. She looked toward the window.

"Lane is out there, riding," she said.

"So I heard," said Rudy.

Irene stared at the window. "It's nuts to be out there on a night like this," she whispered.

"You were saying he was one of the changes," Rudy said. "What's he doing to you, Irene?"

Irene waved the question off, shook her head. Neither of them spoke. They stayed that way, silent, for a long time.

"This your horse?" Rudy asked finally.

Irene shrugged again, noncommittal. "I suppose. I mean, I don't own him. On paper, he's 'Overland Combat Transportation' or a 'Military Heritage Item.' Depending on which books we're juggling." She patted the horse's rump, smiling in spite of herself.

"Irene," Rudy asked, "are they closing this place?"

Irene didn't answer right away. "Sounds like it," she eventually said, her voice distant. She sighed, snapping herself back into the present. "I don't know for sure. I only know Lane's pretty edgy about it."

She glanced toward the window again.

Rudy told her he'd seen the pictures in the colonel's office. He told her what he'd learned about Able and Baker Companies in Korea.

"There were maybe a dozen guys sent here from that battalion," Irene said. "There's only one man left."

"In the bed where the colonel was praying?"

Irene nodded. "Those guys are the reason the Wing is the way

it is. Lane got assigned here after the investigation. Military jus-
tice. He was supposed to take care of the guys whose lives he
screwed up. So he did the army one better. He created the Wing."

"What had he done in Korea?"

"Favors. Nobody could untangle it all. I don't think the army
wanted to. He was holding some equipment for a couple of pals
higher up in Quartermaster who were trying to cut a deal on the
black market. No one was ever supposed to use the stuff. It was
collateral. They knew it was bad. But the deal fell through. The
North Koreans started a big push, the equipment got called up,
and Lane couldn't stop it. The upshot was one of our battalions
ended up with bad napalm, lousy machine guns, and defective
ammunition. The other Quartermaster guys faded into the un-
derbrush, and Lane was left out in the open. The army said he
was a logistical genius and they didn't want to lose him. They
sent him here. The Wing is his penance."

"So what's going to happen to the guys in the Wing?" Rudy
asked.

"I don't think anyone knows."

"What do you think's going to happen to you and me?"

She looked at him. Rudy wanted to read unbounded love and
hope in her gaze; instead he was seeing tentativeness and an attempt at bravery. He couldn't fault her, though. They were all he
had to offer too.

"We're in this together," Rudy said, and he tried to make it
sound more like a sworn truth than a question.

Irene nodded. "Together."

They kissed, and Rudy ached with every fiber to fall down right
there and make love; however, he knew what she meant when
Irene whispered, "It's time I go."

But there was no time. Someone was fussing with the outer
door to the stable. Even through the sound of the storm, they
could hear a horse whinny impatiently. The colonel was back.
Rudy caught a glimpse of Irene as she broke out of his embrace
and ducked behind the pile of hay bales in the corner of the room.

The colonel came in. Rudy had just enough time to grab the pitch fork that was leaning against the wall and to look as if he were just finishing up work.

"Bracing night out there, troop," the colonel said, all hale and hearty. Both he and the mare were frosted from head to foot with driven snow.

"I'll say, sir."

The colonel led his horse into its stall. He began taking off his mittens and parka.

"Place looks good, troop," he said. "I'll finish up here."

The colonel hung his outer clothes over the stall divider and was engaged in loosening the saddle girth. It gave Rudy a chance to check on Irene. Things looked secure over there by the hay bales.

"Sir," he said. "I can do that. Rub down the horse and stuff. I can do it. I mean, if you want to go or something."

The colonel eyed him for an instant. "I said I'd do it, troop."

"Well, it's just I'm here on duty anyway, and I thought—"

"Fall out, troop. No need. Thank you and good-bye."

"Sir." Rudy flipped the colonel a perfunctory salute and began to put on his outer things. He resisted the temptation to steal another peek over at the hay bales. He could tell the colonel was checking on him. He didn't want to leave Irene there, but what could he do?

"There's a Sno-Cat parked outside, corporal. Keys are in it. You can drive it down."

"But what about you, sir?"

"I'll be here awhile giving this fellow a rubdown. I don't mind the walk. The guide ropes are up. Storm's not that bad. You'll see what I mean when winter really kicks in around here."

"Sir, I wouldn't want to—"

"Take the Cat, troop. Now."

"Yes, sir."

The Sno-Cat kicked right over. The headlights panned across the barn annex to the hangar as Rudy backed it around and pointed it toward the main buildings of the post. He looked once in the outside rearview mirror at the receding yard light and at the one illuminated window in the little stable.

The Cat began a diagonal slide on a drift of loose snow, and Rudy had to focus on his driving. As he descended from the rise above the hospital, he noticed there was something hanging from the ceiling of the cab, up by the windshield. He thought it might be somebody's St. Christopher charm, patron saint of Sno-Cat drivers, but when he flipped on the dome light, he could see it was an Eskimo figurine just like the one he carried in his pocket. Someone had drilled a hole right through the little statue's head, threaded a dog tag chain through it, and the figure dangled there from the Sno-Cat's ceiling, swinging wildly, as the machine pitched over the growing drifts. Rudy felt a gust of fear rise in his chest, and he looked again in the mirror, but the hangar and stable were now beyond the rise, out of sight, he was descending so fast.

TWENTY-ONE

Chaplain Captain Brank was putting on his vestments.

"I can come back when it isn't Sunday," Rudy said. He had dropped by to comb through more issues of *Stars and Stripes*. He needed something to take his mind off Irene. He hadn't seen her since he'd left her at the stable, and that was either one, two, or several days ago.

"It's not Sunday," said the chaplain. "I don't know what the hell day it is, but I know it's not Sunday." He led Rudy back among the stacks. The ham radio rattled. The chaplain's robes flowed between the shelves and fanned dust off the paperback mysteries and army field manuals.

"I was just trying these on. I'm thinking of going Catholic." He tugged at the chasuble, smoothed the collar. "Not that these are Catholic vestments. This is just the full Episcopal rig. But it gives you the idea. I've been thinking about my calling. The painting led me to it. What am I trying to say? What am I looking for? Paintings of the sea and sky. Saint Brendan. It occurred to me the direction I'm headed: Roman Catholicism. I'm

going to put in for a leave or a discharge or whatever it takes. Go
to seminary. Come back as a Catholic priest."

"Father Brank," said Rudy.

"Stu."

"Father Stu," said Rudy. The chaplain smiled beatifically, made
the sign of the cross as if he were Lawrence Welk striking up a
bubbly three-four waltz tune, and left Rudy to go through the
stacks of newspapers alone.

Among the dusty and yellowed pages, sitting on the cold linoleum floor, Rudy eventually found stuff about Wonju and the
pull-out from Seoul. It was all vague, with none of the slant that
Guy X had put on it, but this was, after all, an army newspaper.
There was a piece about the new commander of the Second Division but nothing about the dismissal of the old commander. In
an earlier issue, there was picture of some smiling soldiers, all
bearded, waving at the camera. It was slugged, SUCCESS AT
WONJU.

Rudy took the papers with him to the Wing.

Guy X was asleep, so Rudy pulled a chair close to the bed and
leaned over to place his ear near Guy X's chest. The soft, labored
breathing sounded like slow footsteps through wet leaves.

Rudy listened for a while, and a soothing weariness crept over
him. The room began to rock with the wavelike pulse of Guy X's
breathing.

"Greetings," Guy X suddenly wheezed.

Rudy sat upright in the chair.

"You've come back," Guy X said. "So have I."

"Back from where?" Rudy asked, still a little startled.

"My travels," Guy X said.

"Travels where?"

Guy X tapped his own forehead. "Here. Travels from the fits.
The fits I'm subject to."

He told Rudy that he woke up from Korea having them.

"Never had them before," he said. "But now? They send me

back in time. I kid you not. I roll back in time. All over my life. I go back to my own beginning. To my own zygotehood. I see my own cells dividing. Two. Four. Sixteen. Sixteen squared . . . Stop me if you've heard this. . . . I'm here to tell you, *I* sing the body electric. They all think I'm gone. But I'm not. I'm just deep inside. But, you know, I love coming back here, to this place, to this time. Whatever it is. It's home. That's what it is, and I'm a goner. I know that. I'm a goner not goin' nowhere. That's me. I'm Guy X. . . . You should have seen this place when I first got here."

Guy X seemed to be skittering on top of his own thoughts, as if he were under deadline and jamming out copy. He told Rudy about the large extension on the Wing, now dismantled, about how beds had stretched as far as the eye—"and in my case, bub, I do mean *the eye*"—could see.

"This place was packed with Korean War wounded. We had a whole section just for burn cases alone. The Barbecue Pit, they called it. Napalm and flame-throwers really came into their own in Korea. Believe me, I know."

Guy X told how the hospital had bustled in those days. Planes rotated in and out round the clock. A whole section, now dismantled, for surgery. Patients going off to the OR all the time, coming back rebandaged, changed maybe, but hardly for what you could call the better.

"It was a jumping joint back then, but not nicely done up. Not like this. It was all hospital green and white, and that was almost unbearable in the winter. Like the place was turned inside out: ice and green sky and frost fissures in here; and out there stainless-steel mountains and enameled-bedpan snowfields and light the color of plasma-drip bottles. But, oh, was it busy. I kept asking, 'Where am I? Where am I?' and nobody would say until an orderly asks can I keep a secret? And I say I think I *am* a secret, and he nods and says, 'Greenland.' But I don't believe that. Nobody's in Greenland. And then I think, 'Well, why not? Greenland. I'll pretend it's Greenland,' and so it is."

Guy X chuckled and shook, and Rudy had the impulse to lay a hand on his shoulder, but Guy X started in again.

"Then the colonel's guys arrived. The boys he fucked over. I heard about them. And, to top it off, Himself arrives. And boy, do things jack up around here. He spruces the place up. Brave new world that has such people in it. Nicely appointed, yes? But still guys would get wheeled off and not come back. Beds would hang out the vacant sign. Casters on the gurneys would squeak their fare-thee-wells. Attrition. Place got smaller. Men got fewer. Fits got longer. I could see it coming between the fits: death. Getting us down to bare essentials, down to the warm-blooded minimum. . . . And then, the guys stop dying at such a clip. The ones who last are the—what?—we're the *diehards*. We're the keepers of the flame. We won't leave the party and go home. We hang around long after the music stops. Long after the host has gone to bed. Long after everybody has gone back to work on Monday morning. We're still here, and we're here because we're here because we're here because we're here. . . ."

Guy X was sweating, and dried spittle gathered at the corner of his mouth. He lay still until his breathing settled. Rudy had never heard him say so much before, or with such intensity. He sat quietly next to Guy X.

After a few minutes, Rudy reached down and pulled out the bundle of newspapers. Guy X turned his head so he could see what Rudy was rustling and unfolding.

"I found some old issues," Rudy whispered. "I was interested in what you were telling me about Korea. I could read you some of this if you'd like to hear it."

He showed Guy X the headlines. Guy X's eye widened. The tendons in his neck bulged. He seemed about to swat at the papers, but then he grabbed at Rudy's sleeve with his mutilated hand and pulled the paper Rudy was holding closer to his face. He looked at the issue with the SUCCESS AT WONJU photo of the smiling, bearded men. Rudy turned it enough so he could see it too. Guy X pointed to a man standing near the center of the photo. Guy X held his finger on the picture, at the man's chest.

"You?" Rudy whispered.

Guy X nodded.

When Guy X's arm dropped softly back to the sheets, Rudy shifted the paper and studied the man. Dark-haired, with a thick beard well grown in, the man had his head tilted in laughter. His squinted eyes were looking brightly down at a couple of the other soldiers. There was no identifying text with the photo. The cutline read only: *Field officers of the 2nd Div after the stand at Wonju.*

Guy X's eye was moist and almost brimming over. Rudy put the papers down.

"When we shaved," Guy X rasped, "the new commander knew what the hell was up. I got called on the carpet and got relieved of my command. So I upped the ante. I got shithouse drunk, shaved my head along with my beard, and drove a Jeep into the new general's field tent. I ended up in the brig, and in barely more time than it took to sober me up, I was busted and transferred to another unit."

Guy X had closed his eye. His arm with its pale, leathery skin was thrown across his brow as if shielding him from light. He stuttered a couple of times. He'd been speaking so nimbly for so long, it surprised Rudy to hear him have trouble with words.

"I-In a village north of Anyang . . . they'd radioed bad coordinates . . . an F-80. Too low. So low I could see the pilot. . . . I was just a corporal. . . . My unit bought the napalm and bombs that were meant for the village. Turned our position into an incinerator . . . and that changed everything. . . . See? . . . Go ahead, tell me I was lucky."

He looked at Rudy. There was a steely tension around the pieces of his face that could move.

"I can't say that," Rudy told him quietly.

"Sure you can," Guy X said. "Look at me. I was lucky. I could have been killed." And a caustic, hacking laugh came out of his mouth.

Then silence again, until Guy X turned abruptly to Rudy.
"Would you ever do it? If I asked you?"

"What?" Rudy asked. "Do what?"

"Kill."

Rudy looked at him for a second before asking. "What are we
talking about here?"

"You," Guy X said. "And me."

The two men remained motionless. Rudy was not about to
speak. The force of the quiet seemed to mold the darkness around
them as night came on. Time came out of the glacier to move
things along, and Rudy eventually noticed Guy X's body had
shifted into the telltale trembling of a seizure. Rudy rose quietly
from the chair and tiptoed away.

But he didn't leave the Wing. He couldn't bring himself to leave
Guy X completely. The tears welling up in that one eye, the sound
of the small voice spilling out the story, the image of the handsome soldier, they wouldn't let him go. So, instead of heading
past the kiosk and out the double doors, he turned in the opposite
direction, toward the back end of the long room. It was the end
that had the extra beds, the unused equipment, the material left
over from the boom times Guy X had described. It was in shadow
and stood separated from the main part of the ward by several
ornate Victorian dressing screens. Rudy stepped behind them. It
was like sneaking backstage, behind the set. The lit part of the
Wing was framed in darkness. Seen at a distance, from behind
the screens, the Wing was a disembodied square of light floating
in space. The kiosk was a tiny jewel box.

Rudy grabbed a couple of blankets from a mothballed pile in
a canvas hamper and lay down on some mattresses stacked on the
floor. He stretched out and tried to calm himself.

The general breathing and gurgling were barely audible this
far away. Still, if Guy X got agitated, Rudy could hear him and
run to his side. Things stayed quiet. Only a whine and a yelp or

two made it down the ward, nocturnal broadcasts from men wounded beyond understanding what signals they were sending.

Soon the Wing took hold and soothed him. He stared up at the ceiling and felt sleep begin to work in around the edges of his eyes. His own breathing settled. Rest would come.

Familiar dream images stuttered across his sleep. None he could hold on to; none that seemed any different from ones he'd seen in his sleep for weeks now. Until he saw Irene undressing.

He had imagined this so many times: it would occur in his room, in the hay up at the stable behind the hangar, in the hangar on an old cot they'd found, in the old C-47, in the Quonset where the press was—but, somehow, it never happened here, in the Wing. And yet . . . he felt he understood. Here he was. With her.

Rudy looked at Irene. A steadiness showed in her eyes. He felt it too. This was not a dream. She'd found him. She reached for him, he felt her touch, and they kissed. Her hands ran up and down his body. "Let's lie naked," she whispered, and the words were almost unbearable to hear. Together they tugged at his clothes. He kept hearing the words, even as she was humming and moaning softly, as was he, and they were moving their mouths around the planes and hollows and curves on each other.

For a fleeting moment he remembered listening in below the colonel's office window. The clatter of objects swept from the desk. "Reenie." The thoughts scraped him like a gust of cold air, and he shuddered. She told him, "Shhhhh."

He kissed her everywhere, moved his mouth down below as her hands had encouraged him to, stayed there, hearing her above him, and came back up. They were in a hurry now. He was anyway, and she was allowing for that. She held him, helped him. He raised himself above her, and they looked into each other's eyes. Rudy's arms almost buckled from the elation but also from being so close to this precipice. Wind was roaring up from somewhere. It was as if a snowstorm were blowing right into the Wing. It pulled around his face and shoulders and thighs. It tried to pull him away from what was going on right in front of him, underneath him. He shuddered again. But only for an instant. Then he was back. It was perfect again. He was with her.

She looked beautiful to him, yet she was searching for something. He could tell by the way she moved her gaze around his face, his body. She nodded. He wondered at what, but he said, "Oh, yes."

Then Irene slowly rose up. She pushed back as Rudy moved inside her. This was what would give it all a shape and a conclusion. A few short words between them, then they grasped their way toward the end. Rudy first, Irene later; much later really, when he reached over and touched her as they came out of their swoon and made love again.

They were quiet that time, so quiet that all the while, Rudy was aware of the sounds and smells of the ward around him. This time he and Irene never closed their eyes. They never looked at each other but held on and made love as if searching for something in the dark that might come at them from the light down where the war wounded lay. This time Irene called out, one short syllable that she choked off at the end, almost brutally.

Afterward, he watched as she lay next to him and stared at the ceiling for the longest time.

"How did you know I was here?" he whispered.

"A guess. The orderly said you'd come on the ward. I heard a cry or something from back here."

"A cry?"

"Or something. You must have been having a dream. I took a look back here and found you."

Rudy smiled, but he was thinking about what it was that might have made him cry out. He didn't know. He couldn't remember his dreams.

"The other night when the colonel ordered me out of the stable," he whispered, "were you okay?"

She nodded on the pillow.

"Did he find you?"

She shook her head.

"Did you come out?"

"Not until after he was long gone. I must have stayed half the night. Once my nerves settled, I got to like it there, just hanging out with the horses. Listening to the storm."

Rudy lay on his back, one arm behind his head, the other hand stroking her. "I was worried."

She snuggled in closer, but she seemed taut. It was something he knew he could feel under her skin just by being close to her, because now they were lovers.

"We'll have to leave," she whispered.

"Separately," he said. "There's an outer door back here, I think."

She shook her head. "I mean the whole place."

And the enormity of this was like a weight bouncing off Rudy's chest. It crashed down, pressed him into the mattress, but then almost immediately sprung away, making him feel light and lofty.

"We'll do it," he said.

"Together," Irene said. She held him tightly.

Rudy kissed her and felt powerful with promise. She smiled and closed her eyes. *Together,* she'd said.

He looked up, following the crease in the shadows where the wall and the ceiling met. It was up there he saw the dot of light vibrating. It shot around, right and left. Rudy slipped off the mattresses swiftly and silently tiptoed to the nearest dressing screen. He peeked around the corner. The Wing was quiet, framed in darkness, as before. Partway down the right side was Guy X's bed. Rudy had left the alcove lamp on when he'd been there reading the papers. Guy X's head reflector caught the illumination and threw it around the room. Even at that distance, Rudy could see Guy X was out, vibrating in one of his fits, signaling randomly.

Rudy looked back at Irene. She was awake, sitting up, wrapped in the blankets, stiff with apprehension. He signaled to her that things were okay for now, so she lay back down. Rudy looked back up at the little light. It dodged and flickered and darted about, then it descended toward Irene's shrouded body like a weightless falling star.

TWENTY-TWO

Rudy came across Lavone at the mess hall bulletin board, putting up a new poster.

"Now *here* we have film," Lavone said, stepping back to look at the placard. It was for *The Thing*. A shadowy creature loomed over the dripping-wax horror letters of the title. In the background were some buildings that looked a little like Qangattarsa—snow, ice fields, and all.

"Horror in the arctic," Lavone said. "We're the perfect audience."

Then Lavone tacked up the week's KP roster. Rudy's name was near the top.

"I'm sorry, man," Lavone said. "I tried to do something about it, but we're short-handed. Look, I even had to put myself on." He pointed to his own name farther down the list. "The horror. The horror," he croaked.

"What do you mean short-handed?" Rudy asked.

"They're shipping a bunch of guys home toot-sweet. I barely had time to cut their orders. My labor pool's draining."

"Why're they getting shipped?"

"Cutback is all I heard."

Except for the 0430 wake-up, KP wasn't so bad. Desmond was there, drunk but happy, and he saw to it Rudy got cushy jobs. For breakfast, Rudy ladled oatmeal. He had almost no takers. The steam feathered around his face, warm and soothing. He stood in a half-asleep swoon, thinking about Irene. A stream of soldiers' faces drifted past. *The armies of those I love engirth me and I engirth them.* Everyone looked great. Lovely women, hardy men. Even Genteen looked good as he shoved his tray and his little pot belly down the chow line.

Rudy was back at the sinks banging the oatmeal pail in the suds when he saw Irene come through the line for a cup of coffee. She didn't notice him back there, and he only caught a quick glimpse of her, but he felt as if his whole body had been dipped into the washtub—scalded and ecstatic all at once.

He didn't see her during lunch; he was dreamily sorting silverware for the officers' mess. Later, he was on break just before the supper shift, sitting with a couple of guys on potato sacks in the storeroom, when a cook with broken and taped glasses stuck his head around the door and motioned for Rudy to follow him.

"You got an honor assignment," the cook said once he got Rudy out of earshot of the others. "It don't happen every day on KP. Besides, it gets you out of the kitchen."

"What is it?" Rudy asked.

"Cremation detail."

"Jesus."

"Hey, it's cooking, right? Just a little overdone. Take it or leave it."

Rudy reported to the Wing with his outdoor gear. The nurse in the kiosk stood up and pointed toward a bed about halfway down the ward. There was a small package wrapped in sheets in the middle of the mattress. The shift nurse had already shrouded the body.

"You know about our burial custom?" she asked Rudy.

He nodded.

"I'll get the window," she said.

As Rudy expected, the body was light when he picked it up. He tried to picture what the man might have looked like, what had been left of him. Rudy must have seen him. At one time or another, he'd looked at every patient in the Wing. Was this near the bed where the colonel had been praying? Rudy couldn't remember. He looked toward Guy X's bed, but could see only crystalline drip bottles and the soft light of the Tiffanies. He felt light-headed. The smells of suppuration and antiseptic made the room spin. The body in his arms felt too light.

"You okay?" the nurse asked, and a gust of cold air snapped Rudy out of his wooziness. He was standing before an open window. A soldier outside reached through and took the body from Rudy.

"I'm okay," he said.

They rode through the dark to the Fire Department in a white Sno-Cat that looked like a 1930s panel truck mounted on four pontoons with crawler treads. Another Sno-Cat was already outside the Fire Department when they got there. The nurse and the orderly waited in the idling Cat while Rudy carried the body to the door.

Once inside, when his eyes adjusted, Rudy saw he was standing in a gravel-floored room about the size of a school gym. Two bare bulbs hung from the ceiling. There were several Jeeps, a half-track, and a treadless tank parked in the shadows. Before him was a metal box made from parts of army vehicles welded together. On top, a corrugated culvert pipe rose up to the ceiling. There was a door in the front, and inside a banked coal fire of low, blue flame glowed beneath a black grate. Beside the crematorium stood the chaplain, the colonel, and Irene.

The chaplain cleared his throat and read from his prayer book. He was in his full Episcopal rig and seemed to be making the sign of the cross indiscriminately as he progressed through passages about the resurrection and the life, ashes to ashes. As he stood holding the body, Rudy could see the colonel was clasping Irene's hand. When the chaplain was done, he stepped over and took the body. Rudy wanted to see Irene, but she was in the shadows.

Captain Brank crouched before the low furnace door and held the body awkwardly. He hesitated in the heat.

"Hell," the colonel grumbled, and he grabbed the bundle from the chaplain. With a back-swinging, heave-ho motion, he flung the corpse through the opening and onto the grate, where it landed with a soft thud. Then with his boot, he slammed the door shut.

"Crank the bellows," Captain Brank whispered to Rudy and pointed to a large handle attached to the furnace. Rudy was quickly able to get the bellows whining away; the momentum almost made the handle jump out of his grasp. He bobbed up and down with the revolutions, and the fire began to moan inside the furnace.

While he was cranking, Rudy noticed the colonel and Irene head for the door. They left it open, and the headlights of a Sno-Cat swept around as the vehicle departed. The stars were out, and through the door Rudy could see a rain of sparks flying downwind. It was coming from the chimney and the fire he was fanning. When he cranked harder, a few seconds later, up above, there was a thickening of the orange specks of flame and ash.

After a little more fanning and stoking, the chaplain and Rudy shut the flues. They looked into the crematory and winced as the heat hit them in the face. Inside, amid the red glow on the grate, was a pile of white ash.

"The burial crew will be out when this cools down," the chaplain said.

They closed up the Fire Department and got into the remaining Sno-Cat.

"I'll be your chauffeur," the chaplain said. "Hope I can drive one of these babies. I guess the colonel didn't want to hang around after that one."

The chaplain ground the starter and mashed some gears as he lurched the machine around and narrowly missed the corner of the building. In the fan of illumination from the headlights, Rudy could see a faint swath of black flecks on the snow: ash from the fire.

"Does the colonel usually come out to these things?" Rudy asked.

"Rarely. But this one was special."

"Who was it?"

"L. W. Sterner, PFC, Baker Company, Sixth Battalion, Third Infantry Division. Caught in a backfire of his own flamethrower. Left for dead in Korea, 1951. Finally succumbed to pneumonia, Qangattarsa, Greenland, 1959."

The Sno-Cat was approaching Storage Charlie. The chaplain was searching for a way to downshift. Rudy had his hand on the dash to brace himself against the jolt.

"L. W. Sterner was in the battalion the colonel supplied with defective equipment," Rudy said.

The chaplain looked over at him.

"He was the last one," Rudy said.

The chaplain pulled up perilously close to Storage Charlie and found neutral.

"Wasn't he?" Rudy asked.

Over toward the Wing, the pink-orange glow of the lamps shone through some of the sheer curtains. The glow rested in patches like ripe fruit on the snow.

"He was," the chaplain said. "May he rest in peace."

Rudy got out of the Sno-Cat and bolted backward up the steps as the engine screamed when the chaplain threw the machine into gear. Rudy pressed himself against the building. The chaplain sent the front crawler tread up and over the landing, chewing large splinters out of the wood and destroying two entire steps. The Sno-Cat growled away into the night, spitting out chunks of wood and ice.

Rudy was exhausted. He didn't have to go back to KP, and he

didn't even feel hungry for supper. He just wanted to lie on his bunk.

When he got to his room, there were two notes on his bed. One was from Irene.

I loved seeing you,

it read.

It wasn't close enough for comfort.

The other note was unsigned, but it was in the scrawl that Rudy recognized.

Now we've really had it. Our lifeline died. Believe me. Where are you? Report!

But all he could do was lie on top of the bed, the two notes resting on his chest as he breathed. He heard nothing but the sound of the generator becoming the sound of the fire. He saw nothing with his closed eyes but the sparks he'd made, raining down and becoming ash on the snow.

TWENTY-THREE

When the Wing was at its most peaceful, all the patients seemed to breathe together, and the place had the gentle push and pull of a tidal pool. Today, though, the breathing seemed shallow and quick. The room felt on edge.

Guy X was out, gone into a fit. Rudy could see the telltale flutter in his wrist and his neck muscles. The silver reflecting mirror was cocked off to one side to reveal the caved-in part of his face and the sad, ugly, scooped-out depression in the back of his head.

Rudy sat quietly and listened more to the ward. It was as if a stone had been thrown into the tidal pool and the patients were finning nervously behind the rocks, waiting for the water to become clear again.

Guy X, however, seemed to be oblivious. He was breathing at his own choppy pace.

Rudy pulled the copy of Whitman off the bedside table. He adjusted the clip lamp and opened the book to "I Sing the Body Electric." He went through the first stanza, then stopped to look at Guy X. The man seemed almost infantile with his small body and single arm tucked under the sheets and the downy wisps of hair on his skull. The trembling had stopped.

Rudy read as he held the book before him in the clot of light from the lamp. He thought if Guy X were sleeping, perhaps this would wake him gently. If he were still under a fit, then maybe the words would ease him back.

> "They will not let me off till I go with them,
> respond to them . . ."

Rudy spoke quietly, almost to himself.

> "The love of the body of a man or woman balks
> account, the body itself balks account—"

"What is that? I can't hear it."

Rudy looked up. Guy X was still out; the duty nurse was still shut in the kiosk. The voice had come from down and across the aisle, from where the empty beds and equipment were, backstage.

A man was stretched out there. One of the Victorian dressing screens partially obscured him from the rest of the ward. Rudy stood up, and he could see it was the major general. He was lying on a bare mattress near the pile where Rudy and Irene had made love, his hands behind his head, his civilian hiking boots off, his parka draped over a bed frame. He wore a plaid shirt, and he looked as if he were reclining back at the lodge after a successful day's hunt.

"That Shakespeare?" he asked.

"No, sir," Rudy said, not sure how loudly to speak. "Whitman."

The general swung his legs down, got up, and padded over in stocking feet to Guy X's bed. He stood next to Rudy and looked at the patient, then at the book in Rudy's hand.

"You think that'll help?"

"He asked me to read it to him," Rudy said.

"He doesn't look too cognizant, does he?"

"No, sir."

The general sighed almost soundlessly. He walked back toward his things; he motioned for Rudy to follow.

"My chopper got delayed. Storm to the west. So I came in here for a little shut-eye." The general sat on the edge of a bed and began to put on his hiking boots. "It's peaceful in here. You notice that?"

"Yes, sir."

"Strangely . . ." The general jammed his foot into a boot. ". . . peaceful. I like that."

He leaned over and extended his hand to Rudy. "Tolson Vord, soldier," he said. "Major General, United States Air Force."

Rudy shook the proffered hand. The general bent to lace his boot. He continued talking.

"We keep bumping into each other around here, Corporal. What's your name?"

"Spruance, sir. Rudy."

"Any relation to the admiral by that name, Spruance?"

"No, sir. Far from it."

"Good thing for me, eh? Suppose I'd jumped into your shit for dozing on guard duty and you were an admiral's nephew or something. That'd be a can of worms for all of us."

General Vord laughed and shook his head at the prospect. He sat looking down at his lacing job. He hadn't laced the boots with the usual crisscrosses but had done them up in a ladder pattern, the way paratroopers did.

"Strangely peaceful," Vord said again. "You come in here a lot?"

"Some, sir. Not too much."

"You're the editor of the paper Woolwrap set up here."

"Yes, sir."

Vord stood, tucked in his shirt. "I've read it. I saw the issue that had some things to say about the closing of Q-Base."

The general pulled a silver hip flask out of his trousers. He took a swig, offered one to Rudy. Rudy declined.

"Who wrote the letter, Corporal?"

Rudy could hear the puttering of the breathing and all the secretions coming from down the ward. The general had turned on the bed and was staring at Rudy. The man's blue eyes were almost watery. If they were any more liquid, they would have lost their piercing quality and been merely rheumy, the eyes of a drunk or a sad old man. As it was, they were balefully lucent.

"I don't know," Rudy said.

"Yes you do. Of course you do. I know you do."

"It was unsigned, sir."

"Who was it, Rudy?"

"Sir, assuming I did know, what difference would it make? It's just a letter. Just a question."

"The colonel say anything about it?"

"He said I couldn't publish any more unsigned letters."

Vord was pointing toward Guy X's bed. "Say it was that fellow who wrote the letter. The guy in your poetry corner over there. Say it was him. You got a little conspiracy going?"

"A conspiracy? With him?" Rudy asked. "Hardly, sir."

"But the thought occurs to you," Vord said, "that maybe the army will close this place down."

"The thought occurs. Yes, sir."

"And it concerns you."

"I sympathize with the concern in that letter, sir."

"A concerned citizen-soldier," Vord said as he stepped over to the window. He parted the drape and looked out. Over Vord's shoulder, Rudy could see a couple of security lights and the sky, nearly black, with clouds piled like surf up against the wall of mountains. It was midday. This dimness was their brief allotment of light.

"Let me broaden your perspective a little," Vord said. "Let me talk to you about security. About peace. About the way you learned to look at the world. Think back. Picture the world map you used to look at in your old schoolroom. Can you do that, Corporal Spruance?"

"Yes, sir."

"You looked at that map every day, no doubt," Vord said. His voice was soft, almost hypnotic. He was still looking out the window, his back to Rudy. "It was how you came to know the world. Sure, there might have been a globe in the class, but the map hung there right before your eyes. Big. Bitter smelling when you went right up to it and sniffed the ink. Printed on something almost as heavy as oilcloth. The world. Part of your education."

Vord turned to Rudy. "But you know, that map helped you get the world all wrong, Rudy Spruance. It was supposed to teach you about the world, but it gave the whole wrong point of view. A totally erroneous perspective. See, it's the Mercator projection. It screws up our outlook. It's got us believing this hunk of rock and ice, this Greenland, is twice the size of the United States of America."

Rudy thought about it. That's how it did look on those school maps. He seemed to remember one of them even had Greenland colored green. What a joke.

Vord went on: "You sit in your schoolroom, looking up at the map over the blackboard, and Russia is over on the left and the United States of America is over on the right. Or maybe we're in the middle and Russia is split in half. At any rate, those Mercator projections give you the idea the Russ lives in a land divided or, at the very least, on the far side of the known world from us, and so we are safe. She's a distant land. Far off. She can't get us. So, lullaby and good night. . . . Well, that is one piece of class-A foolishness."

Vord began to pace a little, hands in his pockets, casting occasional sidelong glances at Rudy. "Look at the world from where we are. Here. The arctic. Look at it from the top down. The Russ isn't any old distant Eastern bloc on the other side of the map. No. She's our bloody goddamned neighbor. Our land mass and hers are practically holding hands up here, playing ring-around-the-pole up here, with Alaska and Siberia clutching on one side and Scandinavia and the Kola Peninsula on the other."

He clasped his hands together for emphasis. He then loosened them and pressed his palms into the small of his back and stretched a little, leaning backward. His sigh was almost a groan, and he looked around the ward.

"Woolwrap is a piece of work, isn't he?" Vord said.

Rudy looked at all the beds, the lit kiosk, Guy X lying inert.

"And that sergeant of his," Vord said. "What do you think of her?"

"I don't know what you mean, sir," Rudy said.

"Bullshit you don't."

Rudy's jaw tightened so suddenly it hurt.

"You forgetting the first time we met? Done any more of the sneaky-pete under their window? Maybe you get yourself assigned to laundry detail so you can sniff her undies. How about that, Corporal?"

Rudy could feel his face twitch. He said, "Sir, I can't imagine what you mean."

"Ho-ho! Are they drafting enlisted men out of Eton now? 'Sir, I *cahn't* imagine what you mean.' "

Vord was chuckling and shaking his head. He was looking around at the ward again. "This takes some kind of genius, building a place like this on the army's nickel, but what the hell good it does beats me. See, here's my problem with all this."

Vord pulled back the drapes all the way. The twilit wall of black-and-gray mountains loomed in the glass. A gash of white glacier filled a notch between two of the larger peaks. Vord tapped his finger on the pane.

"Polar ice," Vord said. "Zero protection in the Atomic Age against missiles. Even against bombers. And polar ice is all we've got between us and them. After these mountains, pal, it's all flat. Like flying across an empty plate. Of course, their missiles and bombers are easier to spot. They have no cover. But then, we have no protection. So, we need early warning, soldier. Because, mark my words, we're fighting the next one in the air."

General Vord walked away from the window. He was flushed. He walked down the line of beds in the ward, skidding his palm across each white enameled footrail. He was practically calling out to Rudy as he talked.

"The Russ has got sixteen major airfields on the Kola Peninsula alone. There are enough planes and firepower on that little spit of land to blow up the world."

"So you want an air war?"

"Not *want*. But . . . given the choice . . ."

Rudy looked around at the ward. Guy X's eye was closed, but he had moved his head on the pillow. He was at an angle that made his head and face almost appear normal. His little body under the bedclothes twitched once, like a baby dreaming.

"We need warning, Rudy Spruance. We need to buy time. In an air war, time is measured in minutes to target, seconds to impact. The clock looms over schoolchildren under their desks, over citizens making it into bomb shelters. That's what this all comes down to. Time. Early warning. Radar."

"Here?"

"Good place, save for the local populace." He pointed to the beds.

"Well, what about them?" Rudy asked with a petulance rising in his voice.

The general picked up his parka and flung it over his shoulder, hooking the collar with his fingers, Sinatra-style. He looked forlorn and weary, but Rudy had the feeling the look was calculated artifice.

"The Atomic Age is big, Rudy Spruance. Bigger than me. Bigger than you. Bigger than these guys. They're already calling Korea the Forgotten War, and that stands to reason. You tend to forget plenty when something as big as the Bomb is looming," Vord said. He started to walk off through the pools of light toward the door.

"What will you do with them?" Rudy called out to Vord.

"What would you have me do?" Vord stopped to look back at Rudy. "I'm serious. What would you have me do?"

"Well . . . take care of them."

"Yes? *And?*"

"What do you mean '*And*'?" Rudy asked.

"I mean," General Vord said, walking so quickly toward Rudy he looked as if he were going to attack, "something has to come first here. How do I take care of them *and* the defense of our country too? Of them *and* our whole God-blessed way of *life?*"

He stood before Rudy, coiled. His acne scars seemed to have deepened with the flush of his face. Rudy noticed he and Vord were exactly the same height.

"You just do," Rudy said.

Vord stepped backward, nodding. "I just do," he said. Now he looked as if he might burst out laughing. "I just do. Snap the fingers and just do. Spruance, you have no idea of the depth of my problem here."

"No, sir," Rudy said. "Obviously I don't."

But Vord wasn't listening. He had turned to stride down the aisle. The patients' surf noise followed him as he went. Somewhere someone throated a tremulous, two-note aria. After a few moments, it died.

Rudy waited until he heard the door click closed, then turned. Guy X's eye was open now, wide, staring after Vord. Even from across the aisle, Rudy could see the rage.

TWENTY-FOUR

"Help."

"How?"

"I don't know!"

They were whispering. Or at least Rudy was. Guy X was speaking in his dry rustle of a voice, the soft abrasive sound he made with his arid tongue, his reconstructed lips, his two or three teeth. Rudy felt a need for secrecy. Even though General Vord had just left, his presence lingered on the ward, if only because Guy X was still so visibly shaken.

"You want me to read to you?" Rudy whispered into Guy X's ear hole.

"Christ, no," Guy X said. Then he muttered, "That fucker."

"Who?"

"That bastard."

"The general?"

"Is *that* what he is?"

"Yeah."

"Oh Christ, another general to fuck me up. He's going to kill us."

"Who?"

"Us. Not you. Us in here, in this place."

"He didn't say that."

"He didn't have to. You heard him. He said this place is done."

"So?"

"So, they want to shut it down. Who's going to stop them? The colonel's last trooper is gone. So where's the colonel's fight going to come from? They close the place, they'll move us. They move us, how many are going to make it?"

Rudy was leaning forward on his chair, his elbow resting on Guy X's mattress. He looked down the length of the bed. The rumpled sheets were like wind-rippled snow, a tundra.

"How many guys do they *care* are going to make it?" Guy X asked.

"I don't know," Rudy muttered.

"You've got to help me."

"Do what?"

"Don't let them cremate me."

"What are you talking about?"

"Promise. I've had enough fire. Make sure whatever happens they don't burn me anymore."

"How can I—?"

"Bury me. Or put me on a stone out there for the damn penguins to pick at my bones."

"There aren't any penguins in Greenland."

"Greenland!"

"Where we are."

"Greenland? Oh, Christ."

"You forgot?"

"I never thought . . . Look, the hell with penguins. Just no cremation, okay? No fire."

"Listen, I—"

"Promise!"

"Jesus, okay. But what are you talking about? You're not dying."

"Could."

"But you're not. So don't talk—"

"And no one'll know except for you."

"Don't talk that way."

"*You'll* know."

Rudy sat back in the chair. Guy X had him pinned. Rudy reached over and riffled the pages of the Whitman on the nightstand. Guy X's eye swiveled to check the noise.

"Let me ask you something," Rudy said.

Guy X turned his head. The physician's reflector tossed some light at Rudy.

"Who do you talk to?" Rudy asked. "Besides me. Does anybody else visit you?"

"Nope."

"Well, who brought the note you wrote to me?"

This caught Guy X up short. Rudy could see his head twitch up off the pillow. Guy X settled and looked up at the ceiling.

"The redhead," he said.

"So you talked to her?"

"I tried."

"Does she come to see you?"

"No."

Rudy wondered, could Guy X actually be blushing? It was something he'd never seen or even thought a possibility. Rudy didn't know what was left of Guy X below the abdomen. Was it memory or the urges themselves that still affected Guy X?

"Who does she visit?" Rudy asked.

"Nobody. She just sits. I try calling to her but she doesn't answer. Except this time. Maybe she heard me. Maybe I'm dreaming."

"What do you mean?"

"I can't tell anymore. They're not sleeping dreams because I'll see a nurse change my sheets, and I'll call to her and get no reaction, so I think I'm dreaming. Then I'll look later, and there'll be fresh sheets on the bed. So the nurse was real, but my calling wasn't. I *think* I'm getting through to people I see in here, but I'm not. Except with the redhead. She must have heard me."

"And this time. You're getting through now," Rudy said.

Guy X's face pulled into a smile. He wrapped his three fingers around Rudy's cuff. "Then help me. Come back. Promise."

"I have. I will."

"I don't want to leave here. If I go, I'll be done for."

"You don't think you'll survive a move?"

"Might not. But even if I do, where would I go? I'd disappear. Some back ward somewhere. Some VA hospital. Probably give me a name, a biography. Say I was in a car crash or an industrial accident."

"You could tell them your real name."

"They'd love that. Then they'd really have me."

He let go of Rudy's sleeve, and they sat for a while in silence.

"Tell them your name," Rudy whispered.

"No!"

"But if they knew you were cognizant"—he used the general's word—"if they knew, it might change things."

"Keep believing it."

"Then tell *me* your name," Rudy whispered.

Guy X shook his head.

"Well, the hell with it," Rudy said.

Guy X grabbed him again. "Come back. Promise."

"I did."

Guy X's hand was clamped to Rudy's arm. His damaged head was up off the pillow, and his neck sinews were bulging.

"Relax," Rudy whispered.

"You'll be back?"

"Yes," Rudy said.

"When?"

"Tomorrow. First thing."

*   *   *

Rudy went to his room, worked on the paper, had a beer at the club, hoped to see Irene, didn't, went to bed. When he got up the next morning, he headed over to the Wing. He half hoped that maybe Guy X would be under one of his fits. Rudy could just leave him a note. But still, all that Vord had said—all that Guy X had heard—bothered him.

When he got to the Wing, he buzzed the kiosk from the hall and gave his name. Usually they let him right in, but now he was made to wait.

Finally a voice crackled over the intercom. It was one of the orderlies.

"Sorry. Access denied."

Rudy pushed the button on his end of the intercom. *"What?"*

"Says here access denied. They revoked your clearance."

"That's crazy. Let me in."

"Sorry, man. Not by the hair of my chinny-chin-chin."

And the speaker clicked off in Rudy's face.

TWENTY-FIVE

Rudy couldn't remember the last time he'd seen the sun. Day was an hour or so of dusk in the south now; everything else was night. For weeks, the sea had been a black finger of water probing the snow-covered mountains. Slowly, though, as the light disappeared, the cold had turned the brine to a gray, gelatinous paste. And now, finally, the water had frozen, the bergs and floes had become hills and crags locked in a plain that stretched from one mountain wall to the other, and the fjord blended with the rest of the peaked and angular blankness of Qangattarsa.

But the darkness wasn't total. Even on moonless nights, stars illuminated the fjord. In the faint light, the ice was a blue-gray coursed with darker streaks and patches. Exposed rocks were somber, negative spaces, and a person beyond the range of the security lights was a black shape, a presence you felt more than actually saw. Trips outside were rare now, however. It hadn't gotten above zero since before Thanksgiving, and Christmas was approaching.

Delineated time—days, hours, the ticking of clocks, the tearing of calendar pages—seemed to be going on apart from Rudy, beyond some kind of membrane. With effort, he could pass through this barrier and, passing through, could enter time to put out a paper or make it to meals, but he was finding it harder to remember how long he'd been in Greenland and how long he still had to go. It was common, Lavone had said. Take Petri. Suddenly he was a short-timer. There was to be a going-away party for him, and Rudy was invited.

He followed a beaten path through the snow out beyond the parade ground to a pair of glowing igloos. Beef had organized the affair and had hired some Inuit from the settlement beyond the bend in the fjord to supply the party's venue and women.

"The theme'll be 'Screw the North,' " Beef had told Rudy. "Petri will like that."

Rudy hadn't wanted to go, but Beef goaded him and said it was a surprise for Petri.

"I didn't even know Petri was a short-timer," Rudy had said.

"Neither did he," said Beef. "But who does? He and a bunch more guys from Signal and Transport are shipping out tomorrow." He made the fluttering Qangattarsa sign with his hands: Let us fly up.

It was a half-moon night, about twenty below. Snow crunched under Rudy's boots. As he approached the igloos, he could hear singing and caterwauling. A couple of dog sleds were parked in the distance, and the teams were howling in concert with the noise.

Outside the doorway, an Eskimo man was peeing in the snow. As Rudy was about to bend down to go in the entrance, the man turned quickly and nearly soaked Rudy's leg. The Eskimo was drunk. He shined an army-issue flashlight in Rudy's face and said, "Sorry, man. Sorry," as he fastened himself back into his furs. Then he reached out and grabbed Rudy's shoulder.

"Alley Oop," he said and pounded himself on the chest. "Alley Oop."

It took Rudy a moment, but he recognized the man as the Eskimo who'd sold him the statuette at the Bash.

"Alley Oop."

Rudy nodded. He found the figurine in his pocket and held it out for the Eskimo to see. Alley Oop smiled, then turned to puke on the snow. Rudy reached out to see if he needed help, but the Eskimo waved him away between heaves. Rudy ducked through the doorway.

A government-issue Coleman lantern illuminated the inside of the igloo. There were even some Christmas tree ornaments stuck in the snow of the ceiling. Petri was in the center of the small, domed room, shirtless, lying on some furs and bench-pressing a giggling Eskimo woman. About eight GIs, mostly guys from Transport, and several Eskimos were sitting on the blanketed ice shelf around the igloo's circumference. A Wollensak reel-to-reel hooked up to a truck battery played Laverne Baker's "I Cried a Tear."

It was surprisingly warm and dank in the room. It was filled with the odors of beer, bodies, and smoke—cigarette and pot. Lavone had brought out his heavy ordnance. He was offering the Eskimo women amyl nitrite ampules. The women held the little, netted glass vials quizzically and smiled. A PFC was pawing through a shell casing containing yellow jackets and speedballs. He chanted, "Faster? Slower? Faster? Slower? Fasterfasterfaster? Slower? Slo-o-ower? Sssslo-o-o-o-werrrr . . ." He looked at Rudy and keeled over laughing.

Rudy had the impression he might never synchronize with this party, but he found himself a beer and a seat on the shelf near Beef. A sergeant and one of the women crawled through a doorway opposite the igloo's entrance.

"Interested in a little Eskimo poon? Step that way," Beef said, pointing to the door. "It goes to our screwing annex."

Alley Oop had come in and was over with a couple of the other Inuit men with Lavone, who was showing them a pornographic flip book of Horace Horsecollar and Clarabelle Cow screwing. The Inuit looked abashed, but they couldn't resist flipping the book backward and forward.

Petri had put the woman down and was pulling his shirt back on over his blocky torso. He grabbed a beer and came over to Rudy.

"Spru, my man," he said. His voice seemed to pulverize the air in front of Rudy's face. "What would you do if you were me and you were a short-timer? Re-up or out?"

"I don't know," Rudy said.

"You don't know?" Lavone nearly shouted. "You mean you'd consider staying?"

"He was asking about himself."

"Hey. Snap out of it, man," Lavone said. "Don't even mention the word re-up."

"Three hots and a cot," Beef said.

"You stay in," Lavone said, "it's like the army puts you in this book." He flipped Clarabelle and Horace forward and backward. "Any way you look at it, you're fucked."

Bill Parsons's Elvis imitation, "All-American Boy," was on the tape.

"You cats are letting the dark get to you," Lavone said. "This place makes you batshit. It's like a beast squats down on us, and we're all scrambling around under the weight."

Petri picked up Beef's guitar, clutched the neck with his fist, and thwacked at the strings.

"Hey!" Beef yelled.

"I wanna sing," Petri said. "I'm a fucking big-shit short-timer, and I wanna sing." He banged some more.

"That item's still for sale," said Beef.

"So I'll buy it," Petri said. "A going-away gift for a big-shit short-timer." He pulled twenty dollars out of his pocket and threw it down on a fur blanket.

"Now it's mine," he said.

"I didn't—" Beef started to say, but Petri was banging the guitar and hopping around singing a mishmash of Presley songs. The Eskimo started to clap.

"I can feel Elvis's power coming through the strings," Petri shouted. He banged away at the guitar, bashed into the igloo walls, and nearly stepped on the face of a woman peeking in from the annex. Rudy grabbed the lantern to protect it from Petri's boots.

"Hey," Beef yelled.

But Petri tripped, reeled, and landed with his knee on the guitar. The instrument collapsed in a pop and twang of fractured wood and snapped strings.

"You asshole!" Beef yelled. "That was a *relic!*"

"It was a piece of shit," Petri said.

Beef was on his knees looking at the guitar. The Eskimo leaned in to see it better too.

"You son of a bitch," Beef growled. He reached down, picked up the guitar, and in one deft motion swung the dangling mess at Petri's face. Petri leaned back, tumbled over and scrambled through the doorway that led into the annex, Beef in pursuit. There were screams and curses from inside the other room, and Petri and Beef popped out, flying across the main igloo and out the main doorway.

Beef was yelling something about destroying the party of the asshole who destroyed his guitar, and soon Rudy, Lavone, and the others in the main igloo heard scratching and scrabbling on the outer walls. The noise went up the side of the structure, and in a moment they saw a boot come through the roof. Chunks, then whole blocks of packed snow began to fall. Beef was on the roof, grunting and kicking the igloo down. The men inside started to crowd for the exit when the roof collapsed. Rudy threw the lantern clear as Beef came screaming down.

They were all sitting outside in the night like bathers in a tub, up to their chests in the heaps of fallen snow. Beef was buried, kicking, and shouting for help. As long as he kept his feet moving, no one bothered to assist him.

The dogs were barking. Petri was out laughing in the darkness. The lantern had spilled fuel on the snow when Rudy had thrown it clear, and a slithering petroleum fire illuminated the scene. The

annex still stood, and from inside came the grunting sounds of
Eskimos and GIs in rut.

Lavone was sitting near Rudy. He cracked an amyl popper.

"Welcome," he said, "to the Stark Raving Dark."

"Happy Birthday," Irene whispered.

"What?"

He was inside her, standing in a mop closet off the Admin
corridor. A quickie. They'd run across each other outside the mess
hall. It had probably been more than two weeks since they'd been
alone. Rudy'd been living in suspended animation, always waiting
for the next chance to see Irene, worried about Guy X, brooding
about the colonel and General Vord. Rudy and Irene had run into
each other occasionally in the corridors or the mess hall, but ren-
dezvous were difficult, always too brief and always constrained by
the need for stealth. Q-Base had become maddeningly small and
exposed.

Except now, for a moment. The colonel was nowhere around;
no one was. A chance encounter. A wink and a nod. Inside the
closet, lights off, broom jammed up against the door. Maximum
security. Groping excitedly in the dark. Clothes unfastened and
pushed aside. Before they knew it, they were screwing standing
up. The closet smelled like a disinfected cave.

"I checked your 201," Irene said. "Today's the day."

"You're kidding."

"You forgot."

"I did."

" 'Happy Birthday toooooo yoooouuu.' "

"Shhhh."

"Yes . . ."

"Shhhh."

"And a pinch to grow an inch."

Rudy came. Irene laughed softly and sighed, and when they
finished, they sank down and sat on a couple of overturned buck-

ets. She leaned against him and stroked his thigh, tickled it with her fingernails. The darkness swirled rapturously around Rudy. He let his head thump back against the wall.

"If you could be anywhere now," Irene whispered, "where would it be?"

Rudy knew the occasion called for him to answer something like Paris or Tahiti, as long as it was with her—and that part was true, he didn't want to be without her—but the first place that came to mind was the Wing. He told her so.

Irene sat up. It was dark, so he couldn't see her expression. He felt her hand touch his brow. At first he thought she was mocking him, checking to see if he was feverish, out of his mind, but then she settled back down in his lap and hugged him; resigned or understanding or confused, in the dark he couldn't tell.

He started to explain to her about his feelings of peace in the Wing, and then how he'd become worried about the patients, about one in particular. "The one you carried the note for," he said.

"He was lying there unconscious," said Irene, "holding the paper. It had your name on it."

"You read it?"

"Mm."

"He tried to talk to you."

"I never heard anything."

"But he got your attention somehow."

"Well, I noticed the paper. I picked it up."

"What do you think will happen to them?"

Irene didn't answer. She leaned over and felt through her clothes for a cigarette. By the Zippo's light, Rudy could see her face. He wanted to kiss her.

"I don't know," she said. She clicked the lighter closed. Darkness again.

Rudy told her what had happened the last time he'd gone to the Wing, how he'd been shut out.

"Any reason why?"

"I thought maybe you'd know."

"I haven't heard a thing. You didn't ask?"

"I didn't want to draw attention."

"What kind of attention?"

"I don't know. Whoever did it, I don't know why they did it. But I feel like if I asked about it, I'd reveal something."

"Reveal what?"

"I don't know. I want to feign indifference."

"This doesn't make sense."

"Has the colonel said anything?"

"About?"

"Us."

"No."

The word was small and abrupt. It left everything still. The silence made it a challenge to say anything else. They didn't speak for several seconds, and Rudy reached over to touch her forearm. He thought of the way Guy X had held his sleeve.

"I want to get us away from this place," he said. "That's where I really want to be. Anywhere else and with you."

"Me too," she said, but there was something vague and distracted about the way she said it. And he could feel something stir in him. Rudy suspected she was still drawn to the colonel, and he knew that, against all reason and purpose, he felt more drawn to her because of that loyalty or love or whatever it was.

He could feel his pulse rise in his temples. He wished he could see her. "Irene, I need to know what's going on here. Do you still love him?"

"No," she whispered. "I guess not. . . . Oh, hell, I don't know. It's confusing."

"Well, what are you doing with him then?"

"What the hell am I *supposed* to do? It's not exactly easy come, easy go around here. I mean, we *are* in the army, in Greenland, for Chrissake."

"You're right." Rudy sighed. He felt a wave of despair as he listened to the alarm under her words. Then he began to feel restless, crowded. He leaned forward and raked his fingers through his hair. "We're going to get away from here," he said. "We'll start over. Just us."

Irene rocked against him. "I know," she said. "I love that about you. Your hope."

"You think it's crazy?"

Irene was silent.

"Don't spend your whole day on an answer," Rudy said.

"I don't think it's crazy. I only was thinking how it's something I never had before. I always made decisions just to improve whatever situation I was in. Lonely? Get married. Bad marriage? Get divorced. Army life a dead end? Go with Lane. I never had anyone look at me and see . . . well . . . hope."

Footsteps passed by outside the mop closet. A person whistled down the corridor.

"Some birthday," Irene whispered.

"It's okay," Rudy said. "If it weren't for you, I wouldn't have had one at all."

They sat quietly. When they finally got up to pull their clothes together, Rudy asked, "Do me a favor? Go to the Wing for me?"

In the dark, he could sense her surprise. "Tell the guy in there I'll see him, okay?"

"What if he's conked out as usual?"

"Tell him anyway. Whisper in his ear. Over and over. Tell him I'll see him again."

"How are you going to do that?"

"I don't know."

"This I think maybe *is* crazy," Irene said, "but okay."

She left first. Rudy stood in the closet alone for minutes or hours, remembering the feel of her. As he listened for the coast to clear, he quietly hummed "Happy Birthday" in the dark.

The colonel was looking gaunt. The man had lost weight. His eyes looked larger. When his hands weren't balled in fists, his fingers were drumming on any flat surface. He looked both hollowed out and agitated. At meals, the colonel's voice would boom across several tables in forced jocularity. The officers sitting nearby would hunch a little in their seats like anxious courtiers. Rudy managed to steal a glance or two at Irene when she was sitting over in the NCO section during these conversations. She was always staring hard at her meal, glowing a little from the sheen of sweat that had broken out on her face.

Then one day she took a seat right across from Rudy. She had come in with the colonel, but he had gone to eat in the officers-only section.

Rudy was with Beef and a guy from Meteorology who was talking about radioactive clouds and strontium-90 in the milk they were drinking.

"How're you doing, Sergeant?" Beef said when Irene sat down.

"Fine, gentlemen." She smiled at Rudy, who gave her a quick grin and fussed at his beans with his fork.

Beef didn't even notice; he went back to the guy from Meteorology. "This is *powdered* milk," he said. "It doesn't even come from cows. How's it going to be radioactive like you say?"

"I passed your message on to your friend," Irene said quietly to Rudy.

"Thanks. What did he say?"

"He was out of it. I whispered to him anyway. Over and over."

"Good."

"I felt crazy. Usually I go in there for some peace."

Beef and the guy from Meteorology checked for beavers around the mess hall while Rudy and Irene ate in silence. After a minute Rudy felt Irene's foot stroking the inside of his leg. Her foot was bare; she must have slipped it out of her shoe. He could feel her toes caressing the inside of his thigh.

He hoped no one could see them. Beef and the Meteorology guy were looking in the other direction. Irene seemed to be demurely eating her coleslaw. Her foot found his crotch and began rubbing. Rudy's breathing rose into the upper regions of his chest and stayed there.

At that moment the colonel, seated across the room, selected Captain Chaplain Brank for a colloquy. Captain Brank was sitting three tables away from the colonel.

"Padre," the colonel boomed, "you have a midnight mass planned for Christmas? The men might like that."

Irene stopped stroking for a moment at the sound of Woolwrap's voice, but then began again.

Captain Brank turned to face the colonel. His pale skin had instantly become mottled. His hand shot up to dab at his mouth with a napkin. "Well, sir, I hadn't—"

"Oh, I for*got*. You're not Catholic. Are you?"

"No, sir."

"So you wouldn't have a *mass,* would you? Well, how about a *service,* then, Chaplain? How about that? A midnight service?"

"Sounds good," the chaplain said. "Midnight."

"Let's spread the word on that," the colonel said. "Spruance?"

Rudy had a mouthful of baked beans. His jaw locked. Irene stopped rubbing, but she didn't remove her foot. Beef and the Meteorology guy leaned forward to look down at Rudy, who was trying desperately to make everything above the table look normal. He had an erection, but it was fading fast. Irene kept eating.

"Do you copy that, Spruance?" the colonel shouted.

Rudy couldn't speak. The beans seemed to have expanded in his mouth. He couldn't swallow.

"Where the hell are you, Spruance? I thought I saw you in here." The colonel was on his feet turning around looking for Rudy, who was turning red. He raised his hand. Irene still hadn't removed her foot. Except for her fork and jaw, she was motionless.

"Ah," said the colonel. "There you are. Did you hear me?"

"Mmf," said Rudy, nodding, "sir."

"Good. Midnight service. Christmas eve. Attendance optional."

The colonel started to sit down, but shot back up. "And be in my office at 1900 hours tonight, Spruance. Sharp. Attendance mandatory."

Rudy dipped his head once to nod, but then reflexively kept bobbing his chin up and down like a duck trying to get food down its craw. His erection had shrunk to nothing. He was struggling for breath.

The colonel looked at him a moment, then sat back down again. He called over his shoulder, "Somebody slap that poor bastard on the back."

The colonel poured brandy.

"No thank you, sir," Rudy said.

"No?" The colonel held the bottle over the snifter. "It's all right. You're off duty, correct?"

"Yes, sir."

"So?"

"Well, okay. Just a little."

"Just a little it is," Woolwrap said.

The liquid slithered around the broad curve of the glass. Through the slits of the venetian blinds from where he sat, Rudy could see Sno-Cats with huge rollers packing down the runway. It had been snowing again. The drifts were creeping up around the first-floor windows.

Woolwrap handed Rudy his snifter. Rudy had never drunk brandy this way, only sucked the peach-flavored stuff from pints. But from some movie he remembered how to swirl the liquor in the glass and take a couple of whiffs. Actually, he longed for a beer, a beer that he could belt back somewhere other than here. He wished he knew where Irene was. She hadn't been in the outer office when he came in at 1900 hours—sharp. Maybe it was just as well she wasn't there.

Rudy figured the worst Woolwrap was going to call him out for was cuckoldry. And that, Rudy thought, could result in anything from a court martial to hand-to-hand combat right there in the office.

"How's the paper?" the colonel asked.

"Fine," Rudy said.

"Christmas edition's about due out, right?"

Rudy had about enough material at the moment for half an issue. He swirled the drink. He calculated.

"It'll be hitting the streets, sir, in, let's see . . . four to six days," Rudy said.

The colonel furrowed his brow. "That's a little late for the Christmas issue, Corporal. Christmas is the day after tomorrow."

Rudy hadn't known the date. He took a sip of brandy. It tasted awful.

"Yes, well, this is a combination Christmas–New Year's edition. I didn't want to peg the paper too heavily on a religious holiday, you see, sir. Besides, New Year's, as traditionally celebrated, is a little more in keeping with the spirit of this place. At least I thought so. Remembering the Bash and all. Christmas, on the other hand, well, a Christmas issue would probably only serve to make the men homesick, long for family, hearth, home, et cetera, et cetera."

"Corporal," the colonel said, "it's almost sweet to hear you say all that." He slid off the desk and poured himself another drink. "However, it's a crock, isn't it?"

Rudy took another swig and dove in. "Yes, sir. It is a crock. I've fallen a little behind, sir. But we'll be out by Christmas, sir. I promise."

"By Christmas *Eve*, troop," the colonel said. "That's tomorrow."

"Yes, sir. Fine. Tomorrow."

"Even if you have to stay up all night."

"I probably will, sir."

"*Why* did you fall behind, Corporal Spruance?" The colonel was rubbing his eyes as if he were exhausted by what he was about to do. Rudy tensed in his chair and realized he might snap the stem off the brandy snifter if he didn't relax.

"I don't know why, sir," Rudy said.

"That's another crock. You do know."

The man was impossible to read. Rudy couldn't tell if the colonel was about to spring the trap or just settle in for a nice, simple little Q & A between an EM and his CO.

The colonel looked out at the runway. "Every soldier knows the nature of his own fuck-up, Corporal. And he isn't alone. That's one of the nice things about the army. It's contained and containing. You fuck up, guaranteed you'll find other soldiers who fucked up the same way. And by soldiers I might even mean officers. We're all of us soldiers, Spruance. Comrades-in-arms. All capable of fucking up. And the army has a high degree of tolerance, all things considered, for fuck-ups. The army's able to contain them. Use them. Protect them. I suppose it's a fair exchange for putting men in harm's way in battle. The army holds on to its own. Shepherds them through life. That's the reason there are lifers."

Rudy wasn't sure who the colonel was talking about here, himself or both of them.

"They're decommissioning this place, in case you didn't know," the colonel said. "Someday."

"I suspected as much. I'd hoped to have something about that in the paper. Remember, sir?"

"Fuck the paper." Woolwrap made a woozy swiping motion with his hand in front of his face. For the first time, Rudy thought perhaps the colonel had been drinking before their meeting. The colonel sunk into his desk chair and spun around to face the window. Waves of snow spewed off the giant rollers the Cats were pulling.

"Sir," Rudy said in the quiet that had followed. "I understand that the funeral detail I was on, that was for a comrade of yours."

"Who told you?" the colonel asked. He spun back in his chair and seemed to be slightly dazed.

"I pieced it together, sir."

"You did, did you? So . . . ?"

"So, well, I'm sorry."

The colonel's abstraction hardened into a suspicious look. "Thank you, Corporal."

The colonel leaned back in his chair.

"We're shipping people out, Spruance. Sending them home. Want to go?"

"Sir, is that an offer?"

"Not yet. Just a question. Do you want to go?"

Rudy sucked on the brandy glass; nothing was left but fumes. Racing through his mind were the calculations that a yes would mean leaving was more important than anything—especially more important than Irene, if that's what the colonel was driving at, and a no would mean he was either insane or had something going here he needed to stay for—not a good flank to expose.

"Yes, sir," he said. "I'd like to go."

"Well, you can't," Woolwrap said. "I won't let you."

"Okay, sir. Whatever you say."

The colonel eyed him severely. Maybe now he was going to explode.

But Woolwrap smiled. It was a broad, showy grin. "We *need* a man of your caliber here, Spruance. You come here, I give you a newspaper to put out, and you do it. That's not easy, I'm sure. But you are clearly a resourceful and adaptable soldier."

The colonel paused, obliging Rudy to say something. "Thank you, sir," he mumbled.

The colonel stood and seemed to be stepping into an invisible batter's box with an imaginary bat. He knocked mud off his cleats.

"After the Christmas issue, I'm shutting down the *Harpoon*, Spruance." He swung. Rudy blinked.

"Shutting it down, sir?"

"Yep. Shutting it down."

"Why, sir?"

The colonel posed, cocked for a pitch. "Whose stance is this,

Corporal? Meanest swing you'll ever see. Swings so hard, hits himself with the bat in the back. Has to wear padding over his kidneys. Who?"

"Jesus, sir. I don't know. Williams?"

"*Williams,*" the colonel snorted. "No. Jim Gentile." He swung and mimed hitting himself in the back.

"Sir, this closing of the *Harpoon,* does it have anything to do with the Wing being off-limits to me?"

"Nope. Now who?" the colonel said. He was hunched, head down, bat tucked close. "Whose stance?"

"Mantle?"

"Nope."

"Maris?"

"Nope."

"Berra? Skowron? Kluzewski?"

"Nope. Nope. *Kluzewski?* Nooooo. It's Musial."

"Oh. Sorry, sir. Musial."

The colonel swung. "Stan the Man," he said.

Rudy shifted in his chair.

"Let's see your stance, Corporal."

"Sir?"

"On your feet. Let's see you heft the lumber. Step into the box." The colonel pointed to a small oriental rug about the size of a batter's box over near the bookcases.

Rudy slowly rose out of the chair. He put the snifter on the desk and assumed a batter's stance on the carpet.

"Not bad," the colonel said. "Rock a little more weight onto your back leg. There you are. Hold that."

Rudy stood with his invisible bat aloft, facing the venetian blinds. The colonel was somewhere behind him.

"I didn't restrict you from the Wing, Spruance. Those orders came from above."

"Above, sir?"

"Hold the stance. Right elbow up. That's it."

Rudy's neck twinged. He wanted to drop his arms, at the very least take a swing.

"Yes. Above. You've seen the helicopter?"

"Yes, sir."

"Pentagon. Right from Washington, Corporal Spruance. That's what I mean by above. And he said, 'Keep that kid out.' Mine was not to reason why. So, you're out. Why do you think he wanted you out?"

"I don't know, sir. I didn't know that guy with the parka had done it. Until now."

" 'That guy' is a major general. And you knew that. Didn't you?"

"Yes, sir."

"And you've talked with him. Haven't you?"

"Yes, sir."

"So don't bullshit me."

"No, sir."

"I don't like things being done behind my back, Corporal. I have a sense about that. It makes me uneasy. In times like these, I know there are things being done behind my back. And now you know I know."

"Yes, sir." Rudy could feel sweat trickling down his spine and draining out his armpits.

"But you don't know *what* I know, do you?"

"No, sir."

"Let me tell you one thing I know, Spruance. I know how to follow tracks in the snow. Say from Delta Corridor to the stable up by the hangar. Does that give you an idea of the scope of my knowledge?"

"Yes, sir."

"Pretty damn vast, isn't it?"

"Vast enough, sir."

"Take a swing, Corporal. Go on."

Rudy did.

"Not bad. Resume the stance."

Rudy did. But with a small sigh of exasperation.

"Do you like baseball, Spruance?"

"No, sir."

"You know, neither do I. Not really. I suppose it's not martial enough. But, what the fuck? We don't like baseball, you and I. Couple of misfits, I suppose. Right?"

"I don't know, sir. I never thought of myself as a misfit."

"How about me then, Spruance?" The colonel was moving around behind him. Rudy tried to see his reflection in the window between the blind slats, but there wasn't enough light in the room. Rudy held his stance; he had the uncomfortable feeling he was being stalked.

"Couple of misfits," the colonel muttered. "What else do we have in common, Spruance?"

"I don't know, sir."

"Think. There must be something we both like to do."

"I really don't—"

"Think!"

Rudy worked his jaw. "Nothing, sir. We have nothing in common."

"Take a swing."

Rudy did, but as he brought his arms around, his neck snapped and the room careened. He was looking at the floor coming toward him. The ceiling dropped away. His feet were flying out behind him. He crashed on the hard linoleum. There was no carpet underneath him.

The rug was in a pile at the colonel's feet, and the colonel was crouched on the floor, his hands still holding the edge he had pulled. Rudy's wrists and hip stung from his fall.

"We have a metaphor here, don't we, Corporal?"

"What the hell do you mean, sir?" Rudy was breathing heavily from the shock. He was still on the floor, but up on his arms, turned, facing the colonel.

"Everybody's getting the rug pulled out from under them."

The colonel sat back on the floor, knees pulled up, hands clasped. A campfire talk.

"You see, I'm fucked, Corporal Spruance. You might as well hear it from the horse's mouth. I had intended to work out my time here, close the place on my own, or pass it to a worthy successor before I retired and headed out to pasture. I could have kept pulling strings. Worked it all out. Christ, I could have put *you* in charge. A couple of field promotions, a little mumbo-jumbo with the morning reports, some creative paperwork and— bingo!—you're the Qangattarsa CO. I'm good enough to do it, believe me. The army held onto me after that business in Korea because they said I was a bureaucratic genius. And who am I to dispute the United States Army?"

The colonel rocked a little on his butt. He stared up at the lamp on his desk. Rudy shifted on the floor.

"But they caught me by surprise. They want radar. Distant Early Warning. They don't want this. And what can I say? Look at what I've requisitioned. Look at what I built here. Do you think it was all through normal channels? They could make my Officer Efficiency Report read like a felony indictment if they wanted. That's why I'm going quietly. And so far, so good."

"Is that why you're shutting down the paper?"

"More or less."

"So what will I do here with the paper shut?"

"Duties will come your way, Corporal. The army is like that. There's always plenty to do. Holes to dig. Holes to fill."

"But I'm not leaving Greenland?"

"No, you're not. Your work is here. With us. Now, take your base."

"Hunh?"

"Go. Fall out. Dismissed. Carry on. Leave me alone. I brushed you back, fucker. Take your base."

TWENTY-SIX

He got the Christmas issue out on time. He filled it with reminiscences by GIs of their most memorable yule: stories of wards at Walter Reed decorated with wreaths made of surgical tubing, hemostats and wound dressings, tales of heartwarming reunions with girlfriends and wives, of last-minute leaves to see dying relatives who miraculously recovered, accounts of sugar plums and sleigh rides and chaste encounters with angelic USO girls in lonely cities on Christmas eve.

It was crazy. People practically forced their stories on him when they found out what he was after. They gathered around him in the mess hall, dropped by his room, slipped reminiscences under his door. Rudy had no idea if the stories were true, but the intensity, the near desperation with which the troops told him their Dickensian tales left him with no choice but to publish every story. It was as if the whole base was suffering from some kind of undiagnosed yule hysteria. Rudy had to pull himself away from the force of it all to try to write an editorial about the demise of the *Harpoon*.

He failed. He sat for hours at the typewriter, but he'd run dry. At last he said screw it and filled the editorial space with a cartoon by Lavone depicting the Stark Raving Dark as a cross between a giant hyena and a polar bear squatting down on the fjord and all the buildings of Q-Base. *Winter Settles In,* the cutline read. It seemed more suitable.

Something had definitely changed. A beast *was* squatting on Qangattarsa. The colonel, who had been such a force when Rudy first arrived, now hardly ever appeared, even at meals. Rudy rarely saw Irene, and when he did, she looked tense and drawn.

Fights—random, sporadic, and thuggish—were constantly erupting in the mess hall. No one involved could ever remember what had caused the outbreak. People just felt like hitting one another. Usually, nobody tried stopping them. Troops would move the tables back or push the combatants out the door into the snow, where they'd flail at each other in the drifts until exhaustion or frostbite prevailed.

Then there were the crying jags. Several times in the mess hall Rudy saw guys inexplicably burst into tears, just bawl their heads off, sitting at the table, their utensils still clutched in their fists. The weeping soldier was usually left alone. The seats next to him emptied and stayed vacant, as if the weeper were a reeking derelict in a subway car.

"It's the Dark," was always the diagnosis.

Christmas Day, Rudy's new duties began. Lavone came down to his room with the KP roster.

"They put you on for three straight," he told Rudy. "I don't get it. I usually figure out the roster myself, but this came over from Headquarters."

He showed Rudy a buck slip with the colonel's initials ordering Corporal Spruance to be put on KP whenever possible to help fill out the "personnel shortage due to the recent troop movements and manpower reductions. The rest of the time he will be assigned to area policing and sanitation duties."

"Then there's this," Lavone said.

NO ONE THINKS OF GREENLAND

It was another buck slip, same initials. Rudy was to move out
of his room by 2000 hours that night. No more single occupancy
quarters.

"I got you in with Beef and another guy in the last room down
in the EMQ corridor. Petri's old rack. It's a pretty big place and
okay guys. It won't be bad," Lavone said.

Lavone helped Rudy pack up his gear and move it down to the
Enlisted Men's Quarters. Beef was there with his roommate, a
black orderly named Barton from Wilmington whom everyone
called Philly.

Rudy greeted them and threw his duffel down by the open
locker in the far corner of the room. He unrolled the folded mattress on the empty bunk.

"You all set?" Lavone asked Rudy.

Rudy nodded.

"Want your typewriter down here?"

"Don't think I'll be needing it," Rudy said.

"Heard they moved you out 'cause they might be closing that
sector down," Beef said. He was tucking in his bunk, tightening
the hospital corners.

"Sounds like as good a reason as any," Rudy said.

"They close that sector down, ol' Corporal Lavone's shit'll be
in the wind," Beef said. "What's going to happen to your beatnik
pad there, hepcat?"

"I'll get you to build me an igloo, asshole," Lavone said.

"Your newspaper gonna publish any more of Beef's literature?"
Philly asked from over on his bunk. He was smoking, and his
voice rumbled out into the room.

"No," Rudy said. "They shut us down."

"Shut it down?" Beef said. "Why?"

"No reason. Colonel said he doesn't want it anymore."

"Oh, man," Beef groaned. "And just when my writing was
getting good. Wasn't I getting good?"

"Elvis would have been proud," Lavone said.

Philly was laughing. "Bullshit. Woolwrap probably looked at

that crap you was feeding Rudy's paper and said, 'Let the patient die.' "

"Not true. I was getting good," Beef said. He was now lining his boots up on a seam in the linoleum under his bunk. He stepped back to look at his work. The smoke from Philly's cigarette hung in the air.

"Looks fucking perfect, Beef," Philly said. "Now get out of here so I can get some rest. You mind if I sleep, Spruance?"

Rudy said he didn't; he had to get up early for KP. Lavone and Beef headed for the door. Beef said he wanted to make a little purchase down at Lavone's. Something to get him through all-night boiler-room duty. He left saying he was sorry about the paper. "The colonel's fucked up," he told Rudy. "I'm a lifer. I know."

Rudy made his bed and threw his duffel into his locker. He'd unpack some other time. He headed for the latrine. When he got back, Philly was in bed with the lights out. He was still awake because a cigarette coal bobbed in the dark. Rudy climbed into bed.

He lay on his side, facing the wall. The building hummed and settled around them, but this was a different corridor with different noises. The generator sounded strange and dislocated; the pipes clanked differently. There were voices in the hall, beyond the wall. Rudy felt a million miles away from Irene. He wished he could sleep, but it would come hard now. A wave of queasiness slid over him, then an ache, then just a weighty emptiness. He felt better if he curled into a fetal position. Lavone's cartoon came to mind: the hyena–polar bear squatting on him and everything else. *Twat of winter night beast / Covers us all* . . . "Arctic Sutra, Canto Six."

"I remember you from the first day," Philly said in the darkness. His voice rolled in from across the room.

Rudy turned over.

The ember bobbed down, glowed, bobbed away. Philly exhaled.

"The mosquitoes," Philly said. "I was on duty."

"You took care of me?" Rudy asked.

"Part of the team," Philly said.

Rudy could hear the springs squeak, Philly raising up on one arm.

"Hey, is it true you been balling the colonel's chick?"

"Where'd you get that idea?"

"Man, you think things are *private* around here? If they want, people around here can tell how many sheets of toilet paper you use."

Rudy lay on his back. "If everybody knows everything," he said, "why do you have to ask?"

"I just wanted to hear it from the prizewinner himself. That's all."

"Let's just say I don't know what you're talking about."

Philly laughed a low, sighing laugh. "You was one bit-up motherfucker, man," he said. "I was sorry for you. I work on the Wing. I seen hurt-up bodies. But you get used to that. The dead-end hurt don't bother you so much after a while. Funny how all of a sudden seeing a guy who's gonna get better makes you feel sorry. You explain that?"

Rudy thought for few moments. "No," he said.

They lay in silence again for a while.

"Philly?"

"Yeah."

"You work in the Wing?"

"I do."

"Can you let me in there?"

"I thought you been. I thought I seen you in there."

"I'm off the list. No clearance."

"They do that to you too?"

"Yeah. Listen, how about letting me in? Some time when you're on alone. You ever on alone?"

"Yeah. Lot's now. They're cutting back. Why do you want to go in there?"

"Talk to a guy."

"*Talk* to a guy? Which one?"

"He's down the north side. 'Soldier—Unknown Name.' "

"He *talks?* I seen him shake. I seen him roll his eye. I heard he used to read some. What's he say?"

"He says he wants company."

"Oh, man."

"So, how about it?"

"Well, it's a risk. What's in it for me? What you got for me?"

"Forget it, man," Rudy rolled over.

"No. Hey," Philly said. "I'm just asking."

"I got nothing," Rudy said. "I just wanted a favor. For a wounded soldier. Not for me. Why don't you go ask *him* what he's got for you?"

"Okay, okay," Philly said. "You're right."

"So?"

Philly took a last drag on his cigarette. "So, I'll get you in."

Three days of KP and no split shifts like the cooks, just pure straight time: 0430 to 2100 hours. The cooks knew Rudy was being fucked with and gave him easy jobs. He even managed to climb onto one of the storeroom shelves between a couple of meals and, using a sack of rice for a pillow, grab a little sleep.

He saw Irene when he was server on the chow line. She asked how he was doing.

"I'm fine," he said, picking with tongs at the sauerkraut piled on pork chops. "Nah," he said. "I'm not really."

"I know," she said. "Me too."

He was serving her the kraut strand by strand. He hadn't seen her for days. The beast of winter was relenting just a little with her this close. But a couple of PFCs were slapping trays down on the rails at the start of the line.

"I love you," she mouthed to Rudy as she moved away toward a table of nurses. Watching her body turn and stride, seeing her ass move under the skirt as she weaved through the thicket of chairs, he felt pieces of his insides break away and crash through the floor on their way to the center of the earth.

A metallic banging brought him back. The two PFCs were waiting at Rudy's station. They were smacking their trays on the rails, trying to get his attention. "Hey. Hey! What's under this sauerkraut?"

Rudy turned and looked at them hazily. "Swine," he said.

New Year's Eve. Rudy was to mop, wax, and buff corridors at the discretion of the CQ.

No one seemed to be making any special effort to mark the end of the decade or even the end of the year. There was no special New Year's bash, although there was a good deal of drunken barking in the halls. Other than a few shouts of "Happy Fucking New Year," there was nothing organized to ring out the old, ring in the new. The polar beast was squatting squarely.

The officers had taken over the mess hall. The EM and NCOs were roistering in the Quonsets. Rudy rolled the bucket and mops down toward a reported puking incident near a trash receptacle in the Admin hall. He got the vomit cleaned up and was trudging past the access corridor to the Wing when he looked down the hall and saw Philly going in through the double doors.

Rudy parked the bucket and went down the hall and into the vestibule. He buzzed the intercom.

"—ppy New Year," the voice crackled.

"Philly," Rudy said. "Spruance."

"Hey."

"You alone in there?"

"Well, 'cept for a few bits and pieces of humanity lyin' around to keep me company, yeah, I'm alone."

"Let me in?"

There was a pause, then the lock buzzed, and Rudy pushed through the inner entrance. At first the ward looked and smelled as ever, but then Rudy noticed more than the usual number of

Tiffany lamps were off. The darkened, back end of the Wing had grown larger and closer to the doors. The kiosk floated in the half-light. Philly was grinning, leaning out the door, looking like a turnpike toll collector.

As Rudy walked down the aisle, the rustle and sputter of the patients was sporadic and dispersed. Not every bed was occupied. Some of the alcoves had beds that were newly stripped; IV bottles and waste bags were empty, their racks left bunched together like bright metal corn sheaves.

"The population looks down," Rudy said.

"We shipped out a few since Christmas. You musta been on KP," Philly said. "Come on in."

The kiosk smelled sweetly of pot.

"My New Year's medication," Philly said. "I'd offer you some but all I had was a roach I found in my pocket. A rocket in my pocket." He giggled some. "Didn't expect company."

"It's okay," Rudy said.

Philly flicked a switch, and a ventilator fan went on.

"You want to see your patient?" he asked.

"Yeah," Rudy said. "Is he still here?"

"He's probably been moved around. Everybody's been moved around," Philly said. There were hooks below the windows where charts hung; every third or fourth hook was empty. "But he's still here, though." He pointed to a clipboard with the ID, "Soldier— Unknown Name."

"Where they been shipping the guys out to?" Rudy asked.

"Don't know," Philly said. "Happened after I got off duty the other night. Duffy, guy on the late shift, said they loaded them out through the back door into a couple of Sno-Cats. It was Air Force guys on the detail. Never seen them before. Off they went into the wild blue yonder." He made the Qangattarsa let-us-fly-up sign with his hands.

"Was the colonel here?" Rudy asked.

"I guess so."

"And a guy with a crew cut, gray hair?"

"I don't know."

"Wears a ski parka?"

"Hey, man, I wasn't on duty. I don't know." Philly began to giggle.

"What did they tell the nurses and orderlies about all this?"

"Jesus, you're still talking like a newspaperman. Relax. It's a good sign we'll all get out of here soon."

"I'm just curious." Rudy realized he was getting worked up. "What'd they tell you?"

Philly sighed. "They called it troop movement, and, as usual with troop movements, everybody keeps their eyes, ears, and mouths secure. So I don't know. The guys are gone."

"The guys are gone," Guy X whispered.

"I heard," Rudy said. He was seated next to Guy X, his face close to the pillow.

"They're fucking with us, Mr. Editor. They're shutting us down."

"They told me this place is off limits to me. They've shit-canned the paper," Rudy said.

Guy X twitched. The reflector was cocked down over part of his face. One eye blinked: the other was a concave, glaring mirror.

"So you're not Mr. Editor anymore?" Guy X asked. He sounded plaintive, but he might have been mocking.

"No more," Rudy said.

"They're fucking with you too," Guy X croaked.

Rudy sat up for a minute and looked around at the Wing. Guy X was on the edge of the darkened section of the ward. Empty beds and alcoves stretched into the shadows beyond the dark wood partition on the far side of Guy X's bed. Rudy turned back to the kiosk to see Philly with his head down, asleep, on the desk. Ringing in the New Year. It was almost impossible to hear the patients' breathing anymore.

Guy X turned his head away on the pillow. "How long were you gone from here?" Guy X asked.

"A few days," Rudy said.

Guy X shook his head. "Wrong. Thirty-seven and a half," he said. "Exactly. I counted."

"You can keep track?"

Guy X nodded. "They're fucking with us now. I want to keep track of everything. Tell me today's date."

"You sure?"

"Yes."

"New Year's Eve," Rudy said.

"Of what?"

"Nineteen sixty."

Guy X winced, but only slightly; it could have been one of the muscle spasms that continually passed across his face and made his expression so difficult to read. "Auld goddamn lang syne," he said. "Date the letter then."

"What letter?"

Guy X pointed at some paper and a pencil on his night table. "I want you to take a letter for me," he whispered. "A letter. Out of here. For me. You can mail it."

He hooked Rudy's sleeve and directed his arm toward the table with the papers.

Rudy slowly picked them up.

"I want you to say that you are writing for a friend," Guy X said. "This friend wants the person who's receiving this letter to know that the friend has never forgotten her."

And Rudy immediately recollected Guy X mentioning having letters in his pocket in battle back in Korea. Letters from a lover. They were probably there, Rudy thought, in his pocket, the day the F-80 came in too low.

Rudy looked at Guy X but didn't write anything yet. Guy X didn't seem to notice.

"Now this next part is for verification," Guy X said. "It's so she'll know this is for real."

He said the name of a motel, a song title, and the name of a park.

Guy X lay quietly for a while, then turned to Rudy. "Done?"

Rudy took Guy X's copy of Whitman and used it for a writing surface. Slowly he wrote the message.

"Done," he said.

"Mail it."

"Where to?"

Guy X took a scrap of paper from the nightstand and wrote an address, a town in Virginia.

"Put your return address on the envelope," Guy X said. "If she wants to find out more, she can contact you."

"And if she does, what do I tell her?"

"Whatever you want. You don't know my name. You won't know where I am. I won't know where you are. I'll never see her, and she'll never see me, but tell her I'll never forget her."

Guy X picked at his bedclothes, adjusted the head reflector. He covered his face with his hand and stayed that way.

"You want me to leave?" Rudy asked.

"No," Guy X said from behind his hand. His already dry voice cracked even more. He pursed his lips over his three teeth.

"Is this to your wife?" Rudy whispered.

Guy X pulled his hand away from his face, and a faint spasm of a smile twitched over Guy X's features. "No," he said.

"A relative?" Rudy asked.

Guy X actually chuckled. "We had relations," he said. "She was the wife of a fellow officer. She may still be. She and I . . ." Guy X waved his hand. "I just want to contact her. That's all," he whispered.

"Sure," Rudy said. He sat back in his chair. He looked at Guy X, who had composed himself again and was staring off toward where the wall met the ceiling, the way Rudy remembered his own father doing.

"Look," Rudy said. Guy X didn't move, but Rudy could tell

he was listening. "Since this may come back on me, I guess it's okay for me to ask if you really think this is a good idea."

"Of course I do."

"This place here," Rudy said, "you guys in it, you're listed as MIA in Korea. That's the official word. Do you know that?"

"It doesn't surprise me."

"She probably figures you've been lost for years, maybe dead."

"So? That's what I'm writing for. To let her know."

"Yeah, but," Rudy shifted uneasily on the chair, "*what* are you letting her know? She thinks you're gone. Now she's going to think you're back. I mean, who knows what she's going to think? You're just going to drop this on her and then walk away?"

"I'm not *walking* anywhere," Guy X spat.

"I'm sorry," Rudy said. "I didn't mean that. But do you know what I'm getting at?"

Rudy was leaning forward in his chair, elbows on knees. Guy X flopped back down on his bed and grabbed Rudy's hand. He was out of breath, his small chest heaving.

"I got through to you, Mr. Editor. The only one. The others, the red-haired one, all of them, I'd be checked out in a fit or I'd call and they couldn't hear. But I got through to you. So you'll help me. I know you will. You're the only one."

Guy X shifted on the bed, half rolled over to face Rudy. He gripped tighter and pulled Rudy closer. "If the letter upsets her, well, maybe I need to upset somebody."

Guy X, still holding Rudy, rolled back to face the ceiling. He rocked slightly. Rudy felt the tugging. It was like holding the hand of a man who was floating on his back in a vast sea.

"I was thinking the other day, the other year, I don't know," Guy X said, his voice sounding hollow, echoing a little off the alcove around him. "I was thinking that maybe I'm like a ghost already. Maybe ghosts need to upset people. It's either that or disappear."

His hand was shaking now in Rudy's, as if a low-voltage cur-

rent was humming up from the sea through the floating body of
Guy X and into Rudy's arm.

"You're not a ghost," Rudy said. "I'll send the letter."

Guy X smiled and nodded but wouldn't let go. He held Rudy's
hand until Rudy felt the steady hum become a twitching. The
sea had drained away, and Guy X had settled back to his mattress.
He was sliding into one of his fits. Rudy didn't call to him or try
to stop it.

TWENTY-SEVEN

An armed guard had come for him. Philly and Lavone, no less, embarrassed as hell, but carrying M-1s all the same. "They ordered us to," Lavone had mumbled.

"Who's they?" Rudy asked as they'd marched him out of the barracks sector and put him back in his old room in Storage Charlie, now a nearly barren cell with just a cot, his emptied desk, and the old typewriter. He was under house arrest.

"Well, the buck slip was from the colonel," Lavone said, producing the piece of paper. "But it looks like she typed it up." He pointed to the initials down in the lower left corner: *LGW:it.*

Rudy scanned the buck slip. It was an order that he be apprehended by a prisoner detail obtaining M-1 rifles from the armory, confined to quarters, and placed under watch "for violations of the Base Security Operative (BSO:12 [a-e], specifically ¶e.7), detailing the dissemination, distribution, transmission, transporting, issuance or exporting of any unauthorized communications off post."

Guy X's letter. Rudy had dropped it in the wooden mailbox

outside the mess hall, and they'd caught it. He should have been smart enough to realize they must read everything that goes in or out of Qangattarsa. He'd been too naive because he'd never written anyone. He hadn't sent or received a letter since he'd arrived. His whole life had been right there in Greenland.

And now it was right back in his old room. He was allowed out for meals, escorted to the mess hall for chow, then ushered back. A guard sat down at the hall junction where Storage Charlie joined the Admin sector.

Planes were coming and going more frequently. Rudy sat at the window, watching. The aircraft loomed out of the arctic night, their landing lights looking like luminous feelers, slanting down, searching for the runway. Sometimes Rudy could make out loading crews and Sno-Cats shuttling between the base and the landing strip.

He began to feel as if the colonel had done him a favor by shutting him away. When he got out for chow, he could see the usual fights had gotten much worse. The top brass were taking meals in their quarters to isolate themselves. Crying jags were now followed by rages. At lunch once, Rudy watched as a weeping PFC on KP lunged across the steam table, brandishing a serrated carving knife, when a sergeant in the chow line sneezed. Another time, sitting alone as ordered, Rudy overheard a conversation about an officer who'd tried to hang himself from a showerhead in the main latrine; he'd failed, and a day later marched stark naked toward the fjord. That attempt succeeded: he'd died curled in a ball out near the flagpole, and the search party rolled him back to the post as if they were making a snowman.

At every meal there were fewer soldiers, and each time he left his room, Rudy noticed there was less equipment around the post too. But there was no sense to the demobbing, no standing down, no orderly departures, no organization. One day, half the chairs from the mess hall were shipped out, making fighting all the more common as troops battled for seats. A few days later, all the utensils had departed, and Rudy arrived for breakfast to see soldiers eating scrambled eggs with their hands. The next day they were eating with plastic picnic utensils.

Sometimes Rudy would see Lavone or Beef or Philly at a meal, and they'd signal each other with winks or a thumbs-up. The signals became signs that they were holding on, that they were okay. Everything and everyone else seemed unhinged.

He never saw the colonel, and he saw Irene only once, finally, at a supper. It appeared most of the women on the post had been shipped out. Irene may have been the last one remaining. She was on her way out of the mess hall as Rudy was entering. She seemed pale, drawn. Without thinking or checking around, Rudy called out her name. She turned. She looked startled and confused, as if she were surprised to see him and he didn't belong there. Then she was gone.

As Rudy stood back in Storage Charlie worrying about Irene, a C-47 slid down the runway and roared overhead. It banked and headed out the fjord and away. Let us fly up, Rudy thought. He had to get on one of those planes.

A howl came from far off down the hall. A human baying. The lights flickered once.

"Would you like to pray?"

Rudy jerked around. Chaplain Captain Brank stood in the room, smiling. He'd snuck in. Rudy eyed him, tense. The chaplain raised his hands in an I-come-in-peace gesture. "Pray? You? Me?" he asked.

Rudy relaxed a little. "No thanks," he said.

The chaplain shrugged. "Just thought I'd ask. Just thought I *had* to ask." Captain Brank stepped farther into the room. "A pastoral call. Thought I'd visit the prisoner. I'm awfully sorry they've got you shut away like this."

"It's not so bad," Rudy said. "Considering."

The oooooooing sound continued. Both Rudy and the chaplain listened to it fade.

"It's a difficult time," Captain Brank said. "I've never had a posting like this. The darkness, the cold. I rather like it, mind

you. But the men . . . I have to do what I can. I've offered extra
worship services. No takers. Open-door policy for pastoral coun-
seling. No one crosses the threshold. I table-hop in the mess hall.
Men turn away, burrow into their chicken á la king. So I'm trying
the missionary approach. Visiting an inmate in his cell."

"Thanks," Rudy said. He went over and sat on his bed.

"Monks have cells too," the chaplain said. "Maybe you can use
this time for contemplation."

"Believe me, I have," Rudy said.

"Yes. Well. Good. And how's it going?"

"I want to get the hell out of here."

The chaplain nodded, shrugged apologetically. "Feel like crying?" he asked.

"Not yet," Rudy said.

"Good. Weird feeling. It's crazy-making, let me tell you. It hit
me." The chaplain sat on Rudy's desk, leaned his elbow on the
typewriter. "I'd just finally made up my mind to go Catholic. I'd
been rereading the Old Testament, admiring what a kick-ass book
it is, when . . . well, I burst into tears. Out of the blue. Just like
everybody else around here. An upwelling of grief. Woe. Lam-
entation. Bawling like a baby. Then . . . when it was over, the
strange thing was, I didn't feel relief. You don't feel drained.
Damned thing is your blood sizzles. You want to take it out on
someone else. It reminds me of Korea. All that fighting and where
did it get us? It left us feeling like fighting and killing some
more. Metaphorically, I think. Maybe not. Maybe really. Well,
now we have the Bomb . . . *the* Bomb . . . Oh, yes . . ."

The chaplain was grinding his fist into his palm, staring wide-
eyed at the floor. He looked up.

"Ah!" He laughed. "At ease, soldier. I'm okay. Yes. I found the
cure for these heebie-jeebies. Mortification of the flesh. Easy as
pie. I lay down naked, unclothed, on my bed with the window
open. That took the fight right out of me pretty darned quick,
let me tell you. Luckily, I had the example of the Irish saints to
turn to when the killing urge hit."

"Killing urge, sir?"

"It has occurred to me, Rudy Spruance. It has occurred. It's passed now, though."

"Good."

The chaplain hopped off the desk.

"You know, son, I miss the reportage we did together. I truly lost something when they shut the paper down. You did too, I suppose." He looked around the room. "Can I get you anything?"

"Na." Rudy said. He leaned forward with his elbows on his knees, his hands clasped. "Well," he said, "maybe one thing."

"Name it."

"A visitor."

"Ah . . . ?"

"Sergeant Teal."

"Oh."

"Just to talk."

"Indeed."

"Sir, please."

The chaplain let out a soft whistle. "I'm moving in an opposite direction myself. Toward some kind of asceticism. Something pure, I hope. Celibacy for sure. Burning out lust. Or freezing it out, as the case may be. Toward a state of unencumbrance, you know? You seem encumbered, son. Are you?"

"I love her, sir."

The chaplain nodded. "It's written all over you."

"She needs me."

"It's written all over her."

"So . . . ?"

"So it is writ. I'll see what I can do."

The chaplain left, but no one came. No Irene. No escort for a meal. No one. Just the occasional sounds of a plane, shouts, howls, dogs barking now, pipes banging as if tenants were complaining about the noise downstairs, and always the generator grind. Again the lights flickered. Then they went out. There was total darkness for five, maybe fifteen, maybe thirty minutes.

Rudy hollered. No one answered. He banged his head to make sure he was awake. He thought he heard a scream from outside. Not human. Animal maybe.

The lights came back on and with them the normal noises: generator, howls, pipes. How long had it been dark? *Had* it been dark?

Screw it, Rudy decided, time for something to eat. Or, better yet, find Lavone and see how people were getting out of this place.

He went down to the end of the hall where his sentry should have been posted. The doors were unlocked. He opened them and looked into the hall.

No one was sitting on the folding chair. Around the corner, Rudy could hear crying. A man's gut-wrenching sobs. It was, Rudy imagined, how battlefield grief must sound. Punches of woe followed by long, spiraling wails.

He came around the corner and saw a man weeping on a pile of clean laundry. The soldier was sprawled across a mountain of folded white sheets and towels that blockaded the corridor. He lay facedown, spread-eagled, his sobs pounding into the linen.

Rudy approached quietly and, hugging the wall, tried to step over the man and the linen, but his foot brushed the soldier's ankle and the man jerked up. It was Staff Sergeant R. G. Genteen.

Rudy was pinned to the wall, straddling the blockade of sheets. "Sorry," he said.

Genteen coughed and sputtered but quickly wiped the tears and snot away on his sleeve. "Fuck," he said.

"Sorry," Rudy repeated.

"Son of a bitch," Genteen said.

"Look—"

"What'd you see?"

"—sorry."

Genteen jumped up and stood atop the pile of sheets. He started bellowing: "This man fucked with my bayonet, your honor! May it please the court, he fucked with my wheelbarrow!"

"Listen—"

Suddenly Genteen threw a head fake, and Rudy fell for it. Rudy started running but back in the direction of Storage Charlie. He had no choice but to race back to his room and lock the door.

He made it inside and darted around like a damn chipmunk. He cursed himself for losing his head, then stopped cold when he heard the footsteps.

Outside there was the shuffling of boots at a sauntering gait. There was some sniffling, a sigh, a sliding click of well-tooled metal, and a loud, concussive explosion.

The blast made Rudy jump up on the bed. The doorknob bounced across the linoleum.

A moment later the door flew in with a kick of Genteen's boot, and the sergeant strolled into the room with a .45 service automatic swinging in his hand.

He looked up at Rudy on the bed and giggled. "Eeek! You look like you just seen a mouse."

Rudy shifted his feet, and the bedsprings creaked. Genteen shook his head in disgust.

"You know what I hate about this place, Corporal? Hm? *Hmm?*"

"No." Rudy got the word out, and it didn't sound too squeaky, though his throat felt as brittle as cheap plastic.

"Fucking crying jags," Genteen said. "No one ever tells you about that shit. They leave you to discover *that* shit for yourself. You saw me, didn't you? *Didn't* you?"

"Look, I— "

Genteen moved laterally across the room, his arms dangling, gorillalike.

"Leaves you feeling kind of, I dunno, pissed off, I'd say. Agitated, I'd say. Like right now I want to twitch right out of my skin. Got one of my boys in pharmacy to requisition me some Miltowns, but they ain't doing shit, as you just witnessed. I'm way out here. Wanna dial down from where I am. But how to do

it? How? How? How? You saw me bawling back there. I hate
that. That was private. And you saw it."

"Look, Genteen—"

The sergeant kicked the frame of Rudy's bed, hard. The impact
shuddered right up Rudy's spine and made him wince. A pre-
dictable curve of escalation was out the window.

"How about making an escape?" Genteen said. "Then I could
be a hero and save Q-Base all by myself."

"Come on, Genteen."

"What? *What?*" Genteen said. He bent forward like a wrestler
looking for the takedown. He circled the bed one way, then the
other. Then he stood up as if he'd been radioed a command via
some cranial receiver. His eyes glazed over, and wearily he said,
"Ho-hum. What the fuck?" He raised the pistol straight-armed
and pointed it at Rudy.

Panic was shooting up from Rudy's gut on greased rails. He
was about to scream when the pulse pounding in his ears clearly
became footsteps, and they stopped in the door. Rudy did scream,
just a loud animal noise, out of shock over whom he saw. Genteen
spun toward the door, frightened, and he fired.

The shot hurled Irene twisting back and spun her into the
doorjamb. Her eyes and mouth were huge, open, startled. A
sledgehammer blow would have had the same effect. Her legs gave
out immediately, and she slid down toward the floor.

Rudy flew off the bed behind Genteen, who turned the wrong
way at the sound. He looked back to see where Rudy had been.
Rudy was now at the desk. Irene cried out, a half groan, and
Genteen was spinning the other way, toward her. Rudy grabbed
the army-issue Royal manual typewriter, raised it above his right
shoulder, and brought it down on the back of Genteen's head.
The blow drove the sergeant into the linoleum floor. The gun
went off and left a large crater blasted in Rudy's mattress.

Blood began to seep from the back of Genteen's head. The
barbed odor of gunpowder was in Rudy's nose. Its sharpness startled him, almost as if he were being awakened from a sleepwalk.

Irene called his name. She was facing him with her unwounded side. Her head was trembling; her right hand was hovering in the air as if she wanted to feel for the damage but didn't dare.

"Irene," he said, rushing to her. She looked at him through a fog almost as if she didn't recognize him.

He crawled around into the doorway so he could see her left side. The sleeve of her uniform was torn, and the cloth was glistening and black with blood.

"Oh, Jesus," he sighed.

"It doesn't feel bad," Irene said quietly.

He touched her cheek. "Good," he said. "That's good."

It looked like it was a shoulder wound, perhaps the upper arm.

"There, there . . ." he whispered. Then he leaned out into the hall. Not knowing what else to say, he yelled, *"Medic!"*

No one answered. The gunshot hadn't aroused anyone. Genteen groaned from the center of the room. Rudy bent down and picked Irene up. She held him around the neck with her good arm. He ran with her down to the end of Storage Charlie and kicked through the double doors.

The corridors were quiet. He kicked his way through the linen pile and dodged around bedframes and supply crates. There were open boxes of military files stacked in alcoves. Supply closets were unlocked and pilfered. The intercom was on, and the hall speakers emitted a soft, fuzzy hiss.

"Medic!" Rudy yelled as he went, but still got no response. And in a goddamn hospital, he thought.

There was no sign of life until they got close to the mess hall, where Rudy heard whoops and hollers. Irene was looking pale, her eyes half closed. *Treat for shock,* Rudy thought. But he wasn't sure what that meant he should do. The phrase kept bouncing in his head as he ran. *Treat for shock. Treat for shock.*

He ran up to the mess hall entrance and heard laughter from inside. A sign on the door said OFFICERS ONLY. He kicked it open.

A crowd of faces swiveled toward him from the darkened room. There was a projector rattling near the door, and on the screen across the room, a woman dressed in a dirndl sucked the dick of a German shepherd while a nude man in a derby held up her skirt and lashed her ass with a cat-o-nine tails as she pumped his cock with her fist.

Someone up front made barking noises. Irene groaned softly in Rudy's arms.

"Medic!" he yelled into the startled faces.

People moved toward him in the darkness and flickering light.

"Treat for shock!" Rudy yelled as they took Irene from his outstretched arms.

TWENTY-EIGHT

Irene would be okay. A flesh wound. Genteen too. That was all Rudy knew. The officers had ordered him back to his room. They'd sent some medics to pick up Genteen. A few hours later, Philly had come by to tell him the news. Rudy had been lying on his bed, numb, his limbs feeling like lead, his heart pounding and only gradually slowing down. When he recognized Philly's voice, though, he jumped from his rack and went through his shot-up door into the corridor.

Philly had called to Rudy from the hall. He was outside the double fire doors and talked through the crack. He told Rudy about Irene and Genteen.

"I'm not a leper, you know," Rudy said. "The doors are unlocked. You can come in."

"Whoa," Philly said. "You don't want them locked?"

"No. I want to get the hell out of here. Why would I want them locked?"

"Protection, man. You can't get out, but they can't get in."

"Who?"

"Anybody, man. You don't want anybody messing with you around this place. Too weird."

"Where's Genteen?"

"They got him locked up in the dispensary. They're flying him out tonight."

"Philly, find me Lavone."

"It's hard finding anybody at this altitude."

"Philly, you okay?"

"I'm flying, man."

"You high?"

"I'm looking down on all this from way far above it. It's the only way to go. Me and Lavone. Pharmaceuticals. That's how we stay untouchable. Like you, we in isolation. The Stark Raving Dark ain't touching us, man. Just like you. No crying we make."

A howl came from somewhere off in the corridors, then a dog barking.

"How am I going to eat?" Rudy asked.

"Maybe you don't want to," Philly said. "The mess hall's a fucked-up joint. Two days of peanut butter and jelly, then you know what they just served for lunch? Cookies and milk. I'll try to get you something decent before I ship."

"You leaving?"

"Got my orders."

"When?"

"Not sure but soon. Qangattarsa."

Through the crack, Rudy could see Philly's large hands make the fluttering gesture.

Philly sighed, then evaporated. Rudy stuck his head out of the door. The corridor was empty. A ceiling pipe clanked once. He went back in his room.

He must have dreamed. He was lying on his bed. He heard dogs again, lots of them. The sounds made him think of the remnants of the Vikings as Irene had described them: marooned, enduring cold and terrible darkness and invasions of the tribes to the north who were pressed by the expanding glaciers. Skraelings, she'd said the Vikings called the natives. The plague ravaged Europe. No one thought of Greenland. It was the Vatican that finally remembered the lost colony; Rome sent a mission to check on the forgotten diocese. The emissaries sailed into a fjord and found a settlement of stunted, inbred people practicing a twisted form of Catholicism that was more pagan than Christian. They left Greenland, and Western civ turned its back.

In the hall, someone began to sing into the intercom. First it was nonsense scat mixed with static, then it was the line "Bo Diddley, Bo Diddley, have you heard . . . ?" then more static, then a male falsetto doing a few phrases from "When You Wish Upon a Star."

Rudy went to the window. Hell, he thought, wish upon a star. Wish my ass out of here.

Men were outside working. They had a Sno-Cat and a winch. They were pulling a heavy load up from the snow. He could see that the thing the men were winching up was stiff and frozen. It was large, and it caused them great difficulty. Finally, its hoary shape came clear. They were hauling away a carcass of one of the horses.

As the machine churned away, the Cat's revolving yellow beacon became fuzzy and soon disappeared into the swirl of flakes. Then another flashing light began to catch Rudy's eye. He wasn't aware of it at first, and it wasn't exactly flashing either. It came from the Wing. A light there appeared to be fluttering, as if a hanging lamp were rocking in changing currents of air, the way a lantern always swings in a western-movie ghost town when the wind blows through broken windows. Broken windows . . . Rudy took off running.

The ward door was open just a crack. A frigid blade of air streamed through it. Rudy flung the door back.

In the dim, swaying light of the one lit Tiffany, the drapery sheers blew and fluttered on the north side of the ward. The windows there were open, and arctic air was pouring in. The curtains blew on the wind like a phalanx of banshees flying down the long room.

There was no one in the kiosk. Rudy ran toward the first open window. Snow had blown in, and a small drift was forming on the sill. He slammed the window down and ran to the next one. As he went, he tried to check the beds. Many of them were empty and stripped bare.

Many, but not all. There were still a few patients left. None moved or even seemed to be breathing. Their blankets were all pulled halfway down their beds. There were no hisses or huffing sounds. They lay wrapped, bandaged or scarred over, swathed only in sheets and their own cicatrized tissues. He touched a couple of them as he went. Cold.

Rudy shot over to the other side of the ward. He almost overran the bed when he saw the head reflector wink. Guy X was curled facing away from it.

Rudy skidded to a stop and swung into the alcove. He bent close to Guy X's head. He called to him as he felt Guy X's neck. Warm . . . and a pulse.

Guy X grunted. His eye was down, pressed into the pillow. He tried to stir himself to get a look at who was calling him.

Rudy considered yelling for help, but immediately realized that somebody wanted these windows open. He kept quiet and slipped his hands under Guy X to help him turn, and, as he did, he kept lifting him. There was a blanket around Guy X, and Rudy knew that was probably what had saved him: Guy X had been able, with his one arm and remnant hand, to pull the covers up around himself and keep from freezing.

Rudy could see his own breath. There was recognition in Guy X's eye now; a soft sigh came out of his mouth. Rudy found himself saying the same thing to Guy X that he'd said to Irene a few hours before: "There, there. There, there."

Then, before he'd really understood what he was doing, he carried Guy X toward the doors.

"Last looks," he said, and he tilted Guy X up enough so he could see down the length of the Wing. The one Tiffany lamp glowed in the cold stillness. Everything else was in shadow.

"Son of a bitch," Guy X whispered, and Rudy backed out through the double doors.

TWENTY-NINE

"What the fuck you gonna do, keep him for a pet?" Philly was kneeling down by the mattress and looking at Guy X, who appeared to be asleep. Rudy was standing behind Philly, leaning against the shelves in Lavone's storage-closet studio.

"I'm going to help him," Rudy said.

"*Help* him? How the hell you even *get* him?"

"It's not important. What I need is some pointers on how to take care of him."

"You need a fuck lot more than that."

"Look," Rudy said, "you're leaving. I just need to know about these tubes and things."

"He can't stay here forever," Philly said. "*You* can't either. What are you gonna do?"

"I'm getting him out of here. I have a plan," Rudy said.

"You have a plan." Philly grunted and sat back on the floor. He scratched his head and rubbed his eyes. "I thought all these guys were dead."

"What do you mean?" Rudy asked. They were wedged between

the desk and the supply shelves. Rudy had dragged the mattress into Lavone's office and set up a little nest for Guy X. He figured there was less chance of being discovered there. Then he'd taken off to find Philly.

"I mean," Philly said. "There was a big fuck-up. There was a heating failure on the Wing. The shift roster got screwed up. No one was on duty, and the boiler failed or something. You didn't know?"

Rudy shook his head.

"Shit, man," said Philly. "I thought you knew."

"There wasn't a big fuck-up," Rudy said. "Somebody opened the windows."

Rudy told him what he'd seen when he'd been in the Wing. Philly's shoulders sagged.

"Who'd've done a thing like that?" Philly whispered as he turned to look at Guy X. Swaddled in his bedclothes, Guy X lay motionless, asleep, breathing shallowly.

Rudy didn't answer; he didn't know.

"And the bitch of it all is this," Philly said. "Nobody can talk about it, because if anybody does, the army denies everything. None of us is here. Not him, not you, not me. Besides, how easy would it be for someone to convince people that guys who are MIA in Korea turned up nine years later frozen to death in Greenland?"

They sat for a few moments more, listening to Guy X breathe; then Philly got up and started to show Rudy how to change the colostomy gear, how to replace and clean the waste bags, how to feed Guy X and give injections. He said if an infection set in and Guy X needed antibiotics or even painkillers he was fucked, because Rudy'd never be able to get them.

"A lot we shipped out," Philly said. "The rest guys traded for stuff from the Eskimos. So you better get your boy smuggled out of here fast."

"He's leaving soon," Rudy said.

"Good," Philly said. "Me too. I gotta go." Philly extended his hand to Rudy. "Good luck."

"I'll need it," Rudy said.

"You will," Philly answered. Then he dug down into his pocket and pulled out a couple of Three Musketeers bars. "I was going to save these for my flight, but he could probably use them."

He gave the candy bars to Rudy, then bent down and straightened the blanket on Guy X.

"An orderly to the end," Philly said, and he left.

Guy X drifted in and out of consciousness. He never seemed to have a fit, but he never seemed fully awake either. He mumbled, babbled some, moaned a lot. Rudy fed him a mashed-up part of one of the Three Musketeers. Guy X murmured for water, and Rudy dribbled some into his mouth through a surgical tube.

Later Rudy tried to feed Guy X some canned peaches. He'd found a box of K-rats on a foraging trip at the far end of Storage Charlie.

Guy X turned his head away.

"Done," he whispered.

"Come on," Rudy said. "Eat."

Guy X took a weak swipe with his arm at the spoon. He closed his eye. "Done," he said again.

"You need this," Rudy said.

Guy X shook his head. "Done."

Rudy put the can and spoon down. He felt Guy X's forehead with the backs of his fingers. The skin was hot.

Rudy leaned back against the locker. He listened as a plane roared overhead. Probably Philly's flight or Genteen's or maybe even Irene's. He worried about that last possibility as dogs howled and yelped somewhere outside.

"Any mail?"

Rudy looked up.

"Any mail?" Guy X asked again in a dry croak. He reached over and touched Rudy's sleeve. "For you. Back from her. Who you wrote to. For me."

"Not yet," Rudy said. "You have to hang on. Give it a little more time. Hang on."

"I'll hang on," Guy X told him.

Guy X closed his eye and seemed to relax again into sleep.

Rudy turned off the light and sat in the darkness. He'd been bullshitting when he told Philly he had a plan. He wanted to ponder his options, but in the quiet darkness nothing came to him. He could hear his own breathing synchronize with the soft putter of Guy X's. Maybe they could just stay like that forever.

Then, without warning, the door banged open and the room filled with light.

Rudy dove forward, practically covering Guy X.

"Ho-ly shit." Lavone was looking down, hand still holding the light cord, frozen in a Statue of Liberty pose. "What the fuck is *this?*"

"Close the door!" Rudy whispered as he raised himself off Guy X. Lavone shut the door and came around to look at things. Rudy stayed on the floor, and Guy X rocked slightly, whimpering, eye closed. Lavone was hypnotized by the sight of the partial man. Rudy realized that Lavone had never been in the Wing.

"Whoa. Whoa. Whoa," Lavone finally said. He slumped into his chair.

"You've got to help me," Rudy said.

Guy X groaned.

"I can help *him,*" Lavone said. "Right now."

He got up, pulled an enema box out from the lower metal shelf and slipped a beaverboard panel off the wall. He withdrew a Hershey bar box and opened it in his lap. It was packed with ampules and syringes and pills.

Lavone administered a morphine dose to Guy X, whose groan turned to a sigh in almost one breath. They both watched Guy

X relax. He seemed to gain buoyancy before their eyes. Lavone took out a Syrette for himself.

"Are you still the Admin clerk?" Rudy asked Lavone.

Lavone looked surprised. "Of course," he said. "What'd you think?"

"I don't know, man," Rudy said. "I've been out of commission. I don't know what's happening."

"A damn garage sale is what's happening," Lavone said. He winced as he popped the Syrette into his arm. He made a little sucking sound with his lips. "The Danes are going to take over this place when we go because Greenland is Danish property, and the Danes plan to sell off whatever we leave behind to a Norwegian scrap merchant."

"What do you mean, leave behind?" Rudy said. "I thought this was going to become a radar base."

"Up north," Lavone said. "Change of plans. They're putting the radar up north. Up near Thule. They're still phasing this place out, though. I'm assigned to administer the deal. Kind of like executor of the estate."

"You?"

"There's been a breakdown of command, I guess you could say." Lavone was holding the empty Syrette between his thumb and forefinger, rolling it gently, studying it as if it were a fine cigar. "Or you could say we've entered into a new fluidity of leadership. The colonel is a basket case or a maniac, depending whom you talk to. Personally, I haven't seen him for something like three weeks. I get orders from Headquarters anyway, though, and I'm . . ."

Lavone phased out. Rudy waited, the way he'd wait for a radio to pull a distant station back in late at night.

". . . and I'm . . . becoming quite the administrator. I expect it's Vord who's sending me the stuff to expedite. I don't know. Sergeant Teal's still holed up on Delta Corridor recuperating, so it can't be her. It all comes down to one cat. Me. I'm demobbing

the whole place, dig? With my bare hands. Buck slips and bills
of lading and 201 files waving from every fist." Lavone gave him
a sloe-eyed, goofy grin. "Hey, I got your pal Genteen sent to
Indochina. He'll be happy there. I was thinking of getting myself
sent to Saigon. The mysterious East. Warm. Equatorial. Excellent
dope. . . ."

"Lavone, can you get us on a plane out of here?" Rudy asked.

"Us?" Lavone said. "You mean you and him?" They both
looked down at Guy X.

"Me, him, and someone else."

"Who else?"

"The colonel's aide."

Lavone's smile never broke. "Smoking or nonsmoking?" he
said.

THIRTY

The snow was up to his thighs. He wallowed around behind
Storage Charlie and headed into the wind across a side yard lit-
tered with tumbled stacks of freight pallets and propane bottles.
It was dark, and the storm had let up; there were no stars. The
breeze was stiff out of the northwest. The wind had a dank feel
to it even at twenty below.

He was out of breath when he reached the steps to the wooden
vestibule, which served as a kind of airlock around the door to
the building. Rudy shoved against the door with his shoulder,
leaning into a sign that said

DELTA CORRIDOR
♀ PERSONNEL ONLY

Delta Corridor looked deserted. There were signs of hasty departures: a couple of bed frames leaning against the wall, papers
scattered here and there on the floor. A blank lavender sheet of

someone's discarded stationery stuck to the wet sole of Rudy's boot. The faint odor of perfume or bath powder still hung in the air, and someone had stapled a bra to the wall near the fire extinguisher. The rooms he passed were open. Every room was deserted: folded mattresses, empty lockers with doors ajar, a few clipped-out magazine photos still tacked to the walls.

Rudy noticed in one of the rooms a photo of the seven astronauts. It was from the cover of *Life,* the full-color picture of them in their silver space suits. The picture transfixed him. He stared through the door at the seven men. They held their helmets under their arms like football captains, and they smiled, earnest and brave.

Who wants, he wondered, to be the first in space?

Then he heard a woman's voice humming from inside the room. It brought him back. He waited a moment until he was sure. He steadied his breath and stepped inside.

In the far corner, out of sight of the door, was a four-poster canopy bed. The bed was covered with a white ball-fringe bedspread, and Irene, arm in an OD sling, wearing a nurse's blouse and a slip, was sitting on top of the spread. Her hair had been severely cut, chopped down to almost nothing. She was reading a magazine.

When Irene saw Rudy, she stopped humming, and they just stared at each other.

"The princess in her tower," Irene said.

"You're okay?" Rudy said. It was a question sounding like a pronouncement.

"My arm is." Irene let the magazine fall onto her lap, and she touched the sling with her hand. "Or it will be. In time. It wasn't much of a wound really."

"That's good."

Her head was so shorn it was almost as if he could see her skull.

"Irene, your hair."

"I cut it."

Rudy glanced down at the snow crystals melting on the black

rubber of his Mickey Mouse boots. He didn't know what to think. He looked around the room.

"The other women mind you get to sleep like this?" he asked.

"The other women are all gone," Irene said. "Lane sent this over after they'd all shipped out. It had been his."

Rudy nearly laughed at the thought of the colonel sleeping in a four-poster canopy bed; then, in the next instant, the image seemed almost touching.

"Where's he sleep now?" Rudy asked.

"I don't know."

Rudy looked away. There was a heaviness in the air between them; time was slowing down. He thought of clocks and pendulums frozen in the glacier. He felt like an awkward visitor making a call on a vague acquaintance in the hospital. *How's the food? They treating you okay?*

"I've got good news," he said.

Irene looked at him quizzically. With her hacked, feathery hair she appeared monkish, like one of Chaplain Brank's anchorites, a fervent saint of the far north. Her legs were pulled up and pearly smooth under the slip she was wearing. Would he ever be able to touch them again? Her left arm, in its sling, was tucked close to her chest, her broken wing. She pressed her forehead to her knees. A sigh, almost a sob, came up from her chest. Rudy walked over to the bed. Gently, with the back of his hand, he touched Irene's cheekbone.

"We're leaving," he said. "The way I promised. I'm getting us out of here. You and me and Guy X. He's still alive. We're taking him out of here. You and I. Lavone has it all set up."

Irene looked shocked. He felt sweat bloom across his face, but he kept unfolding the plan slowly, steadily, so he'd sound sure of himself.

There was a cargo plane leaving at 2200 hours. It was shipping some of the post's meteorological equipment and surplus rations up to a Danish zinc mine in Marmorilik in a deal Lavone had brokered. From there the plane was flying across the the ice cap,

down to Keflavík, Iceland, then all the way to Rhein-Main Air
Base outside Frankfurt. Lavone was cutting orders that would give
Rudy and Irene clear passage to Germany. He was writing letters
with the colonel's forged signature that would cover any discrep-
ancies in their 201 files.

Irene listened to all of this quietly. As he talked, Rudy sat on
the bed next to her. Laying it all out like that, he was suddenly
terrified of how harebrained the plan now seemed, the halluci-
nations of a dupe and a morphine addict.

"This is all really about you saving your skin," Irene said.

"Of course it is," Rudy answered, surprised at how accusatory
Irene had sounded. "And about us."

"Are you going to leave him swaddled on somebody's doorstep
like an abandoned child?" Irene asked.

"Who?"

"The guy from the Wing."

"We're getting him to a proper military hospital," Rudy said.
He found he had to check an indignant tone rising in his voice.
"Rhein-Main has facilities for Guy X. Lavone looked into it."

"Lavone. Lavone knows all about that stuff?"

"He knows enough."

"But what if Guy X starts to go under before you get him to
a proper military hospital? What if he starts to die? Are you just
going to dump him at some first aid station at a zinc mine along
the way?"

"Not dump."

"Leave him then?"

"No. Stay with him."

"What you're talking about," Irene said, "if it goes wrong or
you make certain decisions, would be desertion."

Rudy didn't answer.

"He may not make it," Irene said.

"Whatever happens to him, at least right now he's alive and
out of pain. He's better off than if he'd stayed on the Wing."

"I guess," Irene mumbled.

"You don't think so?" Rudy asked. He couldn't believe they were arguing; he'd come to carry her away. "Christ, Irene, Vord opened the windows on those guys."

She stared at the canopy above the bed. Her voice sounded exhausted. "I know," she said. "I was there."

"What?" Rudy whispered.

"I was there when he came in." Irene closed her eyes. "I was just sitting. I'd been sutured up from the gunshot, and I couldn't sleep, so I went walking. I felt dreamy from the painkillers. I went down to the Wing. Just to sit. You know. Moonlight. He came in. I saw what he was doing. I wanted to stop him, to say something, but I just sat there. He saw me and smiled and kept opening the windows. The curtains started blowing in. He walked right around me. On to the next one."

"Did he say anything?" Rudy asked.

Irene shook her head. "I tried to move, but I couldn't do it. It was the drugs. I started crying. And that's when I found myself able to move. I was like a zombie. I went up to one of the windows to close it. I had my good arm up when he came up behind me and grabbed me by my bad arm. It hurt so much, I couldn't do anything. I let the window go. Then he very gently led me out of there and back down the hall here and very nicely told me to stay here and be quiet."

"And that's it?"

She nodded, eyes closed, grimacing, obviously trying to shut out the memory. "It was like a dream. I was outside myself. I couldn't reach in and change things. I was there, but I wasn't."

Rudy thought of how Guy X described his life, dreaming he could contact people and change things, but never really being able to.

"So you've been here ever since?" he whispered.

Irene breathed deeply for a time. She settled herself.

"Lane came. Once, I think. He came in to say he'd been relieved of his command. He brought me some food, though. He said he wanted to have a piece of my hair for a keepsake. 'Where are you

going?' I asked him. He said he didn't know. He wanted a locket
of hair, though. I said I would cut it for him. I did. And when
he was gone, I just kept cutting."

Rudy was dizzy. Irene's words swirled in the air around
the bed.

"That was the last I've seen of him."

She turned to face Rudy. "Now you're here. I sometimes think
that if you'd never come to Qangattarsa, never gone on the Wing,
none of this would have happened."

"You took me there," Rudy said. "I asked you to."

They sat so close to each other their whispered breaths mingled.
It was almost impossible for them to focus on each other's eyes at
that distance. Irene's green irises swam in Rudy's vision; her pu-
pils darted around, taking in his face.

"Why is this happening to us?" she asked.

Rudy didn't know if it was her breath that left his face tingling
or a breeze from outside. He thought of the first time they'd made
love, the strange cold blast he'd felt rushing up his skin from
some canyon just beyond his awareness. He sensed something, for
a moment, in the room with them, something dark, looming,
shadowy as a tree. Then it was gone.

The world had become her eyes; the darkness outside, the ice,
the rock and ash, every blessed nautical mile back to some place
familiar had become her eyes.

"Come with me," he said. It was a command, a plea. The force
of her gaze consumed him, steady as ever. But in that gaze he
could see her answer.

She rose, turned from him, and stepped over to the window.
"I can't."

"You said together, we'd leave together."

She nodded, eyes closed.

"I've got your orders practically cut already."

"I can't desert."

"This isn't desertion."

"It will come to it," she said and stepped closer to him, spoke lower. "If you plan to have the slightest chance of saving that man, you're going to have to stick by him until he's in a proper hospital. And that's not a proper *military* hospital. That means chucking Lavone's routing orders and ditching the army altogether."

Now Rudy looked away. He felt his thoughts, his plans hemmed in by the room, the encased heat.

"You're saying," he told her, "this has all the makings of a fuck-up."

Irene rested her hand on his arm. "I don't want to let you go. I've let too much go. Not you too."

"What about Guy X?" Rudy asked.

"Him, *you* have to let go," she whispered.

Rudy shook his head.

"It can't be helped," Irene said.

"Is this you talking or is it Woolwrap or is it Vord?"

"Me. Just me. I love you. I even love it that you think you can pull this off, but there's no way out for all of us. It can't be helped. . . . Besides, I can't desert him."

"Him? The colonel?"

She nodded, her eyes lowered. "That's . . . " she faltered. "That's what I was coming to tell you when this happened." And she looked, almost in bafflement, at her wound.

"Jesus, Irene." Rudy spoke like a man struggling for breath. "But he's *gone*. He's the CO, and he's practically AWOL. Who's seen him? Have you seen him?"

"That's why I can't abandon him."

"Oh, God," Rudy mumbled. He gulped some air, struggled not to plead.

She tilted toward him; their foreheads met. They looked down. She whispered, "I love you."

It was a struggle not to feel nauseated, the room was pitching so. He wanted to keep repeating the words—I love you, I love you—as if uttering them enough would overpower her resolve. But the words wouldn't. He knew they wouldn't, and that knowledge brought back the strangely familiar feeling that he now began to realize was at the bottom of his love for her even as it went against all he hoped for. The very thing that was ruining his chances—her steadfastness, her devotion to her lost man—was making him love her all the more.

Rudy straightened up and rubbed his face with his hands, pinched the bridge of his nose.

"Well," he said.

She turned away from him and opened the shade on the nearest window. The storm had kicked up again, and snow swirled in giant cyclonic patterns against the glass. In the farthest reaches of the security lights, barely visible in the whiteness, was the hulk of the crippled C-47, buried up to its wings. Irene stood looking out at it. Rudy got off the bed and stepped close to her.

"I waited for you out there one of my first days here," he said. "The day you were going to show me around."

"I never did, did I?" she said, still facing the window.

"Nope."

"And now here we are."

Rudy placed his hands on her shoulders. She pivoted under them, faced him. He reached behind her neck and untied the sling. Irene, eyes moist, looked up to watch him. He held her arm a moment then began to unwind the gauze bandage. Around and around her arm his hands went, gathering the pale cloth. The dressing under all the bandage had a small golden stain from the ointments. He slowly peeled the pad away.

He held her arm in his hands, and he and Irene looked at it. There were four sutures, a gentian violet crust of blood around the closed wound, shiny stains from the antiseptics. Rudy could feel Irene breathing close to his ear. He raised her arm a little and at the same time leaned his head down, and as she began to cry, he kissed her wound, touching each suture ever so gently with his lips.

THIRTY-ONE

The wind was picking up. It rattled the corrugated metal walls, and the sound boomed around the cold, dark interior of the hangar. Rudy dragged the sledge carrying his belongings and Guy X through the cavernous space. There were no planes inside, only a Jeep without wheels and a single, broken jet engine: a huge, pitted silver pod unattached to a wing, lying on the floor.

It was warm in the deserted ready room. The propane heater had been cranking away since the morning flight out. Still, the rattling of the metal walls in the main part of the building sent a chill through Rudy. It was twenty-five below outside and dropping. The weather was fighting to get in.

Rudy hauled the sledge right inside the ready room. He and Lavone had made the sledge from a freight pallet. Lavone had helped harness Rudy into the rope traces and had said good-bye back at the door to Storage Charlie. He'd even given Rudy his one poster from *The Thing* and folded it into Rudy's duffel, a farewell present.

"I'll be in touch," Rudy had said, though neither of them quite believed it.

"Dig. I'll be interested to see the postmarks."

They hugged good-bye, and Rudy left for the hangar.

In the ready room, Rudy lay Guy X down on an old sofa near the heater. He unzipped the mummy bag a little. Guy X's skin looked even more mottled than usual—it was still hot and dry— but as he glanced around the room, he looked more alert. Maybe the cold air and jostling had stimulated him.

"We're flying out," Rudy told him. "This is the ready room. We're waiting for the plane."

Guy X tried to lick his lips. He couldn't speak. Rudy got out the tube and bottle rig and dribbled some water into Guy X's mouth.

Guy X nodded in relief and thanks. "Where to?" he asked.

"Safety," Rudy said. "Everything will be okay." And he patted Guy X's sleeping bag.

Rudy looked around the ready room. It was the hangout for pilots and flight crews that passed through Q-Base. On the walls were pinups and weather charts along with old rosters and cargo manifests. On the wall visible to anyone coming in from the airstrip was a sign:

WELCOME TO QANGATTARSA

(INUIT TRANSL.—"LET US FLY UP!")

Under which someone had scrawled:

AND NEVER FUCKING FLY BACK!

Guy X breathed quietly on the sofa. It was about five in the afternoon. Five hours until flight time. Lavone had said this was to be a touch-and-go operation. The plane would only stop, load up, and take off—something about the flight plan not accounting for General Vord's irregular dispersal of U.S. Government property to Danish mining interests. Lavone had made up medical transport papers for Guy X, so getting aboard would be no trouble.

Rudy pulled all the shades down on the windows. He turned off the overhead bulbs and flicked on the one desk lamp. Its light sent a soft glow as far as the sofa where Guy X lay.

Rudy pulled up a chair and sat next to Guy X. He unzipped the sleeping bag and adjusted the waste bag. He tried to make Guy X more comfortable.

"How do you feel?"

"Hot." Guy X smiled a toothless, gnarled grin, and Rudy wasn't sure if it was a grimace or a show of pluck.

From within the folds of the down bag came Guy X's arm. It reached for Rudy, and did it with that uncoiling motion that had so unsettled him when he'd first seen it months ago. The fingers felt for Rudy's sleeve, found it, then worked downward. Guy X took Rudy's hand in his.

"Thanks," he said.

"It's okay," Rudy said and gripped Guy X's hand firmly.

Guy X shook his head. "I'm not going to make it," he whispered.

"Don't talk like that."

Guy X just shook his head again and closed his eye. He lay quiet for a few moments, collecting himself. Then he looked at Rudy again.

"Did you bring the Whitman?" he asked.

Instantly Rudy realized he hadn't. He groped for an answer.

"No problem. I sing the body electric," Guy X whispered. He still held Rudy's hand. He clenched it and shook it reassuringly. He was actually comforting Rudy.

"I got a letter," Rudy said.

Guy X's reaction was slow, but when he realized what Rudy was talking about, he twisted in the bag for a better look at Rudy's face.

"Tell me," Guy X whispered.

"She wrote," Rudy said. "She remembers you."

The lie just spilled out. Rudy couldn't help himself. Guy X's face seemed to radiate light.

"She wants to know more about you," Rudy said. "She said although her life has taken many twists and turns, she still thinks about the time you had together. She said it . . . " Rudy's thoughts gave out.

"She said what?" Guy X demanded.

Rudy wasn't sure he could go on. He prayed Guy X wouldn't ask to see the letter.

"She said the time was what?"

"She said it was wonderful."

"Go on," Guy X said.

"She didn't say much else," Rudy told him. He told himself this was all in the name of hope or peace or a condemned man's last wish. He felt weak inside.

"Is she still married?" Guy X asked.

"No," Rudy said. "That's over."

"Ah," Guy X said, and it occurred to Rudy that he knew, that he'd never ask to see a letter, that he wasn't interested in proof. He only wanted a story.

"She wants me to supply her with more information," Rudy said. He seemed to notice the clanging of the hangar walls more than ever now. "About you," he said.

"Maybe someday you will," Guy X muttered.

A loud feedback screech blasted from a speaker on the wall. It was a hailing signal of some kind. Both Rudy's and Guy X's eyes shot toward the sound. Lavone's voice came on the speaker.

"To whom it may concern: Commo just got word the flight's not coming in. The weather. Probably nothing for a couple of days. Can't tell you what to do next. Lie low at the very least. I'll try to help. Over and out."

The speaker clicked off.

Guy X was still holding Rudy's hand. His grip loosened. He

closed his eye, retreated. Rudy bore the negligible weight of Guy X's arm as he tucked it gently into the sleeping bag. Guy X's breathing was shallow, steady but quick. He was asleep.

Rudy leaned back in his chair. No flight for days. He wanted to think of something, but his mind kept running into walls. Lavone said he'd help. Maybe even Irene would. Rudy felt overcome with fatigue. He felt as though he'd exhausted all his possibilities, foreclosed all his options. This was the dead end. He shut his eyes and listened to the storm.

He was asleep when the door burst open. Rudy jerked awake.

A man stood in the portal, silhouetted by the security lights. He held an M-1 rifle. He was large and wore full arctic outer gear with the hood up and pulled tight. It was a scene right out of *The Thing*.

Rudy stayed in his chair.

"Sir." he said. "You've been gone."

The colonel stepped in and kicked the door closed behind him. He flicked on the lights. His voice came out as a growl. "But not forgotten?"

He began to yank his parka hood back. Rudy kept track of the weapon. The colonel seemed out of breath, flushed, as if he'd been running great distances. His eyes clicked back and forth in their sockets.

"No, sir," Rudy said. "Not forgotten."

The colonel craned his neck to see what was on the sofa. He walked over and, with the rifle barrel, pushed the sleeping bag back from Guy X's face.

Rudy turned slowly to see Guy X looking up, expressionless, into the colonel's eyes.

Woolwrap stepped away to the middle of the room.

"I don't even want to know about that, Corporal," he said quietly.

Rudy shifted in his seat.

"Where have you been, sir?" he asked.

"Out there mostly." The colonel pointed with the M-1 toward the door. "I'm somewhat AWOL. You may have heard. I've been relieved of my command. Have you heard that?"

"Yes, sir."

"Who told you?" Woolwrap asked. "As if I didn't know."

Rudy didn't say anything. The colonel seemed calmer now, but still, he was holding a .30-caliber rifle. Woolwrap flung the M-1's muzzle up so it rested on his right shoulder. He stared at the floor, and he looked like a buffalo hunter pondering tracks in the dirt.

"Militarily I'm fucked. You comprehend that, Corporal?"

"I know things don't look too good, sir."

The colonel laughed. "For either of us, buck-o."

He pointed to Guy X, who had been watching them, eye wide, completely silent. "What's the story here, Corporal?" Woolwrap asked. "I take it back. I do want to know."

"We're leaving, sir."

"Interesting idea. Where to?"

"I don't know, sir. But I'm going to help this guy."

Woolwrap stepped over to Guy X and knelt down.

"Hello, soldier," he said.

Guy X just looked at him.

The colonel leaned closer, spoke quietly. "What can I tell you, soldier? Your chances of making it out of here with that corporal are nil. And you can't go back. I can't go back either. The corporal here, I don't know. Maybe he can make it. Except he'll be AWOL. I'm AWOL, more or less. And you, soldier. You're MIA. What a fix."

The colonel had his hands clasped, and he was kneading them together. He looked like a supplicant before Guy X. The rifle lay on the floor. Rudy thought maybe he should grab the weapon. He could probably make the lunge and snatch it up, but he had no idea what he'd do next.

"What's your name, soldier?" Woolwrap asked.

Guy X didn't answer, so the colonel asked him again.

"He won't say," Rudy whispered. "He's never told anyone."

The colonel looked at Rudy, then back at Guy X. "Good for him," Woolwrap said.

Then the colonel leaned in closer to Guy X. "I did what I could for you and the others," he said. "Do you believe that? It wasn't your army and it wasn't your country. It was me." He stood up and looked toward the shaded window. "I wish somebody would fucking remember that."

Rudy looked down to see Guy X's eye fill with tears. There were drops trickling down the side of his face. He was looking at the colonel. Rudy watched the two of them. He felt left out.

Guy X closed his eye. Tears still seeped out. The colonel looked down at him and saluted, held his hand to his brow for several seconds, then whipped his arm down.

He turned, picked up his rifle and faced Rudy.

"I want you to help me, Corporal," he said. "Button up." He pointed to Rudy's parka and stepped over to open the door. The rubber gasket around the frame made a sucking pop as the door swung in, and a blast of snow roared across the opening.

"What about him?" Rudy said, raising his voice over the wind.

"We'll be right back," the colonel said. "But there's something I have to take care of."

Rudy bent down and tucked Guy X in. Guy X's body shuddered as if he were in a fit, but his eye was open now, and he was fully conscious.

"You've done enough," Guy X said.

"What?"

"And enough is enough."

Guy X turned his face toward the sofa cushion.

"What?" Rudy said again.

But Guy X would not look at him.

"Corporal," the colonel said again. He tapped the rifle barrel against the door frame.

Rudy straightened up and stepped away from the sofa, looking back at the side of Guy X's head. Guy X's respiration was surging more than usual.

"Let's hurry," Rudy said as he met the colonel in the doorway. "He shouldn't be alone."

The colonel pointed with the rifle down the east side of the building and headed out. Rudy struggled to get the door closed, but snow packed around the jamb made it difficult. He yanked and yanked.

"Corporal!" the colonel bellowed from the storm. Rudy gave the door one last hard pull. It held.

"Stay close to the building," Woolwrap called.

Snow managed to find its way inside Rudy's hood and down his neck. It made him shudder.

"What's this all about?" he shouted.

"In here." The colonel reached in front of Rudy and pulled the latch of a sliding door. They had walked along the hangar annex, beyond the ready room to the stable.

Inside, the room was rank with rotted, urine-soaked hay. The heater thrummed softly. Instinctively, Rudy stepped toward it. There was a cot and throw rug in the corner, some discarded K-ration cans and boxes.

"No," the colonel said. "Over here." He opened a stall door.

The creature inside barely looked like a horse. Emaciated, bones protruding everywhere, pasty-eyed, and wobbling on its legs, the animal shied weakly as Rudy and Woolwrap came through and closed the door. There was nothing in the horse's manger or grain trough. Thirty or forty empty Corn Flakes boxes lay crushed in the corner.

"It was all I could get to feed him when Vord cut off my hay flights," Woolwrap said. "Made him sick. And then even the cereal ran out." He kicked one of the boxes.

The animal shifted and made a low, grunting noise that tipped up in a gasp at the end.

The colonel pulled an OD scarf out of his parka pocket and wrapped it gently around the horse's eyes. The animal was too weak to object.

Woolwrap gave the rifle to Rudy and whispered a few words

to the horse. Then he began to lead him toward the door. He held
the horse steady as the animal trembled and backed away from
the frigid blast. With some words to the horse, Woolwrap coaxed
him outside.

They slogged through the snow, Woolwrap and the horse in
the lead, Rudy and the rifle in the rear. Twice, the horse nearly
keeled over as the wind gusted around the back corner of the
hangar. They were moving farther out of range of the security
lights. Rudy could see nothing but sheets of snow beaten laterally
by the wind. Beyond that were the mountains and the Greenland
ice cap in the dark. The hangar banged behind them, and the
wind howled inside Rudy's hood.

About a hundred yards from the building, the horse collapsed.
He toppled stiffly to the right almost as if he were a statue pushed
over by unseen vandals. The snow heaped around and instantly
began to dust his flank. He tried to raise his blindfolded head,
but his body would not follow.

"Shit," the colonel said. "This is it. Come around here. Put it
to his forehead. There's a round in the chamber. Let's get it over
with."

The colonel knelt down and patted the horse's neck. He uttered
soothing words to the animal. Snow had collected on the colonel's
eyebrows and lashes. Rudy couldn't hear what he was saying, but
after a moment, Woolwrap looked up and said, "Come on. Make
it quick."

Rudy came around to face the animal. The distant lights of the
hospital were gray, muzzy dots in the storm. He pulled off his
right mitten, leaving the wool liner on so he wouldn't glue his
flesh to the freezing metal trigger. He felt the cold clamp around
his fingers. He'd have to be quick. He raised the rifle to his cheek.
The wooden stock prickled against his skin. He could kill the
colonel, he thought. The horse would die anyway, might already
be gone. Rudy could just plug the bastard colonel in the head
right now.

But he shot the horse. The animal didn't even move. Rudy

stood looking at the snow already gathering on the carcass, wondering numbly what he'd done. The colonel took the rifle from him and motioned toward the hanger. They started walking back. They were just going to leave the body there.

"That one you shot was hers," the colonel said.

"As if I didn't know," Rudy mumbled. He was feeling his capacity to think slip into the gray world. Or maybe it was that all the thoughts were becoming like the whirling flakes that blotted out an overall sense of depth or vision. Everything inside and outside his head was beginning to blend.

After slogging through the knee-deep snow for about fifty yards, Rudy could see something pierce the blur. A dim light shone from the ready-room door. That was wrong. For that to happen, the door had to be open.

Rudy tried to run. His arms flailed side to side as he attempted to vault through the drifts. The colonel grunted behind him. The storm beat at them. The flakes stung the corners of Rudy's eyes. As he got closer, he could see the door banging against a folding chair inside. An apron of snow fanned into the room. Hazy and distorted in the storm, a pale yellow glow bulged out from the doorway. The door had blown open.

Rudy stopped at the threshold. He raised his mittened hands to steady himself in the frame. On the floor before him lay Guy X. He'd left the sofa, rolled off it probably, and had clawed his way across the room. He was naked because he'd pulled himself right out of the sleeping bag. His flesh was blue. His tubes and bags were strung out behind him, making him look like some kind of tentacled sea creature, stranded on a beach. He had made it all the way to the delta of fresh snow on the floor, where he'd rolled over to look up into the storm and die.

THIRTY-TWO

"Cover him up."

"He's dead," Rudy said. He was stunned by Guy X's nakedness, his genitals, so large and cyanotic, snowflakes blowing on them and on the rest of the body. The corpse looked like a precious stone, smooth and blue, lying on a white sheet. Guy X's eye was open; snow fell directly into it.

"He didn't want to be cremated," Rudy said. "We'll have to bury him."

The colonel said nothing, so Rudy bent down and unfastened the tubing, doing it gently, as Philly had shown him. He took an army blanket that was lying over the back of the sofa and folded it around Guy X. He lifted him up. Light as ever, the body floated in his arms. Rudy stepped toward the exit, but the colonel stopped him.

"Not through the door," the colonel said. He took the butt of the M-1 and smashed the glass of the window. "I'll pass him through. That way his spirit will fly up."

"Qangattarsa," said Rudy.

"Amen," said the colonel.

Once he had handed Guy X out to Rudy, the colonel went to a circuit-breaker box on the far wall and pulled a large switch. Out on the runway, blue landing lights glowed in a pair of parallel lines extending a half mile in either direction into the storm. Rudy stood in the wind looking at the luminous alley and began walking north, bearing the body toward the Viking farmstead and burial ground. The colonel joined him, and without a word, the two men began slogging through the snow side by side.

The storm absorbed the runway lights into an azure penumbra that enveloped Rudy and the colonel like a membrane. It gave Rudy the feeling that he was in an enormous blue room. The snow whipped and dodged about, sometimes diving straight down, other times seeming to rise out of the earth like an immense flock of startled birds.

Rudy felt his fingers and arms begin to get numb from the cold. His feet and legs were okay because they were moving, but his grip on the corpse felt as if it were locking up. He knew he could ask the colonel to take the load, but he didn't want to let Guy X go.

"Corporal." Woolwrap had to half holler in the wind. "I wish there was something I could say."

"No need, sir," Rudy called back.

"One might call this a fuck-up of the first order. Being out here in these conditions."

"One might, sir."

"But *I* wouldn't."

"Neither would I, sir."

"Do you know what you're doing?" Woolwrap said.

"Up to a point," Rudy said.

He looked out to the end of the converging lines of lights. Converging, but never meeting. Up to a point. The snow was piling high around the bulbs; some of them were already covered, leaving patches glowing under the snow like cobalt pools. Rudy could no longer see the lights of the hospital or the ready room.

All that was left were the sinking lights of the runway. The snow was nearly up to his waist now.

"I know what I'm doing," the colonel said. He'd pronounced the words so flatly that it reminded Rudy of Genteen in his derangement pointing the pistol at him. It startled Rudy, and he looked over at Woolwrap, expecting to see the colonel aiming the M-1 at his face.

But the colonel was walking straight ahead, eyes squinting in the blizzard, fixed on some indeterminate distance. They must have walked well beyond the runway because now there was no blue light. Still, somehow, the snow gave off a hint of luminescence. Perhaps it was from the moon and starlight far above the storm, or the hospital lights refracted and rebounded around the millions of moving ice crystals. There was no light, but it wasn't dark.

Rudy slipped and clutched Guy X closer. The ground underfoot began to slope downward. It had to be the berm beyond the end of the runway. Rudy noticed the colonel veering off course. There was a rigidity to his gait as if he'd summoned some deep reserve of military bearing. He faded away.

"Sir!" Rudy called, but his voice sounded impish, muffled by cotton. It got no answer. "Colonel! Sir! Hey! *Lane!*"

Nothing. The snow closed in tighter; the light, such as it was, seemed to drop a notch.

Rudy looked for tracks. He began to get the feeling he was arcing to the right. Maybe he was going in a circle. It was typical for a lost or panicked human to wander in circles. Rudy'd read that somewhere. He tried to figure out where. Maybe a comic book. His own thoughts were beginning to go in circles.

His shoulders ached, so he shifted Guy X over to one hip as if he were a bundle of books. He began shouting again but got no answer. He trudged on.

The shot came from off to the left. The storm dampened and diminished the sound, but Rudy knew it was the muzzle report of the M-1.

He shouted some more, but then the thought struck him that the colonel might have been firing at him. He went silent and bent down, holding Guy X close to his chest.

The storm roared around him. It was absurd trying to detect movement out there. Nothing but stinging flakes bombarded him from all directions at once. Rudy waited for another shot. There was nothing. It was as if a deep quiet had come to exist within the din of the blizzard, an antinoise that filled the spaces between the whirling flakes.

The colonel was dead. Rudy knew that now. The single shot was all he would hear. The colonel had walked in circles, then veered away to shake Rudy off his trail so he could be alone and turn the gun on himself.

Now Rudy was alone. Standing among the dead. This went beyond fucking up, although that was still part of it; it also had elements of ordination and choice, of destiny and duty. We're here because we're here because we're here . . .

But something deep in him wanted to be where he was, beyond help, beyond any ability to return, beyond anything that would hinder or drag against the beautiful exhilaration he was feeling. Maybe he was nuts, but he felt pure. He held Guy X to his chest. He looked up toward the sky. The storm leaped at him.

Judging he was somewhere beyond the end of the runway, he guessed where the Fire Department was. Bearing roughly forty-five degrees to the west of that, he figured he'd run into the Viking farmstead. It was there he'd leave Guy X. He began to walk again.

And he never saw the colonel's body. He never passed the Fire Department. He should have run into the farmstead. For the first time, the thought occurred to him to stop, to quit. He could simply lie down, sleep, lie with Guy X and sleep. Guy X and Rudy X. Brothers in arms.

His thoughts blanked out for minutes, maybe hours, while he walked. He no longer felt his limbs. The pumping of his knees, the burning of his muscles and joints had become a distant rocking, waves that bore him along.

He stumbled. It couldn't have been the farmstead for it wasn't a wall he felt underfoot but a hill, and there were no hills near the old ruins.

He liked the idea of a hill. A climb. A challenge. He pushed on up the rise and hadn't gone far before he struck a large wall. It stretched into the storm to the left and right and loomed above him as well. Rudy felt it with his mitten. It was ice. He had reached the glacier.

Suddenly Rudy saw the dimensions of his situation. He could picture now how far away he was from the hospital, and he could see himself standing next to this wall of ice, a mite up against the toe of a giant.

He rubbed the frozen surface. It had been scoured and buffed by winds for so long that it was as smooth as glazed porcelain. Rudy guessed the wall towered a hundred feet above him. He was under a deep, petrified river flowing down from the Greenland ice cap.

He placed Guy X down and leaned against the glacier. The ice steadied him. He looked at it. If layers upon layers of snow had formed the glacier and he was standing at the bottom, then he was looking at ancient time. He thought of objects and secrets locked in a clear, gemlike tomb: the glacier of his imagination with its frozen pendulums and memories.

But it wasn't that way at all. Here was proof. Time was blank. Time was cold and huge and opaque. It weighed enough to crush stone.

Rudy looked down at the army blanket. This would be Guy X's final resting place. The glacier would eventually swallow Guy X as it moved slowly forward. Guy X's bones would be ground and pulverized by the ice. They would add to the glacier's whiteness.

Rudy would too. He knew now, if he hadn't when he left the ready room, that he'd never make it back. He kept looking down at Guy X. He hardly seemed to take up any space inside the rumpled army blanket that was his shroud. Snow was covering everything.

The ice wall hummed in the wind, a peaceful, white sound. The snow strummed against it. Rudy listened. He began to hear his mother's voice, then his father's. Peaceful. The single report of the colonel's M-1 came fluttering off the glacier. Then the hissing of the men on the Wing. Guy X joined the sounds too, saying in his gentle rasp, *Enough is enough. Enough is enough*.

Rudy sank to his knees. He felt tired. The snow was covering everything. He was becoming sleepy.

Then he heard Irene's voice. He could feel her hand. She was not locked away in the ice like the others. He could sense her looking down at him as if she peered over the edge of the world.

He struggled to his feet. He needed to find her. He knew now what he was looking for when he'd stood in all those houses amid all those other lives back home. He was looking for her.

He stumbled forward. He had to get to her. Simple as that. He had to be with her, even die in her arms if it came to it. He began calling her name.

The sound of his shouts. A whisper. A deafening roar. He didn't know which, but he kept calling anyway. Irene. *Irene*.

He banged along, parallel to the glacier, sometimes smacking it with his left shoulder, sometimes running his mitten along it as if the ice were a tiled wall.

He thought his feet hurt and his fingers too. Then he realized he was feeling no pain there. They were numb. This should worry you, he told himself. But he giggled. What, me worry?

Maybe his eyes had closed, but he didn't think so because he was sure he saw something flicker in the air around him. Maybe there was a new sound coming in under his cries for Irene, under the rush of the storm, under the thrumming of the glacier and under the silence that entwined it all. There was a rumbling.

Rudy turned around to see an aureole glowing from below the slope. It grew brighter. It silhouetted the thousands of snowflakes that blew back and forth across it. Something was about to happen, Rudy told himself, and he felt both an elation that he was about to be saved and a surprising pang of sadness that his solitude was about to be interrupted.

Two headlights and an engine's roar burst over the hill. It was a Sno-Cat. The machine practically leaped over the rise.

Rudy stood mesmerized. Cables, ropes, and poles clung to the body of the Cat, making it look like a breaching whale with severed lines and rusted harpoons stuck in its flanks; the machine must have crashed through and broken the blizzard safety lines down by the base. He could see the snow torrents foaming over the chain treads. The Cat was not just coming his way but seemed to be bearing down upon him.

Rudy began to shuffle sideways. The Cat swerved a little, as if the wind had buffeted it or someone was sawing at the steering wheel. Rudy tried to see who was in the cab. He shielded his eyes from the headlight glare.

The driver was pale, almost white like the glacier itself, and Rudy suddenly knew it was the chaplain.

Rudy started to wave and to run toward the machine that was charging up toward the glacier on a steep slope. He could see the little Inuit statuette swinging wildly from its chain and banging against the windshield. The chaplain looked alarmed. He yanked at the steering wheel just before the Cat slammed obliquely into the glacier wall. The vehicle careened, and the chaplain started screaming something behind the windshield as the machine began to slide sideways down the slope, bearing down on Rudy.

Rudy stumbled and scrambled back up. The engine roar was closer, and with it came the rattle and screech of the chain treads spinning around the pontoons. The Cat was driving forward, but its direction was on a skidding diagonal across the hill. The chaplain had lost control. The Cat was sliding away from Rudy.

The Sno-Cat skidded some more on the slope, and the machine looked incongruously graceful, sliding and sending up spumes of snow. Rudy began to kick and flail toward help, but it was like trying to right himself in heavy surf.

Finally he crawled. It was all he could do. His feet and hands wouldn't work. It was futile. The engine sound had died. The Sno-Cat had disappeared. Gone.

Rudy crawled beastlike for long minutes, maybe hours, until he collapsed. He thought of covering himself with snow. As the colonel had done in his way. As Guy X had done in his. But he had no strength. He would sleep. He heard the motor noise again. No. It was his own voice murmuring, "Irene." He pushed his face into the whiteness. There was no pain.

THIRTY-THREE

The pilot's voice came over the speaker. A storm front to the west necessitated a slight rerouting of the plane out over Cape Cod. There was muttering around the cabin. Maybe thirty guys were scattered about the DC-6. Air force types mostly, a couple of swabbies from a sub base up in Scotland, a marine from the embassy in London, and three or four other soldiers.

Rudy Spruance didn't feel like talking to anybody. He'd been able to get a window seat, and had put his bag in the aisle where he'd leaned his crutches. He had the row to himself.

The crutches were silver and had metal bands to slip around his forearms. They were the kind polio kids used. The doctors at Bishop William said Rudy had to learn to handle them first, then he could graduate to a cane. It would be a while before he would be walking unassisted on a special prosthetic shoe, but he'd make it, they assured him.

Rudy loosened his tie. Though officially a civilian now, he was still in uniform. He had to stay in his Class As for the military hops from England to Pease AFB to McGuire to Oakland. He was heading for the Pacific.

The first thing he'd remembered after the snow was the general standing over him. When would it hurt? Rudy had wanted to know but couldn't ask. He couldn't get anyone to hear. Somebody had told him he would want to scratch . . . no, that was another time. This had been different. The general had been standing over him, and as Rudy's eyes had focused in a lazy way, he'd seen the nearest Tiffany lamp.

"Do you know where you are?" the general was asking.

"Of course I do, you son of a bitch." Rudy's first words. And then he passed out again.

The chaplain had saved him. Later, when he'd come to, Rudy had heard the story from Lavone: The chaplain had driven back in the Sno-Cat and found Rudy, miraculously avoiding mangling him with the vehicle's treads. The chaplain had loaded Rudy into the Cat and had driven him back to the hospital. Lavone told the story as he looked around the Wing. It was his first time inside. Rudy was alone among the empty beds. Once he was truly awake the hurt began, so Lavone had helped him with a little extra dose from a Syrette. Rudy was out again before Lavone had a chance to tell him the worst news. That came when the general visited again.

"You'll be leaving soon," the general had said. "We've got a C-124 Globemaster in on skis for the last lift. I'm flying you to England. To the air force hospital at Bishop William."

"Why not home?"

"Because you need some work. There's a Brit doc there I know. Had lots of practice after the Blitz. He's the best, and he's just what you need. Also, you need some time. Your 201's a lost cause. We'll build you a new file. Then you'll be clear. After that, you'll be free."

"Sounds nice."

"It's not. Now listen up. Brace yourself."

The general pulled up a chair and told him about the ampu-

tations. The first Rudy had heard. Most of his right foot. Most of
the fingers on his left hand. Frostbite.

"That's why I'm sending you to England. For the best rehab
and the Rolls Royce of prosthetics if you need any. Finest Sheffield
steel."

"I have no foot?" Rudy asked.

"You have one," the general said, "and a half. I found a Danish
doc up the coast doing harelip repair on the natives. I flew him
in to see what he could do for you."

"Where's the colonel's aide?" Part of Rudy's mind knew he
should be thinking about what General Vord had just told him,
but there was a blank wall—like the glacier—in his mind. He
turned away from it. He wanted to know about Irene.

"Never mind that," the general said. "Rest."

"Where is she?"

"Transferred," the general said. "I'm dispersing all personnel.
It's best for everyone. Did you hear what I told you?"

Rudy was up on his elbows. For the first time, he realized his
left arm was wrapped in bandages from his hand to his bicep. He
flailed at the sheet with his right hand, trying to fling the bed
covers aside so he could see his legs. The general pulled the sheet
back for him.

His left leg was fine. The foot was a little swollen and appeared
bruised. He moved it. But now he was looking at his right leg.
The foot was blunt, short, wrapped in gauze. It looked like a small
sledgehammer lying there.

Rudy dropped his head back on the pillow.

"You put me in here, you bastard," he said.

"I saved your life," the general said.

"You killed everybody in here."

"We shipped them away. The ones we had places for."

"You opened the windows. You killed everybody, and then you
put me in here."

"Admittedly it has its ironies."

Rudy could feel the pain then. It ran backward and forward

over his limbs, chewing into them, swirling around the tips. He felt a cry rising. He couldn't stop it. He didn't want to. It poured out of him but he couldn't make himself be heard. The silence whirled out of him and over the empty beds and over the general, who was walking away.

In the plane, Rudy was so lost in thought he didn't notice that the white cumulus clouds on the western horizon had changed into a wall of thunderheads. Lightning jumped between them like luminous ropes being thrown across chasms.

"We'll be flying over the Cape soon," the pilot announced. "You can see the turbulence we're trying to avoid."

The plane banked a little for course correction, and Rudy made out the sweep and curve of Cape Cod bending like a flexed arm below the aircraft. It was high summer down there, and Rudy longed to feel the heat after months in Greenland, weeks in England. Slowly he was regaining his sense of time. He missed the sun. He was headed for the Golden State. The Pacific.

They'd outprocessed him at Bishop William. An American army sergeant had come up from London. Rudy met the sergeant on a bench in the hospital garden. The sergeant was so helpful. The papers had Rudy serving his country for nearly a year at a weather station in Scotland. The papers listed the amputations as the result of a boating accident. It was unreal. Rudy just signed the forms. The sergeant never let on he knew the whole thing was a cover. Maybe he didn't know. He smiled and offered Rudy his pen and held the attaché case on his lap so Rudy could use it as a desk.

When they were done, the sergeant snapped the case's locks with a solid click and stood to shake Rudy's hand. Over by the fence, a British army nurse clipped tea roses. The American sergeant stopped on his way out and tried to make time with her. While they talked, Rudy sat on the bench and pulled a small parcel out of his bathrobe pocket. It had been stashed in his belongings. He'd come across it when he first got to Bishop William. He had kept it hidden most of the time he'd been there and only opened it when he was alone.

Inside the parcel, wrapped in papers secured with a rubber band, was the little Eskimo totem. As the nurse and the sergeant talked and laughed over by the hedge, Rudy held the statuette in his left hand, the damaged one. He tried to run his fingers over the figure the way he used to, but it was difficult. He kept thinking he could grip the statue in the old way. The doctors had warned him about that. For a time he would imagine he still had all his fingers, his whole foot. But they would be gone, leaving only a twinge, an itching, sometimes an ache. Phantom pain, the doctors had called it. It's to be expected.

Rudy looked at the papers that had wrapped the statue. There was an assignment order and copies of travel vouchers. They were all under the name Sgt. Irene Teal. She'd been assigned to Ford Ord, California, on the shore of the Pacific Ocean, south of San Francisco.

There was a note written on the back of a discarded manuscript page of the "Arctic Sutra."

Vord had me do the paperwork on her, so I made you a couple of carbons. Thought you might be interested. Plus, you don't want to forget your dolly. Get well soon, man.

Lavone

Rudy looked up. The nurse and the sergeant were gone. He was alone in the garden.

The next day when an RAF liaison came by to set up his travel arrangements, Rudy told him he wanted to see the Pacific.

A clutch of large houses appeared from under the plane's wing. They were on the south shore of the Cape. The houses were white colonials. Most of them were huge with sweeping porches. They seemed separated from the rest of the town. There were wide lawns

that stretched to the sea, a pier, and a long breakwater. It struck
Rudy that the splendid group of seaside estates was like an in-
version of Qangattarsa with its gray fjord, its squat hospital buildings, black water, its ice, cinders, and ash.

"Hyannis," somebody said in a seat behind him. Whoever had
spoken was looking out the window too; the voice had slid along
the curved wall of the cabin to Rudy's seat. "They call it 'The
Compound,' " the voice said. "Kennedy's place."

Rudy looked toward the horizon. The storm wouldn't roll
through for another couple of hours, and he'd be long gone. He
knew that the storm would barrel in, hit the Cape, and maybe
catch the Gulf Stream and swing up the coast. Eventually the
storm would fragment into wastrel squalls that might make it all
the way to the fjords back there in Greenland as rain or maybe
sleet or snow. It would fall on Qangattarsa, its buildings and its
ashes.

Rudy stared at his left hand, the one missing most of its fingers.
It looked a little like Guy X's now. He tucked it into his breast
pocket and touched Irene's stationing papers. They were in there
with the tiny Eskimo statue. He pictured them pressed together.

He wondered if Irene would see him, if he'd even be able to
find her.

White combers, mere threads at this altitude, broke on the
beach below the houses. A sailboat approached the wharf, spin-
naker swollen. Rudy looked down on the Kennedy compound in
the midday sunshine of summer. It was a Saturday. Perhaps Jack
Kennedy himself was down there right now getting ready for his
campaign.

She'd see him. He knew that. He'd find her out there, and she'd
see him, and they'd begin by talking. They'd witnessed some
things together. There was no getting around that. He'd find her;
she'd see him, and then time could begin again.

THIRTY-FOUR

Qivittoq are the evil spirits who live on the glaciers. If you see one and tell about it, you give it power, and it comes after you to steal your soul and eat it away piece by piece. If you see a qivittoq, you must never speak of it. It is a terrible secret you must keep.

Ululluik was feeding his dogs outside the print-shop Quonset. It had been years since the GIs had left Qangattarsa. Ululluik— the one the GIs had called Alley Oop—was now an old man. He was on his way back to his village. He'd stopped to feed his dogs before pushing on. He had been trading goods over in Arsuk. Passing through Qangattarsa with its dilapidated buildings and the memory of what he'd seen always made Ululluik uneasy, but the dogs needed food, so he stopped.

He watched the animals snap at the meat he tossed. He fed them always in the same order, from the strongest dog to the weakest. That way the strong dogs wouldn't attack the weaker ones while they ate. They snapped the meat out of the air, swallowed it in quick gulps, then went back down on their haunches.

Ululluik broke the rhythm by looking over to the horizon. There was a glow in the south. The last light for months. Soon it would be dark all the time. The dogs yelped; he went back to tossing them meat. He was too old for this, he thought. Maybe this would be his last trip.

It had been years since Ululluik had seen the qivittoq in this valley, and in all that time he'd never mentioned it once. He'd seen it after the storm when the Amerikamiut had come to the Inuit and had asked for help. They were looking for a body. A man had died in the snow, somewhere out near the place where the planes flew. There would be goods if the Inuit searched.

Ululluik went out with two other Inuit. One of them, Sammik, found a horse, shot in the head. Sammik later said there had been no meat on the poor beast. It was Anarfiik who had found what the Amerikamiut were looking for. A man, also shot in the head. Anarfiik said the man had blown the top of his own skull away. The rifle was still frozen to his hands because he'd taken his gloves off.

What did you find, Ululluik? Sammik and Anarfiik had asked him.

Nothing.

Sammik and Anarfiik looked at him.

Nothing, he said again. He told himself not to think about the qivittoq when he looked in their eyes. Speak of it, he thought, and you breathe life back into the spirit and it will eat your soul away a piece at a time.

During the search, he had driven his sled out past the last of the qallunaaqs' buildings. He'd made several broad sweeps across the flats that stretched between the frozen waterfalls on the north and the low stone walls to the south. He'd found nothing and decided to follow the faint remains of Sno-Cat tracks. They took him right up to the glacier. He had found places near the glacier where the trail turned and skidded, as if the machine had gotten confused or impatient and had wandered away.

Ululluik left the tracks and drove his sled along the wall of the glacier. After only a hundred yards or so his dogs stopped. He yelled at them. He tried to drive them forward, but they were interested in something in the snow. Ululluik went up to the dogs and found the blanket.

He peeled the wool back and thought for a moment he might be uncovering a baby in swaddling clothes. But instead he found the qivittoq.

It was small and blue. It had one arm, no legs, a round empty mouth, no ears, and one eye that was open and staring at him. It did not chase him, but it did not have to. He backed away, moaning. The dogs edged in and quickly became aggressive, the way they do over a piece of meat. Ululluik had to pull them back, yelling at them. They might have eaten the qivittoq.

He left the place.

Ululluik never went to any of the Amerikamiut to report what he'd seen, and he kept quiet about it with Sammik and Anarfiik too. He'd been quiet about it for years. Perhaps his silence had helped him to become an old man.

The Amerikamiut's buildings at Qangattarsa were in shambles, they'd been left unoccupied for so long. The Amerikamiut had gone farther north to listen with their machines for bombers and missiles. Now, Ululluik had heard, they'd stopped doing that and had left the land altogether.

Before he went to his sled, Ululluik took one last look inside the Quonset. He was old; it might be his last time here in one of these buildings. The place was full of junk, a mess. On a table inside, though, he found a box of tiny letters, thousands of the qallunaaqs' writing symbols locked in a frame. He touched them, and their marks came off on his fingers.

Ululluik picked up one of the slugs of type. He tossed it in his palm and pressed his thumb into the letters. They left marks and dents on his skin.

He put the slug inside his parka. The slug would be his charm. He would carry it with him. He would press its letters into his skin, and it would remind him to be silent for more years. Many more, if he had them in him. In that way, he would be safe from that strange spirit he saw out by glacier. No one would know.

When he was packed and ready to leave, it wasn't even necessary to yell at his dogs. They wanted to leave too. They just leaped up in their harnesses and began to pull.